NIGHT
PASSENGER

David Stanley

PAPER STREET

Published by Paper Street Publishing 2019

Copyright © 2019 David Stanley

The moral right of the author has been asserted

ISBN 978 1 9161763 1 7

www.davidjstanley.com
www.paperstreetpublishing.net

For Lindsey and Connor, my sun and moon

ONE

He fell back, giving the guard more space. No point spooking the man at the last minute. Off the freeway, even a moron like Hanson would notice the same car in his mirrors. They turned right on White Oak Avenue, a single car between them. The traffic crawled a short distance before stopping again. Nobody spoke. Up ahead, the turn signal came on and the minivan cut across onto Martha Street. A line of vehicles streamed past, forcing Blake to wait before he could make the turn. He drummed his fingers on the steering wheel and exhaled slowly through his nose. They were so near the end, he could taste it. At last they were through and he hit the gas to close the gap. The now-familiar taillights swung up onto a driveway in front of a private residence and went out.

Blake pulled over to the curb and cut the engine.

The minivan's door opened and the light inside lit up the bank guard. Hanson was big, easily north of four hundred pounds. The man had to rock himself backward and forward a couple of times before he got out the Dodge onto his feet. The effort seemed to drain him and he stood gripping the open door while he got his breath back. Blake shook his head.

They needed this man, he didn't need them.

Once the guard was inside the house, Blake moved the car into position and glanced at the clock. Seven thirty. At this time of night there was a good chance they could be interrupted by a neighbor. It looked like that kind of street, full of people in each others' business. The smart play would be to come back later, now they knew where Hanson lived. Blake dismissed the idea without verbalizing it with the others.

He was hungry and wanted this done.

Seven thirty five, almost show time. He felt his energy levels building. Another five minutes, he thought. Let the man get settled in after his day at the bank. Give him time to relax, take his shoes off. The guard would still be revved up from the commute home. Driving made people angry, and angry people were harder to control. So you waited it out. Didn't take long.

Five, maybe ten minutes. The calm wouldn't last worth a damn, but it would get them past the opening confusion when things usually went sideways.

Inside the property, light began to pulse against the curtains.

Hanson was watching television.

"All right," Blake said. "Let's do this."

He swung the door open and stepped onto the street. Sara got out next, then Porter. It wasn't his full crew, he wanted to keep it tight and these were the two he trusted most. They walked side by side across the street, with Porter falling into line behind as they came up the path to the front door. Blake drew his Glock and racked the slide. He nodded to Sara and she pressed the doorbell.

A heavyset woman opened the door. She was in her early thirties, had long red hair and wore a loose-fitting floral dress. There was a warm smile on her face but it disappeared fast when she saw the three of them standing there. Before she could say anything, Blake popped her between the eyes with the butt of his gun and she crumpled onto the floor. He listened for movement inside the house then, hearing none, stepped over the woman's motionless body into the hallway.

The house was warm and a delicious meaty smell hung in the air. Nearby, voices droned on, back and forth. The television. He turned and saw Sara and Porter move the woman's legs so they could shut the door. For the first time, Blake noted the redhead wasn't just large, she was pregnant. He supposed this ought to mean something to him, about knocking her out, but all it really meant was that his job had become easier.

"Hon? Who was it?"

Hanson's voice was exactly as he'd imagined it, nasal and somehow fleshy. The man was close, less than fifteen feet away. Probably sitting in front of the television with a beer in his ski glove fist. Not far from where Blake stood, the wall that divided the two spaces ended and was replaced by square glass bricks of a type he hadn't seen for many years. The bricks were thick and cast a greenish light onto the pale wooden floor. It meant Hanson would see them coming and perhaps give him time to reach for a gun.

"Sir?" Blake called out. "Your wife has collapsed."

Hanson charged into the hallway. He still wore his bank guard uniform, complete with sweat circles under the arms. Almost as soon as he appeared, he dropped down in front of the redhead.

"Oh Jesus, oh Jesus," Hanson said.

Blake looked at the broad back of the security guard and shook his head. Hanson's shirt was almost transparent and through it he could see swirls of matted back hair.

"Get off the floor."

2

The man didn't move, not unless you counted a small prayer-like rocking back and forth. He'd shut down, he wasn't in the moment at all. It was something Blake knew about all too well, but he didn't have the time for it, not from this guy.

"Don't worry," Blake continued, "it was just a tap to the head. As long as you tell me what I want to know, she's going to be fine."

Hanson lunged at him, his face scarlet, his teeth bared and clamped together. It happened quickly, faster than Blake thought a man that size could move. Hanson's weight pushed him back, flattening him against the wall. His gun spun out of his hand, bounced off the wall and landed on the wooden floor with a clatter. The guard looked at the Glock sitting next to his foot. The hands on Blake's chest began to shake but he kept right on looking at the automatic.

Sara cleared her throat.

"Don't make me shoot the whore, Hanson."

Her voice was calm and controlled. No panic, no uncertainty. The effect on the guard was immediate, he put his hands on his knees and began to breathe rapidly through his mouth.

"All right big man, take it easy." Blake said. "I don't have time for you to pass out. We got some business to discuss and then we'll be gone. You dig?"

A small nod. The man was losing it, he couldn't even speak. This was a good sign, it told him he wasn't dealing with a hero type. Blake hated heroes, they just made life difficult for everyone. He picked his Glock off the floor. Hanson's head moved with the pistol like they were connected, his throat swallowing repeatedly.

He flicked the pistol to the side. "Move it."

"What about my wife?"

"What about her?"

"You can't leave her like that, she's pregnant for God's sake."

He glanced at the woman on the floor. She looked terrible, there was no doubt about it. Her face was a bluish gray color and her eyes were fixed and dilated.

"Fine, whatever." Blake turned to the others. "Bring her through and sit her in a chair. Make her comfortable."

"Thank you," Hanson said, his voice strained.

Porter and Sara took an arm each and dragged the redhead down the hallway toward him. The woman's head fell back between her shoulders as they walked. She looked dead. Next to him, Hanson moaned. When they drew level, Blake noticed that his gun had left a D-shaped bruise in the center of her head like a smiley face. He wasn't in the habit of hitting people in the head with a pistol and he wondered if he'd hit her too hard.

They got her through into the next room and lifted her into a chair.

3

Blake pushed the guard after them, his Glock aimed at the man's kidneys. If Hanson tried anything, he didn't want to shoot him anywhere that might kill him too quickly.

No matter what, he was getting what he came for.

They walked through the room with the television and into the kitchen. He didn't want Hanson distracted by the sight of his wife's unmoving body. It would be harder to motivate him if he thought she was dead. The kitchen door closed behind them like a full length saloon door. Inside, the smell of food he'd noticed from the hallway intensified. A pot roast, maybe lasagne. His stomach rumbled.

A table with six chairs was set up at the far end of the room to form a dining area. It didn't look like more than two of the chairs had ever been used, the others were pushed against the wall. Not too many parties in the Hanson residence, he thought.

Blake pointed at one of the chairs and Hanson sat. Next door the television was still on, the excited voices bouncing back and forth. Even with the door closed he could still hear it. At first he'd tuned it out, thinking it was about politics but now he realized it was far worse. They were talking about the Lakers.

"Do something about the TV, it's driving me crazy."

A loud bang came from the next room. The voices, however, continued.

"Sorry," Porter shouted. "I got this."

Blake sighed. A moment later, there was silence. He drank it in, it was beautiful. There wasn't enough silence in the world, people were always rushing to fill it with moronic conversation. It terrified some people, being alone with their thoughts, and with good reason. He turned toward Hanson, who took it as a signal to talk.

"You didn't need to hit my wife. What kind of man hits a pregnant woman?"

"Let me explain something. It should be obvious, but apparently it's not. At the moment she's not part of this. If all goes well between you and me, she'll wake up and remember nothing. For her, it'll be like none of this happened. I was never here, we never had this conversation, and I was never forced to hurt an unborn child just to prove a point to you."

The blood ran out of Hanson's face.

"You're a monster."

"That's right. So how about we do this before she wakes up?"

The guard nodded, tears running down his face.

Blake decided to ease off. This was only going to work if Hanson gave him everything and didn't hold back something important. For that to happen, he had to believe he and his wife were going to survive. Out of the corner of his eye, he noticed Porter watching from the doorway. Blake

4

holstered his Glock and removed his jacket. He hung it over the back of one of the unused chairs and rolled up his shirt sleeves. He did this slowly, precisely, so the rolled cuff stayed flat. Hanson's eyes jumped between his smirking face and the muscular forearms that were being revealed. The combination of his bare arms and the black leather gloves had a disturbing quality that pleased Blake. When he finished, he pulled out the chair opposite Hanson, spun it around and sat down so the back of the chair was between his legs.

"What's your first name? I can't be calling you Hanson the whole time."

"Matt."

"Okay, that's better. Soon as we get what we need, we'll be gone. That's what you want too, right Matt? For us to leave?"

"Yes."

"You say yes but your face says no. Why is that?"

The guard swallowed hard.

"I know why you're here but you've made a mistake. I don't have access to anything at the bank. My security clearance is basic. Administrative offices, the kitchen, the restroom. Stuff like that. For the vault, safe deposit boxes, or server room, you'd need the manager's key and it's time-locked anyway. Out of hours, you'd need the president of the bank to get anything to open." Hanson shrugged. "I'm only there to eyeball odd-looking customers and hold the door, I'm nothing. A doorstop. I didn't even buy this house, it was a wedding present from my wife's father. I make seventeen bucks an hour."

Blake sat still, his gloved hands interlocked in front of him. He let time spool out a little before he replied. He'd foreseen this exact moment and he liked the feeling of it now it had arrived.

"Do I look like a bank robber to you, Matt?"

Hanson frowned. "Then, I don't understand. What else-"

Blake ignored him and turned to Porter. "You got the plans?"

"Right here."

Porter put his automatic in his left hand and with his right, unhooked a cylinder that hung diagonally across his back on a thin cord. Blake twisted the tube until it opened and pulled out rolled up sheets of paper. He spread them out on the table in front of Hanson and used salt and pepper grinders to hold one end flat and his Zippo and car keys at the other.

He placed a Sharpie pen in the middle of the top sheet.

"These are blueprints to the Dixie Art Gallery. I want you to mark every camera, sensor, pressure mat and access terminal. I want you to draw, as closely as you can, angles covered by cameras and infra-red, indicating blind spots."

"*The gallery?* That's what this is about?"

Blake sighed. "Get going butterball, we don't have all night."

5

Hanson picked up the pen. His hands shaking.

"I need to stand."

"Go ahead," Blake said. "But no sudden moves. My friend likes shooting people a lot more than he likes surprises and it's gotten so he's pretty good at it."

Hanson stood and leaned over the plans. Blake could smell the guard's body right across the table. In the short time he'd been sitting down, the circle of sweat under each of his arms had doubled in size. If things went on the way they were going, the circles were going to meet in the middle. Hanson's eyes narrowed with concentration, then after a moment the pen went down and started to mark a dotted line on the paper.

"Don't forget external cameras."

"Okay."

Blake got up and turned to Porter. "Keep an eye on him. I'm going to see how the girls are getting on. Make sure he does all ten sheets."

"You bet," Porter said. As Blake left the room, Porter spoke to Hanson for the first time. "So how come you don't work at the gallery anymore?"

"I...I had a health problem."

"You drank, huh? I'd drink too if I were you. Being in the same room as you is enough to make me want to drink and I did three tours in Afghanistan."

Blake smiled. Porter was a funny kid.

The scene in the living room was pretty much what he expected. Porter had put his boot through the television, which had peeled off the wall and fallen onto the floor. When that hadn't done the job, he'd pulled the cord out the wall. Blake turned to face the redhead. What he saw there was less expected. Sara straddled the woman in the chair and was twisting something into her forehead. He watched, speechless, until the twisting movement stopped and Sara drew her arm back to reveal a blood-soaked Swiss Army knife.

"Jesus, what have you done?"

"Horse hoof cleaner," she said. "Can drill through bone."

"That was *not* my question."

"Blood was pooling inside her skull, so I drilled a hole to relieve the pressure."

"How do you even know this shit?"

"House," she said.

Blake moved to get a closer look at what Sara had done to the woman's head. He couldn't decide if he was fascinated, disgusted or just plain irritated. Most likely, a little of each. Next to the chair now, he bent down close. It was a real mess. A thick worm of blood rolled thickly between her eyes and down her right cheek. Unlike in a horror movie, the blood was almost black. He turned to Sara and tried to keep anger from his voice.

"Before it only looked like she was asleep; now it looks like you stabbed her in the head. What were you thinking?"

"I know how it looks but she's going to be fine."

"Yeah, about that," Blake said.

Sara's shoulders sagged.

"You're kidding me, right? The woman's pregnant."

"She's seen our faces. Hanson knows we're hitting the gallery. What do you suppose they'd do after we left here? You think they wouldn't mention any of this to the police? Why do you think we came to *this* guy's house and not the current security guard?"

Sara groaned, realization hitting home.

"Because the gallery won't miss him. They won't see it coming."

"I'm sorry," he said. "I thought you knew."

"I assumed it was because he designed the system."

"Look, clean her up, I don't want Hanson freaking out."

"How much can she remember? She only saw us for a second."

They stared awkwardly at each other. He knew she was right, but was he prepared to risk it? He sighed, vexed.

"I'll think about it."

*

Blake looked through the blueprints Hanson had filled out, flipping quickly past the public areas of the gallery to the loading bay and offices. He'd already decided this was the weak spot. The front entrance was too well protected and was completely exposed to the street. Anyone driving past would see what was going on. He smiled. It looked like the guard had come through for them with some very clean plans. There were no obvious security flaws to exploit, but he wasn't too worried about that.

"Excellent. Now I want the code for the alarm."

"I've not worked there for months, the code will have changed."

"You pass yourself off as this doughnut-eating idiot and maybe that's who you are now, but I bet the Matt Hanson who set up this system put in backdoors and logins people wouldn't know to change. *That's* the shit I want."

Hanson shifted uncomfortably, then nodded.

"Next door."

"Okay," Blake said. "You're doing good, it's nearly over."

He let the guard walk in front of him into the living room. Hanson turned to look at his wife in the chair. To Blake's surprise, the redhead's eyes were open and were gazing blankly up at the ceiling. Sara had cleaned up the blood and lain a thick white cloth across her forehead. Color had returned to the woman's face and she genuinely looked better than before.

7

Seeing this improvement, Hanson seemed to relax and walked to a bookcase of DVDs that lined one of the walls. His finger bounced down the spines until he found the one he wanted. *Never Been Kissed*. He opened the case and took out an envelope.

"I'm not trying to trick you. This may not work anymore."

"I appreciate your candor, Matt."

The envelope was thin with something stiff inside. Blake tore the end off and tipped the contents into the palm of his hand. A plastic security card slid out. There was no branding, it was white with a magnetic stripe on one side. A small cross was inked into the top left corner. Blake looked up at the guard.

"When I was fired they made me return my security pass, along with everything else. I'd known for a while what they were going to do to me, so I'd made another card. They were always underestimating me. On the system it's assigned to the owner of the gallery. She never goes anywhere that needs a card, all she cares about is the art. The way I figured it, they'd never delete her code and if anyone thought to ask her she'd probably assume she'd had one once and lost it. No red flags would go up." Hanson paused, his eyes sliding down to the floor. "I don't know why I created it. I guess I liked knowing I had one over them while they were looking down their noses at me." Hanson's eyes zipped up to Blake's again. "That's why you don't have to worry about me. I *want* them to get robbed. As far as I'm concerned, it'll serve them right for what they did to me."

Blake smiled. He'd half-expected this move by Hanson.

"What's the code for the card? It's not written here."

"2046. It forms a cross on the keypad."

"Uh huh. And if they changed the code, the alarm goes off?"

"It's not like that," Hanson said. "You get three tries to get a code right, then it locks out the ID until it's manually reset. The card's just a key to open doors, nothing else. Once inside, you still have to deal with the alarm. There's no alarm access on the street."

Blake nodded. It wasn't what he wanted to hear, but it was better than nothing.

"There's something you're not telling me. What is it?"

The guard's eyes widened. "There's nothing, I swear."

Blake turned to Porter. "Cut off one of her fingers."

"What? No!" Hanson said. "Please. I'll do anything."

"It's always the same," Blake said, casually. "You always have to cut off at least one finger before people pay attention."

Porter tucked his gun into the back of his jeans and pulled a KA-BAR from a sheath on his hip. Standing beside Hanson's wife, he positioned her right hand palm-down on the arm of the chair, the blade floating above her fingers. The redhead's face was calm, miles away. She had no idea what was happening, but that situation wouldn't last forever.

"Which finger should I cut off?"

Blake sighed. "Start with her little finger, work your way up. She might bleed out when you cut her thumb off, so this way gives Matt four chances to give us what we need."

"Please, I've told you everything."

"I don't have time for games, Hanson. If the next thing out your mouth isn't about the gallery, your wife loses a finger."

The guard swallowed. His face was scarlet and covered with beads of sweat. He looked from Blake to Porter and back like he was watching a tennis match.

"It's about the alarm. I'll tell you what you want, but can you put the knife away?"

"All right," Blake said, dismissing Porter with a wave of his hand. "But you won't get another chance to jerk me around."

Hanson spoke quickly. There were two alarms, he explained, not one. After a moment, Blake smiled. It wasn't bad news at all. Not for what he had in mind. In fact, it was probably the best news he'd ever heard. The guard didn't understand, he couldn't see the angle. A heavy line formed across his forehead while he spoke, as he struggled to see why two alarms was the good news his captors seemed to think it was. His confusion only added to Blake's good spirits. If the security guy didn't understand the problem, there was no way his former arty bosses would see it either. The painting was as good as his.

When Hanson stopped talking, Blake put his Glock under the guard's chin and pulled the trigger. Quick and painless. No fear, no pathetic bargaining for his life. The man had come through for them, it was the least he could do.

TWO

Thorne sat at the bar staring at his Scotch. Season five of *Night Passenger* had just wrapped, yet around him, nobody was celebrating. It felt like a wake. A man wearing a dark suit walked over and sat on the stool next to his. The man smiled at him in a way he didn't much care for, his lip curled up at one side like a big cigar spent a lot of time in there. It didn't happen often, but Thorne supposed he was a fan of the show and merely nodded his head before turning back to his drink. He hoped the man would realize he was in no mood to chat and leave, but when he glanced up he was still there, reflected in a mirror behind the bar.

Nobody ever took a hint these days, not when it mattered.

"It's been a few years, Gunny, but it insults me that you don't recognize a brother Marine when he's sat right next to you."

That voice, so familiar and yet hard to place.

Thorne glanced side-on at the man. Short black hair, mid thirties. Six feet tall, maybe 240 pounds. The man's suit bunched awkwardly around the biceps of his left arm as it rested on the bar. His fingers were thick and brutal, like smaller versions of his arms. A grunt, not EOD. Not with those fingers. Finally, he turned and looked directly at the man's face. Above his left eye, in the tanned leathery skin, was a pale crescent-shaped scar. It looked like someone had left a hot cup of coffee on there and pulled off part of the skin. His heart sank.

"Blake," Thorne said. "Lance Corporal Blake."

"It's just Aidan now."

"*Right.*"

He considered offering Blake his hand to shake, but not for long.

"Rumor has it you jumped off the roof of a building today."

For an instant, Thorne was back in the moment, falling.

"It was amazing. One of the best things I've ever experienced." He paused, their eyes locked together. "You should try it."

A smile flickered at the corners of Blake's mouth.

"I've been watching that show of yours for a while, it's not bad. At first I didn't realize who you were, it's been a while since we last met and once you take off the uniform and let your hair grow out, you are almost a different person." Blake paused to get the attention of the bartender. "I try to avoid thinking too much about my time over there, I'm sure you're the same. Probably why you didn't recognize me just now. You blank it all out. Works most of the time too, but some things are burned in there forever."

Blake stabbed the side of his head with his finger.

"Listen, Blake," Thorne said. "This isn't a good time."

"It never is, brother, but it's the only time we get."

The bartender came over and Blake ordered a pitcher of beer. Thorne sighed. Blake wasn't going away anytime soon. He wanted something, and Thorne had no idea what it could be. Whatever it was, it was bad news.

"This meeting doesn't feel accidental. Why don't you get to it."

"All right. The way I see it, you owe me a hundred thousand dollars."

Thorne smiled. "Really. How do you figure?"

"I was approached in Baghdad by *Ringfire*, a private military contractor. They offered me a job babysitting VIPs. *Protective Security Detail* they called it. It paid a hundred large tax free, for six months' work. I didn't want to spend another second in that country, but for that kind of cheddar, I could do six months. There was only one condition."

"You needed an honorable discharge."

"That's right."

Thorne knocked back the last of his Scotch before answering.

"I'm not sure what you expected me to say at that trial, Blake. You fired your weapon while intoxicated and hit a six year old girl. There was only so much I could do."

"That's bullshit, man! I had one goddamn beer. I was taking fire and I defended myself. I've no idea where that girl came from. One minute she's not there, the next the hajji has her pinned to his chest like a shield."

"So why aren't you asking this *Iraqi* for your money?"

Blake's face darkened. "Is this some kind of joke to you, Thorne?"

"No. In fact, it's safe to say I am becoming less and less amused by this conversation the longer it lasts. I've got bad news for you, friend. I don't know how this scenario played out in your mind, but this acting gig doesn't pay as much as you might think. Right now I have about ten thousand to my name. I rent my apartment, I have no stocks or bonds, and I can double the value of my car by filling it with gas."

To his surprise, Blake smiled.

"Not to mention they've canceled your show."

Thorne clenched his teeth.

There'd been rumors of cancelation throughout production with no denials or comforting words from the network. They'd wait until the numbers came back from the first couple of episodes before they finalized it, but in his heart he knew they'd decided. What would make a difference to the ratings now? It also explained why the last scene shot was the last in the script. It gave them the most time to change the ending before it was made. But here they were, the scene shot, just as it had been in the script, with his character taking two to the chest and falling off a building.

"I've done my research, Thorne. You're finished."

"So why this charade of asking me for a hundred thousand?"

"Oh, it's no charade. I want my money and I will get it. But I didn't track you down after six years expecting you to write me a check. I'm a reasonable man and I can't ignore the fact that you did your best for me when so many others did nothing. We are brothers in arms, I really believe that. However, I have a business venture that requires your electrical skills to complete. I doubt it will take more than an hour of your time and after that you and me never have to see each other again."

Thorne's voice dropped to a whisper.

"You're talking about a *robbery?*"

"I'm only trying to make a living, same as anybody else."

"You're crazy, just like they said."

Blake laughed. His mouth was large and his teeth looked like a shark about to bite. The top two buttons of his shirt were undone but the opening was barely able to contain his neck and the veins that stood out upon it. Thorne noticed many of the cast and crew were openly staring in their direction.

"Why bring me into this?"

"Three reasons, Thorne. First, if I hire someone who does this all the time he's bound to get caught at some point in the future, it's the law of averages. Which means for the rest of my life I got to wonder if this guy is about to roll on me for a lower sentence. Second, I don't know where to contact one of those guys anyway and I'm on a tight deadline. Third, and this is my personal favorite, I'm bringing you into this because the whole thing was originally your idea. In Iraq, you said that after defusing 38 IEDs you could defeat any security system on the planet. That an alarm was a bomb that never exploded, a reward without risk. I believe there was talk of taking candy from a baby."

Thorne sighed.

"Yeah," he said, "I guess I did say something like that. But neither of us are the men we were back in the Corps. I have a life now, a career. Nobody does these things in the real world. Pulling off a diamond heist or whatever; it's a pipe dream, a popcorn movie."

"Relax, it's nothing like that. More like...intercepting mail."

Thorne turned and looked Blake straight in the eye.

"I'm not doing it. Mention it again and I'll go to the cops."

Blake nodded casually, like it was the answer he expected.

"You know, I was here earlier, down the end of the bar. You probably didn't notice me, you had your hands full dealing with that girlfriend of yours, didn't you? Kate Bloom. She really is quite a pistol. I'd say she's even more beautiful in real life than she is on screen. So much passion! I'd assumed it was only the character she played, but she's really like that isn't she?" Blake shook his head ruefully. "I'm also drawn to the independently-minded woman. This one I have right now, she's barely housebroken. Raised by wolves would be my guess. Hell, if they don't slap you every now and then, how can you be sure they feel anything at all? That kind of passion is rare, I hope you realize that. It would be sad if something bad happened to Miss Bloom as the result of a hasty decision."

Thorne eased himself off his bar stool onto the floor.

"What did you say to me?"

"Kate's an attractive woman and I hope she stays that way. There's nothing sadder in this world than a beautiful woman who suffers a disfiguring injury, it's worse than death."

Thorne's fist struck Blake high on his left cheekbone, snapping his head around. Before he could react, Thorne hit him again, this time in the stomach. He put his full weight into it, his right foot counterbalancing, driving his body forward, his hips and shoulders rotating together. The force of the blow tipped Blake backward off his stool onto the floor. The crowd in the bar surged to create space between them, surrounding them. All of them people he knew, people he'd worked with for years. He saw Kate at the front, her face in shock. Seeing him a way she'd never seen him before; his face twisted with hate, his hands balled into fists in front of him. Conversation stopped, seemingly replaced by the thrumming sound of blood surging around his body and the fast stroke of his breathing. Blake got his feet under him and, gripping the edge of a table, pulled himself upright. Blake looked up at him, his head tilted forward.

He was smiling.

Thorne saw it now. Blake had deliberately provoked him and by rising to it, he'd put Kate's life in greater risk. He'd proven how much he cared for her. Blake owned him now. He'd never be free of it and Kate would never be safe, not as long as Blake was alive. Thorne lunged at him, his fury uncontrollable. He landed another heavy blow to Blake's cheek, just missing his eye. Switching to his left hand, he caught Blake by surprise, his fist plowing into his neck below his ear, where the vagus nerve overlapped the carotid artery. Blake's eyes opened wide and his legs buckled. He crashed through the table behind him, flattening it like cardboard and smashing glasses. The crowd shifted again to avoid him, their faces frozen. Thorne wasn't through with Blake, not by a long way. He got down on one knee, grabbed Blake's jacket in his left hand and drew back his right to punch him again. Thick muscular arms grabbed him from behind and pulled him toward the bar. He fought to free himself but the strength of the man that held him was too great and he allowed himself to relax.

Something dug into his back and a voice whispered in his ear.

"Better to keep the girl out of this. Nod if you agree."

Thorne nodded and the gun withdrew.

It hardly mattered, not with Python Arms holding him. Now it was over, he welcomed the intervention. He wasn't sure he could've stopped on his own. He could have gone on hitting Blake, quite happily, even after he was dead. Nobody threatened Kate. It dawned on him that he wasn't injured. Blake hadn't fought back, hadn't even lifted his arms to block the blows. He'd simply let himself take the beating. To Kate, and everyone else in the bar, there'd be no doubt which of them was the monster. Blake had perfectly provoked him, then perfectly isolated him from friends who might have helped.

Thorne had misjudged him, but it wouldn't happen again.

He studied Blake, as if for the first time. His nose and lower lip were bleeding and the whole left side of his face was badly swollen. A lump the size of a boiled egg had appeared over his cheekbone and the skin was so tight there was a shine to it.

Blake stood and arched his back.

"It's okay fellas. A misunderstanding, is all. Totally my fault."

The iron grip relaxed and Thorne pulled himself free. He looked at the creature that had held him. A bear of some kind had apparently mated with an M1 Abrams and an olive green t-shirt had been pulled over the result. He tilted his head back to take in the unpleasant face that looked down at him from a near seven foot summit. Thorne didn't like to think what this titan could do to Kate if he set his mind to it.

"So, Bigfoot, you the brains of this operation?"

A snarl rippled up one side of the beast's face, the small piggy eyes sliding across to Blake for approval of some sort, but Blake shook his head. The giant leaned forward so their faces were inches apart and stared at him while an asthmatic, raspy breath tore in and out of his mouth. Then, with a grunt, was gone, pushing startled people out the way as he went. Thorne turned to the African American standing next to him. Another flashback. Either Blake had problems making new friends, or else he was getting the band back together.

"You remember Porter, don't you, Thorne?"

He looked coldly at him. "Sam."

Porter turned away without meeting his eye.

"Let's take a walk," Blake said. "Get out of these nice folks' hair."

He directed Thorne through the bar, his exit watched by his friends and co-workers. It would be a strange way for him to say goodbye, he thought, if he never saw them again. They left the bar and made their way down the hall toward the restaurant. Blake clearly knew where he was going, that he'd planned it all out in advance. He looked back and saw Porter following behind, but the giant was no where in sight. Porter's right hand was in his jacket pocket but it wasn't alone in there.

"I can't believe you punched me in the neck, man."

Despite what had happened, Blake's tone was light and surprisingly friendly, the menacing edge to his voice now gone. Thorne had experienced similar mood reversals with Blake in the past, but this one set his teeth on edge.

"Where'd you get the freak of nature?"

"Motor pool, Camp Pendleton."

"You sure it wasn't a circus?"

He thought Blake smiled but it was hard to say for sure with his face busted up.

"Watch what you say to him, he has a brutal temper."

"Did the scientists give it a name?"

"His friends call him Foster, except, he don't have no friends."

Blake laughed and slapped Thorne on the shoulder.

They walked into the restaurant. It was late and the tables were empty and set up for the next day's breakfast. There was no maître d' at the door and they continued to the back of the room and into the kitchen.

Unlike much of the hotel, the kitchen was clean and brightly lit. Four men wearing chef whites paused to stare at them before returning to what they were doing. It surprised Thorne how busy they were considering the empty restaurant, but there was always room service to consider.

They passed through a curtain of thick plastic strips into a loading area stacked with boxes. The heat of the kitchen gave way to a cool, dry air. A muscular man, possibly Samoan, stood next to an outer door smoking. His arms were bare from the top of his shoulder down and covered extensively with tribal tattoos. The cigarette looked comically small in his huge hand. Blake walked up to him, his back straight, his shoulders pulled back.

"Beat it chief, we got some private business to discuss."

"So go someplace else, I like it here."

Blake moved a step closer.

"You stay, you die."

The Samoan dropped his half-smoked cigarette onto the concrete and stood on it. He squared off in front of Blake, assessing him and his already bloody face. The man stood for several seconds staring into Blake's eyes and whatever he saw in them was enough, because he shook his head and walked back toward the kitchen without another word. Thorne had to hand it to Blake, he knew how to handle himself in volatile situations. The Marines had given him something no court-martial could take back and

Thorne had a feeling he'd soon be on the other side of it. They walked into a narrow side street. He looked around. Some dumpsters, a smell of piss and rotting garbage. Farther down, he saw a black van with tinted windows and a dent on the side. Next to it stood the giant, Foster.

Thorne turned back to Blake and Porter.

"Why are we here, Aidan?"

Blake indicated the surroundings. "No cameras."

"I'm not sure I like that as much as you."

"It's as much to protect you as it is me. There were also no cameras in the kitchen, nor the section of the restaurant we walked through. It's just us, some old buddies catching up. You realize how few places like this still exist in this country? Hoover would cream his pantyhose to see the society we live in now."

Thorne glanced at his right hand and flexed it, making a fist. The skin over his knuckles was broken and the joints were painful to move. It'd been a long time since he'd been in a fist fight, and he didn't remember this happening to his hand before. He wondered how many cameras were in the bar and if footage of him repeatedly striking an innocent man was, at that moment, being uploaded to the internet.

"How's your face?'

"You have the fists of a little girl, Thorne. Anyone ever tell you that?"

"I think your mother might have mentioned it."

Blake laughed, then shook his head. "I've missed your humor."

Porter's cell phone chirped and he took it out and started to type.

"Come on, man!" Blake said. "If you're going to stand there holding your dick, go wait with Frankenstein."

Porter shrugged his shoulders. "Whatever."

He walked down the alley, head down, typing.

"Fine, you got me here. What are you trying to steal?"

Blake nodded. "Straight to business, I feel you. It's a painting by Picasso. It's not very big, but it's worth a lot of money. They have it in a gallery in Beverly Hills."

"Is this a joke? Art galleries are bank vaults these days. You told me this wasn't going to be a diamond heist."

"Relax. I'll go into detail later, but in the meantime all you need to know is that it will be more like office security, nothing to worry about. I know how unlikely that sounds, but you're going to have to trust me."

Thorne was shaking his head. "I don't know, I don't like it."

"Why not?"

"A Picasso! I don't know anything about art, but I've heard of him. This won't be like when some old lady's car gets boosted and the cops don't lift a finger, people who own Picassos have friends in high places. They'll be trying to solve this."

"Let them try, they'll find nothing. The plan is solid."

Down by the van, Porter laughed, his face still buried in his phone.

"This isn't who I am," Thorne said.

"It's just a painting. Nobody gets hurt. One day it's in a gallery, the next it's on some rich man's wall, what do you care?"

"You make it sound like you're picking up a nickel someone dropped on the sidewalk."

"A nickel, eh? I like that."

"Goddammit, Blake, this is serious."

Blake pinched the bridge of his nose and closed his eyes for a long beat. He nodded, as if he'd decided something, and pulled out his wallet. With exaggerated care, his fingers teased something out from behind a credit card and handed it to Thorne. It was a photograph of a teenage girl with pale skin and long, black hair. She was sitting in a train, her head turned to look out the window, her face reflected in the glass. The lighting in the alley wasn't ideal, but Thorne could see the arteries in her neck, her skin was so clear and flawless.

"Her name's Andrea, she's my kid sister. The picture's about ten years old I guess, she's twenty seven now." Blake's voice seemed to fade out like a radio signal, before coming back. "It's twenty eight that's going to be the problem. She needs money for an operation and this robbery is the only way that can happen. My back's against the wall. I've done bad things in my life, but lifting some painting to save my sister's life will not be one of them. As far as I'm concerned, I earned this money in the Corps with everything I went through and I think you did too. So here's the deal. Get us inside the building and I'll give you a full share of the robbery, less the hundred thousand." His voice softened, became reasonable. "We were friends once, Chris. Can you stop being a boy scout for one night and save my sister?"

Thorne sighed and gave Blake his photograph back.

Nothing was ever simple. A buzz was starting to build in his body. It had been the same earlier on the roof of the hotel before the fall and he liked it. He'd always liked it, it was why he became a Marine. For the rush.

"How much does that leave, out of my share?"

"Nine hundred thousand."

"Wow."

"Not bad for a night's work."

"And Kate, you leave her alone if I do this?"

"Of course."

"Say it."

"I won't touch a hair on her head, you have my word."

Thorne stuck out his hand and, smiling, Blake shook it.

THREE

Thorne walked out the hotel lobby into the searing morning heat. He was wearing the same pale linen suit he'd worn the day before, and for the previous forty six days. The suit was studio property but he'd decided not to return it, not if they were canceling the show. He reached into the top pocket, pulled out his character's sunglasses, shook the legs open and pushed them onto his face. There was a stylized way he did this that he found hard to stop. He did it once in the pilot episode and the producers liked it so much it'd been incorporated into the show's opening sequence ever since.

As he reached the sidewalk, a black Audi sedan pulled up to the curb next to him. He ignored it and walked toward Del Mar station. Blake had arranged to meet him in an hour's time at the hotel bar. Next to him, the Audi rolled along, matching his pace. This couldn't be him, not already. The car made no sound at all, the engine barely ticking over. He stopped and next to him the car came to a halt. So this was how it was going to be. He placed his hands on either side of the passenger window. The glass was tinted and all he saw was his own face looking back.

The window slid open and refrigerated, leather-scented air wafted out across his face. A young woman sat behind the wheel. Her head was tilted over like a dog wanting a biscuit, and if he had one he might have given it to her. She was on the slutty side of beautiful, but beautiful nevertheless. He leant down and rested his elbows on the windowsill so his head and shoulders were inside the car. He took off his sunglasses and glanced into the back.

Blake wasn't there, nobody was.

Thorne felt himself relax, perhaps he had this all wrong.

He turned back to the woman. She was in her late twenties or early thirties and had long brown hair with a curl through it like a rope that had been picked apart. She wore a white shirt and faded blue denim shorts that ended so high up her leg the pocket linings hung out. There was a crazed look in her eyes that suited her in a way he could not explain.

"Thought you were someone else."

The brunette shifted position, turning her hips and shoulders toward him. Her left arm sat high up on the wheel, her long thin fingers almost touching the windshield. The top four buttons in her shirt were unfastened and the unusual angle caused the material to become slack at the front. His drifting attention seemed to amuse her.

"Who'd you want me to be?"

He hesitated. "I think there's been a mistake here."

"Oh, there's no mistake."

"Excuse me?"

"You're Chris Thorne. I got the right guy, yes?"

He frowned. "Who're you?"

"I'm Sara. I'm your ride."

He knew who she was, it was obvious.

"You're Blake's girl."

The smile vanished from her face like it never existed.

"Get in the car, Thorne. You're letting the goddamn heat in."

So this is how his world ended, with a pretty girl and a dirty mouth. It seemed as good a way as any for his descent into crime to begin. He didn't know what he expected. The previous night seemed so much like a bad dream that he'd allowed himself to think he could forget it ever happened. But it was no dream, Blake was for real.

He put his sunglasses back on, opened the door and got in.

"Fine," he said. "Let's do this."

Sara didn't need to be told twice. She stamped on the gas and the sedan shot out from the curb, almost into the back of a late-model white Bronco. She yanked the wheel and the car swung into the next lane, missing the SUV by inches, and continued accelerating. The car was a stick shift and she worked it like a racing driver, her muscular legs dancing the clutch and accelerator pedals, pushing them hard to the floor with each stroke. He looked into the floor well, following her legs to a set of biker boots with oversize buckle fastenings.

"Nice boots."

"Thanks."

"You have a motorcycle?"

"My whole life." She tilted her head back, evaluating. "You?"

"Not since I joined the Corps."

Now the window was rolled up he became aware of her perfume. It was cheap, the kind sold in supermarkets to teenage girls. An invisible cloud of it surrounded her body, like the shields of an alien spacecraft. The scent was strong and several minutes passed before he noticed that beneath it lay another scent. Sex. Now he'd noticed it, he decided she practically reeked of it. That musky, brackish smell, as familiar to him as freshly baked cinnamon rolls. Within the last hour, he thought. There hadn't been time to wash so she'd put on the perfume hoping to cover it up.

Sara turned at Cordova and South Arroyo Parkway, heading back to Los Angeles. He couldn't say he'd missed it, but for sure he wouldn't miss Pasadena. The five days he'd been shooting here had been the unhappiest of his career and had drawn to a close not just his show, but his relationship with Kate Bloom. He hadn't treated her right, and it had taken her ending things for him to realize it.

"How you can wear that jacket, it's like an oven out there."

"It's linen," he said. "Keeps me cool."

"If I was naked I'd still be too hot."

"Ain't that the truth."

She sighed. "You're a lot like him you know."

"Who?"

"Aidan, of course."

Thorne didn't want to hear about how he and Blake were alike.

"So what was that? You skipping out on us?"

He shrugged. "Maybe, yeah. I don't know."

"How can you not know?"

"I'm going through some personal issues right now and I'd rather be dealing with them than planning a robbery with the Marx Brothers."

"Thorne, it's a million dollars. After you're done you can go back to drinking yourself to death or whatever your plan was for the rest of the week, but there's no changing your mind. Aidan will do what he has to make sure this happens. Too much is at stake for you to screw it up with your bullshit."

He looked out the side window once again.

While he'd been in the alley with Blake, Kate had packed up and cleared out. He'd known their room was empty before he opened the door, the silence inside had seeped out like a cold draft. After the way she'd looked at him in the bar, it had been a relief to find her gone. He had no idea what he would have said to her. As much as he hated to admit it, Blake had sold him on the robbery. Explaining the fight without revealing the plan to steal the Picasso would be difficult. Kate saw the world clearly. There were no shades of gray, it was black and white, right and wrong. She'd insist he go to the police, or would do so herself.

This morning, none of that mattered. It'd been so clear to him, waking up alone in their hotel bed. He'd made a choice between Kate and the money, and his decision disgusted him. He had to make things right with her, no matter the cost. But Sara's presence had brought him back to reality. She'd said Blake would do what he had to, and he believed her. The robbery could not be stopped and realizing this, he felt certainty return to his thoughts.

Telling Kate everything stood only to endanger her life. It wouldn't save their relationship, nor would it make her think better of him for the night before. The damage was done. Some space apart was what they needed, some time to heal. She wouldn't be ready to forgive him yet, no matter what he said. While she hadn't left him a note, she had taken his car. There was a hidden message there, he was sure of it. She'd go back to their apartment in Santa Monica. Kate would stop there, she wouldn't keep running. Once this business with Blake was behind him, he'd fight for her and he'd give her everything she wanted.

"You going to tell him what happened?"

"Do I need to?"

He looked at her. "I'm all in. That what you want to hear?"

"It's all I need."

They sat in silence as she picked her way through traffic. It had been a long time since he'd been a passenger in a car and he found that he didn't care for it. Time seemed to pass at a slower rate when you weren't in control. After over an hour, Sara pulled the Audi over to the curb and killed the engine. They were in Culver City. Next to him, Sara continued to stare out the windshield, her hands still gripping the wheel.

"He says you're a rock star with electronics. I hope he's right."

Thorne stared at her coldly. "This us?"

She pointed across the street at a house with an orange tile roof and white stucco walls. He opened the door and got out, then reached down to grab his bag in the footwell. He looked at Sara one last time. It occurred to him he might not see her again. He wasn't sure how he felt about that. At a fundamental level, there was something badly wrong with her. As an actor, he couldn't stop himself from drinking that in. The city was full of fakes. Fake emotions, fake accents, fake everything. To see anything genuine, no matter what, was to learn something about the craft and expand your range.

She turned to him, her gaze piercing and bright.

"Word of advice, Thorne. Don't make assumptions about me based on how I look. I'll do anything for him, anything at all."

He threw his bag over his shoulder and slammed the door. He'd changed his mind., perhaps it would be best if he never saw her again. Thorne crossed the street and walked up an overgrown path to the front door. Out of habit, he raised his hand to press the chime, then stopped himself. It was the wrong play. The more he appeared to be a part of Blake's gang, the better. He needed them to think he was one of them, an old friend, a Marine.

Most of all, he needed them to forget about Kate Bloom.

He tried the handle and the door opened.

21

Thorne resisted the urge to remove his sunglasses. He was in character now, and they were part of his armor. Voices filtered through from the back of the house and he walked toward them. The hallway opened out into a kitchen, dining and TV area. Blake stood with a cell phone pressed to his ear. He wore baggy workout pants and a sweat-soaked gray T-shirt with Everlast printed across the front. His face was swollen and badly bruised and two white adhesive sutures were holding his forehead closed. Blake smiled at him and held up his index finger for him to wait. Porter sat over by the TV on a leather sofa with a man Thorne didn't recognize. The second man was in his mid thirties with long, black hair and incredibly white skin. The man looked over and clenched his jaw. Thorne turned back to Blake as he returned his phone to his pocket. It seemed to him like the call had been about him. Sara no doubt giving him up for his moment of weakness. Blake walked over.

"You're not still on the fence about this are you?"

"No."

"*But?*"

"I don't feel good about it."

"This painting," Blake said, "I'm no expert but it's got to be worth what? Seventy to eighty mill? Somewhere in that ballpark?"

Thorne shrugged. "Probably closer to a hundred."

"No shit. Okay, so some guy spends all that money on a painting...then just leaves it in an art gallery like a book loaned to a friend. That's whack."

"Are you close to getting to the point, Blake?"

"My point is simple. I don't have twenty bucks I won't miss, but this guy has a hundred million in loose change? He may as well have set that money on fire for all the difference it's making to his life. Do you think money like that can be earned? Didn't this guy basically pay for this painting with stolen money in the first place? I'll bet that whatever this guy does, there'll be thousands of regular Joes like you and me doing all the real work and getting minimum wage. This painting we're going to steal? It was paid for by them."

Blake was good, he knew how to hit Thorne's buttons.

Behind him a man spoke in a thick Texan accent.

"He almost makes you wish it wasn't insured."

Thorne turned and saw a man in an open-necked white shirt with a black tie pulled down past the second buttonhole. He was wearing a pair of cowboy boots whose thick heel failed to raise him above 5' 9". His hair thinned at the temples and he had a two day beard you could use to light a match. Based on the grey in his hair and stubble, Thorne placed him as mid to late forties. The Texan smiled and held out his hand.

"Jay Stockton. Big fan of your work."

"Thanks," Thorne said, shaking Stockton's hand.

"He's referring to what you did to my face," Blake said.

Of course he was, Thorne thought. Why'd he still think anyone might've seen his TV show? He caught a mischievous sparkle in Stockton's eye. It only lasted a split second, but he knew he was dealing with a keen intelligence. Thorne had underestimated Blake already and didn't want to make the same mistake twice. There was something else about Stockton, something about the way he carried himself. All this time out the Marine Corps, and he could still sniff it out. An officer. Not too high, not too low.

"So, Stockton," Thorne said. "Is that Captain or Major?"

The Texan smirked. "You got a live one here, Blake."

"I know it," Blake said.

"Our rank is history, Thorne. This is Blake's show."

"All right, how about you give me the 411 on the painting."

Blake nodded.

"Follow me, all the shit's next door." He turned to the two men getting up from the sofa. "Porter, Lynch, you can sit this out."

Blake led him back down the hallway to a room with a closed door, which he unlocked with a key in his pocket. It seemed like a curious detail: locking a wooden door that any of them could get through with the right pair of boots. Thorne noticed Stockton had followed along behind them. This indicated to him that Stockton was second in command and that the others were no more than grunts. The door opened and they went inside.

Thorne took off his sunglasses.

The room had been cleared of furniture, save for an oak table which sat directly under a bare light bulb. Around the walls were boxes and canvas bags, the contents of which Thorne could guess from the smell of gun oil and grease that filled the air. There were no windows. Light from the bulb was harsh and drew his focus back to the table, which Blake now stood behind like a blackjack dealer. Spread out before him were floor plans with pen marks and cross hatchings drawn on top. He moved closer for a better look.

"Okay," Blake said. "At the moment the painting is hanging in an gallery in Beverly Hills. They got security in that place like you wouldn't believe. Lasers, thermals, all that *Mission Impossible* shit. On Saturday, the painting gets shipped back to the owner. It's his birthday this month and wants his picture back to be the big man while he has his party. This will be the third year he's done this, but this year will be the last. The painting is on show all day Friday, then, when the gallery closes up, they take it down and crate it up ready for transport first thing Saturday morning. Overnight they store it in what is basically an office next to a loading dock. Security is minimal. They have cameras, pressure mats, infrared sensors, plus, obviously, the doors are all alarmed."

Thorne snorted. "Minimal, huh?"

23

"Don't you get it? They spend all the money on the fancy security out front where the art is, but the offices around back are all Radio Shack. It wasn't originally part of the same business. Ten years ago the gallery expanded and bought the unit next door. They knocked a couple of doorways through, slapped on some paint and that's about it. Most of the time it's only documents and old computers in there, so they never upgraded the alarm. They figure no one's going to steal that crap and they're right. The alarm in the office is separate from the one in the gallery, so one doesn't trigger the other. We go in through the back and as long as we stay there and don't go near the gallery and a couple of other areas then we're all set."

Thorne frowned. "You have a man on the inside?"

Stockton cleared his throat. "Uh. Not exactly."

"What then?"

"A former employee," Blake said. "His fat ass got fired for being drunk on the job a couple of months ago but the information's still good and checks out."

"And you trust this drunk not to talk?"

"Chill, man. He can't identify us."

Because he's dead.

Silence stretched out between them. In that moment, Thorne knew he'd made a mistake getting involved, but what choice did he have? If they killed this man their threats were all the more real. He decided to start nodding, as if he'd been thinking through the information Blake had given him, rather than making him for a killer.

"You have a buyer in place for the painting once we have it?"

Blake smiled. "Of course, it's a slam-dunk. I wouldn't have the first idea how to move a stolen painting, would you? We only get a fraction of its true value of course, but it's still a lot of money for a night's work."

Thorne stared at the plans with a fixed expression. He was still thinking about the security guard and wondering how many others might have already died. Blake could have the same ending in mind for him when he was no longer needed. Why pay him nearly a million dollars when he could keep it for himself?

"There's something I meant to ask you, Blake. This job will make you a multi-millionaire, even after your sister's medical bills, right?"

"Right."

"So why the big deal about that hundred thousand?"

"Things didn't work out too well for me after the trial. What they did to me, it was unnecessary. My tour was over in a couple of months anyway. After years of service, all I was to them was an embarrassment - a dog that had shat on the wrong lawn. It wasn't enough to end my military career, they had to take away my future." Blake paused for a moment before continuing. "The hundred thousand isn't about money anymore. The loss of that job was pivotal in my life and I figure if I can in some way get it back, my life will return to the way it was meant to be and my run of bad luck will end."

It surprised Thorne that a man as tough as Blake could think like this; as if his life were a fairy tale plagued by an ancient curse. All the same, he'd had his own problems with the Corps and had also left under something of a cloud. It hadn't cost him his Honorable Discharge, but he could understand where Blake was coming from, if not why he should have to pick up the check on behalf of the Marine Corps.

"I think when you're a millionaire you make your own luck."

"I'll just bet you're right about that," Blake said. "Who knows? If this goes to plan I may give you the full mill after all. No hard feelings and all that. For sure you'd deserve it more than that sneaky prick, Lynch. Leave it with me, OK?"

Thorne smiled, made it as natural as he could.

"That'd be cool, man."

Somehow, the idea that he might be given a full share in the robbery was less believable than a share with the bullshit hundred thousand removed. It hadn't occurred to him before, but that cut had provided the $1 million payday with a degree of authenticity. The way he figured it, if Blake hadn't planned to give him the money at the end, he could promise any amount he chose at the beginning and the fact he hadn't had made him immediately trust him. The next thing he knew, Blake would offer him Lynch's share on top. It was manipulation pure and simple, designed to keep him on-side. He couldn't tell if this was a sign Blake intended to kill him, or a reflection on how he did business; through fear and temptation.

Blake put a box next to the plans and pushed it across the table.

A prepaid cell phone.

"That's your burner. Use it any time we need to keep in touch. I already added my number, it's the only one on there and I suggest you keep it that way. Don't use your own cell to call me and don't use the burner to call personal numbers as that will identify you. I paid cash for the burners and bought them all from different stores so they aren't part of the same batch. There's no link back to us from them."

"All right, but why would I be calling you?"

"Any operation needs comms, Thorne, you know that. We can't take our own cell phones with us on the job because they can trace them even when you aren't using them. You might as well leave a business card at the scene."

"Fine. I got it."

Blake passed him a laptop. "Use this for any internet activity connected with the robbery. Google searches, maps, whatever. It all gets saved somewhere. Cookies, processor ID number, MAC addresses, all that. Don't tell me about clearing caches, it's all shit. They can bring back any data they want to, trust me. We use this for everything then, when we're done, we destroy it."

Thorne raised an eyebrow. "A burner laptop?"

"*Exactly.*"

"What about internet connection?"

"Lynch helped the old woman next door set up her computer while she was away on vacation. We're hooked into her Wi-Fi. If we see her getting dragged away by the FBI, it's time to leave town."

Blake had thought of everything. He'd also spent a lot of money so far and he couldn't help wondering where it was coming from.

"Who's fronting this, you?"

Blake stood up, his chest puffed out.

"The buyer. We got a hundred large for costs, any left over we keep."

Somewhere, most likely in this room, was a bag full of money. At least half of it would still be left. He noticed Blake had become tense again, and he didn't want that.

"That's fantastic."

Blake said nothing.

Thorne studied the plans to stop the tension building. There was a stack of pages and he flipped through each one before returning to the top. They were from different floors and sections of the building, at a decent size. The pages had been both rolled up and folded at different times and the paper lay flat with rolled up corners. He looked up and Blake tilted his head to one side. It was the same movement Sara had done in the car.

"I'm going to need to see it beforehand."

"Of course," Blake said, relaxing. "Tonight."

"I'm also going to need equipment. Some won't be easy to get."

"Don't worry, I got a guy. He's not cheap, but he can get you pretty much anything you want, no questions asked. What else?"

"Coffee."

Blake smiled. "Doughnuts?"

"Definitely doughnuts."

*

Thorne sat studying the schematics for the gallery while making notes in a notepad. He'd moved into a back bedroom of the bungalow and was set up in front of a writing desk. He'd been at it for a couple of hours, and the others had left him to work. In his head, something had changed. He was on a mission now, there was no going back. This was how it'd been in the Corps; the self doubt, the fears, it all had to be put to one side. Negative thoughts produce negative outcomes. If you headed down a path believing you'd fail, you nearly always found a way to make it happen.

Having finished with the plans, he opened Blake's laptop and waited for it to finish its start-up. About ten seconds from cold, not bad. It was a Windows machine running an OS he hadn't used before. Thorne had been a Mac user from day one, but it seemed like there wasn't much in it anymore. Using Chrome, he pulled up the gallery on Google Maps. Beverly Hills wasn't a neighborhood he was too familiar with, having neither the budget to shop there, nor the desire to do so. Using Street View, he drove around the neighborhood stopping occasionally to rotate and tilt up to get the full picture. He'd only see the area at night, so it was important to absorb as much detail as he could from the daylight pictures.

The best vantage point would be from the top of the Wells Fargo building, but he was guessing that roof access there would be an operation in itself. That left a six floor parking garage directly next to the secondary building of the gallery. He enabled satellite imaging and smiled as a familiar parking grid appeared on the roof. It was perfect, they'd be able to look over the edge at the gallery below.

Thorne sat back and pressed the tips of his fingers together.

He believed Blake's initial analysis was correct. The front of the gallery was too well protected, not to mention highly visible to pedestrians and passing traffic through the wall of glass that wrapped around the entrance. Attempting a break in there would be suicide, but the rear of the office property appeared was a different story. It had above average security for a an office or store, but inadequate for an art gallery.

He licked his lips, a kind of fever taking hold. It occurred to him that he was looking forward to the heist. It was stupid and crazy and he should have no part in it, yet here he was almost high at the prospect of carrying it out.

The way he saw it, all his money problems were over.

FOUR

Blake decided to take Thorne to the gallery on his own. No one else needed to be there and he wanted to get a better sense of where Thorne was at with the robbery. He'd made it clear that he was on board, but it was obvious to Blake he'd bail given half a chance. Thorne was a straight arrow and always had been. It was a trait that had made him a loyal friend and a dependable Marine, but they were playing by a different rule book now and what they were planning went against everything that made Thorne who he was. Until the two of them were standing inside the gallery, he'd assume nothing.

"I used to think someday I'd live in a place like this," Thorne said, looking around them. "A big time Hollywood actor, you know? A huge house, a flash car. I guess none of that's going to happen if my show's canceled."

Blake said nothing. He liked the sound the AC made as it pumped freezing air into the cabin. It calmed him, and he didn't want to break the spell talking to Thorne about the way his life was panning out. From where he was sitting, his old friend had it pretty good.

"How's your face?"

He glanced at Thorne, the change in direction surprising him.

"I've had worse."

"Only because I didn't finish what I started."

"You still want to finish it?"

"I haven't decided."

Blake smiled. He'd always found Thorne easy to talk with and despite the years that had passed, little seemed to have changed. Sure, the man probably hated him now, but they'd been through bad patches before and somehow it always worked itself out.

"You've not said anything about the gallery. Do we have a problem?"

"I don't know how extensively you looked at those blueprints, Blake, but there are a *lot* of infrared sensors. Close to thirty in the office building alone. Even using the shortest route possible, I figure we're looking at passing eighteen units before we get to the painting. The sensors overlap one another so...no dead zones."

Blake shrugged his shoulders.

"You'll figure something out."

"Thanks, Aidan. You're a big help."

"I know, right?"

He expected Thorne to make a joke but he was distracted by pedestrians on the sidewalk. It was like they'd arrived in a parallel world.

"What's the deal with those guys of yours?"

"My *deal?*" Blake said.

"Where did they come from? Is there a 1 800 number for goons?"

Blake sighed. It was easy for Thorne to mock, he didn't know what it was like. He'd parachuted out of the Marines and hit the ground running.

"This may surprise you, but I used to volunteer at the VA. Our grateful nation has tossed a lot of veterans away like yesterday's garbage. It's not hard to find people prepared to cross the line for a payout. This country owes us, make no mistake." He paused, but Thorne remained silent, his calm face giving nothing away. He felt the old anger returning, thinking about the wounded men he'd met, the shattered lives. "We don't all get to be famous actors when we leave the service. Heroes with rows of medals and a big cheesy smile."

Thorne winced.

"I never asked for no damn medal."

"And I never asked for the *big chicken dinner*, but I got it anyway."

They sat in silence for a couple of minutes, the air between them crackling with bad energy. Blake regretted losing his cool, it wasn't what he wanted from this trip.

"I got to ask," Thorne said, "what does *Lynch* bring to the table?"

"Believe it or not, he was you before you came on board."

"He's an asshole."

Blake grinned. "*Exactly.*"

He saw a trace of a smile pass over Thorne's face.

"Seems to me like the two of us could pull this robbery on our own."

"You're probably right about that, but I've worked with these guys before. I trust them. Besides, they know all the details so cutting them out would be difficult."

He turned into the parking garage Thorne had selected on the internet and began to circle the ramps up to the roof. It was only two days since he'd last cased the gallery, but that time he'd parked some distance away and walked. There were cameras everywhere, and he knew the footage would be studied after the robbery. Coming here was a risk, but if Thorne was right, it was going to be worth it.

The car peeled out onto the roof.

Blake saw three security cameras, two covering the entrance and exit ramp, and one at the far end covering the entire parking area. Lower floors would need cameras to cover blind spots caused by support pillars, but on the roof they were out in the open with nowhere to hide. He gritted his teeth. This better be good. He parked up and they climbed out. As if on some hidden signal, they both performed an identical back arch and shoulder flex. The seats in the car were luxurious, but they were not designed for men their size and build. Thorne noticed their synchronized movement and grinned at him across the hood of the car.

They walked to the edge of the structure and stood side by side at the wall that wrapped around the top of the roof. Blake reached into his pocket and pulled out a pack of cigarettes he'd bought for exactly this moment. He took two out and handed one to Thorne.

"The hell's this?" Thorne said. "Who even smokes anymore?"

"If the security camera back there can pick us out, this is the reason we're standing here. It's not because we're planning a heist."

Thorne smiled. "I wonder if I ever really knew you."

"Nobody ever really knows anyone, don't you know that?"

Blake lit their cigarettes with a lighter and they held them to the side where they could be seen then looked at the gallery beneath them. The sun had gone down and there was no light left in the sky but all the lights burned inside the gallery and there was enough light from street lights to see what they needed.

"What time does the gallery close up?" Thorne asked.

"It's closed already, but the staff don't leave for another half hour."

Thorne glanced at his watch.

"They turn the lights out when they leave?"

"Yes and no. The lights in the main building are on 24/7, but the office lights are turned off. If you want, you can see some of the paintings through the front window even at four in the morning. Not the pricy stuff, but some of it."

Blake brought his arm in, like he was taking a draw on his cigarette, then returned it to where it was.

"It's another layer of security," Thorne said. "Anyone inside is going to be lit up like a Christmas tree to anyone outside, or to the cameras which are probably high definition."

He nodded. "That's what I figured."

"From up here you can see the front and back of the gallery, as well as traffic approaching along north and south Santa Monica, Camden, plus the end of the alley. One of your guys should be up here when it's going down, let us know if things are turning to shit outside."

"Agreed. Stockton's the obvious choice, he's a sniper."

Blake thought again about the infrared sensors. Thorne was right, he'd never counted how many the guard had scribbled onto the blueprints, he'd always just considered it someone else's problem. Thirty was a high number, and eighteen wasn't much better. He was concerned that defeating them all would prove to be either impossible, or take too long.

"You think you'll be able disable the sensors?"

"I don't think you can, that's the mistake I was making."

"What then?"

Thorne smiled. "I'm going to let them go off."

"Is that sarcasm?"

"I don't know, is it?"

Blake sighed. The actor had a fine line in bullshit. No doubt all would become clear soon enough. He dropped his cigarette and mashed it under his heel. Thorne did the same.

"Let's do this, I need to eat."

They took the stairs side by side, their feet synchronized. It felt like old times, the two of them out at night looking for a good time. Too bad that wasn't the case.

They walked onto North Camden Drive. Across the street, a Wells Fargo bank towered over them. The line of cars parked in front of it were each worth an easy hundred thousand. Blake glared at a ninety pound blonde girl climbing out of a Lexus SUV. He turned away, back to the sidewalk. Being broke made him someone he didn't like or want to spend time with, but he couldn't stop himself. At the gallery's window, they stopped and looked in.

Blake saw half a dozen paintings from where he stood, and none of them were any more than a colored shape on the wall to him. He felt nothing. Emotionally, he could be looking at kitchen appliances. He didn't get art, or what people saw in it. They continued to walk toward South Santa Monica Boulevard. At the corner they took a right, heading for the road that serviced the back of the gallery. Neither spoke, the four lanes of traffic was all it took to block conversation. They took a right again, up the alley.

"Blake, I've been thinking. If things go south on Friday night we won't have long to wait for the cops. The Beverly Hills PD is minutes away, I could see the building from the roof. You're talking five minutes tops, and that's assuming a patrol car isn't closer."

They'd drawn level with the back of the gallery.

"You're thinking like a civilian, Thorne. When we were in Iraq, we were surrounded by people who wanted us dead. We drove up and down their streets, we kicked down their front doors, we ripped apart their homes, we screamed in their wives' faces. We did all that knowing that behind every other window was some haji with four teeth and an AK. Yet, here we are.

We're still here, man. We're survivors, you and me. For all your jumping off buildings, you've been domesticated. But you got to trust me, it all comes back. The training, the attitude, all of it. Once a Marine, always a Marine. It's muscle memory, it's part of you forever. Now, in three days, we're going to rob these fools of their dumb ass painting and we're going to get rich in the process. What do you say to that? Are you worried about some linguine-eating motherfucker who hasn't seen his dick in thirty years after what we've been through?"

Thorne laughed. "You're crazy."

"Doesn't mean I'm wrong, does it?"

"It's different, this is our home. You don't shit where you eat, everyone knows that."

"This feels a million miles from *my* home, brother. We probably have more in common with goat herders in Iraq and Afghanistan than these people here."

"I can't argue with that."

Thorne's mask appeared to melt away. In its place, he saw something he hadn't seen in a long time, before all the bad blood and the death of that girl. He saw his friend.

Blake softened his voice.

"Chris, how about we start over, put everything behind us?"

Thorne looked at his feet for a moment, then nodded.

"Let's do that."

Blake smiled and gripped Thorne's shoulder.

This was more than he could've hoped for and vindicated his decision to leave the others at the bungalow. He couldn't imagine this happening while Thorne and Lynch were trying to kill each other. Blake turned and they began picking their way through a small parking lot toward the back door of the gallery. On one side of the building was a fire escape, on the other, a ladder going straight up to the roof. The name of the gallery was written vertically on the wall in two foot wide letters. He glanced around the lot and across the alley to the building opposite.

"Are you seeing any cameras?"

"No, nothing."

"That's pretty weird, isn't it? Even gas stations have cameras."

"I can't say I'm disappointed."

"Still though."

"I know," Thorne said. "Could be this land doesn't belong to them or is shared in some way and they aren't allowed to record people without their permission. I've heard about stuff like that before. There are cameras inside the gallery, I saw that much."

Blake nodded. It didn't make much sense to him, but like Thorne, he thought this was good news. They'd be able to load the painting straight into the van without being seen or recorded. They cleared the parked cars and made their way along the side of the gallery. There was a dumpster right under the ladder that led to the roof. It would be easy enough to use it to bridge the short gap between the bottom of the ladder and the ground. He saw Thorne look at it, then up, obviously making the same connection. They kept walking. The administration building next door was the one they were interested in. As they approached the rear door, Blake noticed something he wasn't expecting.

A keyhole.

"*Fuck!* They added a deadbolt!"

Thorne stood silently staring at it, his hands on his hips. Blake shook his head. The security guard had said nothing about a deadbolt. The keypad and card swipe were there right enough. That looked relatively new, added shortly before Matt Hanson was fired. But the key card wouldn't open the deadbolt, only an electronically controlled latch.

"Can any of your goons pick a lock?"

Blake snorted. Thorne and his *goons* again.

"You kidding? They can barely tie their shoes."

"Yeah, that's what I thought."

"Can't we can kick it in or use a sledgehammer?"

Thorne shook his head.

"The door opens outward. You wouldn't just be breaking the lock out the casing, you'd be trying to force the door through a smaller opening. Besides, the frame is extruded steel embedded in concrete. You kick that, all you get is a busted foot."

"Shit," Blake said.

"It's not the end of the world."

"We can drill out the cylinder?"

"I got better idea."

"All right," Blake said. "Let's go."

He followed Thorne out. The actor was taller and walked faster because of it. They moved south, away from the alley entrance. He supposed they were going in the parking garage from the other side, but they walked past that as well. Thorne was going the long way around.

"Where we going, man? I'm starved."

"We're not through here."

Blake sighed. In his mind he pictured a thick, juicy steak. He could practically taste the meat. Taste the blood that would ooze out from the middle and spread across his plate. The blood would soak into some of his fries, but mostly they'd be crisp and golden and perfect. He turned to Thorne as they made their way out.

"What's your take on the door having a deadbolt *and* a key card?"

"Deadbolt is probably only used when the gallery is closed, the rest of the time the staff buzz themselves in and out with their cards. The parking lot is right next to it, so that makes sense." Thorne said nothing for a moment, before continuing. "Aidan, I got to tell you. That lock did *not* look new. I figure your security guy missed it out on purpose."

"Certainly looks that way."

"You don't sound surprised."

"I guess I'm not. A part of me supposed he was holding something back. He was giving me all this information, maybe because he thought it'd be useless to me."

"You think he missed anything else out?"

"I sure hope not," Blake said. "I guess we're going to find out."

"On the blueprints there's no indication of a magnetic contact on that door, but dollars to doughnuts there's one there. I don't think I've ever seen an alarmed building that didn't have one on a main door. It's like alarms 101."

"You're right. That fat weasel."

They walked in silence. Matt Hanson had set him up, missing out key details of the alarm. Enough to get him caught. Perhaps the guard had seen what was going to happen to him that night and planned a little payback.

"Did you see it?" Thorne said.

"Huh?"

"We just passed a video camera. It's in a black dome enclosure, mounted on the wall. It'll capture every vehicle that drives past."

"And this is a one way street."

Thorne nodded, a wry smile on his face.

"I see a traffic violation in our future."

They exited the alley as a white Prius turned in. Both of them glanced at Rodeo Drive like they'd caught a glimpse of a circus, then turned up Camden to walk back to the parking garage. There was an easy silence between them now. He knew it was easier to talk about forgetting the past than it was to do it, but he had to assume that their previous near twenty year friendship would help offset that. They were back inside the Audi before either of them spoke again.

"Now you've seen it, any idea how we get in?"

"Sure," Thorne said. "As long as your guy can get what we need."

"Like?"

"For a start, I'm going to need a shotgun with M1030 shells."

Blake scratched his chin. His stubble was well on its way to becoming a beard.

"We already got a couple of shotguns. What're 1030s?"

A car exited the ramp and swung around behind them. Thorne turned to watch it go by, his eyes following it as it parked. He spoke, still watching the driver of the other vehicle.

"Master keys."

Thorne had shut down, no doubt thinking about Kate Bloom. She was a beautiful woman and worth thinking about for sure.

"What else?"

"There's going to be a bunch of stuff, Blake, I'll write you a list."

Thorne's voice was hardening up.

"That's cool, but we're short on time here so if there's something on this list that's going to be difficult to get hold of then you should let me know about it now."

He nodded, the tightness in his face easing again.

"I need a couple of high-end radio frequency signal jammers, the best you can get, and an RF spectrum analyzer."

"We're going to jam those sensors?"

"*Right.*"

"Will that work?"

"If they can block IEDs then for sure they can block a $5 sensor made in China."

Blake smiled and started the car's engine.

Thorne was the right man for the job. Perhaps, for any job.

FIVE

Three nights later, they were back. This time, in Blake's van filled with his gang of rejects and bags of equipment. A part of Thorne had supposed that something would've come up to prevent the heist going through, but it was the reverse. Everything had gone without a hitch. At this hour, the drive to Beverly Hills was effortless and soon they were coming up on their turn. Traffic on Santa Monica Boulevard was light and well spaced and the closest vehicle was several hundred feet back, too far to notice their illegal turn. Blake swung the van around the parking lot and reversed back up to the gallery.

Finally, Blake cut the engine and turned to face them.

"All right assholes, this is it. The easiest million dollars you'll ever make. Let's try not to stand on each other's dicks until we're out the other side, okay?"

Porter grinned, his perfect white teeth shining in the dark.

"That's a beautiful fucking speech, man."

"You know it."

Blake put on a baseball cap and they all did the same, pulling the brims down to hide their eyes, nose, and cheekbones from security cameras. Far from bulletproof, but enough to stop facial recognition software. Thorne, Porter, and Blake piled out the front of the van. Blake opened the side door to reveal Foster like a captured grizzly. The giant filled the entire opening and the van shifted noticeably as he climbed out. Behind him, looking considerably less like a grizzly, was Lynch whose pale skin shone like porcelain in the moonlight. His hair hung half over his face and he flipped it over the top of his head with a practiced hand movement. The Irishman's eyes connected with Thorne's and remained connected while he got out.

"See something you like?" Thorne said.

"Your future."

"Do we grow old together? Is that it?"

"You've done all the aging you're going to, Thorne."

Thorne shook his head. Lynch had a serious bug up his ass about him, that was for sure. Perhaps because he'd replaced his role within the gang at the last minute. He wondered what background Lynch had that could be comparable to his. Electronics? Computers?

Blake opened up the rear doors of the van. A dozen bags and cases were lined up ready to go. Thorne reached down to pick up a nylon bag directly in front of him, but Foster pushed past him, his huge hand grabbing the handles first.

"I got this one."

"You're welcome," Thorne said.

When everything was unloaded, Thorne found the grocery bags he was looking for and took it to a clear space to work in. He bent down on one knee and lay a watermelon on the asphalt in front of him. The lot was dark and though his eyes had adjusted to the moonlight, it wasn't enough.

"A little light here?"

The others gathered around in a semicircle and turned on their flashlights. Using a bread knife, he cut the watermelon in two, with one section having 80% of the fruit. He then used the blade to remove a two inch by one inch shaft through the middle.

He held it up for the others to see.

"This look familiar yet, Lynch? *Date night!*"

Blake and Porter laughed as Lynch glared at him.

"Fuck you, Hollywood."

Thorne nodded, a thin smile on his face. The two of them were getting quite the routine going. With a bit of work they'd be able to take it on the road and hit some stand-up clubs. Using the knife he made a final diagonal cut across the bottom. He sat back on his heels to look at it and turn it over in his hands before putting it to one side and repeating the process on another fruit. He figured they would need two, maybe another two inside. When he was through a second time, he stood and unzipped his gym bag so he could reach in for the equipment. He pulled out the shotgun, thumbed open the box of shells and began to feed them into the magazine. Out the corner of his eye, he saw Lynch draw his piece. Clearly they were uncomfortable with him holding a loaded weapon. No doubt Stockton had a bead on him too from his position on the parking structure above.

"Hey," Blake said. "I never did ask what the melons were for."

Thorne put on a pair of safety glasses and racked the slide.

"Observe."

He pushed the shotgun through the hole in the watermelon then turned so that the end of the barrel was at 45 degrees to the deadbolt. He pulled the trigger. There was a muffled explosion and the fruit sprayed out in a wet cone against the door. Thorne tilted the shotgun down and the remains of the watermelon fell off onto the asphalt. He glanced at Blake, who had a big smile on his face.

"*Nice.* How'd we do?"

Thorne placed the firearm on the ground and pulled a small flashlight out his pocket. He shone the beam at the impact site, his gloved fingers wiping pieces of shredded fruit away. The breaching shell had ripped a hole in the outer fabric of the door, but they weren't through yet. He got back to his feet.

"One more ought to do it. It's a tough door."

He recycled the shotgun and added a second watermelon. It was tight around the barrel and he had to use some pressure to get it to fit. He lined it up with the first shot and pulled the trigger. This time, the melon disintegrated in all directions. He glanced back and saw Lynch covered from head to toe in a pink mist.

Thorne grinned. "*Oops.*"

"A rabid dog got more sense than you, Thorne."

He turned away from the Irishman.

"Rabid dogs get a bad rap."

He checked the impact site a second time. He expected to see a mangled lock, but instead saw straight into the room beyond.

"We're through."

When he pulled back, Thorne noticed the shotgun was no longer next to his right knee. He glanced to the side. It wasn't in his gym bag either, or in Blake's hand. It had just vanished. He gave no reaction and instead reached into his bag for the snake scope. Better to carry on like nothing had happened than give them a reason to use it. The scope had a flexible neck and he bent an L-shape in it then passed it slowly through the hole in the door, aiming the lens up at the top of the door frame. The magnetic contact was on the left hand side, exactly where he expected it to be. He pulled the scope slowly out again and nodded.

"Bastard," Blake said.

"What?" Porter said.

"*Hanson.* He missed out a few details when we spoke to him."

Thorne took out an electromagnet he'd made from the electric motor in Blake's freezer. It weighed close to six pounds and was connected by an eight foot cable to a motorcycle battery. He placed the battery on the ground and held the device against the top of the frame in line with the contact. He turned it on and felt the electromagnet snap tight against the metal. In tests, the magnetic force it generated had been enough to carry his weight. Even attenuated by the door frame, he had no doubts it would overpower the sensor.

He looked at his watch: 3:38.

Foster passed him a chunky plastic flight case. Thorne opened the catches and pulled out the signal jammer. Blake had really come through, the jammer was high-end, better than some he'd used in EOD. He didn't question where Blake was sourcing his equipment. With the right budget, you can get your hands on the most amazing toys. As he set the controls, he turned things over in his head. If Blake planned to double-cross him, there were three likely points for that to take place. Once they were inside; once they had the painting; or once they had the money. The last made least sense to him from a strategic point of view. Why keep him around that extra amount of time if the plan was to take him out? On the other hand, none of them appeared to have a suppressor and a gunshot might alert the authorities before they could secure the painting. Perhaps Foster would kill him with his bare hands.

"What's the range of this thing?" Blake said.

Thorne kept working. He was almost ready.

"A hundred feet, less if walls or floors are thick."

"But it's going to work *through this door*, right?"

Thorne glanced up at Blake, surprised.

"I'm kind of curious about that myself."

"You don't know?"

"No idea."

Blake swore.

"What's the big deal?" Porter said.

"Well," Thorne said. "If the jammer doesn't work through the door and we open it, then obviously that will trigger the alarm before the jamming comes into effect."

"Are you kidding me right now?"

"No. However, the office hasn't got a silent alarm. If the jammer doesn't work the control panel will start beeping and a twenty second countdown begins, waiting for the passcode. Since we don't have one, we should use that time to leave before shit gets real."

"We aren't going anywhere without that painting." Blake said.

Thorne turned back to the jammer, his head nodding.

"I figured you'd say that."

He activated the device.

"Come on Thorne," Lynch said. "My eighty year old grandmother could've opened this door by now and her hands never stop shaking."

"Shaking what? Your pom-pom?"

Blake sighed. "Guys? Shut the fuck up and let the man work."

"No need, I'm done."

"Finally. Let's do this."

SIX

Thorne stood on the right side of the door, Blake on the left. His senses sharpened and all distractions went away. This was when he felt the most alive, and simultaneously, when he was most at peace. It had been this way in the Marines, and when he'd taken that fall from the roof of the hotel. He'd tried many times to replicate the same high on fairground rides but nothing ever came close. Blake looked at him and nodded, then swiped Hanson's key card through the card reader. The display lit up, a yellow-green glow in the half light.

ENTER CODE

Blake licked his lips and punched in 2046. There was a brief pause, followed by an electro-mechanical *clunk* as the main lock opened. Thorne pulled on the door handle. Nothing. No movement at all. He glanced back at Foster.

"Bigfoot? You want to give me a hand?"

Foster stepped forward, grabbed the handle and pulled with his left hand braced against the wall. After a second there was a tearing sound and the door opened, scattering fragments of brass and steel onto the asphalt below. They all froze, listening.

No alarm, no beeping.

Blake smiled and dipped his head in a small bow.

"Good job, Thorne."

He followed Blake inside, carrying the jammer in front of him. With the limited range, he wanted to bring it into the building to maximize it's potential. Rebar used in reinforced concrete could reduce it's efficacy and he didn't want to take any chances. One by one the gang's flashlights snapped on, illuminating their surroundings. They were in a small storage space given over to outdoor clothing, boots, and staff uniforms. Along one wall were a series of metal lockers, similar to those in a school.

In the distance he heard a low hum, like an engine running.

He turned to watch the four other men. They were an odd bunch. A freak of nature, a sociopath, and two losers. By his own admission, Blake had used these zeros on previous jobs. Why would he double-cross him, his oldest friend, and let them live? Was it not just as likely that he'd be true to his word? But all too quickly the answer came to him.

Because they wanted to be here.

At the back of the room a door led to the rest of the building. He'd been unable to tell from the drawings if it would also need to be breached using the shotgun, but the door was unlocked and they went through it leaving the unused watermelons behind. They came to a staircase and began to ascend. Thorne kept close to Blake, his thumb ready to kill the jammer at the slightest sign of a double-cross. Now they were moving freely about the building, his role in the robbery appeared to be over and he felt vulnerable.

They came out in a typical office hallway.

From here the jammer would cover them all the way to the secure storage area ahead and back down to the exit. Although he liked having his finger on the kill switch, he'd rather have his hands free to fight off any attack. He set the device down on the floor.

Blake waited for him, his eyes watching him closely.

They moved off along the hallway, their flashlights crisscrossing and bouncing off the polished walls and floor. Framed pictures hung on the wall, all in identical dark wood frames. He swept his flashlight across some of them. They were posters advertising past shows in the gallery, some almost forty years old. These were only for staff and the owners, the public didn't see these. He shook his head. To him, it looked like they'd framed trash.

He turned and looked behind him. The creature, Foster, was there lumbering along. He was stooped over to avoid hitting his head on the low ceiling and it made him look more like a gorilla than usual. As far as he could tell, Foster was the only other person there that wasn't armed, which was pretty ironic since his role seemed to be Blake's bodyguard.

The hum he'd heard earlier grew louder as they approached the end of the corridor. He hadn't thought about it before, it had just been a distant white noise. The kind of sound you hear all the time and tune out, forget. He frowned. It sounded like a generator. They turned the corner and Blake stopped abruptly, causing Porter and Thorne to pile into the back of him.

"This isn't right," Blake said. "According to the blueprints there should be five offices here. Now there are only two doors."

Porter ran his flashlight beam down the wall of the corridor.

"Looks like they knocked the offices together to create a bigger space."

Thorne stood next to the first door and placed his ear against it. The humming sound was coming from inside. The door was made from brushed steel and it was cold against his skin. He knocked on it lightly with the knuckle of his index finger and a deep metallic *thunk* came back. The door was thick. He cleared his throat.

"Either they're storing meat in here, or they have the best air conditioner in the whole of L.A. County." He paused for a beat, like it was a line in his show. "I'm kind of hoping it's the latter because this was a lot of effort just to get some pork chops."

"I don't get it," Porter said. "Why have AC on when nobody's here?"

Blake folded the plans in half and tucked them into his back pocket.

"Isn't it obvious? To protect the paintings."

"But the gallery's on the other side of the building."

"I *know* that." Blake said. "I found out at the same time as you. I don't have any new information. What do you want from me? I don't know. Does it really matter?"

"It kind of does actually," Thorne said, interrupting. "I'm not sure I can open this."

"You could get into the Queen of England's undies if you set your mind to it. Spare me the details, and skip to the part where I'm walking through it."

"Blake, there's no keyhole or gap to get the scope in. I can't tell if bypassing the keypad will trigger the alarm. I'd be lucky to get a playing card down the side of that door. It's solid too. Steel, at least quarter inch, with a keypad lock and recessed hinges. The quality of the installation and the newer tech probably means it's tied into the gallery alarm system, not the piece of shit system we've been up against so far." Thorne turned back toward the door. He stroked the surface, his head tilted over thoughtfully. "The way I see it, we open this door and inside of five minutes, the parking lot will be filled with SWAT cars and guys with coffee breath that want to shoot us in the face with shotguns."

Blake ran his hand through his hair in frustration.

"All right. What do you suggest?"

"I'm suggesting we don't open it."

"Thorne, I didn't come this close to leave empty handed."

"Can I make a suggestion?" Lynch asked.

Blake turned on him, his finger raised. "Not another word, you hear me?"

"But you don't know what I was going to say."

"I know *exactly* what you were going to say, Lynch. Exactly."

Thorne walked to the other door. It was the last remaining office door of the previous layout. No lock. He pushed the handle down and the door swung open and bounced off a box of copier paper. A fish tank glowed softly in the corner. Even before he hit the lights, Thorne saw there was nothing useful in the room. A desk, a PC that belonged in a museum, a photocopier, and stacks and stacks of loose paper piled up ready to start a fire. He crossed the room and stood by the wall that joined the larger room. The smell of fresh paint hung in the air. He peeled off his right glove and placed the back of his hand against the wall. It was stone cold.

Cinder block, not drywall.

"What is it?" Blake asked. "Can we go through the wall?"

"Not easily."

Blake sighed. He took out the floor plan again and flattened it out on the desk. After a moment he was smiling and jabbing at the paper with a thick, gloved finger.

"The window, see? We go out this window here and in through the window next door. The windows are less than fifteen feet apart."

Thorne saw it all right. His old poker buddy was out of his mind. The other three were in the room now, drawn in by Blake's excitement. It was too much muscle for such a small area and Foster towered over them all like a god, his sweat-filled underarms right in Thorne's face. He looked different, calm.

"Blake, that's great." Thorne said. "Fifteen feet with no ledge and a twenty five foot drop. As long as one of us is Spiderman our problems are officially over."

Something passed between Blake and Foster. A look, a head tilt.

Foster turned and punched him in the stomach, knocking him backward onto the floor. Thorne lay on his side, folded up, like a fly that had been hit by a magazine. Over a high pitched whine he heard a sucking sound. Air being tugged in through his open mouth in jagged pulses. He looked up at them, waiting for one of them to do something to help but they just stood there staring at him. His vision darkened at the edges. It felt like an elephant was standing on his chest, pinning him down. The more air he got down, the less the elephant weighed. Slowly his breathing returned to normal, the jags smoothing out. He didn't know how long he'd lain there, over a minute he thought. He was covered in sweat and was very cold. He'd never been punched that hard before and, worse, it was obvious that this was no more than a tap as far as Foster was concerned.

Blake walked around the desk and looked down at him.

"This isn't the Marines, Thorne, but there's still a chain of command. I have allowed you to take point on this because your skills offer us the best chances of success, but I don't want you to forget what's at stake here, or who's in charge. One way or another, we are going into that room tonight. Whatever it takes, even if that means triggering the alarm. Are we clear?"

Thorne nodded. He wanted to be sick.

"You can die from that kind of punch, you know that?"

"I believe it."

Thorne glanced at Foster and smiled grimly. He could see now why the giant looked so calm, so happy. He was was standing up straight, not stooping. The ceiling in the hallway was lower. It was fake.

"I have an idea."

"Excellent," Blake said.

Foster held out his big, brutal hand to help him up, but Thorne ignored it and avoided looking at his face. It might be the face of the man that was going to kill him and he preferred not to look at it any more than he had to. He stood carefully and pushed past the others toward the doorway. Outside in the corridor, he pointed his flashlight straight up. Ceiling tiles and fluorescent panels. It was as he thought. They were such a standard office feature, nobody looked at them twice. He walked back to the door with the keypad lock. The rest of Blake's gang emerged from the office.

Thorne reached up and pushed at a tile with his hand. It lifted straight up. Gravity was all that kept them in place. He caught hold of the edge, tilted his hand and the tile came through the space in the hanging frame. With effort, all of them but Foster could squeeze through the gap without having to saw through the frame. The idea of isolating Foster appealed to him. He put the tile down on the floor and shone his flashlight into the dark space. After a moment, another flashlight beam shot into the same opening. Not much there, some pipes and cables. The true ceiling appeared to be a good three feet higher. He turned to the man standing next to him. Blake. His head was tilted back, looking up. His big mouth was chewing on something like it was a gym workout, the muscles on his jaw flexing. The smell hit him. Licorice.

"I'm thinking your idea is similar to mine."

Thorne grunted. "Give me a boost, let's see what we have."

"Screw that, we got a boost monkey." Blake turned. "Foster, come here."

Foster came over and dumped his huge nylon bag on the floor. Blake had him get on his hands and knees. He did what he was told without hesitation. His broad back was now in front of Thorne like a table. Reluctantly, he stepped up, first with one leg, then with the other. He stood hunched over with his knees bent, as if he was surfing. Of all the scenarios he'd imagined for the evening, this had not been one of them. He looked down at his tennis shoes on the navy-colored flight jacket. There was almost no give in Foster's back, it felt like he was standing on a piece of wood. It scared him. This wasn't fat, this was hard slabs of muscle. There'd be no way for him to beat a man like this in any form of unarmed combat. If it came to it, and he was almost certain it would, he was going to need to shoot Foster. A head shot, or center mass with something like a shotgun; anything else might just make him angry.

With his hand braced against the steel door for balance, Thorne straightened to full height and his head entered the hole in the ceiling. There was a noticeable bump in the sound levels coming from the air conditioning unit. He put his small flashlight into his mouth, grabbed hold of two pipes above his head and pulled himself up through the hole and sat on a small ledge. He was bent over, with rough concrete pressing into the back of his neck, but at least he wasn't hanging on the pipes. The angle forced his head down into Blake's flashlight beam. He flinched at the light and twisted around, assessing his location. In front of him, the wall on the other side of the corridor continued beyond the suspended tile and joined onto the floor above. To his left, at the limit of the flashlight's reach, rose another wall of concrete blocks which he took to be the top of the stairwell they'd climbed minutes earlier. He couldn't make out anything to his right, except for a large black hose that snaked off into the distance.

The air conditioning for the gallery.

He followed the snake back to where it plunged into the room below. On that side of the ledge, in place of ceiling tiles, were sheets of rough untreated particle board nailed onto wooden joists. He frowned and looked more closely at the ledge and smiled. It was the top of the nearside corridor wall.

Thorne looked down through the hole again.

"Hey, Blake, I got a question for you."

"What's that?"

"Who's your daddy?"

Blake laughed. "There's a way through?"

"Improvise, Adapt and Overcome."

"Oorah," Porter said, his voice flat and sarcastic.

"Pass up a pry bar and the small RF jammer. Let's rob these idiots."

"I hear that."

Blake stepped up on Foster's back, his hands holding the pry bar and the jammer. Thorne took them and placed them on the ledge next to him, then reached down to pull up Blake. They were both over 200 pounds and the space became impossibly full with both of them in it. His flashlight in his mouth, he crawled out along one of the thicker joists until he was in the middle of the room below. The jammer was less sophisticated than the other unit, requiring only activation of different frequency blocks. No fine-tuning was possible. He felt Blake watching him from the ledge. His gut told him that neither Blake or Porter would want to kill him because of their previous friendships, leaving that to Foster, Lynch or Stockton. That was half a chance, he thought, and it might be all he needed. Down in the corridor, Porter and Lynch were talking. He couldn't make out their conversation, only that it was light, excited. Tension was easing as optimism returned. A million dollars wasn't what it used to be, but it was still a powerful motivator.

"How'd you know it would be like this?"

He looked above Blake's flashlight, where his face would be.

"What's that?"

"Down in that office, it was like you knew."

"I know contractors. There's no corner they won't cut to shave a dime off their costs and improve their margin. Plus, they could be pretty sure no arty types were going to come up here to check. Security is an illusion, there's always a way past it."

The jammer active, Thorne reached back and waved his hand around until it stopped against the cold steel of the pry bar. It was a thirty-inch octagonal rod with a spike at one end and a wedge at the other. The bar had a nice weight, at least fifteen or sixteen pounds. He imagined dropping through the hole in the ceiling and sinking the metal into Foster's back until it punched out the front. That might be enough to take the big man out.

His watch face caught in the beam of his flashlight.

3:55.

They'd already been inside seventeen minutes.

Twelve minutes until his insurance policy kicked in.

The wooden panels were nailed on from below so he had to work the pry bar in reverse. He worked the flat end into the edge of the joist, then leaned forward over the panel. The confined space allowed him to press his back against the concrete above for extra power. There was a squeak as he pushed down and a gap opened up. He worked the wedge deeper into the gap and pushed again. He moved along the panel, repeating the process. It was tough going and he began to overheat. Clothing chosen to limit trace evidence was not ideal for physical labor.

After a couple of minutes, he paused to wipe his forehead on the back of his sleeve. It wasn't clear to him why he was doing construction work when his involvement was meant to be technical. Doubtless more payback for their fight. As he started to work the pry bar under the joist again, there was a loud groan and the panel dropped down an inch. There was a creak as more wood splintered. Then the panel was gone.

The weight of the wood caused it to hinge open along the opposite side, then tear itself off and fall into the space below. The noise was incredible, like an explosion, and the flat concrete next to his head amplified the sound still further. His heart beat wildly in his chest. He hadn't considered the sound the panel would make when it fell, never mind how he might prevent it. Dust swarmed through the air and he coughed to clear it out his lungs. He pointed his flashlight at Blake and saw a huge grin on his face.

"That was fantastic! Did you shit yourself? I know I did!"

Thorne didn't reply.

Unexpected loud noise was no joke when you'd worked EOD.

His hands were shaking now, a classic shock reaction. He sat back on his heels and let his hands rest on his thighs. He hoped it wouldn't get

46

worse, shock could be extremely debilitating and he needed to be on top of his game. He kept the flashlight trained on Blake's face so he wouldn't see the shaking, but Blake had already moved on and was looking into the room below. Behind him, a wild-eyed Lynch appeared, a nickel-plated .45 clenched in his fist. Without turning, Blake spoke to him.

"Put it away, Lynch, just a piece of wood falling on the floor."

Blake's crew were oddballs, but they were tight.

He crawled back along the joist. Blake had stopped moving his flashlight about and had it trained on something. Thorne turned to look. It was the end of a metal shelving unit, and it made a perfect ladder.

"It's like they put it there to help us," Blake said.

He sat next to Blake on the ledge and let his legs hang down through the hole he'd created. It felt good to stretch his muscles and restore circulation. After several seconds, his eyes settled on the space where he'd set up the second jammer, a space that was now empty. He groaned inwardly. The twisting force of the falling panel had knocked it into the room below, a fall it would not survive. He saw no point telling Blake, the damage was done. If the alarm had been triggered, the cops would arrive before they could get out. All he could do was hope there was no sensor and carry on. He turned to Blake.

"You want to go first?"

"After you, Gunny. Age before beauty."

Thorne sighed. "You're a real hero, Blake."

"I don't know if I ever told you this, but I once considered joining the Navy."

Thorne laughed, he couldn't help it. Some things never changed. Blake and Lynch were laughing too now. The sound was strangely pleasing, like a tide washing ashore. The laughter relaxed him, even though it caused a ball of fire to burn where Foster hit him. If he lived to see the following day, there'd be the most amazing bruise there, no doubt about it. Blake passed him a night vision headset. Thorne took off his baseball cap and stuffed it into the front of his top and pulled on the device. It was a cheap civilian rig, the kind used by perverts and serial killers. He crouched at the edge, judging the distance to the shelving unit.

Five feet out, three feet down.

He put the flashlight in his mouth and launched himself across the void onto the shelving unit. The shelving was either incredibly heavy, or screwed into the floor, because the impact of his body slamming into it caused only the smallest movement in the metalwork. He climbed down onto the floor. Next to his shoes was the battered wooden ceiling panel. Looking up he saw three flashlights aiming down at him; Porter had joined the party.

"Kill the lights, I'm going to do a sweep with infrared."

"Whatever you say, amigo."

The flashlights winked out one after the other and the darkness rushed in. He gave his eyes a moment to adapt, but there appeared to be no available light in the room. Without light, the noise given off by the air conditioning unit was all the more monstrous and overwhelming. He flipped down the night vision goggles and turned them on. A grainy green room appeared before him. He took in his surroundings. There were rows and rows of shelving units, each of them about fifty feet long. The room had to run the entire width of the building, each shelf filled with wooden crates. Hundreds of them. Behind him stood the huge air conditioning unit. He looked at the corners of the room, searching for sensors. It looked clear. He turned his head sweeping the scope back and forth until he found what he was looking for: the remains of the second jammer. He quietly kicked the pieces under the nearest shelf out of sight.

"C'mon man, what are you doing?"

Blake's voice had an unpleasant, hard edge.

"I bet he's rubbing one out," Lynch said.

Above him, he heard laughter.

"You're...not are you Thorne?" Blake asked, humor creeping into his voice.

"He's thinking about Foster's asscrack," Lynch said. "I saw him check it out."

More laughter. He was dealing with morons. The last piece of jammer hidden, he walked to the doorway, deactivated the night vision and turned on the room lights. Panel after panel of fluorescent lights flickered on. After the darkness, the light was brutal. There were groans from above and he allowed himself a smile.

"Jesus Christ, Thorne!" Blake said. "Thanks for the goddam heads up."

While he waited for the others to join him, he clenched and unclenched his fists. The shake was gone now, his body had burned through the spike of adrenalin pumping through it.

Porter came down first.

Thorne noticed Porter's right pants leg didn't sit properly at the ankle. On the outside, the material was bunched up around something roughly the size of a woman's fist. He didn't need to see it to know what it was: a Smith & Wesson .38 Chief's Special. If he'd been ready, he could've grabbed it off him, but then what? Shoot his way out? The truth was, his problems wouldn't end with all of them dead. Blake's girlfriend would still be out there somewhere and he had no way to find her. She'd kill Kate. He believed it, that was no idle threat. The woman was crazy.

Porter got to the floor and turned to face him. His eyes narrowed, seeing Thorne standing so close to him, but they quickly widened again.

"Oh shit, look at the size of this place."

"Just wait," Thorne said. "You haven't seen the worst of it."

48

Porter walked past him and looked down the gap between two rows of shelving units. With the lights on, the volume of items stored was hard to ignore.

"Damn," Porter said. "That's a lot of boxes."

There was no denying it. It was a hell of a lot of boxes and for sure they didn't have time to crack open each one to find the Picasso. There could be 300 crates on those shelves. He glanced at his watch and his eyes widened in surprise. 4:04. Three minutes left. Even if they left immediately, he doubted there was time to get out the way they had come in.

It dawned on him that the robbery was going to be a bust. To his surprise, this realization brought with it a wave of despair. For the first time, his thoughts focussed on the money Blake had promised him rather than threats to his life. He had no idea how he could survive without it. In his mind, he'd already started to spend the money. Pay from this season's show was already half gone, advanced early by the network to head off a previous crisis. It would be months until money from his producer credit started to trickle in and that was barely enough to keep the lights on.

He walked down one of the aisles. Perhaps there'd be something worth seeing at the other end. He didn't believe it, but he figured someone ought to check after they'd come this far. Thorne reached his hand out as he walked along, his gloved fingertips brushing past each box. It made no sense for them to file the box away on one of these shelves if it was being shipped out the next day, that part of Blake's story rang true. Either the crate would be set aside, or the painting was still in the gallery and they hadn't boxed it up yet. He got to the end of the aisle and found what he had expected: a blank wall.

He paused to study the nearest crate more closely.

It was covered in labels from different security firms charged with its transportation. He prodded it experimentally with his index finger. It moved. It was lighter than it looked. Lighter, than it should be. He looped around the stack and came back along a different aisle. A box cutter lay on one of the shelves and he palmed it and put it into his back pocket. All three men had now descended the shelving ladder and were now deep in an argument. Porter stood directly in front of Blake, the top of his body pitched forward aggressively.

"Blake, all these crates look the same. How're we going to find the right one? You said it would basically be on its own in here."

"Clearly the information I had was out of date."

"You think? Your information's so out of date the building's changed shape since it was true. This room isn't even on your blueprints."

"I don't like that tone, Porter."

"Really? My *tone* is the problem here? You going to get Foster to hit me too? Maybe your pet dog won't bite if there's no meal coming. I shouldn't have to tell you this, Blake, but you're only in charge when there's a payoff. This goes south, it's a free for all."

Blake's mouth wrinkled up on the side closest Thorne.

"Porter...*Sam*, we can fix this, this can still work."

Lynch shook his head. "I don't know about that. Porter's right, we aren't going to find Jack in this place. I think they got the lost ark in here somewhere."

"That's enough." Blake turned hopefully toward Thorne. "Find anything?"

"Nothing good."

"Come on!" Lynch said. "Let's just grab a couple of these other paintings and get the hell out. Who cares if it isn't the right one?"

Blake sighed.

"And do what with them, Lynch? Sell them in Venice Beach?"

"I don't know, we can figure that part out later. This stuff is probably worth millions, it'd be crazy to leave it here." Lynch shrugged. "Maybe your buyer would take them."

"He was very specific. To put it in a way you would understand, we were hired to steal a Ferrari and offering him five Toyotas instead isn't going to cut it. This is exactly the kind of amateur stunt that gets us caught. We have to stick with the plan, the plan is solid."

Lynch almost choked.

"Solid? Is that a joke? The plan is *dogshit*. We busted our ass for nothing. What I'm suggesting we will at least have," Lynch paused, "a bunch of Toyotas."

"There's something you need to know about these boxes," Thorne said.

"Yeah?" Lynch said. "What's that?"

"They're all empty."

The three men turned to face him properly, their mouths open.

"What?" Blake asked.

"It hit me. There must be 300 boxes here. I thought to myself, that'd be enough to fill a whole gallery and then I realized. They *are*. These boxes are for shipping them around the country, they don't store them in there. For sure the painting we want isn't in one of them, filed away along one of those shelves. If it's not sitting roughly where you're standing as you originally said, then I got to think it's still mounted on the wall."

The tension on Blake's face melted away. Truth could do that.

"*Fuck.*"

Blake seemed to have summed up the whole night for all of them.

"Isn't that basically a guess, Thorne?" Porter asked.

"Sure, but if you look closely, all the crates have been opened. The lids are resting on top upside down. You can see the nails sticking up."

They all turned to look, except Thorne. He wanted to see their reaction.

50

"I can't believe I missed that," Blake said.

"Wait," Porter said. "If this room only has a bunch of empty boxes in it, why have they fitted the door from Fort Knox?"

"For that," Thorne said, pointing at the air-con unit. "It protects the paintings in the gallery from the hot, dry, air outside. That's at least as important as protection from theft and they don't want anyone coming back here messing with the controls. There's no art stored in here which probably explains the lack of security inside the room."

Lynch was staring at him with open hostility.

"This is all some kind of joke for you, isn't it Thorne?"

"Absolutely."

"Well forgive us for not seeing the funny side," Blake said, "but we need that painting. As I already explained to you, my sister's life is on the line."

Porter and Lynch exchanged glances.

"Blake, it's not here. We need to abort."

"I didn't tell you this before, Thorne, but this is Plan A. Plan B you're not going to like so much. We aren't leaving here without the painting."

"Please tell me Plan B doesn't involve us running into the gallery, pulling the painting off the wall and running for our lives?"

Blake smiled. "*Close.*"

"Oh, you've got to be kidding me."

"Don't worry," Blake continued, "we'll be waiting for you. Engine running."

"That's a terrible plan."

"I knew you'd like it. Didn't I say he'd like it?"

"You did," Porter said.

"No, you assholes. It's a terrible plan because it'll never work. The gallery has a laser grid. You break the laser, it doesn't just set off the alarm, it closes steel fire doors on all the gallery exits. I'd need C4 to get out of there."

Blake was nodding. "Believe it or not, we actually thought about that. We couldn't get any C4, but we got something just as good. Tell him what we got Porter."

"Two AT4 rocket launchers."

That's what Foster had in that enormous canvas bag.

"They make doorways appear wherever you need them," Blake said.

The three of them were grinning at Thorne. He knew they'd held something back, but he hadn't expected this. Anti-tank rockets.

"You're resourceful, Blake, I'll give you that. But if you think I'm going to fire one of those inside a building you're out of your mind."

"We're not giving you a choice, Thorne."

"All you want is the painting, right? You don't care how you get it?"

"That's right," Blake said.

"So if I have a better idea, you'll think about it?"

Blake's head tilted over, a trace of amusement around his eyes.

"Okay, let's hear it."

"We know the painting gets shipped tomorrow. Judging by the labels on these boxes, it will be transported in an armored truck. Depending on where the owner lives, the truck will either transport it all the way to the owner's home direct, or via an airport. The truck is the weak link. Once we know where it's going, we can work out the best place to ambush it. A natural pinch point. The parking lot outside even, there are no cameras. Wave your rocket at them, they'll open right up. By the time the cops arrive, we'll be long gone."

Blake frowned, then turned to Porter. "We hadn't thought about the truck."

"That's not bad," Porter said.

"I don't like it," Lynch said. "It'll be during the day, there'll be people about we can't control. Witnesses. The guards on the truck for one thing."

"So we wear ski masks," Thorne said. "If you like, Lynch, you can wear your mother's pantyhose over your face. Pretend it's a regular Saturday."

Lynch lunged at him. Blake grabbed the back of his jacket and pulled him back. Lynch didn't fight it long. He was six inches shorter than Thorne and at least fifty pounds lighter.

"What is it with you two?" Blake asked. "You can get yourselves a room when we're finished, otherwise I don't want to hear it."

Thorne held up his hands in mock surrender.

"Say we do this," Porter said. "What would we need?"

"The shipping address for the painting. The name of the security company. Flight details, if any. Collection time. The manifest will be on the computer next door."

"I'm pretty certain all that stuff is written on this piece of paper."

Porter held up a pad of paper that was lying on a desk next to him. It was spiral-bound and had tear off sheets and carbon paper. The gallery was the definition of old school. Thorne grabbed the pad and scanned the filled-out sheet.

Ashcroft, James A, 1032 Glen Canyon Road, Santa Cruz County, CA.

There was a crackle in Thorne's earpiece. *Stockton.*

"Guys? A white Impala just pulled up out front."

"Shit," Blake said. "Cops?"

"Uh…negative. Some old dude in glasses as thick as your finger. Looks like he just got out of bed. He's walking over to the front door. Seems kind of nervous, looking around. Okay, he's just sort of standing there staring through the glass."

Blake turned to him.

"Why would he be here if we didn't trip the alarm?"

Thorne knew exactly why; his insurance policy.

One of the key selling points of Blake's robbery had always been its simplistic nature. Get in, grab the painting, get out. On this basis, he'd estimated they'd be looking at no longer than ten minutes inside, beginning to end. If they were still inside after half an hour, it likely meant he'd been double-crossed and lay dead somewhere while Blake's crew goofed around. His insurance policy was a timer circuit designed to cut power to the the electro-magnet thirty minutes after activation. Without power, no force was applied to the magnetic sensor and the alarm would register the door as open.

He shrugged, casually.

"There's something we missed, a secondary system."

Blake glared at him, his jaws clamped together in rage.

"Okay," Thorne continued, his voice calm. "We're in here because we jammed the sensors, right? It's possible the system had some kind of automatic sensor polling. A protocol to ping each sensor unit to check for malfunction or flat battery, not only every time the alarm is turned on or off, but at a set interval, say every half hour. That being the case, it would get no response from any of the jammed units, tripping the failsafe."

"You didn't think of this before?"

"Of course."

"*Really?* Because I don't remember you saying squat."

"Blake, if I told you every possible thing that could happen tonight, we'd still be outside in the van and you'd have scratched right through your head."

He heard Stockton laughing in his earpiece, but Blake bared his teeth.

"Don't get smart with me, motherfucker."

"Hey," Lynch said, "I got an idea."

"Go for it," Blake said.

"Okay, for the old man to check the gallery, he has to switch the alarm off first, right? I mean, he doesn't want it to ring any more than we do. Once the alarm's off, we put a hole in his head and help ourselves."

Blake sighed. "It's not a car alarm, Lynch. The *art* is still alarmed, you can't pull it off the wall without triggering everything. That shit is active all the time, otherwise we'd have come here during the day."

"Isn't that Plan B anyway? Once the interior alarm is off we can walk right in there. No laser grid, no steel doors, none of that. Maybe we can *convince* the old man to disable the alarm on the painting as well. We got nothing to lose."

Blake appeared to think it over, Thorne couldn't believe it.

"You can't be considering this. Do you know what that guy's out there waiting for? Cops. He's not coming in here on his own, he's going to be escorted by L.A.'s finest, or whatever passes for it in Beverly Hills. They'll do a floor by floor sweep of the building and will only leave when they know it's clear. We need to bail before it's too late."

"It's already too late, Thorne. Cops or no cops, I've come too far down this road to turn back now. I've done things that can't be undone. You understand? I can't make this right until we get to the end."

He understood just fine.

"The security guy that worked here before: he's dead isn't he?"

Blake glanced sharply at him but said nothing. Thorne knew it was as close as he'd get to an admission, but the silence bothered him. It wasn't in Blake's nature to let things slide, it was something else.

"It's not just him, is it? Did he have a wife? Kids?"

"Leave it alone, Thorne. We've both killed before. Don't pretend it's different just because some happened on the other side of the world. It's all the same."

"I'm not letting you kill cops or some old man."

Blake squared off in front of him, the muscles in his neck popping out. His head moved in a small circle as it assessed him, as if he were listening to classical music. Thorne stared back. He knew the fight they'd had in the hotel bar had been fake, that Blake had deliberately not defended himself, but it nevertheless felt like a victory. He had the *memory* of beating him and that was enough. He could beat him again.

"This again. You know, there's a reason why I didn't arm you, Thorne. I knew when it came right down to it you wouldn't have the balls. Lynch's idea isn't perfect, but it beats jacking a security truck in broad daylight. We're doing this, and if you have things you still want to say to Kate Bloom, you are too."

He stared at Blake, fury boiling over inside him.

"What happened to you, man?"

Blake turned away from him.

"People change. This is who I am now."

SEVEN

Blake stared at him, braced for a fight. The moment drew out, tension building, until Thorne turned and walked toward the door. It couldn't have gone any other way, he had him outnumbered and outgunned. For a second it seemed none of that would matter. Something elemental had flashed across his friend's face. The desire to kill. Thorne pressed his gloved fists on either side of the door like he was stretching, his head tilted forward until it touched the steel. Blake sighed. It was a pose he knew well enough. Uncontrollable anger burned inside Thorne. He walked up behind him and spoke calmly, as if nothing had happened.

"Can you open that, brother?"

Thorne drew back from the metal and pressed a key on the keypad. There was a *beep* followed by a *click* as the lock opened. Thorne worked the lever and the steel opened into the corridor where Foster stood waiting.

"That's it? One key?"

"That's it."

"Why'd we spend all that time in a crawlspace?"

"You need a code to get in, not to get back out."

Blake sighed. In the end, it didn't matter. They didn't have the painting, everything else was noise. He turned on his Maglite. After a couple of seconds, the light faded and went out. He shook the flashlight vigorously and it came back. He'd had the same thing happen twice before on missions, and each time it was before something went south in a bad way. He pushed the thought aside.

"All right," he said. "Let's book."

They set off down the corridor, back the way they'd come. His mood was dark and there was the bitter taste of failure in his mouth. He didn't need Thorne fighting him every step, or talking to him like he was an idiot. It was hard to ignore the fact that after close to an hour they were no closer to the painting than they were when they started.

In his earpiece, Stockton spoke again.

"Two black and whites just rolled up out front. No strobes."

"How many cops?"

There was a pause.

"Four."

"What're they doing?"

"Talking to the old man. You want me to drop them?"

"Jesus," Thorne said. "I'll do your Plan B. The rocket launcher, the whole bit. Leave the cops and the guard alone. They probably have kids back home waiting for them."

Blake smiled to himself in the dark. You apply the right pressure, you can get someone to do almost anything. They reached fire doors at the stairs and he stopped, his hand ready to push the door aside. They all bunched together.

"The truth is, Thorne, you were right before. It was a stupid idea and since the cops are here now, it's too late. Lynch's plan is the best we got, so that's what we're doing."

"Think about that. A plan of *Lynch's* is the best you got. It's time to go home."

"Screw you, Thorne," said Lynch.

Blake pushed through the doors into the stairwell. If he had to hear one more argument between Thorne and Lynch he was going to shoot them himself. The RF jammer sat on the floor in front of him, picked out with his flashlight. Thorne bent down to retrieve it before they continued down the stairs.

"Will that thing jam the sensors in the gallery?"

"Not if they're wired."

"What about cameras?"

"Same answer."

At the bottom of the stairs they took the second exit, toward the gallery. There was a small section between the two buildings where one alarm system stopped and the next had yet to start. A blind spot. Thorne had theorized the gap prevented one alarm triggering the other. Blake's plan was to hold there until the main alarm was deactivated by the security guard. They soon reached the spot and he signaled them to stop. Ahead, the corridor intersected with another at 90 degrees. Left led to the front of the building, right to the gallery where the painting was located. He saw Porter looking back.

"*What?*"

"I hate to say it, but Thorne has a point. Our original plan had a higher chance of success than this. We should get gone while we can."

"Are you serious? We're literally eighty feet from that painting. You're suggesting we hit the snooze button on a million dollar payout and hope nothing goes wrong next time?"

"Wait, wait, wait," Thorne said. "*What* original plan?"

Blake ignored him.

"It's an old man and some half-asleep cops. We're goddamn Marines!"

"All I'm saying," Porter said, "is that if we shit the bed here our intel will be worthless and we'll be left with nothing."

Blake said nothing for a moment. In his mind, the original plan had remained his fallback position. Without realizing it, he'd assumed it would still be there if everything else turned bad. Like all the best military operations, he'd allowed for failure, even multiple failures. He just hadn't considered the impact of one plan on another. Blake shook his head.

"I can't do it. I can't be this close and not go the extra step."

"So don't kill them."

He turned to Thorne.

"Think about it, Blake. We catch the cops by surprise and get them to handcuff each other. They think this is a bogus alarm check, right? I bet they get them all the time. Most of the time it's a broken sensor, a flat battery, or an open window. It's boring, it's routine. We don't need them dead, Aidan, just immobilized. Whatever happens after that, we're gold. The cops will be embarrassed. They'll want to pretend the whole thing never happened. But you put four of them in the morgue, that's different. Every cop in the state will be after us."

Blake nodded. It made sense. Just the same, he didn't trust Thorne. His old friend had forgotten how to get his hands dirty. Forgotten his own hands had *ever* been dirty. The best thing would be to remove him from the equation until he was needed.

"They're coming," Stockton said.

In the distance he heard *beep beep beep*.

"All right," Blake said. "Porter, Lynch, you're with me. We'll intercept them at the entrance, secure the cops and have a chat with the guard. Thorne, Foster, you go to the gallery and get ready to grab the painting. If the old man can't disable the painting alarm we're switching to Plan B immediately. I don't want to be here a second longer than necessary."

He glanced at each of them in turn, gauging the mood. Porter and Lynch were smiling, their faces animated at the prospect of some action; Thorne, meanwhile, stared at him with lidded eyes and a clenched jaw. Foster looked the same as he always did, like a horse had kicked him in the face as a child.

The beeping stopped.

"Kill the lights," Blake said. "It's time."

He stowed his flashlight and drew his automatic. The hard shape in his hand, the weight. It was an incredible feeling. He felt invincible. If a dozen cops were on their way, it would make no difference to him. Blake walked across the ten foot blind spot into the main east-west corridor. He was now firmly in the gallery building. Even without a flashlight, he could see where he was going. The lights at the front of the gallery bled around corners, reflected off glass, all the way back to where he stood. Porter and Lynch formed up on either side of him, guns front and center. They turned to the left, following the light to the source.

They entered a room filled with sculptures and large items in clear display cases. He'd seen pictures of the same items on the gallery's website and even brightly lit he didn't know what they were. Art, they said. He kept his head down, his baseball hat masking his face from the security cameras mounted on all four corners of the room.

Thorne was right. Dead cops created problems he didn't need. He was here to steal a painting and make money, not kill. Where he disagreed with Thorne, was that they could surprise five people at once. It wasn't possible, not when they were here with the specific purpose of looking for intruders. Maybe cops did deal with a lot of false alarms, but for sure they'd go into every situation hoping this was the time they'd catch someone. Whatever way he looked at it, there was only one play here.

Shooting the cops as soon as they appeared.

As if reading his mind, Lynch spoke, his voice barely audible.

"We're not really taking these fools hostage, are we?"

"No."

There'd be no eye witnesses left to give descriptions, or call for backup.

They entered another corridor with a slow bend to the right. It came out in a second gallery packed with small paintings. The space was considerable, but the floor had only two squat sculptures in the middle to provide any kind of cover. Blake moved to quickly cross the floor and enter the next corridor. A place like this presented few good spots for a shoot-out. He waited for Porter and Lynch to catch up, then moved along the hallway. The next room was the one visible from the entrance. It was the largest space and had small offices off it that would all need to be searched. The cops had to still be there.

They weren't.

All he had to do was sweep his eyes around a complete 360 and it told him everything he needed to know. The cops had come and gone. He glanced to the left, remembering the street outside. They were on full view to anyone walking or driving past. He licked his lips. Not much passing traffic at this time of night, but still. If the cops weren't here, and they hadn't passed them in the corridor, it followed that the cops and the guard had gone the other way around the building, toward the gallery where the Picasso was on display. That room held the most valuable items and represented the best target for thieves. The guard would want to check that first, make sure all the good stuff was safe.

Blake set off in that direction but immediately came up short. The way was blocked by a door with a keypad and a STAFF ONLY sign. He was about to turn back when he thought of the key card for the parking lot entrance. Blake swiped it through the card reader and smiled at the familiar words that appeared. ENTER CODE. He paused for a moment, forgetting what it was. A cross, that's what Hanson said. He punched in 2046 and the door popped open. The three of them entered a narrow corridor and began to move rapidly along it. Rough, unfinished concrete on either side. Strip lights in wire cages were screwed onto the wall, wiring protected by steel pipe. It was basic and industrial. The public weren't meant to see this, so it didn't matter how it looked.

Another scenario came to mind. After gaining access to the building, the guard might've opened the security office and activated the monitors to bring up the feeds from the cameras. They would've seen five serious-looking individuals, three of them armed. That would be pretty much it, he figured. They'd pull back and secure a hard perimeter, bring in more cops.

A huge explosion shook the building. Blake felt the ground shake and a ripple move through the air. He felt the force of it against his chest, his heart. He came to a halt and braced himself between the walls with his hands. Dust floated down from the ceiling like snow.

"Stockton, report!"

Outside, multiple car alarms sounded.

"Nothing at the front. Moving to the back."

The audio was bad, scratchy. Too much concrete between them. He looked at Porter and saw his eyes wide in alarm.

"Blake, man. We gotta split."

Reluctantly, he nodded. The cops would definitely call in the explosion. More would be on their way. SWAT, every patrol car on shift, a helicopter. Explosions were big ticket items, they brought in everybody. The window for their escape was narrowing. They continued their interrupted run down the passage. It came to him what the explosion was and rage tightened his chest.

"Foster, you copy?"

No response. Had the explosion taken out his comms?

"*Foster!*"

Instead, Stockton came back.

"There's a fifteen-freaking-foot hole in the west wall! Broken cinder blocks and drywall cover half the parking lot and smoke is coming out from inside."

Blake heard his own breathing through the earpiece.

"Anything else?"

There was a pause while Stockton took in the scene below with the rifle scope.

"The front door of the van is open about an inch. Nobody visible."

Blake didn't know what to do with that information.

Ahead, the passage came to an end at another door. From what he recalled from the blueprints, the room housing the Picasso was close. Next to the door was a normal switch like a light switch. *A door release.* Blake pressed it and the door silently opened. He gave it a hard shove. A cop stood, back toward him, head tilted as if staring at something on the floor a little ways away. The door swung freely on lubricated hinges until the handle on the other side bit into the wall. The cop jumped and turned sharply toward him, gun coming up. Instinctively, Blake fired three times. Only then seeing the cop's face. A woman. The shots lifted her off her feet and dumped her onto the hard, polished floor.

He looked at the object that had been in her hand as it rolled across the floor and nudged against his boot. Not a gun, a flashlight.

Blake knelt down next to her. Dust from the explosion had fallen against her dark skin like freckles. She was young, barely out of the academy. Looked like she took care of herself. Clean living, hours in a gym. She was lean and athletic, the kind of look he liked. But fate had put her directly in his path and her pretty face was now contorted with pain. He held her hand and squeezed it. He hadn't always been a monster, it was still a new thing for him.

Porter and Lynch exited the doorway behind him, guns raised, like they were clearing a helicopter and taking fire.

"Find Foster and Thorne," he said, eyes fixed on the cop.

When they left, he spoke again.

"Sorry, kid. I should've listened to my friend."

A moment later, she was dead.

He glanced around and saw Porter and Lynch standing next to another body. He got to his feet and walked over to join them. Beyond, a square shape was recessed into the wall. It was a dull silver color, with a vertical line up the middle like huge elevator doors. But it was no elevator, it was the security doors to the room where the Picasso was hanging. The gallery was in lockdown. His eyes came to rest on the second body. Foster.

"*Dead?*"

Porter shook his head.

"No, but I don't want to be here when he wakes up."

Blake closed his eyes. "What about Thorne?"

"He's gone."

60

EIGHT

Thorne stood with his back against the wall of the parking garage on North Camden Drive with a smile on his face. Sirens in the distance were rapidly closing on his position from multiple directions. The show was about to go public in a big way. He reached up to his chest with fanned open fingers. His heart was slow and steady, like a ticking clock. The more danger he was in, the more his body seemed to relax. The first phase was always like this, calm, and totally at peace. He loved this part, this was his addiction. The second phase was more normal, more pedestrian. High heart rate, bursts of energy, and, frequently, violence. But those weren't bad guys coming, and that complicated things.

He'd heard most of what happened inside the gallery through the earpiece, including three gunshots. Thorne knew at least one of the cops was dead, he couldn't see it the other way around. One dead, he thought. What happened to the others? Had Blake tried the handcuff routine? The shots had fallen too close together to be separate targets and it seemed unlikely that the old man had been taken out execution style.

The sirens were louder now, no more than a couple of blocks away. It was time to leave, yet still he remained. He couldn't allow Blake to get caught, that didn't work for him. Their fates were linked now. If arrested, Blake and his gang of rejects would endeavor to see him share their misfortune. As distasteful as it was to him, he had to help them escape. Thorne risked sticking his head out of the cover of the entrance and glanced down the street. He saw two cruisers side by side racing up Camden toward him. A light appeared in the sky.

Whatever he was going to do, he had to do it now.

"Blake, how about we make a deal?"

"You got nothing I want, Thorne. You're a dead man."

"Yeah, well. I'm out on the street and all the cops in the world are about to arrive. How close are you to leaving?"

"That ain't none of your business."

Blake's breathing was heavy, like he was carrying something heavy. Or *someone*. Foster was still down. The background sound of Blake's comms changed from echo-filled hollow to soundless mute. Blake was outside. After a moment, he heard the distinctive sound of the van's side door running along its track and hitting the end stops. Thorne reached into the large canvas sack at his feet and pulled out the second AT4. He removed the safety pin and the front and rear covers. The sights popped up.

It was surprising how quickly it all came back.

"The thing is, Blake, I'm going to give you my half of the deal whether you ask for it or not. You're one of those guys that can't take help when you need it. I'm going to give you a distraction, keep the cops off your back and looking the other way. For old times' sake."

"I'm still going to kill you."

"Maybe."

Thorne shifted the firing rod cocking lever into position and shouldered the weapon. He aimed at the entrance to the bank diagonally across the street, held down the safety and fired. He watched the projectile fly across the asphalt, in through a plate glass window and explode inside the building. The bank shook violently. Pulsing blue strobes lit up the interior and a piercing alarm sounded. After a ten-count, part of the second floor collapsed onto the first and rubble spat out across the sidewalk and into the street. Over the din of the alarm, Blake came back over the earpiece.

"What the hell was that?"

Thorne tossed the AT4 and picked up his backpack.

"Someone appears to be robbing the bank," he said.

He ducked back through the parking garage, toward the alley, head down and the brim of his baseball cap obscuring half his vision.

"You think this makes us square, Thorne?"

The connection was crystal clear, they were less than forty feet apart and without the concrete walls of the gallery between them.

"Whatever your new plan for the painting is, you and your goons can handle it without me. If you succeed and become a millionaire, I doubt you'll risk that coming after me. If you don't succeed, then I figure you will probably all be dead."

He watched them through support pillars as they piled into the van. Foster was conscious now and had one of his giant snow-shovel hands clamped to his head.

Blake got into the van and slammed the door.

"Maybe I come for you now smart guy, *before* I'm a millionaire."

The word millionaire caused Thorne to flash back to the moment they found the shipping manifest for the painting. Blake had shown no interest in the information it contained. It seemed odd at the time, but it was obvious to him now. *Blake already knew who the owner was, and where he lived.*

62

That was his original plan. Wait for the transfer to take place, then steal the painting where the security was at its weakest.

"You know the owner's house will be alarmed too, right?"

Blake started the van, pulling it sharply away toward the alley exit and then out onto Santa Monica Boulevard.

"You're not even close, Thorne. When I'm done, the owner will give me the painting himself. He'll put it straight into my hands, no alarms, no cops. Like I said before, you got nothing I want. And you're dead wrong about what you said before. Millionaire or not, I'm going to enjoy pulling you apart."

Thorne walked out of the parking structure into the alley, then followed the van's route onto Santa Monica Boulevard at a fast run. He was in time to see the van take a right at the intersection, before disappearing again. Blake was about to exceed the range of the comms unit. To his surprise, he heard Blake laugh as the audio began to click.

"I can't believe you choked out Foster, man. That's fantastic."

The earpiece went dead. He pulled it out and tossed it into a storm drain. Thorne took off his leather gloves and tossed them in after it. He crossed over five empty lanes to the other side of the street and tucked tight into the buildings. He held there for a full minute, not moving, until three large Beverly Hills PD SUVs shot past in tight formation. They came to the corner of Camden and split apart in an orchestrated pattern, blocking the road. A dozen cops sprang out the vehicles and advanced toward the bank, which was now partially on fire.

Thorne moved off down the sidewalk.

When he came to a cross street he immediately took it. He knew he looked suspicious and wanted to get as much distance between him and the gallery. He opened his backpack that he'd taken from the van, unrolled his linen jacket, and shook it out. It didn't look its best, but it'd recover. He pulled it on and felt some of the old *Jake Vasco* attitude return. There was nothing that guy couldn't do. Thorne looked at his watch. Almost five a.m., getting late, but still not an ideal time to be on the street.

Even without a dead cop in the vicinity, he would expect to be stopped and asked what he was doing. Because of people like Blake, the land of the free had opening hours. He looked about, figuring out a rough bearing. Seeing no sign of approaching vehicles, police or otherwise, he took a chance and began to run. The shape he was in, he could run like this for an hour and a half, which he estimated would be how long it would take him to get back to his apartment in Santa Monica.

But he wasn't going back to Santa Monica, not yet.

It wasn't hard for him to imagine what Blake had planned. He was going after the owner's wife. Had to be. Kidnap her, force the husband to give them the Picasso. There was a certain inevitability about it. If the thing you want is protected, make that protection irrelevant. It was like a strategy from *The Art of War*.

He saw headlights in the distance and dropped out of his run.

Thorne estimated he was a mile clear now. When he was closer to two miles out, he'd call a cab. He didn't want to have co-ordinates placing him anywhere near Beverly Hills by the cab company, or by police if they asked about pickups. The car slid past. A Volvo the size of an aircraft carrier with a small, worried-looking woman behind the wheel. He waited until it disappeared from view behind him before he began to run again. He'd soon be out of the residential area and there'd be a lot more traffic. He wanted to be through running by then.

His mind returned to Blake's original plan.

Blake had been willing to change course and try a heist instead. That told him that Blake knew the plan was more dangerous, for him and for others. Now that he'd taken the easier option off the table, he'd left Blake with no choice. He'd put the owner and his wife in direct danger, not to mention anyone near them when she was taken. Nine times out of ten, people who are kidnapped are killed by their abductors. Either within the first 48 hours, or at the end, after the criminals got what they wanted. Perhaps it wasn't the owner's wife at all, he thought, perhaps it was a child. He took a deep breath. He couldn't let that happen. A cop was already dead because of him, he wouldn't let Blake kill anyone else.

NINE

Thorne woke just after five, his face sideways on the back seat of his rental and his knees pressed into the back of the passenger seat. He'd spent three days and nights hunting Blake across Santa Cruz County without success and the failure bothered him. His idea was simple. Check motel parking lots for the black van or the Audi sedan, then tip off local police about a group of heavily armed men holding a woman hostage. A SWAT unit would've been dispatched, and Blake and the others would have escalated the situation until they were all dead. Given time, he was certain everything would've fallen into place, but there were only so many motels he could cover alone. That left him with a single stark option; prevent the kidnapping before it happened. If he did that, he'd neutralize the one piece of intel that gave Blake such a high chance of success.

He swung the rear door open and stepped out the vehicle.

The forest around him was impenetrably dark, like a blindfold was tied around his head. The moon no more than a fingernail on the far horizon. Thorne rubbed his arms and legs vigorously to warm them up and get the blood flowing. Despite the hour, he felt wired, energized. There'd be no more sleep, no matter how hard he tried. It'd been the same in the Marines before a mission. He could either get up, or stare at the back of his eyelids.

Thorne took a deep breath and let it slowly out again. The forest air was cool and fresh, and made a pleasant change from the fetid air that filled the car's cabin. It helped him think. He pushed his failure to find the gang from his mind, it was time to start over. He didn't know where Blake had been, but he knew where he would be today.

The same place Ashcroft was, the Capitola Mall.

The idea of calling the police would not work at the mall. Blake would be gone by the time they arrived and Ashcroft's wife along with them. The mall was a fluid environment with too many unknowns, making any form of advanced planning virtually useless. Whatever he was going to do, he would have to figure out a split second before he did it. He knew one thing for sure, Blake wouldn't expect him to be there and that gave him a tactical advantage. Not enough to make up for the lack of weapon, but better than nothing.

He got into the car and started the engine.

Uncovering Blake's plan had taken less than twenty minutes in a Starbucks, including ten minutes waiting in line for coffee. Googling *James Ashcroft Picasso* revealed that he was a US Senator seeking his party's nomination for president at the next election. James Ashcroft was a surprisingly common name, however, and the search brought up a lot of irrelevant matches. He changed his search to *James Ashcroft senator* to narrow the hits but this still produced in excess of eight million results. Too much data. But he knew what Blake wanted: a time and a location where Ashcroft and his wife would be in advance. He also knew that this was in the very near future, so he searched for both their names and added the date to the end of the search, increasing the day with each new search until he found what he wanted.

The intel gave a specific day, but no time. Any way he looked at it, he was going to be several hours early. Time enough to pick up breakfast and a coffee, perhaps even lunch.

He put the car in drive and set off through the trees, the rental's headlights picking out the narrow dirt track. He'd found the place by accident on the first day and had returned to park in the same spot every night when he'd finished his nightly hunt for Blake. It occurred to him that Blake might've found a similar place to dig in, but he couldn't imagine Sara Dawson settling for anything less than a motel room with a comfortable bed, hot showers, electricity, and access to the internet.

At the end of the track he stopped the car and climbed out.

A rusty chain hung across the road blocking access. It was secured at one end to a metal post by a brand-new padlock he'd bought in town. He unlocked it and let the chain drop to the ground. Since he had no further use for the location, he decided not to secure the chain behind him. He got back behind the wheel, rolled over the chain and bumped up onto the highway toward Santa Cruz.

*

Foster. The giant stood towering over other shoppers like one of the redwoods he'd seen the day before. Foster stood fixed, rooted to the floor, staring off up the mall at something, his brow a heavy line across his face. Thorne followed the direction of his gaze to a beautiful woman walking toward them. He saw beautiful women every day, but something about this one caught the air in his throat. It took him a second to recognize her from a picture in his car. Lauren Ashcroft. Sure enough, her husband was right there next to her. Thorne's eye jumped to the figure behind them. Blake. He was wearing a faded red *Doors* T-shirt and had his head turned to one side, talking to Porter. Lauren veered over and stood looking in one of the store windows, Blake almost tripped over her he was so close. *Notice them,* he thought. How can a US Senator be unaware of a threat like this?

Now that they'd stopped, he saw two other figures in front of them also come to a halt. Lynch, and a Latino he'd never seen before. Thorne sighed. He'd hoped for two things above all others. That he'd get to Ashcroft first; and that Blake might have thinned out his crew before he arrived. Instead, Blake had taken the time to replace him.

Five men, assuming you only counted Foster once.

He could also assume that either Sara Dawson or Jay Stockton was outside in the getaway vehicle. Thorne turned and faced away, hiding his face from the gang. There was enough reflection in the glass of a storefront that he could check their positions. Lauren walked into the store and her husband, reluctantly, went in after her. Blake stood guarding the door. He'd be unable to get past him to warn the senator.

He turned his head to take in Foster again.

The giant was carrying something thick in his right hand. The object was about two feet long and had a plastic bag wrapped repeatedly around it. The man's bearlike hand gripped it part way along, with his index finger pressing into a slight hollow. A shotgun. Thorne licked his lips. If he could take out Foster and get his firearm he had a fighting chance at making this work.

Women's laughter sucked his attention back to the reflection in the glass.

Lauren Ashcroft had resumed her walk down the corridor, her face all lit up. She was stunning, something really special. But she wouldn't stay that way if Blake got a hold of her. The senator and his wife appeared to be making their way toward the exit he was standing next to, which probably explained why Foster had been marking the exit.

They'd seen the Ashcrofts arrive, something he'd missed.

In less than a minute the whole thing would kick off and he still had no plan of attack. He stuck his hands into his jacket pockets, searching for something he could use as a weapon. He compiled a mental list as he felt the items; a reusable nylon grocery bag, a stubby flat screwdriver, and a can of Coke. *Shit.* He'd known it would come to this, yet he'd resisted bringing anything better. He checked his pants pockets. A wallet, some coins, his cell phone, and the key fob for his rental car.

He slid the screwdriver into his back pocket where he could quickly pull it out. He put the Coke can inside the nylon bag and let it hang down by his side.

The Ashcrofts passed behind him with their four man escort. He allowed them to pass, then waited for Foster to turn and follow along behind them. They made their way to the exit, the bright sunshine outside silhouetting the figures in front of him. Blake pulled out his cell phone, held it briefly to his ear, then disconnected without speaking.

Signaling the driver.

Calm descended over him. There was nothing left to work out. All there was, was the moment. Out front, a black shape screamed to an abrupt halt. They walked out into the light and he saw Blake's van opposite, blocking the road in both directions. The side door rolled open and slammed against the end stop. A figure stood in the opening wearing a clown mask, tight black leather, and enormous motorcycle boots.

Sara Dawson.

Thorne reached his arm back, then swung it forward as fast as he could. The soda can mashed into the back of Foster's head. The giant stumbled forward a step then stopped and turned around, his face knitted not with pain, but with confusion. Thorne had assumed it would take more than one swing to bring him down, and had already started to swing again. This time, the can crashed heavily into Foster's left temple and the nylon bag disintegrated in a spray of blood. The giant dropped silently to his knees, still apparently uncertain what was happening to him. Thorne stepped forward and thrust the shaft of the screwdriver into his neck. Once, twice. The big man dropped the shotgun and fell to the ground clutching desperately at his neck.

People screamed and scattered in all directions, but he blanked it out. Dipping onto one knee he picked up the shotgun, pushed his finger through the plastic at the indent and found the trigger. With barely any thought, he turned the firearm a small arc and pulled the trigger. The Latino was propelled backward, his body folded around a hole in his midsection the size of a dinner plate. His face was hidden now by his own clown mask, but that didn't hold back the shrill noise the man made before dying.

Two shots sailed past him. Close misses.

Thorne stood and felt a searing heat down first his ribs, then the inside of his left arm. His eyes watered. He angled himself toward the shooter, presenting the lowest profile possible. Porter stood square on, firing constantly. The shots were everywhere. Porter's favored weapon in the Corps was a fifty caliber machine gun mounted on a Humvee, which had given him a passing chance at hitting something.

Thorne brought the shotgun up and felt for the slide to reload. He couldn't find it. The gun had been rolled inside the plastic bag to hide it, but it would take a fatal amount of time to unwrap and pull the firearm clear. He dropped it and dove for the Latino's automatic. He slid across the asphalt, grabbed the pistol and fired twice before he came to a halt. Porter spun to the side and began to crawl along the ground toward the van.

Thorne left him to it.

In less than twenty seconds, he'd taken out two of them and decommissioned a third, but he was still out-gunned and the element of surprise was gone. By going for the pistol, he realized he was now in a wide space at the entrance where buses came and went. He was totally exposed. In front of him, the Ashcrofts had flattened themselves onto the sidewalk, along with several others. If he moved for cover he'd have to abandon them, if he didn't, he'd be dead. It wasn't a hard choice.

He ran to the left, heading north, away from the bus lane. To pursue him, Blake would have to take his eyes off his quarry and risk losing them back inside the mall. Thorne made it ten feet, before his body flew backward and his head hit the ground. Pain radiated out from his stomach, cutting him in half. He touched the area lightly with his hand, then lifted it up to his face.

It was scarlet with blood.

He tried to stand and felt something inside him tear open and a hot liquid pour out. Thorne rolled onto his side and pushed himself up on his elbow. The movement made him lightheaded and he fought the urge to vomit. The pain was sharp and unrelenting, more than he'd ever experienced. He took a deep breath and held it in his chest, teeth biting hard together. It was all he could do not to scream. He took another breath, then drew himself up to a squat. One knee up, one down. His vision grayed, then came back. He got the heel of his gun hand pressed into his raised right knee and pushed himself upright, then fell immediately forward again onto the asphalt, the side of his face scraping along the ground.

There was a high-pitched whine in his ears and his hands were shaking. He thought he smelled frying onions and he shook his head to clear it. He saw Blake move forward, his gun arm lowered, his head turned away. Blake's attention now fixed on Lauren Ashcroft. Thorne noticed that her husband had disappeared. She sat up, her head swinging around, looking for him. Had they taken him? That made no sense; she was the target, he was sure of it. Just then, he saw Ashcroft lying under a green SUV, like he'd been run over. He looked dead.

Lauren's gaze fell on him. Hungry, desperate.

He shouted at her. "Get down!"

Thorne caught a flash of something on her face before she pressed herself back down onto the asphalt. *Relief.* She wasn't on her own.

What he needed, he thought, was a miracle.

Out the corner of his eye, he saw a Buick sedan take the corner of the parking lot, an old man in thick glasses at the wheel. He was driving too fast, and because of the trees at the end of the row, hadn't noticed Blake's van blocking the way. The man swerved to avoid it and came to a stop less than twenty feet from him.

It was the closest thing to a miracle Thorne had ever seen.

He staggered toward Lauren Ashcroft, firing blindly at Blake, forcing him toward the van for cover. Lauren seemed to understand what he was intending, because she rose and raced ahead of him behind the front of the sedan. They were taking fire from inside the door of the van, as well as from Blake. He got to the corner of the Buick and half-dragged Lauren down onto the asphalt, deeper into cover.

Bullets tore into the metalwork around them.

Thorne reached up and broke off the door mirror, then raised it above the hood so he could see the van. Blake was working his way forward, gun angled down in a two-handed grip. There was a flash from the van's side door and the mirror disintegrated. He pulled the mirror casing back down and studied what was left.

Sara Dawson was a damn good shot.

He'd forgotten something, he could feel it in his bones. No, he thought, not something, *someone*. Lynch. On instinct, he turned, his head and arm swinging around together, and in one smooth movement pulled the trigger. Forty feet away, a hole appeared in the centre of a clown mask and a pink mist surrounded the Irishman's head. Thorne dropped back down behind the sedan and leaned his head against the metal. Lynch had been seconds from firing at him. He was at a loss to explain the perfection of his shot.

Muscle memory, that's what Blake had called it.

When experience and training took over.

"What's your name?" He asked, in case he used it without thinking.

"Lauren."

"That's a beautiful name," he said.

In the distance, sirens approached.

Thorne slid out the magazine. Five rounds, another in the chamber.

Six shots, two targets. Could be worse, could be a lot worse.

"What's yours?"

"Chris."

He pushed the magazine back in.

There was a dark red spot on the left leg of his jeans. He frowned. The mark was recessed into the denim and frayed cotton threads stuck out around the edge. Thorne brushed at it with the back of his fingers, like it was a bug sitting on his leg. He winced, his eyes immediately tearing up. When he drew his hand away, a blood stain the size of his palm appeared. Something hot was inside his leg, he could feel it.

Great, he thought, *that's just great.*

"Stay behind the engine, doors don't stop bullets."

"Don't leave, Chris. Please."

Her eyes were wide, her face pale.

"I won't, I promise."

Thorne turned so he was on his hands and knees and crawled forward, flattening himself out on the road. The sedan hid his position from the van, but provided minimal protection. He laid up ready to fire and waited for Blake to come around the side. A second passed, then another. It didn't feel right. He should have seen him by now.

Thorne popped up in a crouch, wide open to Sara Dawson.

To hell with her, he needed to find Blake fast. His head flashed around, scanning the surroundings. To his right were around fifteen people, either running for cover, or lying on the ground. None of them Blake. To his left, a silver station wagon sat abandoned, half up on the sidewalk, all its doors open. He was about to make his way back to Lauren, when he hesitated. The engine of the station wagon was still running, he could hear it ticking over. The car offered a way out.

There was a metallic clatter on the asphalt next to him. A Glock.

Not just any Glock, the one he'd been holding.

His right arm hung limp at his side and his shoulder was on fire. Too late he realized his mistake. Blake had reversed his angle and was approaching from the other side of the sedan. He was ten feet from Lauren, only the car's hood separated them. Thorne grabbed the gun with his left hand and stumbled the short distance back to her. He fired two shots, both missed Blake despite the short distance.

Thorne crashed into the side of the car, denting the metal panel. He'd lost a lot of blood and his heart raced in his chest. He glanced at his shoulder, not wanting to see the damage. The corner of his jacket was torn and through the tattered fabric he saw pink flesh and dark red blood. It was bad. In a matter of minutes, he would bleed out. Well before that happened, he'd stop being any kind of protector for Lauren Ashcroft.

"I don't know how long I've got left," he said quietly. "There's something I need you to remember, will you do that for me?"

Lauren nodded.

"My blood type is AB positive, I can take blood from anyone. If I'm still alive when medics get here, be sure you tell them."

She glanced from his shoulder to the stain spreading across the front of his T-shirt and nodded. She looked terrified.

"*Say it*," he hissed.

"AB positive," she said. "You're a vampire like me."

Blake's voice rolled angrily over the hood of the car.

"I got no beef with you, man. Send out the girl and I let you live."

"Give me a minute to think about it."

"You got five seconds, shitbird. After that, the girl pays for what you've done here. I think you know what that means."

71

"All right! Here she comes."

He stood, gun raised in his left hand. Blake stood there waiting for him, gun pointed back. Thorne willed himself to pull the trigger, but nothing happened. Blake didn't shoot either. After several long seconds, Blake began to laugh. Neither of them could take the fatal shot. There was a shriek of frustration from the van, followed by four bullets that practically combed Thorne's hair.

He dropped back into his cover position behind the car and felt slugs chewing up the metalwork again. Pinning him in place. He heard a splash and a second later caught the distinctive smell of gasoline. The sirens were loud now, less than a minute away. There was a pause, then the bullets continued, it sounded like a full mag.

He glanced over the hood, knowing Blake would be gone.

Thorne saw one last flash from the van's doorway and found himself staring at the sky. He had double vision and his head felt wet. Gunshots continued, but they were different now. Shots were going back and forth. Multiple sources, directions. The police had arrived. Lauren's face hung over him, her blonde hair a halo around her head. He felt cold, distant. She was talking to him, a stream of meaningless words without beginning or end. He concentrated on them, trying to understand what she was saying, but it was too much.

The gunshots faded away, replaced by the sound of helicopter blades.

TEN

Thorne felt himself falling again, the side of the Pasadena hotel whipping past beside him and the ground coming up to meet him. This time there was no airbag, just a parking lot and a circle of people looking up, cheering. He took a sharp intake of breath, his eyes snapping open as he woke up. The room was clean and bright, so bright it hurt his eyes to look at it.

A hospital room.

The inside of his head felt as though it was packed with cotton but the pain from his abdomen was sharp and unrelenting. His head was raised up and he was able to look down at his body and at the wires and tubes that were attached to it.

Then he noticed the shoes. Nikes. They jiggled constantly in the edge of his vision and he turned his head to get a better look. The Ashcroft woman. She was breathtakingly beautiful. A magazine sat in her lap and she flipped through its pages, bored. He cleared his throat so he could speak and felt pain move up his spine like tearing paper.

No words came out his mouth.

The woman looked at him, a huge smile on her face. She moved quickly across the room and sat on the edge of his bed. From the table next to him, she brought over a small carton of juice and held the straw up to his mouth. The carton collapsed in her hand as he drank, their eyes locked together. He drank until it was finished, his thirst unquenched.

"How'd you feel?"

"Terrible."

She held his hand.

"I'm sorry. We're doing all we can for you."

His eyes closed, then opened again. He'd nearly fallen asleep.

"Stay with me Chris, I've waited all day to speak with you. They were working on you for ten hours. I couldn't leave, I had to stay."

"Why?"

She smiled.

"To thank you of course."

"That's not necessary."

She glanced to the side then bent over him, her blonde hair falling around his head as she kissed him. It was so quick and unexpected, that her tongue was inside his mouth before he knew it was happening. He felt his dry lips soften as her lips moved against them, her right hand reaching around through his hair and pulling at the back of his head. Locking it in place. When it ended she smiled at his flustered expression and the light that now burned in his eyes. The fog of sleep retreated from his mind.

"Look um…"

"*Lauren.*"

He smiled, he couldn't help it.

"That's a beautiful name."

"It's funny, you said that before. I guess that means it's true."

"Your name would be beautiful whatever it was."

She threw her head back and laughed. He stared at her exposed throat and the color that filled her cheeks. It wasn't a mean laugh, she was genuinely amused. Her laugh seemed to reach right into his chest and pull something out. He liked it, he could listen to it all day.

"What's the big joke?"

Lauren looked over at a man in the doorway.

"Jimmy! He thinks I'm beautiful!"

"That's not exactly news, sweetheart, anyone could tell you that."

A man stepped around from behind Lauren. The husband. Not dead, then. He saw that Ashcroft was an easy twenty years older than her, old enough to be her father. The senator wore a dark navy suit, a pure white shirt, and a blood red tie. He looked like a million dollars. Ashcroft's hand was thrust out toward him, a quarter inch of shirt cuff highlighting a golden wrist and a chunky Swiss diving watch.

"James Ashcroft, pleasure to meet you. Not every day you come face to face with someone who saved your life."

Ashcroft pumped his hand up and down like a fraternity brother or a gangbanger. His face, however, remained frozen like a mask and Thorne didn't much like the empty eyes that stared down at him. They were like high beam lights, except that utter blackness seemed to come out of them. He thought Ashcroft's expression would be the same if he were holding a pillow over his face and wondered if the display was entirely for Lauren's benefit.

"This is my wounded arm, by the way."

The handshake stopped and Ashcroft laughed.

"Sorry about that."

Thorne wasn't laughing. Instead, he wondered if the other man's age prohibited him from punching him repeatedly in the face. On balance, he thought probably not. He glanced at Lauren and saw that she looked mortified by her husband's behavior.

"Listen," Ashcroft continued, "I spoke to a friend at the District Attorney's Office. We got you covered for the mall, they're sending someone to take a statement and get everything made official. You have nothing to worry about from an investigation, okay?"

An investigation.

"I hadn't thought about that," Thorne said. "I just reacted."

Ashcroft nodded, like it was what he expected.

"Deaths of any kind have to be investigated, regardless of the situation. My friend thinks we can hit this into the long grass. The ones that escaped, *they're* the ones we want. In the meantime, he suggested you don't talk to the police or anyone else about what happened. At least, not until you're interviewed and it's all squared away."

And when they caught Blake, what story would he tell?

"How high up is your friend in the District Attorney's Office?"

A pained expression crossed Ashcroft's face.

"Actually, he *is* the district attorney."

"Oh."

"Jimmy knows a lot of people, but he tries to play it down."

Thorne turned to Lauren and remembered her lips pressed against his, her hand holding his head. As experiences went, it wasn't awful. He felt his face start to color thinking about it and not trusting himself to speak, merely nodded. It never occurred to him there'd be an investigation, he'd had enough on his hands thinking about how to deal with Blake and his gang. But of course they'd investigate, a child could've told him that. What would they find when they did?

He felt the black tide return to claim him and this time he let it come.

*

He woke to the sound of a man's voice. The man was excited, the words out his mouth almost landing on top of each other, as if speeded up. Thorne turned his head toward the sound. A television. His head was groggy and for a moment he struggled to understand where he was. It was the white room with the shades. He was still in hospital. He looked around and once again saw Lauren Ashcroft sitting by his side. Her clothing had changed, which he assumed meant it was the next day. She wore gray yoga pants and a skin-tight black top. Her arms were thin as pretzels, they could snap at any moment.

She saw his eyes moving over her body and smiled.

"Hey," she said.

"You came back."

"I've been here every day, Chris. Don't you remember?"

Was that true? His vision swam for a moment.

"What do you mean *every day*? How long have I been here?"

She looked up and to the right as she thought about it.

"Six days."

His head reeled. It seemed impossible to him that he'd been out of it for so long, but he didn't doubt her. His painkillers spaced him out. Thorne felt a lurch in his chest. He had to get out of here, he was a sitting target. Blake could come for him at any time.

"Oh, hey, don't worry. Jimmy's paying for everything."

She'd misinterpreted his reaction, but it was a fair point. His slim savings would've been wiped out ten times over by now. Thorne nodded his gratitude, an uncomfortable smile on his face. He glanced at the television. He hadn't remembered it being there before and its presence was giving him a headache.

"Have you seen the news?"

"No," he said. "What's happened?"

A crease formed between her eyes.

"*You* happened."

"I don't understand."

"A video of you came out this morning and all the networks have picked it up. They're showing it like every five minutes. You're probably the only American alive that hasn't seen it. I counted ten news trucks in the parking lot."

He flashed back to the pink mist around Lynch's head.

She was watching him closely.

"They're saying you're an actor."

He avoided her eyes and stared down at his right arm as it rested on the bed sheet. An IV line snaked out of a hanging bag and into a plastic plug that was inserted into the fold of his arm. A huge bruise surrounded the area. The bruise was fresh and looked like a pen had leaked ink under his skin and run in all directions.

"I *was* an actor, I don't know what I am now."

"Chris, it's a miracle you're still alive. Give it a little time, this is just temporary."

He was still fixated on his arm. It was numb and felt wet on the inside. His eyes traveled up to his shoulder. Here there was a bulge on the outside. It hid a depressing sight, the bulge nothing more than a lie. Under the thick dressing lay a wound that had removed a quarter inch tube of muscle.

"Sure doesn't feel temporary."

She said nothing to this, which he preferred to a meaningless platitude.

"Your husband didn't look happy last time I saw him."

Lauren nodded.

"You have to understand that what happened at the mall never happens. The good guy with the gun? You're a myth, a failed argument. My husband has fought his whole life against people who push that crap. It's a fantasy for illiterate mouth-breathers with tiny dicks."

Thorne smiled.

"I like the way you speak. You know, with all those words."

Her face flushed and dimples appeared in her cheeks.

"Oh, I wasn't suggesting-"

"If it's important, you're welcome to check."

She laughed and turned away from him, her face darkening still further.

"Here we go," Lauren said, catching sight of the television.

It was security footage from inside the mall. The Ashcrofts walking hand-in-hand with Blake and his goons boxing them in, front and back. Along the bottom of the screen a banner said NEW FOOTAGE OF ASHCROFT SHOOT-OUT APPEARS ONLINE. Twenty to thirty seconds passed before he saw himself for the first time. He looked tired and dirty, he thought. In need of a wash and a shave. He had slumped down to avoid drawing Blake's attention and, as a result, looked uncharacteristically short. Foster, on the other hand, looked enormous, his height magnified by the camera position and the wide angle lens.

Thorne watched events unfold with growing distaste. The video was bleak. While it had been edited to comply with content regulations, it nonetheless showed him killing three men and wounding a fourth. He found it hard to watch all the way to the end, which appeared to show him lying dead in Lauren's lap in a pool of his own blood. The video over, the station cut back to the jovial news anchor, who continued his enthusiastic fluff piece for America's new hero.

Thorne couldn't decide which was worse, what he'd just seen, or this petty little man's reaction to it. He turned to Lauren.

"Can you shut that off?"

She hit a button on the remote and the room fell silent. He noticed Lauren was sitting closer than before. While he'd been watching the recording, she'd pulled her chair right up to his bed. For a moment he thought she was going to hold his hand again, but the moment passed and her head sagged.

"I've watched that clip so many times now," she said, her voice small. "It's horrible. The worst moment of my life and I can't stop watching it. I'm sick."

"It's natural. You want to understand what happened, *why* it happened. So you watch the footage. Hoping this time you'll see something that explains it; some mistake you made that led these people into your life. But nothing changes, it still makes no sense."

Lauren looked down at her hands and exhaled slowly.

She could watch that clip a million times and still not get what she wanted, because what she wanted was to feel safe again. Blake had taken that away from her and nothing could bring it back.

"Chris, how did you know what was going to happen?"

"A cop was here asking me the same thing. *How did you know? What made you take action?* That kind of stuff. I had no explanation for him. There was something off about the people around you in the mall, so I followed them. That's it. By the time I realized the big guy had a shotgun in his bag, there was nothing else to do but take them out."

"I hate what happened. Those people are dead because of me."

He looked away from her, at the window.

"That's not on you, it's on them. And on me."

The hair on the back of his neck stood up. Now would be a good time to come right out with the truth, tell her everything.

"It's not the same. I can tell it doesn't bother you."

He felt blood rush to his face before he turned back to her.

"I'd like you to leave."

His voice filled the room and she sprang to her feet.

"I'm sorry, I'm sorry!"

As quickly as it arrived, his anger vanished. He sighed.

"The way I see it, those men put themselves in the morgue. They were there to kidnap you, Lauren, and after they got what they wanted from your husband they'd all have taken their turn with you before leaving you dead in a ditch. I don't cry for them, not for a second. But that doesn't mean I feel nothing about what happened, or think I'm some kind of hero. I did what I had to and no more. If I'd killed a bear to save your life I'd feel sorrier for the bear than for those assholes."

"Chris, I'm sorry about what I said before. Please forgive me."

"It's fine, I'm over it."

Lauren turned away, a far-off look on her face.

"I never thought a thing like this could happen here. It's unthinkable, a bad dream. We're good people, minding our own business."

Thorne nodded but said nothing. Gun crime was everywhere, being a nice person didn't make you immune to it. He glanced at the IV in his arm, then at a cuff on his other arm that checked his blood pressure. His range of movement was severely limited, he couldn't stand it. Blake would be coming for him, he had no doubt about it. The video on the news made that a certainty, his anger would be uncontrollable.

"Lauren, can you do me a favor?"

"Of course!"

"Get someone in here to take this shit off me, I'm leaving."

ELEVEN

Thorne watched the line of TV trucks and vans trailing along behind them in the Range Rover's wing mirror. The vehicles went back as far as he could see, the true number hidden by the curves in the road. It gave him a bad feeling. This was a big story, he saw that now. Not just because of what he did, but because of who he saved. This was the kind of story that had legs. It wasn't going to go away quickly, it would grow and grow. He knew how it worked, people would want to know more about him. Reporters would dig into his past, looking for something juicy to share with the American people. He could immediately think of at least ten things he didn't want on the nightly news. There were things about him even Kate didn't know about, and he'd rather it stayed that way.

"Look, James, maybe this wasn't such a great idea."

Ashcroft glanced across at him.

"Call me Jimmy, all my friends do."

Thorne left that alone. The man wasn't his friend, he was a politician.

"I'm just saying, maybe I'd be better off at that hospital after all, or a hotel. Somewhere anonymous. I'd no idea there would be all this press interest. At this rate, you could have TV crews camped outside your house for days."

The senator smiled.

"We'll be fine, trust me."

Thorne glanced over his shoulder into the rear of the vehicle where Lauren Ashcroft was seated. She was already looking at him, and he sensed that she had been for some time. Their eyes connected and she smiled before dipping her head down like she'd noticed something interesting on the floor. After a beat her face came back up, both of her cheeks flushed with blood, the smile still there.

He turned to the road ahead.

It was obvious to him that he made them uncomfortable. No more than an unpleasant reminder of what happened to them outside the mall. He knew they'd only offered to let him stay with them because the hospital insisted he was supervised. Perhaps they'd expected him to refuse their offer and were now trapped by an empty promise. People said things they didn't mean all the time, often without realizing it. He'd already given the senator an out and he hadn't taken it, yet the feeling remained; they didn't want him here.

After several more minutes, the Range Rover slowed and Ashcroft swung off the highway onto a strip of asphalt in front of two high metal gates. The gates were mounted on thick concrete posts, which were attached to ten foot high walls on either side. He tilted his head back and saw loops of razor wire on the top of the wall and two overlapping security cameras in armored cases. Thorne felt himself relax. Blake wouldn't get past this lot in a hurry, and neither would any of the press pack that had followed them here from the hospital.

The gates began to open automatically in front of them.

He looked at the passenger door mirror and saw pandemonium breaking out behind them as the penny dropped with the news crews that this was the end of the line. They abandoned their vehicles wherever they'd stopped on the highway in a desperate attempt to capture some footage. Angry pushing and shoving broke out as rival crews jockeyed for position in the narrow space. Thorne shook his head. The nation's media were fighting it out to get the best shot of an SUV driving away.

With the gates now open, the senator drove through and powered up a stone-covered road beyond. Trees were spaced out on either side of them and the late afternoon sun flickered across the hood and windshield as they whipped past. The road had a long gentle curve to the left and it was almost a full minute before Thorne saw Ashcroft's home appear through the trees. It was not at all the way he'd pictured it. He'd known it would be big, but he'd pictured something old. The kind of building made from stone and covered in ivy, maybe with some turrets and stained glass windows. Instead, he saw something that looked like a ski lodge. Very modern, almost industrial, fronted with floor to ceiling glass walls like a skyscraper.

Ashcroft parked next to a couple of cars out front and cut the engine.

"Not bad," Thorne said, looking up through the windshield.

"It's a roof over our heads."

He turned to the senator.

"You honestly don't have to do this. If you like-"

Ashcroft lifted his hand to cut him off.

"It's a long time since I had to do anything, Chris, but I'm pretty sure this falls into that category. We owe you, simple as that. Stay as long as you need."

Thorne nodded, a pained smile on his face. He'd always hated when anyone had stayed at his apartment in the past, and he assumed everyone felt the same way. Even if that wasn't the case, he had little in common with James Ashcroft and he couldn't begin to imagine how they were going to get along. In the end, none of that mattered. He hadn't accepted Ashcroft's offer out of politeness, or because he believed the man owed him something. Blake was still out there somewhere, and as long as he was the senator and his wife were in danger.

"Thank you," Thorne said.

"No problem. As you can see, we have plenty of room."

He looked through the windshield as if to double-check the size of the senator's home. On a list of phrases that made Thorne uncomfortable, *thank you* was right up there with *I'm sorry,* and, *I love you.* When he went to say one of them, it was like there was something jammed in his mouth preventing the words from coming out. Much of who he was revolved around an attempt to avoid saying any of the phrases.

He twisted in his seat so he could reach around his sling arm to pull the door release lever with his left hand. It was a difficult movement, and the raised side of the seat pressed hard against his wounded shoulder causing pain to shoot across his body. It took him a couple of tries before his finger caught the lever and the door opened a couple of inches. He used a handle to pull himself out. His vision swam for a moment and he remained in a half-crouch until it sharpened up.

He was kidding himself if he thought he'd be able to protect the Ashcrofts a second time around, he could barely stand.

The senator appeared next to him.

"Put your arm across my shoulders. The chair won't work on the gravel."

He turned and saw Lauren standing in the mansion's doorway next to a hospital wheelchair. Between them, were ten feet of stones and a couple of shallow steps. He'd known the chair had come with them, but he wasn't pleased to see it again. Something close to anger flared in his chest and he struggled to contain it.

"I'd rather use the crutches."

"Maybe tomorrow, Chris. I don't think we're there yet."

The man had a voice like an airline pilot. Calm, reassuring. The kind of voice that you could trust in a crisis. Reluctantly, Thorne nodded. There was no one else here to see him like this and the odds seemed to favor the couple seeing a lot more of him in a bad way before they were through. If he didn't get used to it now he'd only be creating problems for himself later on. He placed his arm across Ashcroft's shoulders and felt the other man's arm around his back. They shuffled awkwardly toward Lauren, his left leg dragging in the stones like it had fallen asleep. When they reached the front door, Ashcroft took a step back leaving him standing on his own.

"You okay?"

"Yeah."

"I'll just get your bags out the trunk."

As Ashcroft turned away, Thorne saw a smile on his face.

This is making the senator feel good, he thought.

Thorne had misjudged him. Despite knowing nothing about the man or his politics, he'd automatically assumed the worst; that he was only helping him to help himself. It made him feel bad, because he hadn't done any of this for James Ashcroft, who he assumed probably had it coming in some way. He'd done it for Lauren, who he'd taken for an innocent.

He lowered himself into the wheelchair. He was tired and wanted to curl up somewhere like a dog and sleep, preferably for a week. It occurred to him that he'd pretty much done that already and that he needed to be more on the ball. Lauren squatted down next to him, her face inches away from his and spoke softly.

"You won't tell Jimmy about what happened will you?"

Thorne had no idea what she was talking about.

"No."

"Good. He wouldn't understand."

Thorne nodded. *Him and me both.* Lauren remained in front of him, like she was waiting for him to say something else, but he had nothing. Her eyes flicked up, over his head, toward her husband. The stones crunched under his feet as he approached. She got to her feet and spoke at a normal volume.

"How about I show you around, Chris?"

"That'd be great."

Lauren opened the door and wheeled him inside. A chirping sound kicked off as soon as the door opened and she stood on tiptoe to type a five digit code into a control panel on the wall. There was a long chirp, then silence. Her calm reaction and speed of number entry told him the alarm was always on, the Ashcrofts weren't putting on a big show for him.

He looked around for the first time.

They were in a large entrance hall with a polished marble floor. The room was cold and empty except for a full-size piano covered in framed photographs, and a console table with a selection of car keys on a silver plate. In front of them, a staircase rose up to the second floor, while to their left a corridor opened up. Lauren pushed him toward the corridor. He was tired, and the sunlight pouring through the glass wall hurt his eyes as though he were hungover.

For a moment, he considered pulling out his sunglasses and threading them onto his face Jake Vasco style, but decided against it. These people were reaching out to him, trying to repay him, and sunglasses would be too much. He'd look like an ungrateful douche. As they moved along the corridor Lauren spoke constantly, like a torrent of water. About her move to Santa Cruz from Los Angeles, about meeting James Ashcroft, about the architect of the building. In less than a minute, she'd spoken more than he had the previous month.

Three doors opened off the corridor and Lauren seamlessly interrupted her own monolog to show him a large gymnasium, a steam room, and a combination shower and dressing area. The corridor opened out in a vast space filled with hot, humid air. In front of them was a swimming pool surrounded by an outdoor-style deck with loungers and low tables. Beyond, lay plush chairs arranged around a TV, and a kitchen with a breakfast bar. He could tell that this was the room they spent most of their time in. Lauren parked the chair and walked past him into the kitchen. The wheelchair put his eye line at the same height as her ass, which appeared to be one of the seven wonders of the world.

"You want some water?"

"Sure," he said.

Lauren opened a stainless steel refrigerator and bent down, disappearing entirely behind an island unit. She passed him a bottle of water and began to talk about the kitchen renovation they'd just had done. Thorne smiled and tried to make it convincing. He looked at the bottle of water. She hadn't opened it, it was still sealed. He eased the sling off his right arm and straightened it out in front of him. It immediately began to shake so he let it drop down the side of the chair where she couldn't see it and began clenching and releasing his fist to restore blood supply. His fingers felt weak and the touch sensation of his fingertips against his palm was almost non-existent. He brought the arm up into his lap again and used the hand to grip the soft plastic of the bottle as his left hand gripped the lid. It was harder than he imagined. He was right handed and had never opened a bottle this way before. Finally, he got the lid off and drank gratefully from the bottle until it was empty.

"Wow, you were thirsty."

He hadn't noticed Lauren watching him.

"It's the medication," he said. "Makes my throat dry."

"Have mine. I don't really need it."

She reached out to him, offering her bottle. The seal was broken but there was barely any liquid missing. He went to take it but she continued to hold on to it, like she'd changed her mind. Their fingers were touching.

"You don't mind that I drank from it, do you?"

"Not really."

"There might be spit from my mouth in there."

"I can only hope."

A smile spread across her face. She let go of the bottle and looked up.

"What about you, Jimmy? You need a drink?"

83

"Yeah. A Scotch," Ashcroft said.

"Hon, it's four in the afternoon."

"I'm still on D.C. time I guess." The senator walked past him and into the kitchen where Thorne could see him. Ashcroft set out two glass tumblers on the counter. "Chris, you want something stronger? You a Scotch man?"

"I'm good thanks."

"Fair enough."

They left the senator sitting in front of the TV watching news, a glass of Scotch in one hand, remote in the other. He was relaxed, in his element, yet the shift in posture made him look older and more troubled than he had just moments earlier. Everyone had their problems, he thought, even rich people. Lauren wheeled him out the room in silence, her conversational flow at an end. He glanced through the large glass windows to the tree line beyond. Both the glass and the thick forest that surrounded the property represented a security problem, one Blake was sure to get through. The alarm made little difference, police response times out here had to be at least a quarter of an hour, by which time Blake would be long gone. Blake was out there somewhere, and he'd be coming.

"Are you an alcoholic?"

The question pulled him back into the moment.

"I try not to be."

"I'm being serious, Chris. If you're staying here I want to know."

"You've nothing to worry about."

They were in the entrance hall where they'd begun.

This time, Lauren pushed him through to the back of the room where another passage lead off to the other side if the building. The corridor was as wide as it was tall, a long square pipe with no windows. Paintings hung on the nearside wall, eight in total, with the last one protected inside a glass or composite case. He could guess which held the Picasso. Lauren rolled him quickly along, zipping past the art without a word. Thorne marveled. They had a painting worth a hundred million dollars and she said nothing yet, minutes earlier, she'd taken the time to explain a faucet in the kitchen that dispensed boiling water.

Blake was right, the painting made no difference to their lives.

His mind turned the new information over. If the Picasso disappeared, it was conceivable they might not notice for several days, perhaps longer. His eyes rotated to watch the protective case go by, but he kept his head static, giving nothing away. He was low and saw nothing but a vague blur. He guessed that the corridor was used as a gallery precisely because it lacked windows whose light might damage the art, but the location also likely meant that the Ashcrofts barely came to look at it.

The corridor took a sharp right and dead-ended after thirty feet in a long, narrow window. There were two doors on his left and a third on his right. Lauren pushed the first door open and he saw the end of a bed and an antique dressing table with a large mirror. Ashcroft had placed his backpack on the bed, next to a white plastic bag with no branding on the side. His medication.

"This is it. Sorry it's so small, we have better rooms on the second floor, but with the stairs…we thought this would be easier."

She wheeled him into the room and swung him back to face the door. Fury was boiling over inside him. He was *through* with being pushed around like a piece of goddam furniture. Better he shuffle along like a train-wreck meth addict than fucking *roll*.

He kept his face calm, his eyes bright.

"It's perfect, Lauren. Really."

"The bathroom is directly opposite. The hot water takes a while to come through, but the shower's pretty good."

He said nothing and she shifted awkwardly from foot to foot.

It seemed to him that beautiful women were frequently uncomfortable with silence, preferring to surround themselves in a bubble of often meaningless conversation. Kate was the same way, but she'd grown used to his quiet presence. At least, so he thought. It now appeared she'd wanted to talk about her feelings and where they were headed as a couple. She'd wanted them to marry and have kids.

Why did she have to break up with him to tell him that?

"Can you help me out of this thing?"

"Of course," she said.

Lauren held his left hand as he stood, quickly wrapping her right around his back the way Ashcroft had. The move brought them together in an embrace, the front of their bodies briefly pressed together. He shifted unsteadily as his wounded thigh went into spasm, but it passed and he was able to straighten to his full height. She was strong, he felt her arm muscles flexing against his back.

"Lauren, you can let go. I'm okay."

She looked up at him and her cheeks filled with blood again, her mouth slightly open. *This face,* Thorne thought, *this is why I'm here.* She smiled.

"I forgot how tall you are," she said.

He wasn't sure how to respond to this, so gave a small nod. She remained uncomfortably close to him. Either Lauren had some serious issues with personal space, or she was doing it on purpose. He began to feel light headed.

"Lauren, I hope you don't mind, but I'm wiped out."

"I'll bet."

She didn't move. He glanced at the door and back.

"I thought I'd try get some sleep."

"Oh, sure."

She hesitated for a moment, then leaned in and wrapped her arms around him, her face pressed into his chest. Her grip was tight, like a kid doing a bear hug, and he winced as her arms tightened around his fractured rib. The hug lasted no more than a couple of seconds, after which she turned and walked out the room, pulling the door closed behind her.

Thorne moved to the edge of the bed and sat down. What the hell was that? Was she thanking him again, is that what that was? He pulled his cell phone out the backpack they'd brought from the hospital. The battery was almost flat, it'd been on for days. It dropped from 8% to 7% as he looked at it. He sighed and selected recent calls. As he expected, there hadn't been any, but it always seemed to be the easiest way to bring up Kate's number. His finger hovered over her name until the screen dimmed and went black.

He lay back on the bed and stared at the ceiling.

TWELVE

The entrance to the Ashcroft place was closed, the tall steel gates blocking his path. In front of them, news crews milled about hoping to get footage of their new hero. Lieutenant Cabot slowed to a crawl as he left the road and began to nose his cruiser through the crush of reporters and camera crews. A camera turned his way and a light snapped on. Within seconds, other cameras did the same, the reporters perhaps sensing that footage of him coming and going might be the only thing they'd capture all day. Cabot sighed. When he reached the gates he swung open the door and stepped out into the glare of the camera lights. An intercom was built into one of the gateposts and he made his way toward it, surrounded by a swarm of cameras and reporters.

"Lieutenant Cabot! What progress have you made on the case?"

"Is there an ongoing threat to Senator Ashcroft?"

"Was this a kidnapping or an assassination attempt?"

They moved alongside him, microphones held out to capture any response. He regretted not sending Detective Barnes to deal with the gate, but it was too late for that. He decided to say nothing and act as if they didn't exist. It was better that way, if you engaged them you risked getting pulled into their world and drawn down to their level. They could take something you said and twist it around to mean something else.

Cabot was almost at the intercom when he saw the reporter from Channel 9 News standing waiting for him. He tried to remember her name. She was a light-skinned African-American, attractive, but styled to minimize her looks. Her hair was folded up on her head and clipped in place. She smiled, but not in a way he liked. He ignored her and pressed the intercom button, looking at the lens embedded in the post. He felt the reporter lean in toward him, the cameraman just over her shoulder. They were close, he could smell her perfume.

"Do you honestly believe the Sheriff's Office is capable of carrying out an investigation of this kind? Wouldn't this be better handled by the FBI?"

He bristled. *Fuck the FBI!* The special agent in charge of the San Francisco field office had called twice already, offering assistance. He spoke of a joint task force, increased manpower, and a bigger budget. But he knew what that added up to. They'd take over and squeeze him out. That smug bastard wanted all the glory and Cabot refused to give it to him.

"Sheriff's Office has jurisdiction, ma'am."

The panel buzzed and Ashcroft's voice came out a speaker.

"Hey, Victor. Come on in."

The gates began to open and the reporter spoke again.

"If you're on *this* case, who gets lost cats out of trees?"

A ripple of laughter went around the press pack. He pushed his way back to the car, teeth clenched. His face was scarlet, he could feel the heat on his cheeks. The woman had made him a laughing stock. Jocelyn Cooper, that was her name, he remembered now. They called her Coop. *Coop with the scoop.*

He got into the Ford and slammed the door.

"What did she say to you?" Barnes asked.

"Never mind," he said, not wanting to get into it. He drove through the gates and paused on the other side, his foot on the brake, eyes fixed on the side mirror. If anyone followed them through the gates, he would arrest them. He willed them to follow. They wouldn't be laughing then. "This whole thing was a mistake, I should never have agreed to it. We should be doing this in interrogation."

"You never explained why we're doing it at all. I already interviewed Thorne at the hospital. He knew nothing, or as close to it as makes no difference. He was just in the wrong place at the wrong time. It happens."

"You answered your own damn question, Barnes. We're here because you interviewed him without me and didn't record his answers."

"I took *notes*. He's a witness, not a suspect."

The gates finished closing and he took his foot off the brake and hit the gas. Hearing Barnes talk about Thorne made his skin itch.

"We got Thorne on video murdering three people in cold blood and seriously wounding a fourth. What would you have me do? Give him a goddamn parade?"

Mason Barnes stared at him for several seconds.

"I don't get you, man. He nearly died saving your friend's life."

Cabot pulled up in front of Ashcroft's huge home and cut the engine. In truth, he wasn't certain if he and James Ashcroft were still friends and it made him uncomfortable to hear the word from Barnes. Six months earlier, he'd said something to Lauren after too much Scotch and he hadn't heard a peep from either of them since. Ashcroft had been busy, sure, but it was an unusually long break in their communications. He had to assume she'd told her husband what he said and that neither of them appreciated it.

"Barnes, listen. I want to try something when we go in there. I don't want you to engage with Thorne at all. I want to throw him off balance and I figure he thinks you believe him. Nothing personal, okay, just the way I want to play it."

"You're the L-T."

Cabot got out the car and walked toward the mansion, leaving Barnes to bring the flight case and tripod. On the whole, he had no problem with the informal way the younger man spoke to him. He was the best detective in the department and that was all that mattered to him. Sometimes, however, this informality strayed dangerously close to insubordination and it struck him how often around Barnes he had to pause and wonder if he'd just been insulted.

The front door opened and James Ashcroft emerged wearing a crisp new suit and an off-the-rail smile. Cabot swore silently to himself. The smile was as fake as a porn star's breasts and it confirmed that his friend knew all about his comment to Lauren. He tried to return the smile, but he wasn't sure how natural it looked.

"Thanks for this Victor, I know it's probably not protocol."

"No problem," he said. "Just tiding up loose ends."

"Of course. Chris is waiting up in the library."

It shouldn't have surprised him that Ashcroft would be on first-name terms with the actor since the man was living in his home, but it was jarring to his ear. *Chris.* He was instantly annoyed. It felt personal, as if this new friendship replaced the lost friendship with him. They crossed the entrance hall and began to climb the staircase to the second floor. At the top of the stairs they turned down a hallway and entered the large room Ashcroft called his library. Thorne sat stiffly in a straight back dining chair, staring straight ahead like he was watching a television. His head was covered in bandages, and his right arm was in a sling. Thorne looked in a bad way and Cabot tried not to react as he turned to look at him.

"Good morning, Mr Thorne, I'm Lieutenant Cabot of the Santa Cruz County Sheriff's Office."

"Yeah, I saw you on the news."

Cabot flashed back to his encounter with Jocelyn Cooper at the gate. It took him a second to realize that Thorne was referring to previous coverage.

"I've seen a lot of you on the news too. Quite the action hero."

Thorne grunted, but said nothing.

"Well," Ashcroft said, "I'll let you guys get on with it. Victor, I'd like to speak with you before you leave. I'll be in the den, look in on me when you finish up here."

"Sure thing, Jimmy."

Cabot sat in a chair across a table from Thorne. He noted with displeasure that the actor's natural height and the elevated seated position of the dining chair combined to make him significantly taller than him. Unless he tilted his head, he'd be looking at Thorne's chest. He watched Barnes set up the video camera. The device was tiny and looked ridiculous on a tripod, but he knew it was capable of recording amazingly sharp 4K video. Thorne watched the camera being set up with growing alarm.

"You're recording this?"

"It was a condition of the deal I struck with Senator Ashcroft, I assumed he told you. If you prefer, we can continue this in the presence of legal counsel. Is that what you want?"

"You know I have immunity for defending the Ashcrofts, right?"

"Of course. I'm just clarifying a few details for the final report, you know how it is. Paperwork, paperwork, paperwork. What do you say? Can we get started?"

The camera was bullshit but to choose the alternative would make Thorne appear guilty before he said a word. There was a tense moment as he appeared to think it over. It was a well established trope that innocent people had nothing to fear from police scrutiny, but even Cabot knew that wasn't true. For the same reason he preferred not to talk to the press unless he had to, he knew there was no upside for an innocent person to talk to the police.

After a beat, the actor nodded his approval. Cabot felt waves of anger radiating from Thorne and he couldn't be happier. The camera was paying dividends already, the so-called hero was on his back foot before they even got started. Barnes indicated with a look that the camera was recording, and sat to one side out the way.

"Witness statement with Christopher Thorne, conducted by Lieutenant Victor Cabot at the home of Senator James Ashcroft on Thursday November 12th. Case number six eight four nine seven eight. Also present, Detective Mason Barnes. A copy of this recording will be made available to Mr Thorne at his request." Cabot paused and made a show of removing a notebook from his inside suit pocket. He turned to the first blank page, popped out the nib of his pen and looked at Thorne. "All right, perhaps you can start by telling us why you came to be in the Santa Cruz area."

"My girlfriend broke up with me and I needed to get out of L.A. for a while. I came up here, seemed as good a place as any."

"What's your girlfriend's name?"

Thorne glanced at Barnes.

"I already gave him this information at the hospital."

"Let me explain something to you, Mr Thorne. Every investigator has their own way of carrying out an interview. This is essentially a conversation between you and me, and it is easier for me to start afresh as if no previous interview has taken place, than it is for me to fit in with

90

someone else's conversation. Do you follow? As you answer one question, it leads me to think of another and so on. If I ask only for answers I know are missing now, I will end up having to come back later when that next question comes up as a natural part of my investigation. I don't have time for that, and I am sure you don't either, so how about we get through this as quickly as possible?"

Thorne nodded. "That makes sense. Her name's Kate Bloom."

Cabot wrote this down, as if it were new to him.

"She's an actress on your TV show, correct?"

"Yes."

"Why did she break up with you?"

Thorne lifted his left hand and touched his forehead, his fingers stroking the edge of the bandaging. It appeared to Cabot as though Thorne had forgotten the bandage was there until the last second. His eyes lost focus and no answer seemed to be forthcoming.

"Mr Thorne?"

"Because I'm an asshole, all right? That's why she left me."

Cabot said nothing for a moment and let his eyes wander over Thorne. It occurred to him that he might be watching him act. He expected some form of deceit from interviewees, but he'd never questioned someone before who lied for a living. He would need to watch a few episodes of his TV show to get a feel for Thorne's acting ability.

"Perhaps you can clarify something for me. I'm having difficulty understanding the connection between the two of you breaking up, and your desire to leave L.A."

"We live together. As far as I know, she's still at the apartment. It's as much her place as mine, we rent it together. I doubt either of us can afford to run it on our own, we'll both have to leave." Thorne shifted awkwardly in his chair, wincing in pain as he did so. "I didn't go back there because I wanted to give her some space to cool down."

"You hope to save the relationship?"

"She has a temper. Sometimes she says things she doesn't mean. We work together, we live together, there's no room to breathe sometimes. I understand that. I thought if I gave her time to herself she might start to miss me."

"All right. Why Santa Cruz?"

"Kate used to study here. She was always talking about it, trying to get me to come and I always found some reason to put it off. I don't know what I thought, maybe I'd understand her better. Maybe she might decide to come join me here to patch things up after she'd cooled off a little. Listen, I know how this sounds. I just didn't want to sit in some seedy L.A. hotel a mile from my own apartment, drinking Scotch to forget her. I didn't want to be *that guy*. I wanted to feel like I was doing something constructive."

Cabot nodded as if this made sense. In his notebook he added *Kate Bloom, UCSC?* It was a detail Barnes had failed to uncover, or had neglected to mention. No matter how tenuous, it was a prior connection to the area that helped explain Thorne's presence. The story itself was pretty stupid, he thought, but that didn't mean it wasn't the truth. He'd heard a few strange tales in his time that had checked out, this could be no different.

"Let's move on. You flew Delta to San Jose and picked up a rental at Enterprise, correct?"

"Yes."

"Your flight was on an open ticket. Why was that?"

"Because I didn't know how long I was going to be staying."

"No idea at all?"

"No. I had no idea how much time Kate would need to herself. I was going to play it by ear. If things went well I could fly back without much notice."

"You must've had some idea. A couple of days? A week?"

"Maybe a week, I hadn't thought about it."

"You rented the car upfront for two weeks."

Thorne smiled.

"Right. They had a deal, 14 days for the price of 8. I took it."

"I see. You realize you can drive here from Los Angeles without having to worry about flights, reservations or deals."

The smile on Thorne's face faltered for a moment, before recovering.

"When Kate left she took my car with her. I didn't want to take it back, I thought that sent the wrong message. As far as I'm concerned, the more things she has around her reminding her of me, the better."

Cabot paused. There'd been something there, he was certain of it. A moment of panic. He couldn't wait to see if the camera had captured it. The girlfriend might have his car right enough, but Thorne's reaction suggested he hadn't thought of it before now. Time had definitely been a factor in his trip to Santa Cruz, and it seemed unlikely to him that Thorne's stated reason required any urgency. He wrote *Thorne in a hurry?* on his notepad and circled it. When he looked up he saw the actor was studying him closely. His left hand, the one not in a sling, was clenched. Interesting.

"All right, Mr Thorne, how about you tell us what you did in the three days between picking up your rental and the day of shoot-out at the mall?"

"What has any of this got to do with catching the people responsible?"

"Perhaps nothing at all, but that's for me to decide."

Thorne sighed and shook his head.

"Not long after I landed my mood nosedived. I realized how futile this was. Kate had wanted to show me the area herself, by being here without her I stood to damage some future bonding moment. The trip had been a stupid idea and a huge waste of time. I had imagined it would feel like a vacation, but I hadn't been on a vacation without her in five years. Everything felt empty and pointless. I was not in a good place. If you want a list of different things I did you're going to be disappointed. I drove around, listened to music, and I drank beer. On the second day, I went into the redwoods and got lost there for a couple of hours. It was getting dark before I found my car again. Those hours were miserable, but they were also the closest I'd come to peace since I arrived. I believed I'd accepted that I'd lost her. It felt like a relief."

"Why do you say believed?"

"Because when I woke the next morning I needed her back."

This was the first thing Thorne had said that rang true for Cabot, it reminded him of the months following the death of his wife. Some days the grief would ebb away and he would feel better; the next it would return like it had never left to crush him without warning. The actor obviously cared for this Bloom woman, that was no story, he just couldn't make the same connections. You couldn't win someone back if you weren't with them. If anything, the break-up gave Thorne a reason to stay in L.A., not leave it.

Cabot turned the page on his notebook and crossed his legs so his right ankle lay across his left knee. It was a physical signal that they were moving into a different section of the interview, that this was the important part.

"Run me through the day of the shooting. Leave nothing out, no matter how trivial. If you picked your nose, I want to know it."

Thorne sighed.

"When I woke that morning I decided to get Kate a gift. A piece of jewelry, something like that. She'd always hated statement gifts; she thought it implied ownership, or that she could be bought off, but I was desperate and felt I had nothing to lose. I'd been at the mall the night before and thought I'd try there first. When I got there, I found the place closed and the parking lot deserted. The mall didn't open until ten and it was a little after six, so I decided to go for a walk to clear my head. I found a McDonald's that was open and bought breakfast. I'm not sure how long I stayed there. They had free Wi-Fi and I sat on my phone checking messages and emails. My data service up here has been patchy, so I took advantage of the connection. There was nothing from Kate so I checked flight departure times thinking I might cut my losses and go back early." Thorne paused. "You want me to jump ahead?"

"No, this is perfect. Keep going."

"After leaving there, I walked down to the beach."

"What beach is that?"

"Off the Esplanade, Capitola, I don't know what it's called."

Cabot nodded. "Continue."

"I sat on a wall down there that looks out over Monterey Bay. The clouds were huge and dark like it was going to thunder. No one else was there. I guess I sat like that for about an hour listening to music and watching the clouds roll in. It was pretty dramatic."

"I'm sure it was," Cabot said, sarcastically.

"When I got up to leave I realized how cold I'd become sitting on the wall. I considered returning to the McDonald's for another coffee, but in the end went back to my rental and sat there with the heat turned up. I must've fallen asleep, because the next thing it's after ten and the parking lot has about 20 cars in it. That's when I went inside."

"Just a moment. How long were you asleep?"

Thorne shrugged. "Ten minutes?"

Cabot made a note of this in his notepad. The report from Barnes had contained no mention of Thorne's visit to the beach, or of him falling asleep in his rental. It wasn't to say he hadn't turned up this information, but if it wasn't in his report the difference was marginal. He'd need to talk to the detective about what he left out of his reports. Thorne hadn't appeared tired in any of the security footage he'd seen. Cabot suspected that almost everything he'd heard so far was a lie. He could check the visit to McDonalds, but that was it. Walking about town and listening to music at the beach; it was for the birds.

All he'd heard was an unverifiable story, with no witnesses or alibi.

The part of the story he knew would be true, was that Thorne had arrived in that parking lot hours before the mall opened. It would be true, because everything else about the story felt like it was only there to support the car being somewhere when it had no reason to be there. Thorne wouldn't know if the car had been recorded entering the lot, or if anyone had seen the vehicle sitting there on its own, so his story was vague enough to fit in with whatever evidence might turn up.

Thorne stating that he'd fallen asleep bothered Cabot. It was an element in the story that could be adjusted later without compromising his honesty. If he proved a discrepancy in Thorne's timeline, it would be a simple thing for the actor to claim he must have slept longer than he originally thought or, equally, for less time. Nobody would be able to draw any conclusions from this. Unless you looked at a clock before and after sleeping, it was often difficult to tell how long you had been unconscious.

"Tell me about the mall."

"I saw the tall one first. At over seven feet he was hard to miss. After I noticed his size, I noticed he was carrying what I took to be a sawed-off shotgun wrapped in a shopping bag. He was watching a man and a woman, who I know now were James and Lauren Ashcroft. I then noticed four other men watching them. They didn't look like good guys. The Ashcrofts were walking toward me and the four men were moving along with them,

94

two in front, two at the rear. The giant stood near the door I had just come in. It looked like a security screen, except they were all wrong for it.

"Lauren stopped to look in the window of Victoria's Secret. James appeared to be embarrassed and looked around like he wanted to be somewhere else. I thought he'd seen the men following him but he looked right through them like they weren't there. Lauren went into the store and James followed. The four men nodded to each other, like they were getting ready. I put it together that it was a kidnapping. They were going to grab one or both of the couple and kidnap them. Since the giant was next to the door, I thought they'd wait until the two were near the exit, then bundle them into a van. This meant there had to be another person driving the getaway vehicle, making six people total."

Cabot interrupted. "That's quite a lot to put together, isn't it?"

"If they were there to rob a store they wouldn't be following the Ashcrofts, anything else you could do with one or two guys. They had enough people to take on a security detail, cops, or mall security. I guess they assumed the senator would have protection."

Cabot nodded. It wasn't far off his own analysis from viewing the tapes.

"Why did you think they'd have a van?"

"It would have to be big enough to transport them all - even a van would be a tight fit with eight people on board. That big guy would take up a lot of space on his own."

He made a note of this. They still hadn't identified the make and model of the vehicle used, never mind found it. This rankled with Cabot. People just didn't seem to notice vans in the same way as other vehicles. He assumed the gang had dumped it and switched to cars after they got away, but there was no trace of it yet.

"Carry on," Cabot said.

"I checked my pockets. I had no weapon, but I looked to see what I had anyway. It wasn't much: a can of Coke, a screwdriver, and a reusable nylon bag. I put the screwdriver in my back pocket and the can inside the bag. The Ashcrofts had left the store and resumed their walk toward the exit. As the giant walked past me, I heard tires skidding out front and the metallic clang of a side door slamming open. This would be the getaway vehicle. I fell in behind the giant and walked with him through the door. I needed to be sure everything was the way I pictured it before I did anything. When I saw the van in position and the driver wearing a clown mask, there were no more doubts."

Thorne paused to drink from a bottle of water, then continued.

"I used the Coke can in the bag to drop the giant, then finished him with the screwdriver. I grabbed his shotgun and pointed it at the closest of the men and pulled the trigger. He went down hard. A bullet burned its way down the left side of my chest and the inside of my arm. I tried to reload the shotgun but the bag prevented it, so I used the second man's automatic to tag one of the other men. One, maybe two shots. I don't think it was bad but he made a break for the van, he'd had enough. I was hit again, this time in the stomach. I found myself lying on the ground, the pain was incredible. I managed to get back on my feet and saw Lauren was still in danger. I shouted at her to get down and moved toward her.

"They were firing at us from the van now as well. We took cover behind a black sedan. I remembered I'd only got one of the two men that had been following the couple. I turned and saw him aiming a revolver straight at me so I shot him through the head. Then I got hit in my shoulder, causing me to drop the gun. My arm hung limp and useless. I pressed my back against the sedan. The car was taking a lot of hits and I could smell gasoline.

"I reached out and grabbed the gun with my left hand. I'd tried shooting with my left a couple of times in the past, and I'd sucked each time. There were three of them left, including the guy I wounded and the driver. It didn't look good, but I could hear sirens now. All I had to do was buy time. I saw one of them working his way toward me. He was wearing a *Doors* T-shirt. I'd figured him as the leader earlier. I swung out from behind the car, exposing both of us. We aimed at each other, but nothing happened. His gun jammed and my finger wouldn't cooperate; I couldn't make it pull the trigger. I heard him laughing through his mask as he ran back to the van for cover. I followed him with the gun, but I still couldn't shoot. It was too late by the time I saw the driver, she shot me in the head and I went down."

"Wait, what did you just say?"

Cabot couldn't believe his ears. Thorne had zoned off, re-living the day. He hadn't interrupted with questions, because Thorne's story fitted with the footage he'd seen and the witness statements he'd read.

"I said I was shot in the head," Thorne said.

"No. You said '*she* shot me in the head'."

"Why would I say that? I never saw the driver's face."

Cabot felt something inside him, it was electric.

"The shot to your head was a graze, correct? It basically missed?"

Thorne's eyes narrowed.

"Didn't feel that way at the time."

"Almost like the shooter couldn't take the shot."

"Is that a question?"

"Like the shooter is a woman."

"Women can fire guns just fine, Lieutenant."

"Sure, in a military or law enforcement environment. I have no doubt about it. Perhaps at a gun range with paper targets. But I'm talking about homicides on the street, one stranger killing another. You're six to eight

96

times more likely to be shot dead by a man and that's a fact. Once you remove crimes of passion, the gap only widens."

Thorne sighed. "*Maybe*, I don't know."

"Finish you story, Mr Thorne. It gets better every time I hear it."

Anger flashed across the actor's face.

"I don't think so. We're done here."

Cabot was delighted. He'd got under Thorne's skin and the man was making mistakes. It was a good sign. He didn't care about the rest of the story, he knew how it turned out.

"You know, you said something earlier that's not correct."

Thorne grunted. "Oh yeah? What's that?"

"The man you wounded, or *tagged* as you say, was seriously injured. About a mile down the road his friends left him for dead at the side of the road. He's at Dominican Hospital right now connected to the wall. *Medically-induced coma* they call it. Despite how that sounds, I'm told he'll make a full recovery." Cabot paused, noticing Thorne's frozen face, and smiled his first genuine smile for a long time. "It's going to be interesting to hear what he has to say when he comes around, don't you think?"

Thorne turned toward the window. The stubble on his face caught the light as he turned, like facets on a diamond. He spoke without turning back, his voice calm and measured.

"Sounds to me, like all you have to do is sit and wait."

Cabot closed his notebook and returned it to his suit pocket.

"That's pretty much what I thought, Mr Thorne. Not much longer now, I figure. A week, maybe ten days on the outside. Well, Barnes, I think we should be heading off to get some lunch. If you could pack up here I'm going to have a quick word with Jimmy."

"Sure thing, boss," Barnes said.

It was the first time the detective had spoken since they'd got out the car. Cabot was pleased to note that his colleague's tone was light and agreeable. He got up and walked to the door then stopped to face Thorne again. He found the actor looking straight at him. His jaw was clenched, and his eyes were narrowed. It was not, he thought, a friendly look.

"Oh yeah," Cabot said, casually. "Forgot to mention. That wounded man, Samuel Porter, turns out he was a Marine too. Served the same time you did, in Iraq and Afghanistan. What are the odds, right? Popped right up on AFIS. The world is a small, small place."

Thorne stared back silently.

Cabot nodded slowly, like he was agreeing with something that was being said. After a beat he winked at Thorne and left the room.

THIRTEEN

Cabot. The man was bad news, Thorne could smell it on him like a cheap cologne. The lieutenant wasn't buying his account of the shoot-out like everyone else, he saw his lies for what they were. He'd been too slick, he could see that now. In his experience, most people prefer a story, even a true story, to be presented with a small amount of style. But others, like Cabot, don't like everything neat and tidy with a bow on top. To them, it feels like they're being sold an angle, rather than being trusted to work out the truth for themselves. His story had been too well thought-out. It sounded rehearsed, scripted. But the world wasn't like that, it was rough and spontaneous. Real life had edges. He should've given less detail. He'd sustained a head wound; forgetting some of what happened or getting it mixed up would've been believable. If he'd done that, Cabot would never have noticed his mistake.

But he had noticed, and nothing good could come of it.

Thorne watched from the second floor window as the lieutenant walked out to his cruiser with Ashcroft. The senator had his hand on Cabot's back between his shoulder blades. It was a light touch; friendly, but in control. Presidential. When they reached the car, they turned to face one another, Ashcroft talking a mile a minute. Thorne wished he could hear what was being said, convinced it was about him. But a moment later, both men laughed and he felt himself relax.

The senator had told a joke.

He'd sensed an awkward tension between them when Cabot had arrived, but this now seemed to have dissipated. Now, the two were laughing and joking like old friends. Thorne knew all about old friends, and how the line between friends and enemies could become blurred. Friendship could be faked, used to serve an end.

Friendship could be control.

Ashcroft shook Cabot's hand, the now familiar energetic fist pump. It was strange to see a man almost in his fifties do this type of handshake, but it reassured him that there'd been no hidden message for him at the hospital. When he was through, the senator turned and walked back toward the mansion. Ashcroft didn't appear to see him at the window, but when Thorne glanced back at the lieutenant, he saw him smiling grimly up at him.

The longer he stayed in Santa Cruz, the more this fat worm was going to dig up. There were some questionable holes in his story, most of which Cabot hadn't even dreamed of yet. It could only be a matter of time before the noose started to tighten.

The simplest thing would be to leave town. The cop was small time, and without easy access to him his investigation would stall and fall apart. Cabot obviously suspected him of some kind of involvement, but that wouldn't be enough. The hunt for the remaining gang members would have to take priority and while the lieutenant looked for them, he could slip away. He should return to L.A. and try to work things out with Kate.

Cabot drove down the driveway and out of sight.

But he couldn't leave, not while the painting was still in play. Blake would remain a threat to the Ashcrofts as long as there was any chance he could complete his robbery. Only when the painting was back in the gallery would they be safe. He had to convince Ashcroft to return the painting before his birthday, before it was too late. But how could he do that without exposing his involvement? Nobody so far had made the connection to the painting and he was inclined to leave it that way.

"He got to you, didn't he?"

Thorne turned and saw Lauren standing behind him holding two highball glasses. She was wearing a man's pale blue shirt with the sleeves rolled up to the elbow, and light pink bob socks. He tried not to stare at her legs and focussed on her face but there was something strange about it that he couldn't identify.

It was Lauren, but at the same time, it wasn't.

"He made me go through that day again. I already went through it at the hospital with that other guy, Barnes." Thorne sighed. "I misspoke and he thinks it *means* something. He thinks I lied to him. The guy's infuriating."

"That's probably because of me."

"How's that?"

Lauren turned and walked over to the sofa. She placed the glasses on the low table and flopped down where Cabot had been sitting. She folded her legs up under her like a Buddha. Somehow, folded up, there seemed to be more leg than ever. She seemed blissfully calm, and there was a smile on her face like she was in on a joke he didn't know about. He'd seen this look before and it made him smile too. He crossed the floor and sat opposite her, laying his crutches on the floor. Sitting next to her looking like this would've been a mistake; at least with a table between them there was a chance he might not make a fool of himself.

She was watching him closely, as if sensing his discomfort.

"He's in love with me," she said. "Has been since we first met."

Thorne stared at her.

"Cabot," she added, a sparkle in her eyes.

He felt his face turn scarlet.

"Isn't he in his sixties by now?"

"Oh, at least."

Lauren leaned forward and picked up her glass. Ice tinkled as she lifted it from the table. It was a nice sound, an angel getting its wings. She took a sip, swirled the glass, then took another, longer pull. He watched her throat move up and down as she swallowed. The hairs on his neck stood on end. If he was honest with himself, his reluctance to leave Santa Cruz was a lot less noble than he was prepared to admit. She put the glass back down, leaving a pink bruise on the side where her lipstick had rubbed off.

"I made you one too," she said. "Thought you could use it."

"I see that. What is it?"

"Gin and tonic."

"Lauren, I can't drink alcohol. It screws up my meds."

"Oh." Her face fell. "You want me to fix you something else?"

He glanced at the drink again. Gin had been Kate's poison, he'd always been a Scotch guy. But this, this looked good. As much as it tempted him, he knew it wasn't worth more pain. He had all he needed.

"Don't worry about it," he said. "So you were saying before that Cabot is being a hardass because, what? Because he's jealous of me? Because he wants me out the way? You're already married, it's not like I'm a rival."

Her smile reappeared.

"I think the he has a clearer understanding of the situation than you do."

She was getting him all turned around.

"Lauren, are you *high* right now?"

She giggled. "What gave me away?"

"I've not seen you this relaxed before, it suits you." Thorne paused, then continued. "I also couldn't help noticing that you're not wearing any pants."

Lauren looked down at her legs and laughed. She appeared genuinely surprised to see her own bare skin and she stroked her legs experimentally. When she glanced back up at him she had a serious expression, like she were about to testify in court.

"Do you want to get *fucked up?*"

A smile spread across his face and he nodded a couple of times, amused at the idea. He hadn't been high since before he joined the Corps. Lauren stood and held out her hand to him across the table. He took it and let her lead him out the room. Her grip was firm, confidant. In the hallway she looked back at him and made a *shhh* face, then glanced toward Ashcroft's office. The door was pushed over, but not closed. Music played softly through the gap, something classical. A tug on his hand brought him back and they were once again moving down the hallway. At the end of the hall they turned into the master bedroom, then through a side door into an en-suite bathroom.

The walls and floor were white marble, large square slabs joined together by thin lines of gray cement. A shower stall, a bath big enough for two, a sink, and a toilet and bidet side by side. A window ran the full length of the bath without a ripple pattern for privacy. Lauren let go of his hand and shut the door behind them. There was a lock, but she didn't turn it. She reached into the shower stall and turned the water on, and the room filled with the static hiss of the droplets crashing onto tile. She bent down on one knee in front of the sink and from a wooden cabinet underneath, took out a cardboard box with the name of a detergent on the side. She passed this up to him, before returning to the cupboard again, this time for a double A battery and a strap designed to wrap around a suitcase at an airport. Thorne looked at the strap, his eyebrows knitted together in concern.

Lauren saw his reaction and smiled.

"Don't worry, it's not that kind of party."

She put her hand on his left shoulder to steady herself and stepped into the bath. He saw her feet were now bare, the bob socks lay discarded on the marble floor. A white shadow crossed the top of her foot where sandals had blocked the sun's rays. It was the first sign he'd seen that her honey-golden skin tone was not her natural coloring. She slid the long window open and pulled herself out through the gap in a smooth, cat-like movement, twisting around so that she could sit on the window frame. Her shirt become hitched up and Thorne found himself staring at the pink satin briefs she wore underneath. Lauren paused to do something outside, then swung her left leg sideways through the opening into the sunlight, followed moments later by her right.

A better man might've looked away while she did this, but he was the only man there. She dropped down out of sight, making no sound on the other side as she landed.

He pulled off his shoes and socks then stood in the bath and looked out the window. A white stucco shelf stuck out below like a balcony formed by the roof of the room below, which Thorne figured to be the southern corner of the pool. The space formed a right triangle with walls on either side and an open outlook into the woods on the third side. As it wasn't a balcony, there was no wall or guardrail. A series of brightly colored rectangles covered the majority of the white stucco. Padded tops for sun loungers, he realized, a single empty lounger frame sat to one side. Lauren's face looked up at him with a big smile on it.

"Pass me the box."

Thorne passed it to her and she was able to take it out of his hand without him having to toss it. The drop wasn't as far as he'd imagined.

"Stay away from the corner coming out," she continued.

He wasn't sure what she meant until he looked. Top left was a magnetic sensor for the alarm system. It had been disabled in a very simplistic manner; the two units had been glued together and the magnet part detached from the sliding window. The tops of the screw heads had been left in place, giving the impression while the window was closed that nothing was wrong.

He shook his head.

Why would they disable their own alarm like this?

But all too quickly the answer came to him: because James Ashcroft knew nothing about it. That's why she'd shut the door and turned on the shower. He moved over to the edge of the window to follow her out, and noticed that she'd pushed the double A battery into the track of the window and hooked the suitcase belt around the far edge of the window. He smiled to himself. It was obvious to him what she intended to do and it was ingenious.

Thorne wasn't as flexible as she was, and he tumbled out the narrow opening onto the lounger cushions below. He lay still on his back, waiting for pain that he felt certain was to follow. Nothing. He hadn't fallen far, just badly. Lauren's face slid into view above him. She was close, the ends of her hair touched his face.

"You okay?"

"I think so," he said.

Her face was against the light and he couldn't make out her expression. For a moment he thought she was Kate. The mess of blonde hair, the proximity. Kate Bloom was all he'd known for so long, that his brain hadn't adapted to his single status. Thorne felt her breath brushing against his cheek, the faint flowery scent of gin washing over him. He wished he'd taken the drink she'd made him. She'd done something nice for him, and he'd rejected it. Thinking about the drink made him remember his crutches, he'd left them next to his chair and he hadn't even noticed.

"Let me close the window," she said, softly. "I'll be right back."

Her face disappeared. He turned to find her again, rolling over onto his side and propping his head with his hand. She was standing on her toes and the bare insoles of her feet were right in front of him like two pale curls of butter. His eyes flipped up the length of her legs to the two half moons of her butt, where they stopped. Her shirt was lifted up as she worked. After a beat, his eyes continued up her torso to her head and arms. Lauren was pulling on the suitcase strap to close the window shut behind them. The large area of glass would've been too heavy for her to move from this angle; but with the strap it slid easily along the track until it hit the battery, just short of the window frame. She jiggled the material lengthwise to disengage the end and pulled the strap out through the gap. The window looked closed, it was perfect. If James Ashcroft walked into the bathroom he'd never notice.

Lauren turned and saw the way he was looking at her.

"What?"

"Nothing," he said.

"Jesus, Thorne. Spit it out."

"Falling out your window is the most fun I've had in a long time."

Her smile returned.

"Let's see what we can do about that."

She picked up the detergent box and walked around the end of his feet and sat on the padded matting next to him, her back up against the hard stucco wall. Their positioning reminded him of the end of the shoot-out, so he pushed himself upright next to her and watched her hands expertly roll two joints. She lit them both and passed one to him. He took a long draw. The smoke burned his lungs and he had to fight to control his body's desire to cough. The high hit him immediately, with no latency. He felt mildly dizzy, but at peace. Neither of them spoke and after a while Lauren tucked herself in tight against him, his right arm around her like a protective wing. They looked out into the distance together, across the tops of the trees, and into the blue nothingness of sky above.

FOURTEEN

Today it was a black Lexus. Blake watched it flash through the gaps in the pines as it sped down Ashcroft's driveway. A compact, nothing fancy. Totally anonymous and forgettable. It looked like the senator was trying to blend in and disappear. A wise move. If he hadn't been watching the mansion directly he would've missed it. He tracked along, following the car's progress. The sun obscured his view of the driver, but he caught a glimpse of Thorne in the passenger seat. He was hard to miss, half his head was covered in white tape. Blake lowered his binoculars and turned to Sara, who was already looking at him. They'd waited over two hours for this moment and an unpleasant tension had grown between them. But now, Sara was smiling. The plan was back on track.

He wrapped both their binoculars in a grocery bag and placed the package in a hollow he'd prepared next to a tree, spreading loose soil and pine needles over the top. They weren't going to need again unless they came back here to check on Thorne, which hopefully would be never. Behind him, Sara started the motorcycle and revved it a couple of times. She was keen to get going. Recon work was not for everyone, doing nothing for long periods of time wore you down. You lost focus, becoming first bored, then angry. She turned the lime green Kawasaki to face downhill and looked over her shoulder at him. He smiled as he pulled on his helmet. She looked amazing, like a comic book villain. Tight black leather, large black boots.

Practically unstoppable.

He got on the motorcycle and they took off through the trees.

The forest road was rough. Heavy vehicles had torn up the muddy surface, forcing Sara to weave from one tire track to another to avoid the deepest holes. Despite the conditions, she took it fast. He knew she needed excitement after the long wait, but it wasn't the kind of riding you wanted to do as a passenger. She stopped at the edge of the tree line, thirty feet back from the junction with Glen Canyon Road. She was such a pro, she always knew the right move. The angle prevented them from looking at approaching vehicles, but it hid them from the road.

He glanced at his watch.

They'd timed the journey from the mansion's entrance to where they sat at a conservative fifty mph. Any longer than two minutes meant the car had turned north, toward Scotts Valley, and they'd have to race to catch it. The forest road had taken them less than a minute, so they wouldn't have long to wait one way or another. He was about to check his watch again when the black car shot past. Sara drove down the last of the track then gave the car enough time to round the next bend before she popped the motorcycle up onto the asphalt and followed.

The road was slow and narrow with forest on both sides. Where it widened, cars and SUVs were parked, most of them at least ten years old. Shade from the trees reached across first one side of the asphalt, then the other. He wondered why people willingly choose to live in a place like this, surrounded by trees, when they could live in a city and be part of the real world. What was there to do here? Was there any work? He wanted to know, the question begged to be answered. They couldn't all run gas stations or hardware stores; there had to be something else.

At the city limit sign, Sara started to close up on the Lexus.

Beyond this point the number of possible destinations opened up dramatically and she couldn't let Ashcroft get out of sight. In the center of the city, the streets formed a typical grid and the Lexus was going up one street then switching across and going down the next. It didn't seem like Ashcroft had a particular destination in mind, but was driving about for the hell of it. They were on a street they had been on over five minutes' earlier. It was one-way and had vehicles parked on both sides.

A twin deck bus pushed out in front of them at an intersection.

The bus was long and the turn forced it diagonally across the width of the street, where it stopped. It hid the Lexus completely. A tightness built in his chest. To lose Thorne now would be a disaster after the hours they'd invested in tracking him. Sara moved across to look down the outside, but the bus driver had left only a couple of inches next to cars parked at the curb. After a moment the bus moved forward, but instead of moving to the left to unblock the street it straighten up to the right. The rear of the vehicle was now coming toward them and Sara had to back off to let it through. Blake caught a glimpse of the Lexus, then it was gone again.

He started to relax, at least it was still there.

Twenty to thirty seconds passed before the bus moved again, it felt like an eternity. Sara ducked to the left to go down the inside and almost hit a dark brown delivery truck that was blocking the left side of the street. Blake gritted his teeth. Between the truck and the bus he could see the next intersection. He stared at it while they waited. Ashcroft didn't turn off on the cross street. The small black car had to still be in front of the bus somewhere. Finally, the bus moved forward again, clearing the truck, and Sara flew past. Blake knew what he was going to see, but it was no less dispiriting when it happened.

The Lexus had disappeared.

"Fuck!"

He wanted to shout it loud enough for the bus driver to hear. Instead, it was little more than a hiss. Just the same, Sara stiffened between his hands. He cursed her caution. There'd been a moment at the intersection when she could've nailed the throttle and got in front of the bus. She'd hesitated, and that was all it had taken. Thorne would certainly have made them had she done so, but remaining undetected meant nothing if the target got away. He tried not to think about it. There was no way she could've anticipated the bus blocking them. Getting blocked on a motorcycle was rare. Sara pulled over to the side of the street. It was pointless to continue without a plan. He looked up as the bus rolled past and saw the driver shaking his head at them. They had nothing.

Thorne could be anywhere by now.

"Don't start with me, Aidan. I'm not in the mood."

"Yeah," he said. "Me neither."

Up ahead, in front of a Chrysler sedan, he saw a curve of high gloss black bodywork. Relief washed over him, it was the rear of the Lexus. Ashcroft had parked. It looked like wherever they were going, they'd arrived.

Blake took his right hand from around her waist and pointed.

"There. Go past like we're looking for a parking spot. Slow so we can see if anyone's inside, then pull over a short distance after."

Sara pulled out into traffic. They turned to look as they passed the Lexus. The car was empty. As Sara brought the bike once more to a stop, he glanced up and saw the side of Thorne's head. He couldn't believe it, Thorne was sitting right next to the window of a cafe. Across from him, sat the Ashcroft girl. There was no sign of the old man and judging by the way the two of them were looking at each other, he wasn't anywhere close. Blake smiled. He'd expected his next encounter with Thorne to be unavoidably violent, something that could jeopardize his new plan, but this? This was going to be sweet.

Sara twisted around, visor open. "What now?"

"Stay close, this won't take long." Blake dismounted and passed her his helmet. "Park where you can watch the entrance. I'm not expecting any problems, but if things go south I might need to leave in a hurry."

She nodded and he walked back up the street.

He was certain Thorne hadn't seen them ride past and he'd never see him coming from this direction. He slipped into the cafe and into a booth

106

against the far wall. It was nearly noon and the place was packed. A long line of people snaked down the middle of the store. There was no waitress service, you had to order at the counter. Normally he hated places like this, but today it suited him just fine. He'd be left alone with no one bothering him for an order he didn't need. Blake stared across at his old friend, partially screened by the moving line of people. The window seat had probably been chosen so that Thorne could keep an eye on people coming and going, but that was never going to work when you were seated opposite Lauren Ashcroft. The woman was seriously into Thorne, her hand kept reaching across the table to touch his hand or his face. Since they were in such a public space, Blake wondered if she even knew she was doing it, or if she did it without thinking.

He wasn't sure what he was waiting for until he saw it.

The woman leaned across the table and whispered something to Thorne, before standing up and heading for the back of the cafe where the restrooms were. Blake moved quickly, crossing the floor and looping around the line of customers until he was standing next to Thorne's table. Only several seconds had passed and he could still smell Lauren's perfume hanging in the air. He glanced to the right in time to see her ass swinging one way then the other as she walked away. Thorne was staring at a menu with brightly colored photographs of doughnuts, cinnamon rolls, and other baked goods.

"This seat taken?"

"Yeah," Thorne said, without looking up.

Blake waited for the bandaged head to tilt up and look at him. He didn't want to blink and miss the moment it dawned on Thorne who was standing next to him. It was quick, no more than a flicker between his eyebrows, as the actor's subconscious processed his voice. The head came up, followed almost immediately by a body braced for action. The man's reflexes were damn fast, even in this condition. Blake pushed his automatic forward inside his jacket pocket, so that the end of the barrel became obvious.

There was no need for any kind of misunderstanding.

"Easy, brother," he said. "This is just a conversation."

Thorne froze, his eyes fixed on the pistol.

"Sit down, buddy," Blake said. "It's probably better we get through this before that little cheerleader gets back from the restroom. These liberal types are compassionate, but there's only so much they can understand. Wouldn't you agree?"

Thorne eased back down onto the cafe's bench seat, his face flushed, arteries pulsing visibly on his neck. Blake knew it meant Thorne's system was wired with adrenalin and that he'd have to be careful. Even with the Glock, he wouldn't be guaranteed victory. If the actor came at him at this range he might only have time to fire a single shot and that hadn't been enough before. He slid onto the seat the Ashcroft woman had been sitting on and smiled. It was still warm from her perfect ass. She was well put together all right, and it told him everything he needed to know about why his friend had turned on him.

"You look like shit, Thorne."

"Feel like it too."

"They got you on any good drugs?"

"Oh, sure. You could shoot me now and I wouldn't feel it until a week on Tuesday. That why you're here? To score some pills?"

"I thought we should have a little chat is all."

Under the table, Blake took the pistol from his jacket and laid it sideways on his thigh, the barrel aimed at Thorne's crotch. If he needed to use it he didn't want it stuck in his pocket while two hundred pounds of Marine flew at him across a narrow strip of wood. Thorne's eyes followed his arm's movements with interest. Looking for weakness, planning moves should he need them. It wasn't hard to work out what he was thinking, they had similar training and background. He only to imagine what he'd do in the other man's shoes.

"I'm not very happy with you, Thorne."

"For what it's worth, I didn't like doing what I did but you gave me no other choice."

"All you had to do was look the other way. These people were nothing to you, what do you care what happens to them? Before this started you didn't even know they existed."

"I guess that's true, but I didn't like the idea of having to live with their deaths if things went wrong. I am sorry about Sam, he didn't deserve that."

Blake shrugged, indifferent.

"Porter knew the risks going into this. I don't feel bad about it. I'd rather die here, like that, than in another country in a bullshit fight over oil. Wouldn't you?"

"He's not dead, Blake."

"*What?*"

"Yeah, he's at the hospital in a coma. I'm told he'll make a full recovery. What do you suppose he'll tell the cops when he wakes up?"

Blake said nothing. He knew exactly what would happen when Porter woke up; he'd sing like a goddamn bird. What else could he do?

"Where's your charming assistant today, Blake?"

"Oh," he said. "She's around."

"If she sees me looking this bad, she might leave you."

He smiled. "She might at that, old man. Damned if I know what makes her tick. I'm almost certain she's crazy but I wouldn't have her any other way. She hides nothing from me; anger, joy, disappointment. It's all there on her face, and in her actions. There's no pretense, no agenda. It's so refreshing to have that kind of honesty and passion."

"The two of you are a regular American dream."

Blake found his eyes drawn to the bandage around Thorne's head. It looked bad. There was a blood stain the size of a silver dollar just below the surface. The blood dark, almost black. This, he thought, this was what happens when you do the right thing.

He'd been that guy once, never again.

"How many times were you hit?"

"Five."

"Shit, Thorne. Don't you have *any* vital organs?"

"Apparently not. I do have some cool new scars though, thanks for that."

"What are we going to do with you, my friend?"

"*Friend?* Is that a joke?"

"You know it's funny. There was a moment in that parking lot where you had a shot at me and didn't take it."

"You're imaging things."

"I don't think so, and I'm not just speaking from memory here either. Have you seen the footage? It's all there. You had me dead to rights and you didn't take me out."

Thorne sighed. "What do you want from me Blake? An apology? Revenge? If you came to cheer me up you wasted your time."

"There's still a chance to save this. Don't you see? You're on the inside now, they trust you. This couldn't have worked out better if we'd planned it. You walk freely about that huge house, yes? Is the painting just hanging there on the wall? I guess they have alarms there too, but you have all the time in the world to work out how to run a bypass without having to worry about getting in and out. Don't you see? Half the job is already done." Blake pushed the automatic under his thigh and sat forward, both hands on the table between them. A gesture of good faith. He dropped his voice to just above a whisper. "You were on board with the robbery but not with the kidnapping. It's two different things, I get that, I really do. This new plan, it's back to where you like it. Nobody gets hurt and the two of us get rich. What do you say, brother? Can we put all this behind us and make some goddamn money?"

Thorne glanced back toward the restrooms before replying.

"Who else is involved?"

Blake smiled. Thorne had a hero complex, but he was still flat broke.

"Just you, me and Sara. Large crews are more trouble than they're worth, trust me. You spend as much time looking over your own damn shoulder as you do looking forward. Who needs that?" He paused for a moment as his cell phone vibrated. The warning signal. He plowed on, regardless. "I'm prepared to honor our original deal, but the rest comes to me and Sara. Let's call it a cool million and forget that 100,000 bullshit, I'm over that now. I think this is more than generous given the shit you've put us through."

"And if I refuse?"

"Then I got no more reason to keep you alive."

Outside, across the street, a sheriff's car pulled up. They both glanced at it. Through the glass Blake saw the old cop from the news, Cabot.

"Is that what you've been doing, Aidan? Keeping me alive?"

The sarcasm was thick and hard to take, but he ignored it.

"It seems like our time's up. What's your answer?"

Thorne sat back and let out a slow breath, his head tilted to one side.

"Two million, that's my answer. If you don't like it you can go fuck yourself."

Blake stared at him for several long seconds then burst out laughing.

"You got balls, man. All right, two it is. Now-"

"Just a second. Say we do this, I don't want to see your cracker ass ever again. I'm not going to be your go-to guy whenever you need an alarm fixed. We're *done*, okay?"

Cabot was halfway across the street now, heading straight toward them.

"Believe it or not Thorne, you aren't that much fun to be around. As for other jobs, you got nothing to worry about. After this, I'll never need to work again and that suits me just fine. I'm fixing to retire here, not start a new career." He slid the automatic back into his pocket, got to his feet and stood next to the table. "Listen, turn on your goddamn burner phone so we don't have to meet like this again. Next time, I won't be so polite."

He turned and walked toward the door.

This was the pinch point right here. He had his back to Thorne and the cop was about to arrive. It was the perfect opportunity for his friend to take him out the picture and clear any doubts over his name with the police. He knew it wouldn't happen, though. He could think of two million reasons why it wouldn't. Not to mention the story he could tell the cops about Thorne if he was arrested. The way he'd tell it, he'd just be a pawn doing what his old friend told him to do. For once in his life, his lower rank would work for him. No, he had Thorne over a barrel and he was certain the actor knew it.

Blake was in the doorway now and in front of him Cabot's head was down, fighting the wind. He was holding his hat onto of his head with one hand, and blindly reaching for the door handle with the other. Blake got the handle first and snapped the door open. As the two passed each other, he leaned in and rolled his shoulder so that it dug hard into the cop's chest, spinning the shorter man around and hard against the store's large glass side window. It rang out with the impact.

110

"Excuse me," Blake said, without stopping.

"Hey, son. Turn around."

He kept walking. He had a huge grin on his face. The lieutenant sounded really winded and it was all he could do not to laugh. If he turned back now he'd laugh for sure and that wouldn't sit too well with the cop. There was a fine line between an accidental bump and assaulting a police officer. Laughter probably tipped the balance.

"Something wrong with you, boy? I'm talking to you."

Blake ignored him.

He reached the corner of the building and walked around it, out of sight of the lieutenant. One of two things would happen now. Either the old man would sigh and go into the store for coffee and bear claws, or he would decide to pursue him for a more sincere apology. Of the two, he knew which he'd put money on. To be on the safe side, he drew his weapon and tucked it discreetly under his left armpit, his right arm diagonally across his chest like he was scratching himself. Nobody passing him on the sidewalk would look twice at him, but he could fire the gun in less than half a second by straightening his arm. He picked out a spot on the building's stonework that he imagined was the same height as Cabot's head and stared at it.

If the cop came after him, he was happy enough to shoot him dead. He wouldn't have a choice, the man had probably spent most of the morning looking at grainy stills of his face. There was no way he wouldn't be recognized. Besides, blowing the lieutenant's brains all over the sidewalk might even be the smart play. He knew how cops worked; one of their own gets killed and they pretty much forget about all other cases they're working on. The bungled kidnapping would go on the back burner until new evidence came to light, which it wouldn't because they would've stopped looking for it.

Sara drew alongside and flicked up the visor on her helmet. There was a light in her eyes he hadn't seen for a while and it was good to see it back. He put the Glock back in his pocket. His helmet was hanging on her arm and she tossed it to him. He pulled it on and swung his leg over the seat and his arms around her waist and they tore off down the street. Around a minute later, she peeled off the main drag into the gloom of a parking garage. The flat concrete walls bounced the deep boom of the motorcycle engine at them from all sides.

His thoughts drifted from the lieutenant back to Thorne.

Two million dollars. He almost shook his head in amazement. It was half what he'd expected Throne to ask for - didn't the man know how to divide twelve by three? Perhaps he was playing it smart, not pushing his luck by asking for too much. There was a point when it became easier to kill someone than pay them and he didn't feel that was the case here. He and Sara would walk away with a perfect ten mill. Double digits. Breaking into that ten for another two would've been hard but two million off the top? He could live with that, particularly since his share of the payout was set to double from the previous heist.

Sara stopped next to a space and rolled them backward into the spot with her boots on either side so that the motorcycle was facing out, then killed the engine. He dismounted and took off his helmet then silently watched her wrestle with the bike. Every time, the same routine. The motorcycle was heavy, but he knew better than to help her get it up on its stand.

"What did he say?" Sara said over her shoulder. "Are we good?"

"Yeah baby, we're good. But let's be ready with Plan B just in case."

She finally got the Kawasaki on the stand and turned to him.

"Aren't we already on Plan D?"

"Well, shit," he said. "The waffle waitress can count."

Sara slapped him hard across the face. He'd known it was coming but he let it happen anyway. Knowing how a joke ends doesn't stop it being funny. He ran his tongue around his mouth in a practiced movement. Sometimes she made him bleed. Not today. His cheek pulsed from the slap, which was right where Thorne had hit him during the bar fight. If he knew her like he thought he did, he'd say she aimed for that spot on purpose. She removed her helmet and shook loose her long brown hair. It spilled out across her shoulders like a liquid, sliding about on the polished leather as it uncoiled itself. He loved her hair, loved its feel between his fingers and against his skin. Most of all, he loved when she told him to pull on it when they were fucking. Her eyes were piercing now, her lips peeled back to show her teeth.

This was no smile, this was a wild animal preparing to bite.

He held her tight as they kissed.

FIFTEEN

Thorne's body felt like it was on fire. He lay on the bed, teeth gritted, waiting for the pain to pass. A low growl forced its way out of his throat and through his teeth. He couldn't stop it any more than he could stop the pain. Minutes passed before it eased off again. He lay still, listening to the sound of his own breathing. His body was covered with sweat and the sheets stuck to him. He sat up and swung his legs onto the floor. Immediately, the pressure across his chest eased. Thorne raised his hand up and touched the bandage encasing his head. For a second there'd been a wet feeling like he was bleeding and instinctively he checked his fingertips for traces of blood.

Nothing.

He got to his feet and paused to check his balance. The dizziness was still there, but not as bad as before. No worse now than after a couple of drinks. The space next to him was narrow and he was able to use the wall to steady himself as he moved toward the end of the bed. He couldn't keep lying there, he had to move around. A charcoal gray robe hung on the back of the door and he put it on. It was small and the sleeves stopped halfway down his forearm. He lifted the lapel, buried his nose into the soft fabric and smiled. *Lauren.* Her shampoo, her moisturizer, her body.

The door of his room opened silently, with a viscous dragging from the thick carpet that made him think of a good milkshake. Thorne set off toward the kitchen. His mouth was dry and he craved a glass of water with chips of ice in it. Halfway down the hallway, he came upon the Picasso in its security housing. It was a small picture, not much larger than a sheet of legal paper and the frame probably doubled the space it occupied.

Thorne put his face up to the armored glass and peered at the contents.

He hadn't been sure before but he was now.

He *really* hated the painting.

There were three other pictures hanging on the wall, but none of them had protective cases over them. It didn't mean they weren't worth something, but probably not a hundred million dollars. He tried to imagine having that kind of money to blow on a painting, but he just couldn't. He remembered that security cameras were pointed at the painting and moved off down the hallway as casually as possible. He avoided the temptation to look up at them and continued down the hallway as he had before.

He was almost at the east side of the house when he saw bright moving shapes dancing across the dark stone wall. The pool. He could hear it now too; the gentle hum of the filter pump and a soft slapping of water. When he turned the corner, the room was not quite as he expected and he stopped to get his bearings. To his left, the large floor to ceiling windows were now black, like a movie screen showing deep space. Above the windows lights shone on the blond wood of the slanting roof space, causing a golden glow to fall down on the rippling surface of the water. To his right, a series of small lamps he hadn't noticed before were scattered around, emitting small pools of light. Thorne was so absorbed taking in the scene that it took him a moment to notice Lauren watching him from the far end of the pool, just her head above the surface. Her hair was stuck to her skull and it made her eyes look bigger and her face younger. She looked startled.

"I was getting a glass of water."

"I trust you, Chris, I just wasn't expecting to see you."

"Kind of early for a swim isn't it?"

"Jimmy snores. Either I come here and swim or I pull a plastic bag over his face and wait for him to stop thrashing about. This seems easier."

"You're pretty dark, Lauren."

"Thank you."

She sank beneath the surface for a moment then reappeared. Thorne wondered what she was thinking but her eyes gave nothing away. He felt awkward staring at her but he couldn't help himself. She made him forget his injuries and for that reason alone he wanted to keep the conversation going.

"So, how bad is it?"

Lauren tilted her head to one side.

"How bad is what?'

"The snoring."

"Oh, it's terrible. Worse when he's been drinking like he was tonight. He's been drinking a lot recently. I think he's worried about something but he never speaks about it. Sometimes he talks in his sleep as well, you know? Real nasty stuff. I don't like it, but I'm not sure telling him about it would do any good." Lauren paused. "When I told him about the snoring he just shrugged and said it's natural, that it's designed to discourage animals from attacking us while we sleep."

Thorne nodded. "I've heard that before."

"Even when he's asleep I hate him."

Lauren's words seemed to hang in the air between them. In his mind it was like a door opened, but a door to what he wasn't sure. Nothing good.

"Normally you sleep where I'm sleeping don't you?"

"Yeah, sometimes. It's cool though, don't sweat it. You save a girl's life, she owes you forever, right?"

"You don't owe me anything, Lauren."

"That's precisely what I do owe you. Anything."

Heat fanned out inside him like after a good Scotch. *Anything.* It was such a dangerous word and the way she said it, the eye contact…he turned his head away from her, as if that alone could turn off the thoughts that were now filling his mind. Anything. Jesus Christ. He walked to the edge of the pool and sat down, dropping his feet into the water. It was a lot cooler than he expected, but it felt nice against his skin. He found his thoughts drifting back to the kiss she'd given him at the hospital. It was one of the best kisses of his life, he was certain of it. He could see she was waiting for him to reply.

"Okay," he said. "A kiss. Then you owe me nothing."

Lauren smiled and swam toward him. Her arms and legs were lean, with clearly defined muscles, no doubt from hours in the pool and from the gym down the hall. She was carrying a little extra padding around the hips and chest, but he had no problem with that. Curves were good. Lauren slowed and began to tread water in front of him as she appeared to look him over. He didn't envy her, he wasn't at his best. After a moment, she smiled again, her mouth small and pinched. He amused her, like the punch line to a joke. Another guy drawn in by her looks, willing to do what she wanted. He wondered what that must be like, to have that power. Thorne supposed it all depended who was looking, it was a tough world out there.

She let her legs sink to the bottom of the pool and rose up, walking the last couple of steps to where he sat. The water came to the bottom of her ribcage. He couldn't take his eyes off her, she was stunning.

Lauren put out her hands and held his knees as if to balance herself. Her hands were cold and wet. She looked down at his lap, from knee to hip. He saw her problem. He was tall, and his long legs created a gap between them. Thorne said nothing, she'd figure it out. Her hands slid slowly up his thighs, pushing the robe up, and pulling herself forward.

Pushing his knees apart.

A shiver went down his spine. She was between his legs now, his feet touching her hips, his knees gripping her chest. The robe pushed high, barely covering what it needed to. His legs moved with her as she breathed, a slow rhythmic pulse. He couldn't say he disliked it.

Lauren looked into his eyes, then down to his mouth.

She was in front of him, no more than a foot. He felt her breath brushing against his cheeks. Before he thought too much about it, he leaned forward and kissed her. It was a tender kiss, but there was no passion in it. Not like the kiss he wanted to give her. But a kiss like that, it wasn't something you did without knowing the reaction of the other person beforehand. She might not like it. This was a gift, after all. A toll for having saved her life. She seemed happy to offer it but that wasn't the same as giving it on impulse, like at the hospital.

The kiss ended and he drew back to look at her face. Her eyes crinkled with amusement and a wet hand gripped the back of his head, pulling them back together, holding him in place. Her tongue pushed past his teeth into his mouth, forcing it open.

This is a kiss, he thought.

Finally, she broke away and smiled again.

"I still owe you, Chris. Maybe I always will."

Lauren pushed herself backward through the water, her honey-colored body turning as it disappeared below the surface. Kissing her had been a mistake. Instead of scratching an itch, he found himself more consumed with her than ever. Worse than that, was the knowledge she'd really liked it. Lauren sat on the pool steps opposite, studying him. He realized he could hear himself breathing. His mouth was open and he was breathing through it like an animal.

"Can you bring me my towel and the robe? They're on the chair behind you."

"Sure," he said.

Thorne pulled his feet out of the water and stood awkwardly. Over by the chairs he picked up the towel and a white silk robe that lay next to it and held them in front of him as he walked around the corner of the pool. He looked away while she dried herself and when he looked back she was knotting the robe's belt around her waist.

There was a trace of sadness in her eyes.

"They're not real you know, Jimmy had me enhanced."

"That doesn't matter to me. You're kind of beautiful."

She pulled a face and threw the towel at his head.

"Kind of, huh? You're such a dork, Thorne."

He followed her to the kitchen, his legs moving as slowly as they could. Lauren had a way of walking that made her ass twitch from one side to another, as if she were wagging an invisible tail and it was one of the most delightful things he had ever seen.

116

SIXTEEN

Cabot stood in front of the evidence wall and stared at the faces of those pinned to it. The wall was a cork noticeboard five feet long by three and a half feet high. Most of the time this board was used to log bowling tournaments between the Sheriff's Office and the Police Department. A tournament that was characterized by the SCPD thrashing them at every opportunity. He didn't remember how the wall had come about, though he suspected it might owe a lot to TV cop shows who had repeatedly proved its potential as a way of quickly summarizing a lot of information in a single place.

On the left hand side of the board were photographs of Lauren and James Ashcroft, then Christopher Thorne, Samuel Porter, the three dead men; Lucas Foster, Ricky Martinez, and Taylor Lynch. That left the two unknowns who were still in the wind. He noticed this had changed. *Morrison* was now written over one, while *Chelsea DiMarco* was written over the other. The other photographs were all pin sharp, but that's where their luck ended. Morrison was a grainy security picture, while Chelsea was a silhouette. The driver had never left the van so there were no photographs, grainy or otherwise.

Mason Barnes approached and stood silently alongside.

Cabot had never liked numbering unknown subjects of an investigation, he found the practice caused a barrier to form between his officers and those they were chasing. There would often be multiple unknowns of the same sex which could lead to a lack of clarity over who someone was talking about at any given moment. Additionally, if there was more than one investigation ongoing at the same time, a situation could arise where different suspects could be confused for one another due to generic naming. The best solution he'd found, was to give the subjects aliases that would be changed when their real identities were known. It was an approach that Barnes had enthusiastically endorsed and he had since allowed the detective to come up with all the names.

Cabot tapped the grainy picture of the man Thorne couldn't shoot. "Why *Morrison?*"

"That's easy. He's wearing a *Doors* T-shirt. Jim Morrison was-"

"I know who Jim Morrison was," Cabot said, cutting him off. He was annoyed with himself for not making the connection. "What about this *Chelsea DiMarco?*"

"It was the name of a girl at school. The guys used to debate whether she was a he, on account of her mustache. She had a mustache before most of us did, it was embarrassing. Anyway, I figured since we don't know if the suspect is male or female, this was a perfect compromise. If we confirm he's a man, we can call him DiMarco."

Cabot nodded. "I like it, but let's drop the DiMarco part. I want to keep the naming format consistent; single names for aliases, double for real names. Surnames for men, first names for women. We can't risk mixing them up in the field. I'm not worried about the driver being male, I'm a hundred percent we're looking for a female."

Barnes looked like he was going to comment on this, then obviously thought better of it. Cabot knew what it meant, that *nobody* thought the driver was a woman. It hadn't taken him long to discover this, all he'd had to do was walk around the department, it was everywhere. The sidelong glances, the conversations that mysteriously dried up as soon as he was near enough to hear. He didn't care. People could have their opinions, but the facts would speak for themselves and he knew how they'd shake out.

*

Cabot sat watching the interview footage again. He'd watched it at least ten times already, and every time he did it made him angry. The sound was muted now, he was watching Thorne's body language, facial movements, anything that gave him away. So far, he didn't have much. Most of the time, the actor had spoken continuously, relating events from the day, his face flat, relaxed. The only time anything was different, was after he'd caught the actor making a mistake. His eyes had flickered up and to the right, and his smooth, line-free face had scrunched up in worry. It was his favorite part of the video.

Barnes sat on a chair opposite him, his body reclined way back and his right ankle resting on his left knee. He had his left arm out straight along the back of the chair next to his, like he was at the movies with a sweetheart. Cabot glared at him over his desk. Whenever Barnes came into his office he seemed to own the space, like he belonged there and that it would be his very shortly. As long as that happened after he became sheriff, he had no complaints.

"I pulled Thorne's service record, you should take a look."

118

Cabot sighed. Not only did he not want to read it, he didn't want to hear about it either. He could tell from Barnes' face that it had impressed him and he was going to hear about it no matter what.

"Let me guess, your big hero now was a hero back then?"

"He has a Medal of Honor, two Silver Stars, and a Bronze Star."

It was worse than Cabot had imagined possible and he was forced to look away. It felt like he'd been punched in the gut. The more they dug into Thorne, the cleaner he became. His perception of the actor was so at odds with the facts that it seemed like they were different people. The detective wasn't finished, however.

"I hate to say this, but if Thorne was still on active duty he'd get a Purple Heart for what he did at the mall. They might yet find a way to do it, the people love their new hero."

"You know who else was a decorated vet?"

Barnes smiled. "John Rambo?"

"Timothy McVeigh."

The smile slid off the younger man's face.

"You can't seriously compare Thorne with the Oklahoma City Bomber."

"Just making a point. In my experience, a positive past offers no useful information to a criminal investigation. Good people turn bad, it's as simple as that. Tell me, what was Thorne's speciality in the Marines?"

This, Cabot already knew.

Barnes sighed. "Explosive Ordinance Disposal."

"There you go. The man could blow us up ten times over."

There was a silence between them for a moment, during which time Barnes seemed to study the nails on his right hand. Eventually he looked up, his face caught somewhere between amusement and confusion.

"Boss, what is it about Thorne you don't like?"

"Pretty much everything."

"I meant in terms of the case."

"I *know* what you meant, Detective, and I don't like your insinuation that my problem with him is based on some kind of petty personal dislike. Are you actually telling me that you think it was chance that put him in that mall?"

"Chance? No." Barnes shrugged. "It's a mall, he went there to buy something, just like he said. Jewelry, for his old lady."

"You buy that whole *accidental hero* story?"

Barnes stroked his chin, like there was a beard there.

"Yeah, I guess I do. It happens sometimes. A good guy comes along, does the right thing. It's not so hard to believe, is it? We have it all on video. They show it a dozen times an hour on every network."

"Porter and Thorne were both Marines. That's how this thing's connected, they go way back is my guess. Are you going to tell me that's just a coincidence?"

Barnes nodded slowly, as if conceding the point.

"Do you know Carl Sutter?"

Cabot frowned, thinking.

"The Capitola Police Sergeant?"

"That's the one. He was in the mall that day with his wife and daughter. Off duty. Was less than a hundred feet from the action when it started. He was strapped too, the man has a concealed carry permit. In any case, by the time he arrived it was all over."

"What's your point?" Cabot said. "Who gives a shit?"

"Sutter was in the Marines at the same time as Thorne. He served in Afghanistan and Iraq. I believe his deployment pattern matches Thorne's, although I'd have to check my notes. So here's the thing: if it's not a coincidence for Thorne to be there at the same time as Porter, how can it be a coincidence for Sutter?"

Cabot leaned across his desk and pointed his finger at the detective.

"Get the fuck out my office."

Mason Barnes looked at him, his eyebrows raised in surprise.

"Lieutenant…"

"*Out.*"

Barnes sighed and got to his feet. From looking like he owned the place, he now looked crushed, like a scolded puppy. Cabot almost felt sorry for him, the little prick. He felt his reaction had been fair, but perhaps some of his anger was due to the detective having a point. There was a difference though, Carl Sutter lived here, he hadn't just arrived from Los Angeles. He hadn't sat in a cold parking lot for two hours waiting for the mall to open. Thorne had no business being there, *he* was the anomaly.

"Barnes, just a second."

The deputy turned back toward him, braced for another attack.

"Yeah, boss?"

"How'd you ID those clowns anyway?"

"From their wallets. Credit cards and driver's licenses."

"You run the names through NCIC?"

"Yeah," Barnes said. "A couple of hits, neither of them particularly helpful. Ricky Martinez did eight years for armed robbery at Victorville, while Taylor Lynch did two and change at Lompoc for showing his wang to a six year old girl."

"Charming."

"Ain't nobody mourning these assholes."

Cabot ignored this comment, and the folksy way Barnes had said it. The subtext was not complex. Thorne had taken out the trash and they were all the better for it. An opinion that appeared to be widely shared by most of his fellow officers, as well as the public at large. He didn't know what it was about Thorne that made him reject his actions as heroic, but it was hard to ignore the fact that the Ashcrofts would likely be dead without him.

"All right, Barnes. Let's put the subject of coincidence to one side for the moment. If I'm wrong, I'm wrong. But right now, we have precisely jack shit and nothing to lose. So how about you run their prints through AFIS. My bet? They're all ex-military."

Barnes nodded. "I'm sure you're right, Lieutenant. I'm just not convinced it'll make any difference to Thorne either way. It's circumstantial and he has immunity."

The kid was a straight shooter, he'd give him that.

SEVENTEEN

Lauren stood next to his bed staring down at him. She was wearing skin tight black yoga pants and a long sleeve gray T-shirt that hooked around her thumbs. Thorne blinked a couple of times to clear the fog of sleep. It didn't help. Had she woken him up? How long had she been standing there looking at him?

"Watching someone sleep is pretty creepy, Lauren."

"It's eight o'clock."

"And?"

"We're going for a run. You and me. Eight o'clock is when I go running. I've brought you some clothes. They used to be Jimmy's but they should fit you just fine. He never wore them and I doubt he'd get into them now, so consider them yours."

"Are you kidding me?"

"Two things. One, no I am not; and two, my face is up here."

He felt his cheeks burn. Damn, she looked good in those pants.

"I can't run with this leg. It's hard enough to walk."

"Then we walk. I'll wait for you in the kitchen. You got five minutes. If you're not there by then, I'm coming back here with a bucket of ice water. Don't worry about showering or changing your dressings, we can do that when we get back."

She walked out the room without waiting for a reply. Thorne sighed. He lifted the cover and swung his legs out onto the carpet. He'd developed a way of hooking his right foot under his left ankle so he could use the strength of his right leg to move his left. It wasn't perfect, but it was something. He paused on the edge of the bed and stared at his taped-up left thigh. After tearing a hole through the old man's Buick, a subsonic fragment the size of a pea had buried itself in his leg and it felt like it was still in there.

Lauren had left a pair of sneakers and some neatly folded clothes on top of the dressing table. He felt a strange coolness below his left eye and when he touched it with his fingers, he found his cheek was wet. He wiped it dry with the back of his hand, and shook his head. He knew how she'd waken him up: she'd licked his face. He smiled to himself. Lauren Ashcroft could lick his face any damn time she wanted.

He caught his reflection in the mirror and his smile faded. It reminded him of the countless hours he'd spent in front of mirrors in makeup, or practicing lines for his TV show. *Kate*. He hadn't called her once since he'd been in hospital. Was she worried about him? He began to mechanically dress in the clothes Lauren had laid out for him. He'd call Kate when they got back from the walk. Even if their relationship was over, she'd still want to know he was okay, wouldn't she?

The clothes fitted him perfectly, as he knew they would. These had never belonged to Ashcroft. He was four inches taller and forty pounds heavier than the senator, they weren't exactly twins.

Thorne fed his head and arm into the sling, and set off after Lauren.

He found her standing at the window next to the swimming pool looking into the forest beyond. The sky was slate gray with dark, heavy-looking patches in the distance. It didn't look like weather for yoga pants but for sure he wasn't going to say that to her. He checked to make sure James Ashcroft wasn't standing in the kitchen watching him, then turned back. Lauren was facing him now, looking at the clothes he was wearing. He held the Nikes up in his left hand and she nodded apologetically. Tying laces had become difficult since the shoot-out because reaching down stretched his damaged deltoid and compressed his abdominal wound, causing him incredible pain. He could still do it, but Lauren was keen to help and he liked the way she looked crouched in front of him.

After she tied his shoes, they walked out the front door and she turned right, away from the driveway. He followed along behind her. She was going too quickly for him, the jarring impact of each footstep caused pain to shoot up his leg as he attempted to keep pace. At the corner of the building, she stepped sideways through a gap in a hedge into the darkness beyond. On the other side was a hard packed mud track that lead off into the trees. Soon they were in the forest, the uniform vertical lines like bars around him, sunlight filtering softly down from the canopy above. He turned his head and every direction looked the same.

She stopped and let him catch up before continuing on, side by side. They walked in silence for several minutes before she spoke.

"I've been thinking about that kiss last night."

Here it comes, he thought.

"I'm sorry, Lauren, I should never have suggested it."

"That's not where I was going."

He looked across at her.

"It wasn't?"

123

"No," she said. "After I went to bed I lay there thinking about it. How it felt, you know, all that. That's when it hit me, I kind of screwed you. It was a bad kiss."

Lauren turned toward him, a strange half-smile on her face.

"What are you saying?"

"I'm saying you saved my life."

"Oh, Jesus. Forget it."

She shrugged her shoulders. "I can't."

"The kiss was amazing, Lauren. We're all square, you and me."

"I can do better."

"That's not necessary. Come on, let's just walk."

"Forget I said anything," she said.

He nodded. "Already forgotten."

A moment passed, then another.

"Was it really amazing?" she asked, finally.

"I don't know what you're talking about," he said.

She turned to look at him. "What?"

"You're not very good at this are you?"

"No," she said.

The path curved to the left, the gradient increasing and the trees closing in on either side. She passed him to lead the way. They were now headed in a southeasterly direction, away from the mansion. The ground here was covered in layer upon layer of pine needles, he could feel the softness of them underfoot. He knew she was still thinking about the kiss, it was probably the whole reason she'd got him out here into the woods in the first place. She wanted to talk about it somewhere isolated. She wanted to kiss him again. It was there on her face, that half-smile. It was a complication he didn't need. He couldn't afford to be distracted from Blake or Cabot, too much was at stake. His gaze drifted down and he watched her ass move through the tight skin of her pants. It seemed to writhe with every step, like two snakes were fighting to the death beneath the surface.

He heard a swishing sound up ahead. The path was approaching the road. After all the twists and turns, this represented the first bearing he had on where they were. All the trees looked the same that it was hard to know how far they'd traveled. Over two miles was his guess, which had to mean they were approaching the road at a diagonal, well down on where the security gate was located. Suddenly, there it was through the trees. He saw a flatbed truck go past. Lauren dipped away again, away from the road at another angle. They were still going away from the mansion, every step they took, a step they'd have to repeat coming back. He was slowing. The pain from his leg was constant and there was tightness there that was causing him to limp. He wasn't ready for this, he hadn't healed. The

124

minutes ticked by, more and more distance covered. If he'd been on his own, he would've stopped long ago. For several minutes he entertained the idea that the path they were on was circular and that they were already heading back to the mansion. The idea got him through a bad patch, where it felt like he was being electrocuted, but he knew now he'd been kidding himself.

"Look," he said. "I'm beat. If you want to run on, that's fine. I'm sure I can find my way back from here."

"If you quit now, you won't see it."

"See what?"

She smiled and shook her head. Rather than slowing down for him, she was now walking faster, pushing him to keep up. His thigh burned like it was on fire. It wasn't warm out, but beads of sweat covered his body. Pain could be like a fever, and it seemed to be eating him alive. Out of misguided pride, he was trying to match her new pace. In a detached manner, he wondered if they would get to their destination before he passed out.

After five minutes, he saw the light change ahead where the forest came to an end and sunlight broke through in a blazing curtain. It was no more than fifty yards, if this was her destination he was going to be fine, if it was any farther, he was going to have to lie down. Lauren increased her speed again and he let her leave him behind. His tanks were empty, he had nothing left, not even pride. She looked back at him.

"That all you got, Thorne?"

Lauren, the drill sergeant.

"I think so."

"I never had you down as a pussy."

Her tone was pitch-perfect. It got to him, at some prehistoric part of his brain. He found some strength to go faster, like loose coins lost down the back of a chair.

"I take five bullets for you, and this is the thanks I get?"

"Oh, please. Two of those were basically paper cuts."

He laughed. She was good.

They broke through the tree line side-by-side into an open glade covered in wild grass. In the middle of the area, an old tree lay on its side, its thick trunk rising four feet off the ground. When the tree stood, it would've been a monster.

Lauren walked across the glade and up to the tree. This was her turnaround, the place where she ran to, before heading home. She pulled herself up onto the trunk and twisted so that she was sitting on it with her feet hanging down the side. It was something he was unable to do with his arm in a sling. He walked along the length of the truck until he got to where some branches stuck out and he was able to use them as hand and foot holds. He walked back along the top and sat down next to her. He was glad to be off his feet. He estimated they'd covered five miles. All of it, apparently within the boundary of Ashcroft's property. It blew his mind that anyone had this much land.

"All this belongs to you?"

"None of this belongs to me," she said.

"You know what I mean. To James."

Lauren sighed. "Yes."

He studied her face in profile. Lauren was beautiful and perfect, but she was also sad. He wondered if part of her beauty *was* the sadness. It gave her a depth. She felt his eyes on her and turned to look at him. He changed the subject.

"You miss L.A.?"

"I miss my friends."

He nodded. Part of the hunger he saw in her eyes was loneliness. Ashcroft gave her everything she could want, except what she needed most. It partially explained why she'd bonded to him the way she had. Her life was boring, routine, but all that had changed. Now it was exciting and she had him to thank for it.

"When I joined the Marines, I felt the same way. I was rarely home and everyone I knew seemed to be moving on. Whenever I saw them, we had less and less in common. I regretted joining up, and I missed my old life. One day, I returned to my old neighborhood on leave. I'd been looking forward to it for months; meeting up with the guys for a drink, catching up, telling each other old jokes. Instead, I sat there in my rental and watched some of my friends come and go from their homes. They looked broken by their lives. After an hour, I started the car and left. I never returned."

"That's a terrible story, Chris."

"No, it isn't. You're missing the point. I'd escaped and it took my coming back to realize it. The past is the past. Leave it there."

"I shouldn't miss my friends?"

"How long's it been? Ten years?"

She shrugged. "Close enough."

"If you hadn't left, you think you'd still be friends?"

She looked away, down the glade.

"I don't want to talk about this anymore."

"You don't miss them, Lauren. You miss who you were when you were with them. It's not the same."

"Maybe."

He'd pissed her off. He put his hand next to hers on the tree trunk. After a moment, he lifted his small finger up and laid it over the top of hers and curled it slightly underneath. She curled hers too. Their two smallest fingers were twisted together like lovers on a bed. They sat like that for several minutes without speaking. Her muscles flexed against his, like they were hugging each other. It felt good and it was with reluctance that he lifted his hand away.

"We should head back," he said.

Thorne pushed himself off the tree onto the ground. He took the landing on his right leg, but nevertheless felt a shockwave pulse through his left thigh. She dropped quietly onto the ground next to him. Lauren set off in a slow jog and he was able to match her pace without difficulty. It was easier on his leg than a fast walk, and it would get him back to a hot shower faster. He wasn't unfit, but the pain in his body was exhausting. He needed sleep.

After ten minutes, they were back to running single file and Lauren used it as an opportunity to increase their speed. He saw the road once again. This time there was no swish of cars going past, just the low, steady rumble of an engine turning over. He frowned, it didn't seem normal. It sounded hollow, empty. Lauren kept her head facing forward, her ponytail flicking left and right in a steady rhythm. As they reached the closest point to the road, Thorne turned and looked back through the trees to the source of the sound. A black van. He couldn't tell for sure that it was Blake's, but he knew it would be. What was he doing? Is this how he'd followed them before? Just parked up at the side of the road and waited for them to drive past? Wouldn't he have noticed that?

Thorne continued without stopping.

He couldn't confront Blake with Lauren present, and he was in no condition to fight him if things turned sour. He thought the deal they'd made in the coffee store would've bought him more time, but Blake was not a patient man. He couldn't afford to be. Between the news reports and the police, a small army of people were trying to track him down. He'd want to get as far from the area, as soon as possible. It would only take one person to recognize him from pictures on the news and things would start going wrong for Blake very quickly. Suddenly he understood. The van wasn't surveillance, it was a power play. Blake *wanted* him to see it, he was applying pressure. Blake was assuming he would drive past at some point in the day on the way to Santa Cruz and would see the van at the side of the road.

It was his way of reminding him what was at stake.

Thorne took a deep breath and held it for a beat before letting it out again. He'd known men like Blake all his life. Not too smart, but brutally efficient. They were like sharks. One way or another, they got what they wanted.

He and Lauren had re-entered the stretch covered by the blanket of pine needles and silence crowded in on them. He could no longer hear the van, but the sound of the engine stayed with him. It went around and

127

around in his head like a bad pop song. Something was bothering him, and it took him a minute to work out what it was. There'd been twenty feet of trees, branches, and vines between him and the van, but there'd been no fence. Ashcroft's security gate and camera system were worthless. If Blake wanted to, he could push his way through to this path, then follow it around to the back of the mansion unseen. No cameras covered the narrow angle between the path and the front of the house, only at the front door itself, and he was certain there would be a way past that.

He'd given no thought to stealing the painting since his meeting with Blake. It had been in the back of his mind, like a squeaky brake you know needs fixed. He was putting it off, but he couldn't do that for much longer. Setting aside the two million dollars he'd been promised, it was clear to him that the root cause of everything *was* the painting. With it gone, Blake and his demented sidekick had no reason to stay. If they left happy and rich, it seemed unlikely they'd put it all at risk with further conflict. Staying alive was a good deal for everyone. He had to do it, there was no alternative. At the end of the day, as Blake had said, it was just a painting. This path, and the security blindspot it represented, would be an essential element in the robbery. The investigation of the theft would quickly find this hidden access and focus would move away from him as prime suspect.

He'd contact Blake on the burner phone, tell him he was working on his end of the deal. Make all the right noises. Assure him that he was working on a plan and that he had nothing to worry about. He'd betrayed Blake once already, it was understandable that he needed reassurance. Thorne smiled. He'd ask Blake for some piece of equipment he needed for the robbery, keep him busy getting hold of it. Anything that kept Blake looking the other way was going to be better for both him and the Ashcrofts.

Lauren looked over her shoulder at him.

"Hey," she said. "You're smiling."

"It won't last."

"Nothing does."

EIGHTEEN

Cabot had a legal pad in front of him on his desk. He'd made a timeline of Thorne's activities starting with his departure from Los Angeles and ending with him lying in a pool of his own blood in Lauren Ashcroft's lap. He'd broken it down as much as possible, trying to get it down to the bare bones. For the most part, they were key phrases, some a little more detailed than others. He'd used information that Thorne himself had provided, but he'd put those parts in parenthesis. He assumed the actor knew the key to lying was to make up as little as possible. Therefore, a lot of what he'd been told would turn out to be the truth. Inevitably, there would be a lot that was unverifiable or irrelevant, but he needed as much as possible in front of him to see where to go next with the investigation.

He preferred to work things out using pen and paper, to feel the friction of the ink being dragged across the page, to scribble out mistakes and replace. Put in arrows, circle some words, underline others. He couldn't get close to that experience on a computer.

He tapped the point of his pen next to the first item on the timeline; *Thorne leaves L.A.,* and wondered if he was starting the timeline too late. He didn't buy the story about why he left Los Angeles in the first place, so it stood to reason he should try and track down Thorne's activities before he left, see if anything unusual was going on. Perhaps he should dig into the man's financials, see if he had any money problems, or if he suddenly received a large sum. He wrote *Financials* to one side of his list and circled it. Hollywood actors were the same as everyone else, they could find themselves in a tight spot over money. He didn't know how much Thorne made, but it mattered little. Those with more money than others usually found new ways to spend it.

His thoughts were interrupted by a one-knuckle knock on his office door. Summersby stood there, his mouth open and part of his tongue sticking out. Just what he needed, he thought, another conversation about missing overtime payments with this idiot. He noticed that the detective had a notebook in his free hand, one of his fingers inserted into the pages like a bookmark. Things were looking up.

He motioned for him to enter.

"You got something for me, Summersby?"

"A buddy of mine in patrol passed this to me, Lieutenant, I thought you'd be interested. Yesterday morning, a 911 call reported a man having a heart attack down by the wharf. When the paramedics got there, they were jacked. Guns pointed in their faces, the whole routine. The thieves took off with their vehicle and left them standing at the curb like a couple of fools. Fast forward a couple of hours, another 911 call. This time, a car crash down in Twin Lakes. Again paramedics turn up, get jacked. No shots were fired in either case, and patrol has already recovered both vehicles."

"What did they take?" Cabot said, trying to cut the story short.

"Defibrillators."

He sat back in his chair and studied Summersby. The man was grinning, like there was some punch line coming. There had to be, why else was he hearing this?

"Okay," Cabot said. "Tell me the good part."

"The thieves wore clown masks."

"The *same* clown masks?"

Summersby nodded. "I think so. One of them had blood spatter on it."

"Goddammit!"

His voice was louder than he intended and heads turned to look at him through his office windows. They could all eat a big bag of dicks as far as he was concerned, this wasn't the bloody Rotary Club. He sighed and looked up at the ceiling.

"This is good news though, isn't it?"

"How do you figure that, Detective?"

"Well, it means they're still around. We can still catch them." Summersby paused, his face lighting up. "Do you think they're locals?"

Cabot grunted. He felt it was bad luck to verbalize the hope that dangerous people would stick around so they could be caught, knowing that this increased the risk to his community. Nevertheless, it was a reality all cops faced, and he wanted these people badly.

"They're not locals, I know that much. They're from L.A."

"How do you know?"

"Because Thorne is."

"He's one of them, isn't he? Has to be."

Cabot stared at the younger man for several seconds to see if he was jerking him around, but he could see he wasn't. Of all the people that could be open to his theory on Thorne, why did it have to be this asshat? He'd rather fight Barnes' skepticism, than suffer this man's support. He grabbed his coffee mug and, finding it empty, stood and walked out his office to the break room for a refill. Summersby tagged along silently behind him. There was a jug of coffee on the hotplate that had probably been sitting there cooking for over an hour. He filled his mug without rinsing out the half inch of cold grounds and took a mouthful.

"I don't get it," Cabot said. "*Defibrillators?* Why?"

"You got me, Lieutenant. Maybe to sell."

"How many are we talking about?"

"Four. Each crew caries a backup in case their primary fails. I'm told that the cost to replace them is close to ten grand. These were top of the line."

Cabot shook his head. Ten grand. It was a decent haul for a couple of minutes' work. You find somewhere quiet, call 911, and the victims come to you like you've ordered pizza. He took another swig of coffee, already forgetting how bad it was. To his way of thinking, it didn't seem likely that a gang who'd tried to kidnap a US Senator and his wife were now pulling low-level robberies. It wasn't that he doubted that the same people were involved, he just couldn't see the angle. His gut told him it wasn't for the money, but then what?

"All right," Cabot said. "Go interview the paramedics. Take Liu, people seem to open up to her. Obviously, I don't give a flying fuck about the defibrillators, but if those were the same clowns from the mall, then these medics could have vital information. When you're done there, check the crime scenes to see if patrol missed anything and, finally, see if you can track down any footage of the robberies. Stores, traffic cams, ATMs, whatever. Find out where the thieves came from, where they go. If we're lucky, we'll get some clearer stills of these assholes without their masks; perhaps a make, model, and license plate number for their getaway vehicle."

"Traffic cams are live, sir, you can't rewind them."

Cabot sighed. "Just get me something I can use."

"You got it."

"This is good stuff, Summersby, keep it up."

The detective smiled and nodded. It wasn't a good look for him, Cabot thought. Too much gum showing between his lips, not enough teeth. Probably no one had ever complimented him before, so he didn't have the practice. They walked through the squad room together and Summersby peeled off toward Liu's desk, while he returned to his office. It would be ironic if this car-crash of a detective would be the one that tied up the case, but that's how it was sometimes.

You find the right thread, and you pull on it.

Next to his keyboard someone had stacked some papers on top of his notepad. There was a bright yellow post-it note on top with a smily face drawn on it. He peeled the post-it off and stuck it to the edge of his

131

computer monitor. This would be the database lookups he'd asked Barnes to get him. He found what he wanted on each page, Barnes had circled it for him. Lucas Foster and Taylor Lynch had both served in the Marines. No military service was listed for Ricky Martinez. Including Samuel Porter and Christopher Thorne, he was now dealing with four former Marines at the scene of the shoot-out and they weren't done yet. He knew there'd be one more: the man they now called Morrison.

Cabot sat back in his chair, rejuvenated.

When he thought about catching the two remaining clowns, what he really thought about was how that would then enable him to nail Thorne. They were little more than stepping stones for him to get to who he wanted. He knew it should be the other way around, but the results would be the same. He drank his coffee, allowing his buzz to build. Experience told him that you had to enjoy moments like this while they lasted, because all too often they went nowhere. When he was finished, he put his mug down and moved his mouse to clear the computer's screensaver. Thorne appeared on screen. The interview footage again. Playback was frozen with the actor looking off to the side, out the window of Ashcroft's library. He remembered the moment, he remembered every moment of that interview now. He'd just told Thorne that the wounded man, Porter, would soon be able to give a statement. Thorne had turned away. *Turned away to hide his face.*

Cabot smiled. Thorne was vulnerable on this Porter thing.

NINETEEN

Best steak in the county. That's what Ashcroft had promised him, that was all it took to lure him out of the mansion and back onto the streets of Santa Cruz. He was staying at the man's house, it didn't hurt to play nice every now and then.

Traffic moved slowly on Chestnut, it looked like there'd been a collision on the opposite side of the street and cars bunched up as they past it. They were starting and stopping. Thorne turned to watch a man and woman walking down the sidewalk next to them. The couple were carrying a large mirror with a dark wood surround. It appeared heavy, yet they matched the speed of the Range Rover with little difficulty. The mirrored side faced toward him and sunlight occasionally flashed at him, depending on their positions.

The SUV ground to a halt and the couple pulled ahead.

Thorne looked away, bored. First, through the windshield, then across to Ashcroft behind the wheel. The senator had a smile on his face, like he was thinking of something that amused him. Thorne thought he'd smile the exact same way if he was James Ashcroft. After a moment, they moved off again, and he turned back to look for the couple. They'd stopped behind a Volvo station wagon. The mirror was on its end, tilted to rest against the vehicle's open tailgate so the couple could catch their breath.

Thorne saw the street behind reflected on its surface.

Near the top of the mirror, was a black van.

The van looked *very* familiar.

Ashcroft turned off at a cross street, heading east, toward the centre of Santa Cruz. Trees leaned in from both sides of the road. Thorne watched the passenger door mirror, his eyes fixed on the crossing. He mentally counted down in his head; five, four, three, two, one. Just then, the van made the turn and popped out behind them. Thorne felt calm pour through him like ice water. Stage one of his unusual reaction to adrenaline. He became alert, his eyes unusually sharp. It cut right through the fog of

Fentanyl. Thorne wet his lips. It was impossible to tell at this distance if it was Blake, vans had a way of all looking alike. The van was 40 feet behind them and was now partially hidden by a silver Chrysler.

Thorne didn't like it. Why would Blake follow them now? This only stood to put their deal in danger. Didn't Blake realize that Cabot could have people watching the senator in unmarked cars, waiting for this exact scenario to play out?

It occurred to him that since he'd made the deal with Blake he'd stopped preparing for another attack. He'd assumed an attack wasn't coming, that he had it handled. But what if that reaction was *precisely* what Blake was counting on? If Blake hit them now, today, he was completely unprepared. The kidnapping would unfold as it had before, only this time around, there'd be no interruptions. Without the element of surprise, he'd be killed immediately.

Ashcroft turned south on Center Street. Again, he watched the mirror. He knew that once you became sensitized to something, you saw it everywhere. Thorne told himself it was nothing, a coincidence and no more. It was reasonable to assume that a vehicle might make a couple of the same turns without it meaning anything. Part of their routes might overlap, it must happen all the time. But with every repeated turn the odds of this shortened.

The van turned on Center.

It was still there, not closing up, not falling back. He swore silently to himself. If this really was Blake, and he didn't see who else it could be, there might still be time to stop him before he started. A single police cruiser could be enough to spook Blake. Make him re-think any plans he might have and revert to the deal they made.

He leaned close to Ashcroft and spoke quietly.

"Make a left at the next junction."

Ashcroft glanced at Lauren in the back seat before replying.

"What is it?"

"Hopefully nothing," Thorne said.

The senator nodded, his body language changing in a heartbeat. He got it. His face hardened and his mouth became a thin, flat line. Thorne looked again at the mirror, waiting for Ashcroft to make the turn. He wanted to be wrong. He wanted to see the van flash through the intersection behind them, and out of their lives. Ashcroft turned sharply onto Lincoln without using his turn signal. He gave it more gas than normal through the turn and continued to power down the near-empty street. They shot through the Cedar Street crossing seconds later at over 60 mph, forcing a white Camry across the corner of the sidewalk and into a fire lane to avoid hitting them. This wasn't exactly what he had in mind.

The street was clear all the way back to Center Street. They'd opened up a gap, but it wasn't going to last. Up ahead, a line of cars waited to feed onto Pacific Avenue. This had been the wrong way to come, the traffic here would box them in. In another shoot-out there'd be nowhere to go. At the front of the line, a car got out and they all crept forward. It was painful; they were never going to get through before Blake arrived. The white Camry pulled up behind them. Thorne wondered if the driver would get out and start something with Ashcroft. This wasn't L.A., people here expected you to be human. When they wished you a nice day, they meant it. The moment passed, and the driver stayed where he was. Another car got out at the junction, leaving only two vehicles. Again they moved forward. His eyes were fixed on the mirror now. The Camry blocked most of his view, but he could see enough.

The van had turned onto Lincoln.

Doubt vanished from his mind; it was Blake, it had to be. The van was accelerating hard to catch up and would be with them in seconds. Their burst of speed had been for nothing. Just then, a gap opened up in the traffic and they got out onto Pacific, which Ashcroft immediately turned off onto Soquel Avenue. It was almost perfect, but they hadn't had enough distance. Blake would've seen the extra turn. Sure enough, he caught a glimpse of the van as they turned down Ocean. The traffic here was lighter and faster and he had to lean forward to see the intersection in the mirror.

Ashcroft had the Range Rover's revs up high, he was flooring it. For a tank, the thing really moved. A couple of seconds later, he saw the van appear, leaning hard over as it cornered. To his surprise, another van followed the first, this one light gray. The black van had blocked his view of the one behind. The sun bounced off the sides of both vehicles as they turned, illuminating the logos of two television networks. Thorne sat back in his seat and let his breath out in a sharp blast.

"Jesus," he said. "It's only TV crews."

After a pause he and the senator burst out laughing.

"Never thought I'd be glad to see them," Ashcroft said.

Lauren leaned forward.

"Perhaps you assholes can let me know what the hell's going on next time. I'm not a child or a piece of goddamn luggage. I have the right to know."

Thorne looked around. Lauren's face was scarlet, and her hair was all messed up.

He'd forgotten she was even there.

"Sorry, Lauren."

"Yeah babe," Ashcroft said. "My bad."

Lauren glared at Thorne, ignoring her husband. She was breathing through her mouth and he could see the rapid rise and fall of her chest. Her cheeks were flushed. She was angry and frightened and though he was disgusted with himself, he'd never been more attracted to her.

Thorne returned his eyes to the road.

They were traveling parallel to the San Lorenzo River now, heading south. They were close to the beach and he saw the curving track of a rollercoaster to his right. The television vans continued to follow, but had fallen back. There were no stop lights and intersections here, less chance of them losing their quarry.

Ashcroft hummed quietly to himself. He seemed relaxed, like he'd forgotten all about what had happened. Thorne supposed that from the senator's point of view it was just a minor blip. A misunderstanding that might later become an amusing anecdote for the campaign. He could forgive Ashcroft for thinking that way, but he knew better. They'd been lucky this time. He'd made a mistake about who was following them, but the reasoning behind his mistake was sound. This was a wake-up call, not a time to relax. He'd dropped his guard with Blake, even after being ambushed in the coffee shop. But that couldn't continue. Blake could double-cross him at any moment, just as he'd betrayed Blake at the mall.

He needed a backup plan.

TWENTY

They were at a marina. Masts swept past in a blur, the senator's foot firm on the gas. Thorne's eyes scanned the scene before him, looking for threats. Some adrenaline still remained in his system and he felt it in the form of hyper vigilance. This was the legacy of combat, of PTSD. It didn't come up too often, but it was always there, ready to come back without warning. Everything was a little too bright, a little too colorful. Ashcroft swung the SUV into a parking spot and killed the engine. It dawned on him that the senator was exactly the kind of person that would own a yacht, and that they were likely about to go out on it.

"I thought we were going to a restaurant?" Thorne said.

"I only promised you the best steak, Chris. I didn't say where."

"Right."

Thorne turned to get out. Inwardly, he sighed. This again, he thought. He reached across his body and pulled on the release lever with his left hand. The door was heavy and he had to twist to the right and give it another shove with his foot to avoid it closing again. His shoulder dug into the corner of his seat and he bit his teeth together to stop from crying out. He hadn't sworn once while he was being shot, but the urge to do so since was almost constant. He'd be damned if he was going to show his pain to the very people he'd saved.

Outside the vehicle now, he straightened to full height and slammed the door shut behind him. As he readjusted the sling's position, he turned to look back toward the road. The news vans were almost on them. A small twister of dust rose up behind the two vehicles as they picked their way through the lot toward them. It appeared that the press had lost sight of them in the zig zagging parking lot, but it wouldn't take them long to find the large SUV.

Ashcroft pulled two iceboxes from the back of the Range Rover and passed one to him. There was a forced friendliness about the gesture that made him wonder where the day was headed. He nodded then followed the senator down the pontoon. He spotted what he knew would be Ashcroft's yacht almost immediately. It was a large stealth bomber in white fiberglass. Sure enough, Ashcroft went alongside it and climbed on board.

Thorne glanced at the name written on the stern.

Questionable Things.

"Please don't ask him about the name," Lauren said.

He turned to her. "Why not?"

"Because he'll tell you," she said.

Thorne understood. Everyone asked Ashcroft about the origin of the name, and Lauren was sick of hearing it. He walked down the side of the yacht and held the icebox up to Ashcroft with his left hand. He heard doors slamming shut and raised voices. The news crews had caught up with them. He climbed on board, then turned to help Lauren, only to find her right there next to him. When she saw what he'd done, anger flashed across her face.

"Don't do that shit with me again," she said.

He shrugged and said nothing. When you were in a hole it was best to stop digging. Up front, Ashcroft was untying one of the lines that held the yacht in place. Thorne didn't want more engagement with the press pack than could be avoided, so headed toward the stern to finish the casting off process. He leaned forward and used his knee to brace himself while he untied the stern line and threw it over the side onto the pontoon. It landed at the feet of an African-American woman who was studying him with interest.

"I'm sorry," she said, earnestly.

"Excuse me?"

"For earlier. We didn't mean to scare you, it was stupid. We thought you knew who we were but you didn't, did you? You thought we were...*them.*"

It was the reporter from Channel 9. A man in his late twenties was running toward them from her left, a camera already up on his shoulder. Up in the parking lot, blisters had opened on top of the vans and satellite dishes had appeared. The reporter was trying to stall him. He stood from his crouching position and turned away. James Ashcroft was smiling at him and as they made eye contact, the senator nodded. A moment later, he felt the engine come to life through the deck. He stared down at the woman as the yacht pulled away from her. What struck him most about her was that she too was smiling at him, a big cheesy grin.

This is what I do, I make people happy.

The boat swung around into the main channel out to sea, and he walked slowly forward to where Lauren sat. Now they were underway he had to concentrate to keep his balance. Having his arm in a sling made simple things difficult to the point of absurdity. He knew that, soon, he'd stop wearing it no matter the pain. He stood watching Lauren, a smile on his face. One of the iceboxes was open at her feet and she was in the process of mixing what appeared to be the world's largest gin and tonic. He guessed that sailing wasn't her thing and she'd rather be anywhere else. She leaned into the icebox again. This would be for the tonic, he thought. Every time she leaned in, her top fell open exposing a lot of cleavage.

"Earth to Chris."

"Hi," he said.

He'd zoned out for a moment, remembering the pool, the kiss. She had her head tilted forward, looking at him over a pair of sunglasses.

"Where were you?"

"Casting off."

"No," she said. "Just now. You were miles away."

"I was, but you were right there with me."

She let out a long breath. "Oh God, I wish."

"What does *that* mean?"

Lauren shrugged, casually. "You started this, Thorne."

"I'm going up front with James."

She took a sip of her drink, her eyes fixed on his.

"If you push him over the side, I'll tell them it was an accident."

"I love your sense of humor."

Lauren sighed, her gaze shifting away from him. It was his cue to leave, and he took it before she said anything else. He thought she'd nailed a perfect dry delivery of her line, but as he moved forward he knew there *was* no line.

He entered the cabin. It was large, with tinted glass windows all the way around and overhead. He walked through a galley kitchen to an eating area with off-white seats arranged around a table in a square. Beyond lay a cockpit area, with two black leather chairs and a steering wheel. Ashcroft sat in one of them, and Thorne climbed into the one next to him. They sat in silence as Ashcroft navigated them out of the marina. They moved slow enough that when he turned his head and looked out the side window he could see the TV crews running alongside, perhaps hoping to set up their cameras to get footage of them heading out to sea. It surprised him that news channels were still covering the Ashcroft story. To Thorne, this spoke to a subconscious knowledge that the action was far from over.

The *Questionable Things* cleared the marina and they headed out into Monterey Bay. The transition in speed and setting seemed to break a spell he and Ashcroft were under. The senator turned to him as if noticing him for the first time.

"You want to steer?"

"Sure," Thorne said.

They swapped seats, Ashcroft holding on to the wheel until the last second to maintain control. Thorne made several small course corrections to get a feel for the steering. It was the first time he'd been in control of any kind of ship and he couldn't help but be disappointed.

"What do you think?" Ashcroft said.

"I thought the directions would be reversed."

"Would be with an outboard motor or a tiller, a wheel's the same."

"You ever open her up, see what she can do?"

Ashcroft nodded. "Sure, but not too often. Mostly what happens is that plates and glasses slide onto the floor and break. I come out on the water to relax and get away from the world, not to zip about like a racing car. Did you want us to do that?"

Thorne shrugged. "Just the way she looks. Streamlined. Fast."

Ashcroft said nothing and their conversation once again came to an end. After about ten minutes, Ashcroft turned off the engine and the yacht slowed to a halt. The water was like glass with no detectible swell.

"Let's get the grill on," Ashcroft said. "I'm starved."

They walked through the cabin to the deck where Lauren sat. She looked like she'd melted into the seat. She still held a glass in her hand, but it probably wasn't the same drink. The senator opened a cover, exposing a large grill and began setting it up. Thorne sat next to Lauren at a small table. He chose to sit at the end as it was the farthest he could sit from her without appearing rude. It also allowed him to keep an eye on the senator as he prepared lunch. He allowed himself to study Lauren's profile. As near as he could tell, it was perfect.

Ashcroft turned to them holding a pair of tongs.

"How do you like your steak, Chris?"

"Burned to a cinder on the outside, dripping with blood on the inside."

"Good man."

Ashcroft laid two slabs of beef down on the grill followed by a piece of salmon. A cloud of smoke rose into the air and swirled around them. Under the table, Lauren put her hand on his thigh and ran it slowly back and forth. She continued to look over the side of the yacht, a neutral expression on her face. She was toying with him. His sling prevented him from brushing her hand away. He moved his leg in an attempt to get her to disengage, but her hand only crept higher, toward his crotch. The senator turned toward them.

"Sorry about the smoke, it's only like this at the beginning. Usually there's a breeze that takes care of it, but it's so calm today." He turned to Lauren and frowned. "Hon, perhaps you could fix us *all* a drink?"

It wasn't a subtle dig, but it bounced right off her without comment. She turned to face Thorne for the first time, her hand still resting on his thigh.

"You want anything, Chris?"

"I'm good thanks."

Her hand was almost touching him.

"I think you need to relax. Tell him, Jimmy."

"She's right you know. We got a couple bottles of the most beautiful Pinot. Goes perfectly with steak."

"Come on guys," Thorne said. "I'd love a drink, but I can't."

"All right," she said. "But we'll get you eventually."

"I have no doubt at all about that."

*

As Ashcroft had promised, the steaks were amazing. If politics didn't work out for him, there was a future there as a chef. He caught himself staring at Lauren and noticed she was staring right back. Her mouth was open, her lips full and juicy. He looked away, off over the back of the yacht, to where the sea merged into the sky. It was nothing. They'd been through something intense together and it made them feel close. If Kate hadn't broken up with him, it would be a different story. He'd have considered it flattering, then moved on. But the breakup had changed something in his brain, he couldn't stop thinking about Lauren and the way she was when they were alone together.

Lauren stood and had to steady herself. She was half cut.

"If you boys don't mind, I'm going up front to catch some rays."

"That's fine, honey," Ashcroft said.

He had a feeling the two of them had arranged this beforehand. Ashcroft wanted to talk to him alone. This was why they were here, everything else had been for this. Lauren paused to pick up a bag, then worked her way around the side of the yacht to a raised section of decking beyond the cabin. She unbuttoned her shirt and dropped it at her feet, then did the same with her shorts. Underneath she was wearing a bikini that was at least one size too small. She took a towel from the bag and laid it out on the deck. Her feet were set wide apart to combat the roll of the yacht and the amount of alcohol she'd consumed. He was staring at her again but he couldn't help himself. She stood gazing into the distance and pulled a pair of sunglasses out of her hair and onto her face. After a beat, she noticed they were watching her and waved. Finally, she lay down on the towel and disappeared from sight. He turned and found Ashcroft watching him with hooded eyes.

"There's something I feel I should tell you about my wife."

"What's that?"

"I'm in love with her."

Thorne smiled. "I'm not surprised. She's adorable."

"That's nice of you to say. In fact, she's vulgar and a bit on the slutty

141

side. I can't exactly hold it against her, it's the reason I married her. The thing you have to understand about Lauren, is that she bores quickly. Right now you're new and exciting; next month it'll be something else. I just don't want there to be any misunderstanding in the meantime."

"Misunderstanding?"

Ashcroft sighed. "Without you my wife and I would be dead. You know it, I know it, and Lauren knows it. We are immensely grateful to you, but my gratitude does not extend to you sleeping with my wife. Clear enough?"

"Crystal."

They fell into an uneasy silence. He didn't know if Ashcroft had picked up on something between him and Lauren, or if his warning was more generic. She was easy enough on the eye that the senator could assume he was interested in her without having to see it. Ashcroft lifted his wine glass and took a long swig, as if to rid himself of the previous conversation. When he put the glass down it made a loud noise on the table, causing them both to flinch.

"Sorry," Ashcroft said, about the glass.

"Don't be," Thorne said, about Lauren.

He looked at Ashcroft and saw that he understood. The senator smiled and nodded once, the air between them clear again.

"Did you want to talk to me while Lauren was away?"

"I'm not sure I need to after what happened earlier."

"You were going to ask if I thought the gang would be back?"

Ashcroft nodded again. His hands were resting on the table on either side of his body, his fingers smoothing out the tablecloth over and over again.

"I trust your instincts on these people. How long do you think we have?"

"Two weeks," Thorne said. "Maybe less."

"That's all?"

"I've been thinking about this since that stupid chase. It'll depend on whether they have to replace any of the men that died. If they had specialized skills, for example. From what I saw, the only skills they had were in firearms and there's no shortage of people like that."

Ashcroft stared at the table, his face pale. Thorne felt bad for lying to him, but he could hardly tell the senator that he'd met Blake in town the day before.

That he *was* the replacement man.

"Unfortunately, Chris, you're probably right. It's funny, I intended this to be a send off. A nice meal on the boat before you went on your way. I figured you'd want to get back to L.A., back to your normal life. This is unfair, but I wanted you gone. I spend so much time in D.C. that my time here is limited. I hate that. This is *me time*, you understand? I love Santa

Cruz, it's the only place I can relax and leave everything else behind." Ashcroft paused. "Anyway, if you're willing, I'd like you to stay for a while until the situation here is resolved. I feel safer with you around and know Lauren feels the same way."

He wished Ashcroft had stuck to his plan and told him to get the hell out. That way he'd be off the hook for anything that Blake might do later.

"I'll think about it," he said.

Ashcroft nodded. "Can't ask for any more than that."

He wondered what James Ashcroft expected of him if Blake did decide to make another armed attack. Last time around he'd nearly died. Wasn't that enough?

"Cabot doesn't think they'll be back, does he?"

"Ah, Victor!" Ashcroft said, as if talking about a circus dog that could walk on its hind legs. "To be honest, I got the impression he was more interested in you."

He felt his pulse quicken. "Oh? In what way?"

"I assumed he was a fan of your show."

Thorne smiled. Nothing seemed less likely to him than the lieutenant being a member of the Jake Vasco Fan Club. It was so unlikely, that he wondered if he was being tested. Had Cabot shared his suspicions with Ashcroft? Thorne wanted to talk more on the subject, but now was not the time. He had to be careful, appear unconcerned.

"Last time around was just business for those men. A job, nothing more. Next time, it's going to be personal. Three of their friends are dead and another is in hospital connected to a wall socket. I don't see this having a happy ending."

"Me neither."

"Any idea what it was they were after?"

The senator looked surprised, as if he'd never thought about it.

"Money, I assume. A kidnapping."

"Why now? It's months since you announced your candidacy. Could it be anything else?"

Ashcroft picked up his glass, his hand shaking slightly. He drained it from half full then poured out another.

"No," he said. "Just money."

TWENTY-ONE

Thorne stood in the hallway staring at the Picasso. He'd decided to stop worrying about the security cameras. The painting was famous, not to mention insanely valuable, and it was reasonable to assume that any visitor to the house would stop and look at it from time to time. Hadn't Ashcroft brought it back from the gallery for precisely this purpose? No, he thought, it wouldn't seem either odd or suspicious for him to be seen looking at it. At least, not until it went missing. If Blake's plan had a hole, that was certainly it.

Given enough time, he knew he could defeat the security system. It might not be easy, but it would be possible. The challenge would lie in deflecting attention away from himself as the obvious thief. For one thing, he'd have to hang around after he'd taken it. Store the painting somewhere safe nearby, then come back and face the music. If both he and the painting went missing at the same time, there would be no mystery as to what had happened.

Thorne saw two scenarios.

The theft could take place at night, while the others slept; or during the day, while the Ashcrofts were out. The latter option gave him the best access, but the poorest alibi. He would need to frame it as a conventional robbery and that would take extra time, faking a break-in. Afterward, Cabot would have him under a microscope as never before, and moving the painting at that point would be somewhere between difficult and impossible. Lauren's running path offered investigators a convincing route in for thieves, as well as an easy way out for him to hide the painting. To sell the story in any credible way, he'd have to injure himself. A knock-out blow to the head, something like that. It was all very well to say you slept through a robbery when the owner did too, but who'd believe him if he did so alone? He was reluctant to sustain any further injuries and from that point of view the day-time robbery was a bust.

The painting depicted the head of a horse, rearing back as if in terror.

Its teeth were fanned out like a hand of cards and its eyes were bulging. Thorne had always had a soft spot for horses but this one did not appear to be having a good day and it was beyond him why anyone would want to have such an image on their wall. Blake said it looked like a child had painted it, and he wasn't wrong. He wondered what made it worth so much money. A hundred million dollars. Thorne couldn't get his head around it. He'd have to work for nearly two thousand years to make that amount of money, and here it was on the wall in front of him. He was no socialist, but he knew this was wrong.

The case was roughly three inches deep and wrapped around the outside of the painting before bonding seamlessly into the wall. There was no hinged panel providing access; there appeared to be no access at all. However the painting was added or removed, it didn't appear to be through the case. He frowned. This made no sense at all. There had to be a trick to opening it, the painting had to come in and out somehow.

He moved closer and closer to the painting until his face was right up against the armored glass then turned as if to look down the hall. The left side of his vision was now filled by a grayish-green blur, that ended in a sharp black line where the case folded in on itself. His right eye, however, could see past the reflections to the interior edge. He saw light blue dots spaced out down the edge of the frame. Lasers. He sighed. Dealing with lasers wasn't a part of explosive ordinance disposal. He pulled his head back a fraction and they disappeared. If he hadn't looked for them, he wouldn't have known they were there. It was the signature of a good security system that it didn't advertise itself. Hidden lasers on the front end told him that the back end was going to be top-notch. The best money could buy. He caught a glimpse of himself reflected in the glass and noticed he was smiling again.

He liked a challenge, it was who he was.

Outside, two car doors slammed shut. He jerked away from the painting. The Ashcrofts had returned from San Jose. He heard their voices before the front door opened. It sounded like they'd been fighting the entire way back. He made his way down the hall, past the pool and into the kitchen. Ashcroft was holding a bottle of Scotch in one hand.

"Jesus, Lauren. Sometimes a cigar is just a cigar."

"A cigar! It's a goddamn gun."

Ashcroft turned to Thorne. "This is what I get for trying to protect myself. What do you say Chris? Do you think we should sit around and wait for those men to attack us again, or do you think we should be prepared?"

Next to the senator, on top of some dirty rags, was a pistol.

"I hate to say this, Lauren, but it's unlikely this is over. Last time we were lucky, we need to be more proactive. James is right."

She sighed. "Big surprise, soldier boy likes the gun."

He looked at it again. Even from where he was standing, Thorne could see it wasn't new. It looked like it had fallen into some mud and been driven over by a truck.

"Where'd you get it?"

"I bought it from a guy on Craigslist."

Thorne laughed. "You're kidding."

"No."

He pinched the bridge of his nose and closed his eyes for a moment.

"Okay, I'm just going to ask. Why didn't you buy one in a store?"

Lauren and Ashcroft exchanged an awkward expression.

"He doesn't know," Lauren said.

"Know what?"

"Lauren and I are well-known campaigners against the Second Amendment. If it got out I'd bought a firearm it would set the movement back years and make me a laughing stock. My run for president would be over. You may think this hypocritical, but my anti-gun stance is stronger now than ever before."

Thorne shook his head in disbelief.

"All you had to do was ask. *I* could've bought it."

The senator flinched. "I never thought of that."

"Do you mind if I take a look?"

"Of course. In fact, I'm hoping you'll train me to use it, there's no one else I can ask."

"It's not that complicated, but sure."

Ashcroft passed it to him handle first.

"James, you're pointing the gun at your own chest."

"It's fine, it's not loaded."

"You checked?"

"The guy said so. I bought bullets from him too."

Thorne slipped the sling off his right arm and took the gun carefully out of Ashcroft's hand and, pointing it at the floor, checked the chamber. It was empty.

"Look, forgive me for being a dick, all right, but a firearm is only empty when you've checked it's empty. Take *nobody's* word for it, least of all some creepy dude you just met off the internet. I know you're new to guns, but that's just retarded."

Ashcroft nodded. "You're right. I need to hear this."

Thorne examined the gun. It was dirty and badly scratched, but there was little doubt in his mind it could kill people. As it moved, light caught on what appeared to be a clean area. Something mechanical had gouged into the metal and scooped out a half-inch long trench, like a screw you were meant to turn with a coin. He knew what it was, what it signified.

"How does it look?" Ashcroft said, opening the Scotch.

"It's a Smith and Wesson 1911 CT semi automatic pistol, firing .45 ACP rounds. A good, solid firearm, nothing fancy. You won't be shooting a gun out of anyone's hand with it, but if you aim center mass you're going to hit something important." Thorne paused for a beat. "Did you notice this mark on the side?"

"No, what is it?"

"It's where the serial number used to be."

Ashcroft shrugged.

"I'm saying," Thorne continued, "that it's illegal to have this."

"But it's illegal anyway isn't it?"

"This is different. There's only one reason to do this to a firearm, and that's to hide the identity of the owner. You don't do this if your intention is to protect yourself or to fire it at a gun range. Given how dirty and marked it is, I'd say it was dumped somewhere and that the nimrod you bought it from found it."

"I'm still not sure I understand."

Lauren shook her head. "Jimmy, he's saying you bought a murder weapon."

Ashcroft's face paled.

"No, I can't be sure about that," Thorne said. "It might've been tossed before it was used, or it dropped out of someone's bag, it's impossible to tell. But if you are caught in possession of a gun that ballistics can tie to a murder then it doesn't look good for you, and the story of how you came to have it is not very believable."

Several seconds passed before Ashcroft spoke again.

"It changes nothing, we still need to protect ourselves. We can say the gun belonged to one of the attackers, that one of them dropped it during a struggle and we were able to grab it. Just like you did in the parking lot."

Thorne smiled. "That's crazy enough to work."

He put the pistol on the counter and took the glass Ashcroft held out to him. He lifted the glass to his nose, swirled the contents and inhaled. To him, Scotch smelled like a mixture of urine and gasoline, but he enjoyed the sensation as it rolled down his throat.

"Out of curiosity, what section of Craigslist did you see it?"

"Sporting goods."

"My husband is a collector of sporting memorabilia," Lauren explained.

"Aren't you concerned this guy can identify you?"

"Give me some credit, I wore a baseball cap and sunglasses."

"For a minute there I was worried."

TWENTY-TWO

When he got back to his bedroom he saw he'd three missed calls from Blake on the burner phone. It wasn't a total surprise. A full week had passed since he'd agreed to steal the painting and so far he'd done nothing about it. He sighed and dialed the number.

"Thorne, *buddy*, good of you to call back."

"What do you want?"

"*Updates*. I got that shit you asked for days ago and you've not been in touch. Not even a goddamn text message. Maybe you're having a blast up there with that old man's wife, but we're sitting on our asses here doing nothing. We want this done and dusted so we can get the hell out of here. What's the delay? What am I meant to do with this stuff?"

"Nothing. I have to do it, just like everything else."

"You should remember what's at stake before you speak to me like that."

Thorne smiled. He was all broken up about Blake's feelings.

"Whatever, man. I still have some details to work out. Probably no more than another couple of days. I have questions for Ashcroft and if I don't space them out it's going to get suspicious, especially after it goes down. When I got all I need, we can meet and I'll fix up the gear. That's the easy part."

There was a long silence at the other end.

"I read about your immunity deal with the DA. I hope you don't think it means you can cut me off, or stall me indefinitely with endless problems."

Thorne sat on the edge of the bed and let out a long breath. Rather than deny it and risk Blake seeing through it, he decided to push back and see where it went.

"And why's that, Blake?"

"Because I still want my money, *fucknuts*, and I'm going nowhere until I get it. The longer you put this off, the more chance Sara and I have of getting caught. Believe me when I say this, but if that happens, we're taking you down with us. That immunity deal won't be worth shit."

Thorne smiled again, then lay back on the bed and stared at the ceiling. He felt Blake's anger right through the cheap plastic handset and could clearly picture him in his head. Blake would be shaking, his face scarlet. The thought of it alone was like warming himself next to an open fire, he could feel his skin prickling, his hairs standing on end.

"It'd be your word against mine, *amigo*. How much do you think your word is worth? I'm a hero. In case you haven't heard, the sun shines out my ass."

When Blake's voice came back it was calm and precise.

"Perhaps. But you're forgetting the gallery and that dead cop. Even without breaking your immunity deal, I figure you're looking at spending the rest of your life in prison. That cop's not the only one either, they'll pull you into all the others. Conspiracy murder, they call that. Good luck proving you weren't involved because that's not what we'll be saying."

Thorne's smile disappeared.

"So you're saying what?"

"This robbery is happening with or without you. If we do it my way it's going to get messy. Real messy. I'd prefer to avoid going down that route but if you give me no choice, that's the way it goes. You feel me? If I get what I want, you get what you want."

Thorne sighed.

There'd be no leaving this behind, he was in it until the end.

"I'll be in touch."

He cut the call and tossed the phone across the room.

It was clear to him now as never before. Another attempt to steal the Picasso would join everything up for investigators. The bungled gallery heist, the shoot-out at the mall, and the final theft of the painting. What appeared to be unrelated events would condense into a single pattern. If he could be placed at the scene of two of the three, it wouldn't take long for someone to wonder where he was the night of the gallery break-in. He had no alibi for that night, nor the days before it. As tempting as Blake's two million might be, there was no way to get it without exposing his involvement in the death of the cop. The deal with Blake was worthless, there was only one option open to him.

Survival.

TWENTY-THREE

Cabot heard raised voices outside his office. Excitement, not anger. As a seasoned cop, he knew what it meant: there'd been a break in the case. He sprung to his feet and raced around his desk for his office door and turned to the source of the feeding frenzy. To his surprise, he saw Summersby standing there with a huge grin on his face. He held a clear plastic evidence bag aloft like the severed head of a conquered enemy. Inside, a clown mask. Cabot smiled. Finally, they had hard physical evidence tied to one of the surviving gang members. With luck they'd pull DNA and fingerprints from it and with that, a positive database match.

He pushed through deputies and administration staff that had poured in to see what was going on. There was a real buzz in the air. This is how cops got high, he thought. Liu stood next to Summersby, her eyes dancing nervously about as people crowded around, while her normally calm face showed a kooky smile and perfect white teeth. It was the first time he'd seen her smile in the eighteen months she'd worked in Investigation.

"Amazing," Cabot said. "Where'd you find it?"

"In the footwell of the second ambulance," Summersby said. "It'd gone under the seat. I guess they lost it or forgot about it."

Cabot took the bag and carefully turned it over in his hands. It was light as a feather. Since it was Summersby's find, he walked over to the detective's desk and sat in his chair. People gathered around him in a circle to watch. There was a lamp on the desk and Cabot pulled it over and turned it on to get a better look. He moved his face in close and inspected the mask through the bag, turning it to catch the light. There was something on the inside, he thought. A powder of some kind. It was whitish-pink in color, it barely showed against the moulded plastic until the light hit it at an angle, when it showed as a dull area with no shine. He turned it over to see the front again. No blood. It was the first thing he'd noticed about the mask and he couldn't help but feel disappointed. He knew if they did get an ID there'd be no connection to Thorne.

"What do you think, Victor?"

He looked up and saw Carson looking down at him.

"It's the getaway driver's mask, Sheriff. The woman."

The sheriff stroked his mustache while he processed this. Cabot knew the woman-driver angle was unpopular and generally viewed by his coworkers as part of his one man theory implicating Thorne. They all seemed to believe he was focussing on a mistake the actor made in an attempt to make him seem guilty.

"What makes you say that, Lieutenant?"

"The other mask had cast-off blood spatter and misting across the front due to wounds sustained by Samuel Porter, the man in the coma. That blood-covered mask was reportedly seen by the paramedics during these robberies, so we know it wasn't cleaned off and is still out there somewhere. That leaves this one, which logically must belong to the driver. There appears to be a trace of some kind of compound on the inside where it pressed against the wearer's face. Specifically, the cheekbones. I believe this compound will turn out to be makeup or sunscreen."

"What about fingerprints, DNA?"

"I guess we'll see," Cabot said. "The mask could easily hold both sets of fingerprints if one passed the mask to the other to put on."

The sheriff smiled thinly, his head nodding. It seemed like a less than enthusiastic response, sarcastic even. Not for the first time, he wondered if Carson wanted this investigation to fail in order to damage his reputation ahead of any bid he might make for sheriff when the post was up for re-election. This didn't seem like much of a stretch considering Carson's narrow victory over the previous incumbent and the animosity of the campaign that preceded it.

"Well done, Victor. Good work."

"Actually, sir, credit goes to Summersby and Liu here."

Carson bristled, clearly irritated by his public generosity.

"That's very fair of you, Victor. An investigation is a team effort of course."

The sheriff turned and pushed his way through deputies that stood around him. He seemed to do this a lot, Cabot thought, suddenly leaving a room like he had better places to be. Most likely, this was because he knew little of real police work, and feared being discovered by those under his command. Cabot looked back and saw Summersby grinning from ear to ear while, beside him, Barnes looked decidedly irritated. It appeared the golden boy didn't much like being sidelined.

His cell phone began to ring in his pocket.

"All right people, show's over," he said, already standing. "Summersby, get this mask tested. Put a rush on it, this is important."

He pulled out his cell as he walked back to his office.

"Cabot."

"This is Robert Brookridge at First National. I received your request this morning for financial statements belonging to one of our customers; Mr Christopher Thorne of Ocean Park Boulevard, Santa Monica."

He was in his office now. Instead of sitting at his desk he stood facing the wall. There was a tone to the man's voice that he didn't like and he had a feeling he wasn't going to enjoy the remainder of their conversation.

"That's right."

"There was no warrant attached to this request and the subject is still alive. Am I right to assume that this is a fishing trip and you don't have enough evidence to convince a judge?"

"Now wait just a minute," he said, his voice rising.

"No, you wait, Cabot. I ran this past our legal department and their advice was clear. If I give you what you want, I'd be breaking the law. Mr Thorne has rights, which as a police lieutenant I assume you know. Either re-apply when you have enough evidence for a warrant, or forget it."

He thought about knocking it back and forth with Brookridge for a couple of minutes to soothe his damaged pride, but he could tell that the banker was smart enough to see through that. Since he was likely to lose the argument anyway, the only way forward was to admit it and hope that this created a positive room for movement. People were more forgiving if you treated them with respect and were gracious in defeat. It was a lesson that had taken him most of his life to learn, and still occasionally forgot.

"All right, look, you got me. What you're saying is true, I apologize for not being straight with you. That said, I have a single question that I don't believe will invalidate Mr Thorne's rights. If you answer the way I expect, I'll be able to discount him as a suspect and avoid any awkward publicity for either your bank, or your customer. Now, I'm sure you're aware from media coverage that the case I'm working on involves the attempted abduction of a US Senator and his wife. I know we both want the same thing, Mr Brookridge."

There was a pause on the line and he wondered if he'd laid it on too thick.

"What's the question?"

"In the last six months, has Mr Thorne received any irregular large sums of money or series of sums below the reporting threshold? A yes or no will be sufficient."

"I still have to run this past legal."

The line went dead. He returned the phone to his pocket, fury building in his chest. There was a time when people would sign off in some manner before disconnecting. A simple curtesy that didn't cost a dime, and allowed both parties to know the conversation was at an end. Now, one person seemed to always get boned, and that person always seemed to be him.

"That didn't sound good," Barnes said.

Cabot turned and saw him standing in the doorway.

"Not great, no."

"Did he answer your question?"

"He's going to ask a lawyer first."

Barnes snorted. "Of course."

He knew the detective didn't share his suspicions about Thorne, but he appreciated his support nevertheless. Cabot supposed that if he was wrong about Thorne, then Mason Barnes stood to benefit from his disgrace as the most likely candidate to replace him as lieutenant. On the other hand, if he was right about Thorne then Barnes could claim to be a key member in the investigation that brought him down. Whichever way it went, Barnes would somehow come out the other side covered in glory.

"Was there something else, Detective?"

Focus seemed to return to Barnes' face.

"Right. I sent you an email, I figured you hadn't seen it yet."

This, he knew, was the younger man's way of reminding him that evidence no longer needed to be transported in file folders. It was well known in the department that he had yet to fully engage with the electronic medium and sometimes needed to be prompted. He sat down at his computer and opened his email. While he did this, he noticed with displeasure that Barnes came around the desk and stood behind him so that he could see the screen. It annoyed him, not because he had personal or embarrassing emails that might appear in his inbox, but because close to 50 unread emails then appeared which would only help cement the idea that he was out of touch.

It took him several seconds to locate Mason Barnes' name in the long list and punch it up. The email had no text and consisted of three attached photographs which he recognized as coming from the mall's security system, before the gang put on their masks. The pictures were zoomed in on the man known as Morrison.

He glanced up at the detective for an explanation.

"I've been going through the mall footage again and decided to try and enhance some stills of this guy using Photoshop. It was mostly a waste of time because the quality is so low and we have to magnify it, but something did come out of it as you can see."

Cabot flipped between each picture. He didn't see anything.

"What am I looking at?"

"There's something on his face. A scar maybe."

Cabot saw it then, like half a circle.

"You're sure that's not a reflection? It's very regular."

"I don't think so," Barnes said. "Once I knew what I was looking for I went back to the footage again. It's faint, but it's there. Moves with him as

153

he turns his head. A reflection would move somewhere else."

Cabot nodded. "Looks old. A broken bottle wound maybe?"

"Yeah, maybe. Or shrapnel."

"Can you feed this into AFIS for an ID?"

"NGI."

"Whatever. Can you use it?"

"This picture is too noisy, we'd need something sharper. Something closer to a mug shot, not this high angle. Even then, I don't know. It's not like fingerprints or retinas that stay the same. This guy Morrison could be on the database from before he got this injury. You'd get no matches. Equally, you could get over fifty partial matches of random people."

Cabot nodded. Technology could only get you so far, eventually it always came down to bashing heads and kicking down doors. Somehow, he found this reassuring.

"All right, update the composite sketch for Morrison to include this scar and print it out. A dozen copies, so we can show it around. Send a digital version to the press. Who knows, it might ring a bell with someone and flush these jokers out into the open."

After the detective left his office, Cabot sat back in his chair and put his feet on his desk. He began to slowly peel an orange. The skin kept breaking off in chunks but he didn't mind, he was used to it. Oranges had become a strange part of his process over the years, his mind was able to drift away while his hands were busy removing first skin, then individual sections of the fruit. Despite the fragile skin, the flesh inside was juicy and delicious.

At the back of his mind he was getting an uneasy feeling about the C-shaped scar that Barnes had identified. It resonated with him as something he'd seen before and he couldn't think from where. He tossed another section of orange into his mouth and chewed down on it. It was somewhere recent, not an old case. He reached up and fished a stone out his mouth, then pinched it between thumb and forefinger, firing it across the room.

It would come to him eventually, it always did.

TWENTY-FOUR

As he drove past the Live Oak on ramp, Blake was astonished to see Ashcroft's cobalt-blue Maserati merge into traffic right in front of him. The car was a distinctive vehicle, there was no mistaking it. On impulse, he began to follow it, slowing his pace to match the senator's careful driving. He checked his mirrors to see if anyone else was following the senator. After what happened at the mall, he would've expected Ashcroft to hire some kind of security detail. Remarkably, that didn't seem to have happened and he wondered if Thorne had dissuaded the senator from taking further steps as part of his plan to steal the painting.

On the other hand, Thorne had gone dark again. There'd been no response to any of his recent texts and his cell phone never seemed to be on when he called. Blake couldn't help think his old friend was playing for time. Perhaps Thorne would tell him the job was more difficult than he'd foreseen, that he wanted more of the payout. It was a theory that made a lot of sense. The more time that passed, the closer they got to the end of their window for stealing the painting, and the more leverage Thorne had over him. Once it was returned to the gallery, it was game over. There'd be no time to get another team together to have a second run at the painting there; he'd have to agree to any terms Thorne wanted.

It was unfortunate they needed him at all, but his own knowledge of electronics was pitiful. Even knowing the answer lay, somehow, with the stolen defibrillators, he didn't have the first clue how to take the plan forward and Thorne was keeping his cards close to his chest.

Ashcroft took the Santa Cruz fork and the highway looped around in a tight loop. Blake fell back, his eyes fixed on the Maserati in the distance. The posted speed limit was twenty miles per hour and the traffic around him was obeying the limit. He felt strangely exposed on the motorcycle at the slower speed. Motorcycles were Sara's thing, not his. After the endless northerly curve, the road twisted around to the southwest. The senator kept to the right, the lanes marked Half Moon Bay, and Blake fell in behind him. After several minutes, Ashcroft turned south onto River Street, which had a clot of slow moving traffic on it. He made the turn and maintained a constant two car gap to the senator.

He had no idea what he was going to do once they reached their destination. Most likely, nothing at all. It didn't benefit him if the target was constantly afraid of another attack. It was always better to catch someone by surprise, assuming that was still possible. He was just taking advantage of a situation to find out all he could about his mark to avoid any surprises later. The slower speed allowed him to glance to either side and take in more of the location. On the opposite sidewalk, a sign read *Do you have a pinched nerve?* He frowned. There was something about this that didn't feel right, and pinched nerves had nothing to do with it. The cars between them turned off together, leaving him directly behind the Maserati with no screen. The small car shot forward, and Blake had to struggle to keep up. He'd lost his focus and had been made. Logic told him to abandon his tail, but he couldn't bring himself to do it. The change in the way the car was being driven was incredible, and he hated the thought of being out-driven by the senator.

Up ahead, the traffic light changed, forcing Ashcroft to stop and wait for the intersection to clear. Blake smiled to himself. He had him. As he drew close, he flipped up his visor so he'd be able to see the senator more clearly through the car's tinted glass. He rode slowly down the left turn lane, next to the driver's side of the car. The side window powered open and he looked into the shaded interior of the car. He blinked. From his high position, the first thing he saw was a tanned, muscular arm and the carefully rolled cuff of a shirt. *It wasn't Ashcroft.* There was an explosion of movement and Thorne shot out through the open window, a long hunting knife clutched in his fist. Before he could do anything, Thorne slammed the blade down, deep into his thigh. He felt the metal jolt against the bone. He stared at the half-submerged knife for a second before screaming. A thick red tide rose up around the steel as Thorne pulled it out, and he felt the jagged edge of the blade tearing his muscle as it left his body. The pain was unbelievable, and his breath caught in his throat. He clamped his right hand over the open wound, while his left hand flailed behind him for the Glock stuffed into the back of his jeans.

It was too far around; it was set for a right-handed draw.

The blade was between their bodies now, an inch below his ribcage and angled up toward his heart. Thorne's eyes were wide and fixed, his teeth visible through peeled back lips. He'd flipped. With one more push, Thorne could finish him. Blake attempted to grab the knife with his right hand and felt the hot flow of blood pour from the open wound and down his leg. It was a weak gesture and he knew it, but Thorne drew the weapon back out of reach. Playing it safe, not taking any risks. Some things never

156

changed. Behind them, a horn sounded: the stop light had changed. Thorne smiled at him playfully, then shrank back into the car and hit the gas. The Maserati raced forward, tires screeching, crossed over his lane, then turned hard left across the Water Street bridge.

Blake gritted his teeth.

He was in no position to pursue Thorne to exact revenge, he had to deal with his leg as soon as possible. He u-turned and pulled into a parking lot behind Bank of America. Without dismounting, he unfastened his belt and looped it around his thigh to slow the bleeding. He didn't need to stop blood flow, just hold the sides of his wound closed until he could do something about it. He tied the belt as tight as he could bear. There was a burning void in his leg. It felt like a huge yellowjacket had stung him and the stinger had broken off inside.

In his mind, he replayed his ride down River Street trying to remember stores that could help him. The selection he remembered were of little use. Auto body repair shops, lumber specialists, furniture stores, beauty salons...nothing jumped out at him. There was no denying it, Thorne had stabbed him in a really inconvenient part of town. He'd laugh at this thought if his situation wasn't so serious. Blake considered calling for proper medical attention. He couldn't afford to spend time driving around looking for something that he could use to patch himself up. The way his luck was going, it would be one of the ambulance crews he'd jacked. Would they recognize him without the mask?

He'd feel the blood loss in his fingers and toes first, as his body shut down to preserve his core; then his vision would begin to suffer. These two together would make riding Sara's motorcycle incredibly difficult. If he was going to call for help, he had to do so while his body was still able, and soon enough that he wasn't too far gone when they arrived.

He cranked the helmet visor full open to get more air.

Blake was getting lightheaded. He closed his eyes and took several deep breaths. Deep and slow. It helped him focus and would help manage pain. They didn't tell pregnant women to breathe like this for nothing. It took nearly a minute, but he could feel his body begin to relax, the extra oxygen easing his symptoms. River Street, there was something, he was sure there was. Yes. There'd been a red rectangle on one of those multi store listing posts. OfficeMax. He'd been in one of those stores before, he'd get most of what he needed there. Some tape, bandages, general first aid supplies. Somehow, people in offices were getting seriously injured and they were going to the stationery store to get themselves fixed up.

He put the motorcycle in gear and pulled out of the bank's lot.

It felt good to be back underway. He knew roughly where the store was but it took longer than he expected to get there when he wasn't being distracted by his pursuit of Ashcroft. He corrected himself: his pursuit of

157

Thorne. For the first time, it dawned on him that his arrangement with Thorne to steal the painting was over. Had the actor already made up his mind not to go through with the plan, or had he simply reacted to the tail? He might not have liked being followed himself, but he wouldn't have put two million dollars at stake over something so trivial.

OfficeMax was around the back of another store, an island in a sea of asphalt. He drove around until he found a parking spot that was shielded on two sides by two flat bed trucks and on a third by the store wall.

It wasn't perfect, but it would do.

The store exceeded his expectations. Painkillers, wound wash, tape, bandages. Aside from antibiotics, it had everything he needed. He filled a basket with over a hundred dollars' worth of products. Rather than compare items he chose to grab anything that looked good, even if it duplicated a product he already had. He noticed he had a pronounced limp and it was so cold inside the air-conditioned building that he had begun to shake. He bit his teeth together to stop them clattering together.

At the checkout, a bored-looking girl rang it all up and put it in a bag with barely a glance at his leg. The only thing she said was the price, delivered in a flat monotone. He paid cash and it nearly cleared him out. She didn't bother to wish him a good day, perhaps sensing that ship had already sailed.

Back outside, he sat heavily on the asphalt and leaned back against the wall with his legs straight out in front of him. He felt dizzy and tired. Despite a cool sea breeze coming up from the south, beads of sweat covered his face. He stared grimly down. The right leg of his jeans was soaked in blood from mid-thigh to mid-calf. He could feel the extra weight of it in the fabric and it had already hardened at the edges to form a blackish tide mark. It looked bad, it looked real bad. He'd lost a pint of blood, maybe more.

He arranged his purchases next to his leg so he could grab them quickly when he needed them. He took a deep breath and slowly let it out as he removed the belt from around his thigh. Blood surged painfully through his leg into the wound, but he had to keep going, there was no time to waste. He pulled his jeans down past his knees then lightly re-tied the belt around his thigh. He took the wound wash and sprayed it straight into the injury, using the fingers of his other hand to hold the sides open. He flinched as the liquid hit the exposed flesh but he kept going, into and around the cut. He was able to fill the cut with the antiseptic fluid then manipulate the sides of the muscle to flush the inside out.

He'd had field training and knew that after blood loss, infection was the next biggest killer with traumatic injury. However painful it was now, it was worth taking the extra time to get any dirt out. When the canister was almost empty, he filled the cut with everything that was left and let it sit

158

there for a moment. It appeared to bubble inside the cut. A sign, he hoped, that it was doing its magic. He flushed it out again and cleaned the top carefully with cotton pads. He squeezed some antimicrobial wound dressing into the cut then applied superglue to the outer edges and pinched the sides shut. The chemicals in the glue burned like all hell and brought tears to his eyes. He held it closed for two minutes, far longer than he believed was necessary. The cut needed to be sutured closed, but he couldn't have anyone asking what happened to his leg. He released his grip slowly and took his hand away. The cut stayed closed, but his skin buckled awkwardly. It looked like it would hold, but he knew that the real test would be when he stood up and used the leg. As a fail-safe, he stuck a square trauma pad over the top and wrapped an elasticated dressing around and around his thigh. He could feel the tape hold the muscle closed beneath the skin.

He let his head tilt back against the wall, his face looking straight up.

Above, a cloudless blue sky.

He knew he should get moving again, in case the girl or someone else in the store had taken issue with his appearance and called the cops, but there was something he needed to do first. He reached into his pocket and dug out his burner phone. His hands shook as he held the cheap, rubberized plastic. Thorne should've finished him when he had the chance, because he wasn't going to like what came next. This was war now, and the gloves were off. At some level he'd always known it would come to this. Right from the beginning, he'd seen the actor struggle with their arrangement. Even after what had happened at the mall, he'd still hoped to bring Thorne back on board. To do things the easy way. Now that point had passed, things were clearer. In a way, Thorne had only made what had to happen easier for him. Blake hit the call button and held the cell phone up to his ear. It rang a long time before Sara answered.

"Do it," he said.

"You sure?"

"Burn it to the ground."

She paused for a moment. "Tonight."

Blake cut the call. She could probably tell something had happened, but he didn't want to get into detail. He knew she wouldn't want to hear about it anyway, she'd think he was a fool. Sara Dawson was not a woman you went to for sympathy and chicken soup. At a pinch, she'd reload your gun or pass you a beer. He looked up from the phone's blank display. A man in his seventies with a bald head and a thick gray beard looked at him over a half loaded cart. The old man's mouth was hanging open.

"The fuck do you want?" Blake said.

TWENTY-FIVE

Thorne waited ten minutes before he turned Ashcroft's car around and returned to the intersection where he'd stabbed Blake. The light turned red on the car in front and he sat there waiting in the turn lane ready to retrace his steps back up River Street. His eyes flipped up to the gantry and he felt his heart sink. Traffic cams. They covered all four corners of the junction and would've been pointing straight at him when he'd had his altercation with Blake. He tilted the sun visor down to cover his face and re-ran the scene in his head. It had been brief, perhaps only 15 seconds. Blake rolls up, he stabs him, he drove off. It seemed to stretch out at the time, but he knew it was quick.

The light changed and he followed the car around onto River. There was no sign of Blake at the side of the road, nor in the parking lot alongside. He continued north, the route he expected Blake to take. When wounded, you go with what you know, you don't go forward hoping for something to appear, there's no time for it.

He drove slowly, his eyes scanning both sides of the road, the sidewalk, and cross streets. Looking for any sign of Blake, or an ambulance. Nothing. His thoughts returned to the traffic cams. What would they have captured from their position? The cameras were mounted high on the opposite side to oncoming traffic. They had been at the front of the line, which made the camera over Blake's left shoulder as he turned to face into Ashcroft's car. There was a good chance that most of their interaction had been blocked from view by the width of Blake's own body. That first stab though, the blade slamming down, that would've been on camera. He sucked his lower lip in and began to chew on a piece of dry skin. He was driving Ashcroft's car, it wouldn't be hard for the police to trace it back to him.

He glanced at the knife that still sat on the passenger seat.

The whole reason for his trip had been to buy this weapon. It was a token weapon against a Glock, but he wanted some kind of backup to Ashcroft's untested automatic. Now the knife tied him to a crime he knew he should get rid of it. He shouldn't even think about it, he should toss it in a mailbox or down a storm drain at the first opportunity.

He turned off River into a retail park. A large anonymous area, with warehouse sized stores. He needed to think, to be free from the distraction of driving to work this out.

He was reluctant to lose the weapon. If Blake was still alive, and he had no reason to think otherwise, then he still needed it. The store he'd bought the knife from had security cameras and even if it hadn't, it wouldn't matter. The man behind the cash desk had recognized him and asked to shake his hand. If the traffic cams put him in the frame, then the police would be able to prove he bought a weapon matching the description of the one used, and his inability to provide the knife later for testing would be damning. Short of driving outside the county and replacing the knife with one exactly the same, he was stuck with it.

He parked up and went into one of the stores.

Inside, he bought a bottle of water, a can of lighter fluid, and a disposable lighter. Back out in the parking lot, he used the water to wash the knife and his hands. There was a trace amount of blood, no more than would come out a bug on your windshield, but that wasn't what he was concerned about. He knew it was what you *couldn't* see that you had to worry about. He set the knife down on the asphalt and sprayed the blade with the lighter fluid until a film of it coated the blade, then set it on fire with the lighter. The flame flashed across the metal and went out. He turned the blade over and repeated the process. He sat back on his heels. The liquid was so volatile it began to evaporate immediately. Parts of the blade would be untouched. He looked around to make sure no one was nearby then lit the spray of fluid direct, playing the flame over the blade like a blowtorch. It wasn't foolproof, but it was better than nothing. When he got back to the mansion he'd give it a proper clean.

Thorne started the engine and spun the car around and out the parking lot. As he rejoined River Street, a brief vibration through the steering wheel triggered a physical memory of the knife blade cutting through Blake's leg muscle. The jolt as it hit bone. He sighed. However bad things were, they were about to get a lot, lot worse.

*

He walked into Ashcroft's office with the keys for the Maserati and found him silently holding a telephone against his head. The senator looked up at him and nodded, then held up his hand, fingers spread out. *Five minutes.* Then pointed through the wall at the library. Thorne went into the next room and stood at the large window. He'd only planned on dropping the keys off, he didn't need a big conversation about it. Was the call about the

161

car? Thorne shook his head at his own stupidity. He'd stabbed Blake without thinking about it. He'd bought the knife and was immediately presented with an opportunity to use it. It seemed perfect, but it'd been a huge mistake for two reasons.

He'd done it in public, in front of a camera.

He hadn't finished the job.

"Did you get what you wanted?"

Thorne turned to see Ashcroft behind him.

"Yes, thank you."

"How'd you find the car?"

He relaxed. Ashcroft just wanted to talk about his car.

"It's a real peach to drive, James. Beautiful."

"You caught me off-guard with your request, I wasn't ready."

"I don't understand."

"Walk with me," Ashcroft said.

He followed the senator down the stairs, through the large hallway and out into the bright sunshine. Ashcroft turned left up the drive, then left again around the side of the mansion. He'd never been around this side of the building. It was in permanent shade and he felt the cool air through his thin cotton T-shirt. At the back of the building, the thin strip of driveway widened out again and another building appeared. Three double garages joined together, each with their large steel doors closed. Since he'd arrived, the Ashcrofts had done nothing but park their cars out front, but it stood to reason they had a garage for their vehicles when they were in D.C.

The senator took a remote from his pocket and pressed a button. One of the metal doors powered open. The interior of the garage was dark and the mansion behind cast a heavy shadow. There was a car inside, he could see that much. Ashcroft walked forward, speaking over his shoulder.

"Just stand here a second."

After a beat, the car started and pulled forward out of the garage. It was another Maserati. Same size, same color. There was no dirt anywhere on the bodywork, even the tires shone. If he had to guess, the car was brand new. As the car drew level with him the engine stopped again and Ashcroft got out and walked around the hood to stand next to him.

"What do you think? Arrived yesterday."

A smile played across Ashcroft's face.

Thorne studied the new car, as if he'd missed something.

"It's beautiful, but isn't it the same as the car you have?"

"In every detail except one."

The smile on Ashcroft's face widened and was threatening to get out of control.

"Which is?"

"This one's yours."

162

The ground seemed to fall away below Thorne's feet. He turned and looked again at the car as if this would clarify the situation for him, but the information remained the same. He knew little of Maseratis, but he figured the car had to be worth an easy $100,000.

"Are you *serious?* You're giving me a car?"

"I know what you're going to say. That you can't accept it, that it's too much. But I won't hear of it, okay? What I owe you I can never repay, this is my way of saying thank you."

Thorne smiled.

"Trust me, James, none of those sentences were about to come out my mouth."

"*Good.* How about we take a test drive?"

They got in the car. The cabin smelled strongly of leather and something he couldn't identify. This would be the *new car smell* he'd heard all about. He closed his eyes for a moment to drink it in. It was intoxicating. If the other car had smelled of anything, it was Ashcroft himself. Sandalwood, something like that. He opened his eyes and ran his fingertips around the wheel like he was touching a woman for the first time. Knowing the car was his changed everything. He turned to Ashcroft and saw he was studying him closely, the same big smile on his face.

"Thank you."

"You're welcome."

Thorne put the car in gear and hit the gas. The mansion's driveway flowed past under the wheels and they arrived at the gate, which began to automatically open. The new car already had a security tag fitted. At the highway, the asphalt was deserted in both directions. He swung north, away from Santa Cruz. He'd had enough of the city for one day.

"I was going to give you this car at my birthday party. Make a big deal out of it, you know? My way of saying thank you and acknowledging what you did for us."

Thorne could picture the scene, it would've been horrible.

"But after you borrowed mine," Ashcroft continued, "I realized it would be a mistake. A gift should be a personal thing, from one person to the other. The only people that need to know about it are me, you, and Lauren."

"That's the way I prefer it, James."

"You're never going to call me Jimmy, are you?"

"There was a guy in my unit in Iraq called Jimmy. *That's* who Jimmy is to me. You're James. I don't mean anything by it."

They sat in silence for a moment, the Maserati trailing behind an old pick-up.

"He's dead, isn't he? Your Jimmy."

"Yeah. He's dead."

TWENTY-SIX

Cabot was back at the mall, walking the route made by the Ashcrofts that day. It was his eleventh such trip to the scene and every time he came away feeling renewed. The visits served to restore his anger, which helped maintain his focus in an investigation that increasingly appeared to be going nowhere. He came to a halt in front of Victoria's Secret, where Lauren had stopped to look in the window. By this point, the senator and his wife had been identified by the gang.

He frowned. It was almost as if the Ashcrofts had arranged to meet their kidnappers here, because what else was this? He'd have to look at the Ashcrofts' timeline. The gang must have followed them around all morning, looking for the best opportunity. From a kidnapping point of view, the mall presented a good grab point with multiple escape vectors. Supposing the gang had followed Ashcroft here, it opened up the possibility that evidence existed at other locations visited by the senator that day. Evidence that would help to identify this Morrison character. Clearer security footage; a credit card transaction.

Something concrete.

He moved off again, toward the exit.

It didn't do for a man like him to be seen staring at women's underwear, no matter the pretext. They were something else, the clothes in that store. He'd already found himself wondering what items Lauren had chosen and what she looked like wearing them. He forced the thought from his mind. On the tapes, Morrison and his men surrounded the senator. To James Ashcroft, with other things on his mind, it would appear as if they were in a natural flow of pedestrians moving through the mall. Only from the elevated vantage point of the cameras did a more sinister perspective reveal itself.

Then there was Thorne.

He'd arrived separately from the gang, that was clear enough from the recordings. But hadn't he said he'd fallen asleep in his rental car? Perhaps that was actually true. He'd fallen asleep with the heating turned up, and woken to find he was late for the party. He'd walked in and seen the Ashcrofts coming toward him, and everything else had unfolded. But the way he appeared on the footage entering the mall made him look like he *expected* to see them, or the gang, walking right toward him. He didn't have the casual, distracted walk of someone at a mall, killing time. He had the energized, almost frantic thrust of a man who knows something bad is about to happen and that time was against him.

Once again, the actor became a sticking point in his creative process.

Thorne *hadn't* followed the Ashcrofts here from somewhere else. In fact, he'd arrived first, before anyone else. Barnes believed chance alone had brought Thorne to the mall that day and when you looked at it objectively, chance was the most obvious explanation. The *Occam's Razor* solution. But if you discounted the notion of the accidental hero, as he did, then something impossible reared its head. For his hypothesis to be correct, Thorne would need to have known the senator's plans hours if not days in advance. How could that be? How had he not seen this flaw in his reasoning before?

Did this clear Thorne?

Cabot followed a young woman out through the exit, into bright sun and the cool fall air. As he walked, he pictured in his mind where the three men had died. There were no blood stains or bullet holes, no hint of the carnage that had taken place. The only thing that had changed, was that the area appeared a lot cleaner than it had before. Over at the curb, three teenagers stood laughing at the spot where Thorne had fallen. Normally, the spot was part of his walk-through, but he decided to give it a miss this time. He'd seen enough of it anyway from that video. There was something magnetic about the clip that made you want to keep viewing it. This didn't make him like Thorne any more, he'd just watched the clip more times than was healthy. He walked toward his cruiser in the parking lot. As he drew alongside the teenagers, he saw that two were now lying on the asphalt; one of them, a male, with his head resting in a girl's lap, while the third took a picture.

Recreating Thorne's final shot and his death-like gaze.

He got into his Taurus and fed a stick of gum in his mouth. There was a flavor in there he just couldn't get rid of, no matter how much spearmint he chewed. When he returned to the Sheriff's Office, it was to find that someone had parked a cherry red Prius in his usual spot. He glared at it for several long seconds, before moving down the lot to another space. It was trivial, yet it needled him just the same. When he came back out he knew the red car would be gone, but would likely be replaced by another. That was part of the problem; the rogue car establishes a precedent that other drivers soon follow. If he wasn't careful, it would be open season on that spot, one he'd been using without a problem for ten years.

He walked inside the building, head down and hands in his pockets.

The inconsistent timelines were a problem. He *knew* Thorne was involved, he felt it in his bones. Thorne Arrived First. He could almost see the words, as if he'd already written them on his notepad. How had this fact and its obvious implications escaped him for so long? Almost immediately, the answer came to him: *rust*. He hadn't investigated a case like this since he'd arrived in Santa Cruz. There weren't that many homicides in the county. If he was being honest with himself, that was what had drawn him to the area in the first place. Now, approaching retirement, he craved it. He hadn't been this fired up in years. Whether he ran for sheriff or not, this would be the last big case of his career and he wanted a good result.

A new thought came to him, from the dark fringes of his mind. He assumed that there was a point of intersection between the gang and the Ashcrofts prior to their meeting at the mall, and that the gang had followed them there from somewhere else. But what if that wasn't the case? What if both the gang *and* Throne met the Ashcrofts through the same impossible foresight? Wouldn't that help prove a link between them rather than destroy it?

He sighed. It was ridiculous, he was grasping at straws.

Could he be wrong about Thorne after all?

In front of him, Barnes sat at his desk talking into his telephone. As ever, he was tilted way back in his chair with his feet up on the desk, the telephone's curly cord stretched almost straight. To his surprise, he noticed the detective was wearing snakeskin cowboy boots, a fact that momentarily caused his mouth to stop chewing. The tone of the conversation seemed to change as he approached and he sensed that the call was a personal one. Across the narrow divider, he saw that Summersby's chair lay empty. Cabot sat in it and stared across the low wall at Barnes who hastily wrapped up his call and hung up.

"*Detective*," Cabot said, reproachfully.

"*Lieutenant*," Barnes said, in the same tone.

The younger man grinned, and Cabot couldn't help but smile back. The bastard had a boyish charm just like his big hero, Thorne. Perhaps that's why he can't see through the actor, he thought; it was too much like looking in the mirror.

"So, boss, how're things down at the mall?"

Cabot nodded, the bitterness immediately back in his mouth.

"Kids are taking *death selfies* where Thorne collapsed."

Barnes laughed. "No kidding."

"Oh yeah. Cold dead eyes, outstretched arm - the whole bit."

He could tell that this news had entertained Barnes, and he regretted sharing it. By doing so, he'd somehow validated the stupidity of those kids and given their act an audience.

"I don't know if you've noticed," Barnes said, "but it's a lot busier than usual out there for this time of year. People are coming here from all over because of what happened."

"You mean reporters? TV crews?"

"No, no. *Normal* people. It's like a sort of crime tourism. The place is on TV every day for two weeks, suddenly everyone wants to come visit for themselves."

Barnes was right, the area had become jammed. He hadn't thought too much about it, but it felt like it was peak season. Slower traffic, lines of people in stores - it all made sense.

Cabot leaned forward and spat his used gum into Summersby's coffee mug. It would be a nice little surprise for the detective when he came to have his next break.

"They probably hope to see him walking down the street."

"Oh, I'm certain of it. There's a Thorne autograph on eBay right now. Last I looked, it was sitting at $13,000."

He could almost feel his blood pressure rising.

"Do me a favor, Barnes. Keep shit like that to yourself."

His cell phone rang and he was glad of the interruption.

"Cabot."

"This Robert Brookridge again at First National."

Thorne's bank, he'd forgotten all about it. "Go ahead."

"The answer is no."

Rage swept over him. "You're refusing to answer my question?"

"I *am* answering your question, Cabot. No is the answer. Christopher Thorne received no unusual funds to accounts held with our bank. I trust that this information will help you with your investigation, and you can move in a *more productive direction*."

Brookridge cut the call. Cabot sighed and returned his cell phone to his pocket. Even this banker in L.A. thought Thorne was innocent. Nobody could see past that video. They saw a hero and that was enough for them. Why wasn't it enough for him too? He ran his hand back and forth over the top of his head as if he could massage ideas into his brain. Video, that was it. He'd been approaching this all wrong. Thorne knew there was footage of everything after he entered the mall, he was relying on it to sell his story. But there was little on that clip that was helpful from an investigative point of view. What happened *before*, that was what he needed to concentrate on. That part of the story was bullshit. He needed to pull it apart, expose it for what it was: a work of fiction. Only then would he make progress. Have other people questioning Thorne's actions, his motives.

167

"Saddle up, Barnes. We're heading out."

Mason Barnes stood and picked up his jacket.

"About goddamn time. Where we going, boss?"

"McDonalds."

The detective's face fell. "I already ate."

"This ain't lunch, asshole."

*

It was after 1 p.m. when they arrived at the McDonald's Thorne mentioned in his interview, and the place was busy with lunch traffic. In a restaurant like this, you could expect to find people in line for lunch anytime between 10 a.m. and 2 p.m. As it was, the line snaked through the eating area and more than half the tables were occupied. It was a small McDonald's compared with some, but the food would be just the same. Somehow, the food was the same wherever you went. He walked past the line up to the front. One of the servers was just finishing with a customer and he cut in front of a tall, blond surfer. He raised the palm of his hand to the man's chest.

"Police business, mac. Stay in line."

He turned back to the server.

"Get the manager."

The kid nodded and, without saying anything, left the counter and went through in back. Cabot stared at the ice cream machine. It looked good, he could really do one right now. The surfer was standing next to him now, waiting for his order. He could feel his presence looming over him without having to look. Tall people, he thought, they all have such a god complex. Like they became tall through some great effort of theirs, rather than by the genes they were born with. Thorne was the same way. Cabot saw the surfer's muscled forearm out the corner of his eye. His skin was a deep caramel color from constant sun exposure. In a couple of years he'd start to look like leather, he had seen it before. Sunlight made you old, if it didn't kill you first.

The kid was back, followed by a slightly older kid. This one had to be mid twenties, if that. This was the manager? Jesus Christ. The manager had Clark Kent glasses on beneath a flap of hair that hung over his left eye. He stuck his chin forward.

"Help you, sir?"

His face was bored and Cabot didn't have time for it.

"Is there somewhere we can talk privately?"

"Not really. Just the tables out front."

"This is a murder investigation, son, not a complaint about your food. I figure you don't want to discuss dead bodies next to your customers."

The color drained from the manager's face. Cabot could see the man's Adam's apple moving up and down, trying to work something down his throat.

"I suppose you could come into my office. Public aren't supposed to be back there, but I guess you're okay. Go to the side, I'll open the door for you."

Cabot and Barnes stepped away from the counter and walked to where a door was set into the wall. After a moment, it opened and the manager waved them through. The area beyond the door did not have a pleasant vibe and reminded him of a prison. Broken dreams, depression, and the constant smell of grilled meat. Well, most parts were the same. They followed the kid back to a small office. The manager and Cabot sat on either side of a desk and Barnes stood by the door, arms folded. The kid brushed the flap of hair away from his face.

"What's this about?"

"I'm investigating the shoot-out at the mall across the street. One of the gunmen claims he ate here beforehand and I'm here to check it out."

"One of those men was here?"

"That's right."

Again the Adam's apple pumped up and down.

"What do you need from me?"

"I need to speak with anyone that was working that day."

"Of course." The manager turned to his computer. "What date was that?"

Cabot told him and the manager typed this into his computer. After a moment, he turned and wrote four names onto a pad of paper that sat next to his keyboard. He typed some more and then looked between the pad and the screen.

"You're in luck. Two of them are working today. Want to speak to them?"

Cabot nodded. When he was sure they were alone, he picked a trash can off the floor and swept items off the desk into it, creating space to work. Car keys, pens, tape. Everything went in. Whatever the man wanted he could pick out later. He pulled a wad of photographs from his pocket. There were a dozen pictures about the size of an old Polaroid print.

"What's your thinking, boss?"

Cabot glanced at Barnes.

"Thorne said he was here, let's see if he was."

"That's it? How does that help us?"

Cabot returned his attention to the photographs.

"If he said he was here and he wasn't, I want to know. Then I'd want to know where he *actually* was, because that might be important."

"And if he was here?"

169

Cabot sighed. "Then I'd want to know if he was on his own, or with these other clowns planning the whole thing. I'm just doing my job, Barnes. If my investigation clears him, the two of you are free to soap each other up in a shower, or whatever the hell it is you want to do with this guy, I really don't care."

To his surprise, Barnes laughed. Cabot couldn't help but smile as he heard it. The detective was still laughing when the manager returned with two African-American women.

"All right ladies," Cabot said. "Who's first?"

The routine was the same with both employees. He laid the photographs out on the end of the desk, revealing the faces slowly like a tarot reading in three rows of four. The pictures were of Thorne and of all the other players, including Ashcroft. For those that were dead, he'd used pictures provided by the DMV, rather than pictures from the morgue. Death really caused problems when it came to facial recognition, people couldn't get past it. For Morrison, he'd used the grainy still from the security camera above Victoria's Secret. He'd thrown in some pictures of some local ex-cons for unbiased filler and, to mix things up, a publicity picture of Charles Grodin from the movie *Midnight Run*.

Both women picked Thorne out immediately; both smiled as they did so.

"Him!" Said one.

"Mmm. That one," said the other, in a dreamy far-off voice.

Thorne was the only one they recognized, neither recognized Ashcroft, Morrison, or even Grodin. Both thought Thorne had been seated on his own, but couldn't be certain. Cabot told each of them they could leave. He looked up from the chair at Barnes as he came in through the door from the hallway.

"Well?" The detective asked.

"Charles Grodin hasn't eaten here. Didn't even recognize him."

Barnes shook his head. "That's appalling. How about Thorne or Morrison?"

"Just Thorne, nobody else." Cabot touched his forehead with the thumb and forefinger of his left hand. It was either to help him think or to stop him shaking his head. "Get that manager kid back in here, there's one more thing I want to check."

The manager must've been listening at the door because he appeared right away. He squeezed past Barnes then paused for a moment before sitting down to look at the blank space on his desk and his full trash can.

"Show me footage from your security cameras."

"For that same date?" The manager looked at Cabot as if he was joking. "Look, you got to realize, our system has a fixed retention policy."

"Meaning what? How long do you keep the footage?"

"Depends where it's from. For example, footage from the camera covering the parking lot and the outside of the building is only kept for 24 hours."

"Why so short?"

"Because we know almost immediately if we need to keep anything. You're talking about customers fighting, or damage to the restaurant or vehicles. Any problems, we flag the file and the footage gets saved, otherwise it just takes up space. There's also the legality of long term storage of personal activity without permission. This is McDonald's, not the NSA."

Cabot could see where this was going. "And inside?"

"Well, yeah, I was getting to that. The footage inside the restaurant is split into three areas; public, in back, and the tills. We keep the tills footage the longest, 60 days. It's used to spot patterns of usage that might point to staff taking money. A lot of employees have little to lose and work unsociable hours. The cameras help keep them honest."

"Look," Cabot said with growing impatience, "I don't give a shit about your hourly rate. A man who killed three people and put a fourth in a coma said he ate here. How long do you keep footage of people ordering food, sitting there eating, all that?"

The manager licked his lips nervously. "7 days."

Cabot swore. It was 22 days since the shoot-out. Any definitive proof Thorne had been here was long gone. He had the word of two young women who probably didn't know what day it was today. Thorne's story could not be proved or disproved: it was the worst possible outcome. With two witnesses independently picking him out, the balance favored the actor's version of events, but not a hundred percent. People were unreliable.

All it meant, was that they recognized Thorne.

Did it mean he'd actually been there, or that they'd seen him on TV? After a short period of time, memory became fluid. Unlike facts, memories became distorted, jumbled up. This raised another, more troubling possibility. Thorne had been purposefully vague during the interview about his activities in the days before the shoot-out. If he'd been in the restaurant on either of the two previous days, it would be a simple matter for him to use that in his story to conceal what he'd really been doing that morning. He'd be able to describe the restaurant with convincing detail if asked, with the bonus that a member of staff might alibi him by misremembering which day he'd been there.

"Bring up footage from the tills," he said.

"From when?"

"Right now, I want to see the angle."

The man selected a feed and enlarged it. "This is camera 1. Camera 2 is pretty much the same but from the other side."

The image shrunk down and another image appeared. Cabot shook his head in dismay. The camera clipped off the customer and recorded only the tills and items on the trays.

"This is all digital, right?" Barnes said.

"Right."

"So it's not like a tape that gets reused. It can be recovered?"

"Maybe someone can, but it's not me."

Cabot sighed. Recovered files were problematic at best anyway. It was easy to present it as tainted evidence in court. The files were changed to bring them back to life. Who was to say how much had been changed. Dates? Times? People knew how much can be changed using a computer, they all photoshopped their faces for Facebook.

"All right, how about credit card transactions? It's possible he didn't pay with cash, right? Maybe he's one of those dicks who pays for everything with his cell phone."

"You'd have to speak to someone higher than me about that. We're not allowed to show financial information without permission from corporate, or a warrant."

It was useless. He didn't have the evidence for a warrant, the evidence was on the other side. Chicken and egg. A perfect loop that seemed to do nothing but protect criminals from legitimate investigation. Cabot got to his feet.

"Come on Barnes, this is a bust."

Out in the parking lot, another sheriff's car was parked opposite theirs and a couple of patrol deputies sitting inside shoveling food into their faces. Neither of the two acknowledged him in any way, despite prolonged eye contact. This neither shocked him nor angered him, it was just the way it was. He didn't mess with patrol, and they didn't mess with him. He unlocked the door of his cruiser, climbed in and waited as Barnes got in next to him. There was a sense of weary resignation about the younger man as he put on his seatbelt and slumped in the seat. They were no further forward. Thorne had been recognized, but he hadn't expected anything else. The man seemed to be everywhere right now.

Cabot pulled the car out of its spot and swung round, toward the exit.

Identification of Christopher Thorne was going to suffer from this problem wherever he went, whether they remembered the shoot-out footage or not. Witnesses might be pre-inclined to give favorable testimony because at some level they remembered his heroism. He frowned, thinking about the two till cameras. They had the same underwater quality as the feeds at the mall and it came to him what it meant.

"Something bothering you, boss?"

He glanced at Barnes, surprised. "Why?"

"You have that *face* when something's going on."

"It's that security footage, it reminded me of the recordings at the mall. Something was the same, and something else was different. I couldn't place what it was until just now. On TV, the mall footage has sound, but the official footage is silent. I never noticed before."

Barnes smiled. "God, you're right! I hadn't noticed either."

He pulled the cruiser out of the parking lot and swung it across the street, back toward the Sheriff's Office.

"Where do you think the sound went? Did someone remove it?"

Barnes appeared to think about it.

"You know what? I'll bet it's the other way around. That there was never any sound on the store security, but it was added later from another source. On TV it's an edited clip, right? Not separate streams from different cameras. It's the exact same one that's up on the internet, the TV companies didn't make it. I reckon whoever put it together pulled the sound from a cell phone or somewhere else and stuck that on over the top. The sound volume doesn't change between cuts, it's constant which means it has a single source."

Cabot nodded. "Some damn kid in his bedroom."

"It's always some kid in his bedroom. No doubt about it."

He glanced at the detective to determine if he was being mocked. Instead, he saw Barnes writing something rapidly in his notepad. He smiled. That's what he liked to see; it was the tell-tale sign of a good cop, always making notes.

"What you got? You think of something?"

"Yeah. I just thought of a really great tweet."

Cabot didn't speak to the detective the rest of the drive back.

173

TWENTY-SEVEN

Thorne sat at Ashcroft's breakfast bar with a bottle of beer, checking news coverage on the senator's tablet. He'd been at it for nearly half an hour, searching for news about a stabbing on River Street. Nothing. Not even a generic search for witnesses to an unnamed incident. He'd passed the scene within ten minutes. First responders should still have been there, but they were not. For his own reasons, Blake would've wanted to avoid all contact with police and paramedics. He'd managed to skulk off, back to wherever he was lying low, hopefully to bleed out in private.

Satisfied, he looked for items related to the shoot-out. This had become part of his daily routine and he found himself going back to it whenever there was time. He told himself that he needed to keep tabs on Cabot's investigation, and the enquires of journalists, but he knew that was less than the whole truth. He'd grown used to seeing his name in print and, like any junkie, was chasing his next fix. Again, he struck out. The last piece was from three days earlier and contained no new information, only a summary of events and personalities.

The story was old, and the investigation stalled.

He set the tablet down and looked over at the pool where Lauren was doing laps. She mixed her strokes like an Olympic athlete. Crawl, butterfly, breast, and back. Ten laps of each stroke, before starting over. She swam like this for an hour without resting and did so three times a day. James Ashcroft sat in one of the poolside chairs drinking Scotch, looking not at Lauren's athletic body cutting through the water, but at a muted television displaying an endless stream of financial information. Stock prices; risers, fallers. It appeared to Thorne to be the most boring channel ever.

Thorne took a long swig of beer and returned his attention to the tablet to check entertainment websites. A reality star had slit her wrists in her hot tub. It was everywhere, wall-to-wall. He flipped past it, unconcerned. He was about to close the tablet again when his eye caught a headline.

Kate Bloom in fist fight with photographer.

He tapped the link without reading the teaser paragraph.

A picture loaded of Kate standing in the doorway of a restaurant. She wore large mirror sunglasses and held her hand outstretched toward the camera to block the lens. Her lower lip was caught under her top teeth and he guessed the picture was taken while she was telling the photographer where to go. It wasn't the most flattering picture of her he'd ever seen, but it made him smile nevertheless, particularly since it was accompanied by another picture of a creepy-looking man with a black eye. He read the article quickly. She'd been out with an unnamed friend at a steak place on Wilshire called *Pacific Dining Car*, when a man began to take pictures of her inside the restaurant. He was quickly ejected by staff, but remained outside waiting for her. After her meal he approached her again on the street and was immediately punched in the face. The man gave pursuit along the sidewalk, then began to take pictures of her in the Camaro, knocking heavily on the glass in an effort to make her open the window. Instead, she drove off over the top of his foot, crushing four toes.

Thorne smiled again. He could see the scene so clearly in his mind. Kate was beautiful, but she was no delicate flower and suffered no fool gladly.

The article mentioned him in two places; once as her co-star and partner of five years, and second as the hero of Capitola Mall. Their out-of-date relationship information caused a deep sadness to open inside him and he was filled with a desperate need to speak to her. Perhaps this incident would prove to be the perfect icebreaker between them and offer him a way back into her heart before too much time passed.

He stood and walked around the island unit and along past the pool area. Lauren had stopped swimming, but he didn't turn his head to look for her, he didn't want to get sidetracked. He walked through the mansion, back toward the guest room. It amazed him that he hadn't spoken to Kate once since he'd gotten out of hospital. Every time he'd thought about it, he'd found a reason not to call. He closed the door and sat on his bed, his cell phone in his hand. Without thinking through what he wanted to say to her, he dialed her number. The call went straight to voicemail. It was a default message provided by her carrier which she'd never changed as a security measure. He hung up without leaving a message and squinted his eyes to make out the tiny digits on his cell phone clock.

00:14.

It was late, sure, but Kate charged her phone next to her bed and never switched it off. He thought about calling the landline. If she was asleep and he woke her up, she'd be annoyed. The landline was out in the hall, she'd have to get out of bed to answer it. Kate could be pretty cranky when she was woken up like that. Thorne decided to risk it anyway. He needed to hear her voice, even if that voice was removing his spleen for ten minutes.

He navigated through the address book to find the number. He hit dial and waited for the call to connect, it felt like the signal was going out into space. After an eternity, an automated voice came on. *The number you dialed is not a working number. Please check the number and dial again.* He cut the call and stared at the screen. How could the number be wrong? They rarely used the landline, but he must've called it before from his cell. It looked right. The number ended with a triple six which he'd always made a joke about.

He sighed and lay back on the bed, vexed.

The story about her and the photographer had likely generated plenty of interest. Not just with friends and family, but with the press pack. Kate had no more love for the press than he had. It was, after all, how the situation had started. She would turn off her cell and unplug the landline, wait for things to calm down. In Los Angeles, people moved on pretty fast and there was no shortage of things for the press to cover.

His theory seemed to fit the facts, but in his guts he knew it wasn't true. The automated message came back to him. *Not a working number.* If she'd left the phone off the hook or unplugged it he'd get a busy signal, wouldn't he? What did that leave? His thoughts drifted for a moment. News of their break-up had yet to come out. If the press had pursued her since the shoot-out she might've decided to change her cell number and cancel the landline account. He didn't know what happened to numbers that had been canceled, but he supposed they could easily be tagged as not working.

His cell phone rang and he jumped. He lifted it to his ear, but it remained black and silent in his hand. His eyes moved over to the burner cell on top of the dressing table. The display was lit up, its cheap ringtone like a fairground ride.

Only one person knew the number.

"Turn on the news, asshole."

Blake disconnected without waiting for him to respond.

He ran back through the mansion to the east wing. The Ashcrofts were both still there next to the pool, ignoring each other. Their heads snapped around as he ran in.

"Put on the news," he said.

"Which channel?" Ashcroft said.

"Any channel."

Ashcroft changed to KCAL9. On screen a large building was on fire. The flames licked out through multiple windows, devouring walls and soaring up into the night sky. In front, five towering palm trees were also on fire. It looked like a movie. He felt sick. Even like this, he recognized his home. The camera swept around to face Ocean Park Boulevard, which was choked by fire trucks and a crowd of shocked residents. As the camera moved he saw a glimpse of his Camaro parked at the curb. His eyes probed the figures on the street looking for Kate. If his car was there, she was there. His building had it's own parking garage but she rarely used it as it was cramped and had thick unforgiving pillars. He searched for her blonde hair in the crowd, knowing he wouldn't find it. Along the bottom of the screen the banner changed from BLAZE IN SANTA MONICA to FIRE AT HERO ACTOR'S HOME. The sound came on. Ashcroft must've realized it was still muted. An excited male voice was narrating the visuals from off-camera.

"Fire broke out just after eleven and spread rapidly through the building. Early reports indicate that the sprinkler system failed. At this stage, it is believed that the fire started in the apartment belonging to Chris Thorne before spreading into neighboring units. Residents were forced to flee wearing whatever they had on. Kate Bloom, actress and partner of Thorne, as yet the only confirmed fatality."

"Switch it off!"

His voice was loud and cut across the droning voice of the reporter. Ashcroft immediately hit the power switch and the screen went black, its shape disappearing into the black window behind it. Silence filled the room. He stood frozen, still staring at the blank screen. A poison entered his body, he could feel it spreading out with each beat of his heart. The Ashcrofts stared at him from their lounge chairs, he could feel their eyes on him. Several seconds passed before he turned toward them. Tears were running down Lauren's cheeks and when he looked at her, she began to sob. She'd never met Kate, but she could cry for her. His own eyes remained dry. Within him, rage was building and building, without end. Ashcroft stood and walked over to him, his face pale and frozen. Thorne knew what was coming, and he was in no mood for it. He held his hands up to block the senator's embrace.

"Don't. I can't do this. I can't be around people."

He turned and walked out the room.

Lauren called out after him. "Chris! You can't be on your own."

Thorne continued to walk away. He felt himself shiver. The muscles in his body were tightening up. His jaw was clamped shut, like he was holding a scream inside.

He should have killed Blake when he had the chance.

TWENTY-EIGHT

Thorne walked next to Lauren down the small path of pine needles as they finished another run in the woods. It had been a run marked by impenetrable silence and unspoken sadness. As they popped out through the gap in the hedge, Thorne saw a man in his late sixties sitting on the step in front of the mansion. He was facing down the drive, as if waiting for someone to arrive by car. He wore faded blue jeans and a leather jacket, both of which were baggy and ill-fitting. Rather than projecting an image of strength, his outfit did the opposite, drawing attention to his thin frame and wasted muscles. Despite the obvious lack of threat, it was nonetheless disconcerting to see someone randomly appear inside Ashcroft's security gate. For all he knew, the man could have a gun in his pocket.

The crunch of gravel under their feet made the old man's head spin around. Thorne recognized him from a framed photograph inside the mansion. It was Adam Mathews, Lauren's father. Mathews rose to his feet, his face twisting up in disgust.

"Look at you two, all sweaty and out of breath. Did I interrupt something?"

"*Dad!*"

Lauren's face colored and Mathews saw it.

"There's that red face of innocence!"

"You're embarrassing me, is all."

"No, I don't think so. In fact, it's the whole reason I came up here, to talk to you about *this guy*," Mathews said, looking at Thorne with undisguised hostility.

Inwardly, Thorne sighed. It seemed like there was a solid 25% of men that hated him on sight due to the way he looked. He'd worked hard his whole life to look the way he did, it wasn't some genetic lottery like this type of man seemed to think. They were in front of the old man now and he could smell alcohol coming off Mathews every time he exhaled.

"I guess you're not here to thank him for saving my life."

"That's a joke, he was probably in on it. You need to open your eyes!"

"What the hell's your problem?"

"Do you really need me to spell it out?"

Lauren straightened her back and put her hands on her hips. At five nine, she was several inches taller than her father and her new posture made muscles pop out on her arms and shoulders.

"You know what? Yes. I want you to say the words to my face."

"Don't act so high and mighty with me. I've seen the pictures, just like everyone else. The two of you are obviously *fucking*." Mathews leaned into this last word like he was pitching a baseball, a grim pleasure carved into his face. "You've turned yourself into a real whore, Lauren, I hope you're proud. First that sugar daddy, Ashcroft, now this guy. I'm glad your mother isn't alive to see this, it would've broken her heart."

Thorne grabbed the front of the man's jacket, twisted it a quarter turn and lifted him off the ground like a sack of potatoes. Mathews' mouth dropped open in shock and he looked at Thorne's emotionless face, then the single arm that held him aloft.

"Jesus!" Lauren said. "Put him down."

But he did not. Instead, Thorne moved his face closer to her father's. He saw his own bared teeth reflected in the small, dark eyes in front of him. These were the eyes of some kind of burrowing animal, designed for perpetual darkness. He wanted so much to hurt this vile little man. What kind of dad calls his daughter a whore?

"Chris, he doesn't know any better. Let go."

He released his grip and Mathews fell backward on his ass.

Lauren's father lay there breathing rapidly through his mouth. Thorne noticed that both of Mathews' hands vibrated nervously at his side, his eyes fixed on him as if he expected more violence.

"What a hero! Beating on an old man!"

Thorne smiled, causing Mathews to recoil. Lauren's father saw who he really was, the way he saw himself. Without Kate in his life, he was capable of terrible things. Death was inside him, and the only way he could think to get it out was to kill Blake. A life for a life. Even then, he wasn't certain it'd be enough; the anger he felt toward this man he'd just met was extreme. If he were to hit Mathews he knew he'd enjoy it. He'd hit him, and as it was during the bar fight with Blake, he wouldn't want to stop. Part of him longed for it to happen, to let the monster inside take over so that he didn't have to be here.

Lauren put herself between them and placed her hand lightly on his chest. He felt his heart beating against her palm. It was slow and steady, same as ever. Despite the depth of anger he felt toward Mathews, he was perfectly calm. Her father was no threat to either of them and he knew it. He had better things to worry about than this old fool talking trash about someone he cared about. Lauren moved her head in small, birdlike movements, trying to get his eyes to lock on to hers. When they did, he saw compassion and love.

"Go inside," she said. "This battle I can fight for myself."

Thorne nodded. He didn't know what to say to her. He couldn't admit that he needed the rage, that it was all he had left. That if she robbed him of it with her empathy, that he'd be unable to continue. He turned away and went back to where he'd dropped the backpack. He saw Mathews out of the corner of his eye getting awkwardly to his feet. Thorne picked up the bag and walked toward the front door of the mansion.

"Come home with me Laurie. You aren't safe here."

"Thanks, but no thanks."

Thorne fished around in his pocket for the keys. He was taking his time, waiting to hear what Mathews said next.

"That guy is bad news, honey. He's a stone cold killer and he's under the same roof as you. What do you think is going to happen? Is this the prince you used to dream about?"

"Dad! That's *enough*. Chris saved my life and was badly wounded in the process. You ought to be ashamed of yourself."

Mathews laughed.

"You'll see. That clown in the coma? He's *awake* now. It was all over the news while I was driving up. The cops are interviewing him as soon as the doctors finish up with him. I'm guessing your boyfriend here will be in jail before lunch."

Thorne froze.

Porter.

"I want you to leave. In future, I want you to call in advance before you show up here. And dad? You better be sober next time."

"Maybe there won't be a next time. That's what I'm thinking. Maybe you're planning to run off and play *Bonnie and Clyde* with this asshole."

Thorne snapped out of the spell he was under, opened the door and went inside. The control panel of the alarm lit up and began to beep and he calmly entered the code. It was a sign of how long he'd been here that this was now second nature. The alarm deactivated, he tossed the backpack to the side of the door and walked back through the building to his bedroom. He cursed his bad luck. To prevent himself hearing about Kate again and again, he'd avoided news. He hadn't looked at a TV, tablet, or cell phone for over twelve hours.

Back in the bedroom, he stripped off his clothes and crossed the hall into the bathroom. He turned on the shower and used the time before the hot water came through to remove his dressings. The room was small and unventilated and quickly filled with steam. It was a feature that he liked because the mirror almost immediately misted, hiding his new appearance from himself. On previous occasions, he'd also found the thick, soup-like atmosphere useful to his thought process. He could tune-out and think things through without distraction. But he no answers came to solve his predicament with Porter. Instead, the only thing that came to him, was a resurfacing desire to hurt Mathews. It felt like the man's animosity had brought this whole Porter situation about. It was stupid, yet the feeling was hard to shake. Somehow, like Cabot, this old alcoholic had seen straight through his act to his initial involvement. Mathews had managed this just from watching him on television, where he should be most convincing.

Thorne stepped into the stall and pulled the door closed.

The old man was right about one thing, Lauren wasn't safe here. He'd misjudged Blake and because of that, Kate was dead. If she wasn't safe, nobody was. Blake didn't just kill people in his way, he'd kill people to make a point. By being here, he was giving the Ashcrofts a false sense of security. They were relying on him to protect them again whether they knew it or not. He made them feel safe, and they should be afraid. The best thing he could do was leave. It would force them to wake up, he did nobody any favors by staying. He nodded his head to himself, his decision crystalizing.

But that was for a different day.

He couldn't leave until he'd dealt with Porter.

Thorne tilted his head back and let the water pound against his face.

The heat was set to maximum and it was almost too hot to bear. His skin seemed to burn around each of his injuries. Porter! He swore out loud and the fast moving water seemed to snatch the word right out the air and down the drain. He realized he'd made a critical mistake. He'd heard the word *coma* and allowed himself to forget about him as if it were the same as *dead*. But of course it wasn't, not even close. Soon, Porter would wake up and find himself looking directly into Cabot's grinning face. He wanted to scream. There'd been plenty of time to deal with the situation but he'd pissed it all away and now it was too late.

He'd shot Porter twice, he probably couldn't rely on his silence.

Thorne was dressed and in the Maserati on the way to the hospital before he thought too much about what he was going to do when he got there. In his mind, he still thought he could convince Porter not to mention his role in the gang to the police. There was no reason to after all. They'd been friends for years, would it be asking too much for a favor now? He shook his head. It was ridiculous to expect Porter to keep him out of it, and any promise he might make to that effect was likely worth nothing anyway.

Only one course of action would keep him out of prison.

TWENTY-NINE

The man lay stretched out before him on the asphalt between two cars. A doctor. His white coat fanned out underneath him like a cape. Down, but not out. He tried to crawl backward, away from him. His eyes wide and terrified. Blake walked forward so that he stood over the doctor, ready to hit him again. He saw the man glance at what he was holding: a rubber dog bone. It made a pretty good blackjack. It had a nice weight and an end that was easy to grip. You could pick one up just about anywhere, and without any problems with law enforcement. Blake swung it again, hard, and it bounced off the side of the doctor's skull. The man's body sagged as he passed out. Blake moved quickly to pull down the doctor's scrub pants in case the man wet himself and he'd have to start over on someone else. The scrubs were baggy enough for him to pull straight off without undoing the man's shoes. Underneath, the doctor wore only boxer shorts. Once they were off, Blake pulled them on directly over his jeans. They were a little on the small side, but they'd do.

"Help me get his coat off," he said.

Sara bent down next to him and they began to strip the doctor. The man's muscles were clenched, making it difficult to remove his arms from the sleeves of his coat. Blake wished he'd asked the doctor to do this before he knocked him out. Once it was off, he hung the coat over the passenger door mirror of the car next to him, then began the process again with the scrub top. This came off easier as it had larger openings around the arms. He pulled the top on over his t-shirt and felt the heat from the other man's body transfer to him.

Sara studied him closely.

"That actually suits you," she said.

Blake smiled as he pulled on the coat.

"Fuckin' A."

"You ready?" she asked.

"Just a second."

He unbuttoned her shirt by two more buttons. The first fastened button now lay below the line of her bra. He adjusted the material of her shirt to provide the best view of its contents.

"I'm not sure this is the place, Aidan."

He picked up on her sarcasm without seeing her face.

"Sorry, hon, but this was how we met in the first place so I know they work."

"When we get back, I'm going to punch you right in the face."

He looked at her face and smiled. "No doubt."

The man at his feet groaned. Blake kicked him until he stopped making any sound, then threw in an extra kick free of charge. He didn't know how long this was going to take, and he might need the man's wake up alarm snoozed for an extra five minutes.

"What if someone sees him lying there?"

"I'm not too bothered about that," he said. "Let's go."

They walked toward the hospital entrance. The doctor's scrubs were tight, forcing him to walk slower than normal. The white coat helped hide an inch of jeans above the scrub pants, not to mention the Glock in the small of his back, but heat was already beginning to build with all the layers of clothing. Two cops stood smoking at the corner of the building where they'd abducted the doctor. They both hid cigarettes behind their backs as he approached but their eyes switched quickly from him to Sara's chest. He couldn't say he blamed them.

Inside, the hospital was chaos. He saw a dozen more cops, and double that number of journalists and cameramen. The media circus had arrived. At the front stood a red-faced Cabot who appeared to be getting reamed by a tall woman in dark-framed glasses and a business suit. Some kind of administrator or lawyer he thought. The lieutenant faced away from him but Blake pushed on past anyway, his arm around Sara's shoulders. He couldn't discount the possibility of being recognized from the coffee store incident, or even the security footage. As they planned, she was now dragging her leg as though injured.

A man in his early twenties approached. He looked tired and his scrubs were wrinkled, but his face was open and friendly.

"Can I help?"

"Yes," Blake said. "Get me a wheelchair."

The man sank back into the crowd without a word. Moments later the man was back, pushing a wheelchair in front of him. Sara lowered herself into it slowly, and with shaking arms. Blake felt she was overdoing it, but the shaking made her breasts jiggle in just the right way and the man stared at them, mesmerized.

"What happened?"

He was asking Sara, but Blake answered.

"She was hit by a motorcycle."

They'd worked out a whole backstory for her fake accident but he decided to ditch it and keep it simple. He wasn't certain Sara would be able to stay on point.

The man glanced up at him and frowned.

"Are you new here? I don't recognize you."

"Started today," Blake said, looking back at the media scrum.

"You chose a good day for it."

Blake nodded. The man took his cues well.

"I see that. What's going on?"

"You don't know?"

"Just got here. Found this one out front as I arrived."

Even this casual reference to Sara caused the man's face to get sucked into the gravity well of her chest. He couldn't take his eyes off it.

"They got a guy up on the fourth floor under armed guard. He was one of the gunmen at the mall shooting the other week, with the senator and his wife."

Blake nodded to Sara. They knew where to look for Porter.

"I heard about that," Blake said. "Saw it too actually."

The man turned to him, a smile on his face.

"Oh my god, I can't stop watching that video, it's amazing. Must have seen it about 30 times. That other guy was here too, the good guy, but he's gone now. He's walking around like nothing happened."

The nurse was looking straight at him, at one of the men in the video. All he saw was a doctor. It gave Blake the confidence he needed; this would be easier than he imagined. He just needed to get on with it, before Cabot made his move. Blake moved around the wheelchair so that he was standing behind it, his hands lined up with the handles. It wasn't a subtle move, and the man understood their conversation was over.

"What's your name," Blake said, his tone friendly.

"Mikey."

"I'm Charles. I'll catch you around once I'm settled in. I'd like to talk with you some more about that video, it fascinates me."

Mikey's expression lifted.

"You bet."

The man noticed something to the side and shot off to deal with it. Blake smiled. He couldn't have asked for anything better. The man would be too busy working to ask anyone about the new doctor. He began to push Sara deeper into the hospital.

"I never had you down as a Charles," Sara said, dryly.

"First name that came to mind."

"*Charles* was the first name that came to mind?"

"The wheelchair, made me think of the X-Men."

She sighed.

"I'm learning new things about you, Aidan. Terrible things."

Blake resisted the urge to laugh, as they were coming up on two cops at the elevator. A man and a woman. They held coffee in tall paper cups, and stood against the wall. Neither of them were waiting for the elevator, they were just talking. Cabot had brought a lot of foot soldiers with him for his big interview. The Sheriff's Office lay only a couple of minutes' drive from the hospital and many had obviously thought the trip worthwhile. Blake ignored the two deputies and pressed the button for the elevator. Behind them, conversation stopped. He knew the cops were looking at him. Fooling civilians was one thing, police was another. Cops were like bloodhounds, they could sniff you out. He had fastened the doctor's coat up the front to hide the ill-fitting scrubs, but this prevented him from quickly accessing his Glock. If things kicked off, the automatic might as well be on another planet.

He put a friendly look on his face and glanced back at the cops and gave them a small nod. In his experience, it was all most of them needed to let them know you were on the side of the angels. His gaze lingered briefly on the female officer, like he was checking her out. She smiled and bowed her head in embarrassment. He turned back to the elevator as the doors opened. He pushed Sara on and hit 4 using the knuckle of his index finger. The cops they were talking again. The female officer laughed and put her hand over her mouth, her eyes glancing at Blake as she did so. He didn't care if they were laughing at him, as long as they were laughing. He had no animosity toward the police as long as they left him alone. The doors closed and he caught a glimpse of himself reflected on a strip of chrome. He had to admit, he looked pretty damn convincing as a doctor. His wide neck didn't really work, but if you needed a doctor that could bench 380 pounds, he was your man.

"I hate being in this chair by the way."

He looked at the top of her head like he was looking at her face.

"I figured. It's only for a while longer."

"If we pull shit like this again then next time *you're* playing the part of the dumb-ass princess that needs to be rescued."

"I feel ya babe."

The elevator stopped and the doors slid open. Blake expected more cops to be standing there, but there were none. He pushed Sara out and began to wheel her along. He supposed that moving patients like this was not something a doctor would normally do themselves, but he couldn't worry about that now. At least as a doctor he'd be less likely to be challenged, or told to do another task. His plan was to walk along looking for the police guard that would mark the room he was after, but after several minutes of fruitless search, Blake decided he'd have to change his

185

tactics, or risk Cabot getting there first.

"This is taking too long, I'm going to have to ask someone."

"No shit," she said.

Up ahead was a nurses' station. A single nurse sat there, almost hidden behind a vase of flowers and a computer screen. She hadn't seen them yet, which was perfect. The problem with Sara on a wheelchair, was that it didn't fit with the narrative of him needing to see a patient that had been in a coma. The accident victim ruse was now working against them. He pushed Sara over to the wall and stopped.

"All right, Princess," he said quietly. "Ride's over."

Sara sprang out of the seat, like she'd been fired from a cannon. She wasn't waiting for him to change his mind. He glanced around to check no one had witnessed this miracle, but judging by the calm way people were walking about, no one had. He used the cuffs of the white coat to wipe down the chair's handles.

"Okay, hang back while I ask about Porter."

He approached the nurses' station and let his hands hang over the top of the counter so that he was invading the space of the woman who sat there. She looked like the type that would sit there blanking him, pretending he didn't exist, and he didn't have time for that.

"Help you?"

"I'm trying to locate a patient," Blake said.

The woman's head turned to a computer screen.

"Name?"

"Sam Porter."

She looked back up at him without typing anything in.

"Samuel Porter is in 446."

"Thanks."

He turned to leave when she spoke again.

"Did they add your name to the list?"

"What list?"

"You know he's a criminal under armed guard?"

"Of course," he said.

"Only people on a list are allowed in. It's updated every day."

Cabot was smarter than he looked.

"I wasn't told about a list. Can you check I've been added?"

She turned to her computer again and began to type. While she did this, he came around to her side of the desk, so that he could see the screen. She glanced up at him, her eyes narrowed and her cheeks sucked in like she'd bitten on a lemon. He ignored her and glanced at the screen. The list of names was in front of him.

"Excuse me," she said.

"Shit, they haven't added me. All right, thanks anyway."

The woman was looking him up and down now. She stared at his running shoes. There was dried mud along the tops from when he was up in the forest watching Thorne. Her eyes moved to the quarter inch of jeans that above the scrub pants. He'd been made. Asking about Porter, walking around the desk, the clothes; it didn't take much to put it together. He unbuttoned the top two buttons of the white coat, reached inside, and pulled out the dog bone. She looked at it, her eyebrows raised in confusion.

He'd been willing to play nice with her, even thank her for her help and move on. But that wasn't enough, she had to get all up in his business, stick her nose where it wasn't welcome. He couldn't have that. She watched him lift his hand up with the bone, still not understanding what it meant for her. He brought it down fast on her head and she folded up onto the floor without a sound. He put the rubber bone back in his pocket. Best $3 he'd ever spent. He used his foot to push the woman's legs under the desk where they wouldn't be seen. She'd twisted as she'd fallen and her head had shot right underneath, out of sight. As long as no one sat at the desk, they were golden. Even then, he figured most people would assume she'd simply passed out and hit her head. He looked up and saw Sara shaking her head.

"Couldn't you have tied her up?"

"With what? I didn't bring any rope, did you? We're on the clock here, I don't have time to be nice to people who would happily throw both of us under the bus the first chance they got. Besides, I don't remember you saying shit when I did the same to that doctor. You knew what you were getting into, we're not here to sell Girl Scout cookies."

"I'm tired of watching you hit women."

"I've not noticed you holding back violence against anyone, male or female. Shit, you burned a woman alive a couple of days ago."

Sara's face turned scarlet.

"That was a mistake and you know it!"

He nodded. "How about we call this quits, eh?"

"No," she said, "let's *not*. You're way stronger than I am, stronger than any of these women. *That's* the difference. It's wrong. This isn't equality, it's abuse."

"Fine. But for the record, I didn't hit her as hard as the guy outside."

Blake came out from behind the desk and they set off for Porter's room. He considered pointing out to her that he was stronger than the men he fought too, but he knew it would've gained him nothing. The truth was, equality meant treating everybody the same, not treating some better. He'd protect himself, protect both of them, from threats in whatever form they took. When they were on the other side of this and the $12 million was safe, *then* he could afford to be a more rounded human being. Until that point, all bets were off.

187

He looked across at Sara and saw her face was fixed, her mouth a thin, flat line. Probably too soon to make a joke about boning a nurse, he thought.

A man in his mid twenties rushed toward them at something between a jog and a run. He was wearing an expensive suit and looked vaguely familiar, but Blake couldn't place him. When he passed them, Blake let out a sigh of relief. If the man had recognized him, he would've been able to identify him to the police later. Blake would've been forced to take him out right there in the corridor and things would've got messy very quickly.

He was a cop.

It came to him suddenly. The man in the suit was the guy who stood next to the lieutenant during press conferences. A deputy. He never spoke, just stood eyeballing the camera. He didn't recognize him without the uniform. Blake glanced back and felt his heart lunge in his chest. The man had stopped running and was halfway down the hallway looking back at them with his hands on his hips. His stance caused his suit jacket to pull apart and expose the seven pointed star that hung in a leather wallet over his belt. There was a small movement of his head toward Blake and the man smiled, then turned away and continued down the hall.

He'd been looking at Sara, not him.

"What is it?" she said.

"Nothing. Just another fan of your ass."

"Another?"

She was warming up again. She couldn't stay mad at him for long.

"Never mind that," he said. "The way these doors are numbered it should be coming up on the left."

They were at the other side of the building from the elevator. A corridor lead off the main hallway, and the room number told him it was off this corridor. He stopped short of the junction, then glanced quickly around it and back. The police guard stood next to the door looking bored. It was exactly the way he'd pictured it in his mind, except the cop had no chair to sit on, something he looked like he needed. He turned to Sara and spoke quietly.

"You know what to do?"

"Please. I've been doing this shit my whole life."

Sara walked around the corner, humming gently to herself.

He'd give her twenty or thirty seconds to get the man's interest, then he'd show up asking to see Porter. That would be enough time for her to work her magic. It was all the time it had taken her to get him on the hook, and he'd never thought of himself as an easy mark. The timing of his arrival would be annoying for the cop; he'd want to get rid of him as quickly as possible in case Sara wandered off. It was a thin plan and he knew it, but he had nothing else.

After what he thought was long enough, he walked around the corner with his head down, toward the floor. He hoped it would look like he was preoccupied with something, and not a threat. It also allowed him to hide some of his height. He was almost at the cop when he glanced up and saw the man looking at him. His face wasn't hostile, just irritated. Blake caught a glimpse of Sara's face; she was smiling and her eyes shone and twinkled. She was so good he almost got sucked in himself.

"Can't let you in if you're not on the list," the cop said.

His voice was bored, almost automated, like he'd been telling people the same thing for days. Perhaps people like Mikey, coming to have a look at one of the famous gunmen. He noticed the man's name badge: GARRET.

"I'm on the list. Raymond Jensen."

Garret sighed and pulled a notepad out his pocket. It was folded over ready for use with a thick rubber band holding the bent over pages flat. Blake could see the list of names from where he was standing. There were about a dozen and he saw the one he needed upside-down at the bottom. It was slightly different from what he was expecting.

"What did you say your name was?"

"Raymond Jenkin," Blake said, correcting himself. He must have misread the computer screen the nurse had pulled up. Next to him, Sara scratched herself lightly between her breasts. Her false nails made this sound like ice being scraped off a windshield.

"Go on in," the cop said.

Blake wanted to smile; Sara was the best. He opened the door and closed it quietly behind him. The room was small, with a single bed and no window. It looked like it had started life as a storage area, before being used for dangerous criminals. A chair sat in the corner facing the door. He reached down and touched the seat with the back of his hand. There was a trace of heat still on it. The detective had sat here. If he'd left to use the john, he might be back at any moment. He looked at Porter and he appeared to be asleep. He walked around the end of the bed so he could look at Porter's face. Saliva ran out the corner of his mouth and he could see part of his tongue. It didn't look like a normal sleeping face, but there probably was no normal when you've been in a coma.

Blake looked down to where the other man's feet tented up the bed sheet and pinched the big toe, hard. There was a grunt and a fast intake of breath, then Porter's eyes opened. First by a small amount then, seeing Blake standing there, by the full amount. He blinked several times, then frowned. Porter didn't seem to be with it. The look on his friend's face was vague at best, with no obvious sign of recognition. Blake knew his disguise wasn't that good; Porter's noodle was cooked. This whole thing had been a waste of time. Cabot was kidding himself if he thought he'd get anything useful out of Porter. There'd be no formal statement given today; no identities of gang members revealed. He'd worried for nothing. Perhaps in time, Porter would do more than drool, but he wasn't there yet.

An unpleasant thought rolled through his mind.

This is a trap.

Now the thought had entered his head, he couldn't shake it. Why else would Cabot publicly announce Porter's recovery when it was plainly not true? Controlling access to the room would limit a leak over the true condition of the patient. Porter was bait, and he'd taken it. He couldn't believe he'd been so stupid. It explained something else too: he'd seen cops all around the hospital but only one of them was directly guarding Porter. Two if you included the detective. The rest had been goofing around, or in the lobby with the TV crews. Cabot had let them get this far; the further in he was, the harder it would be to get out.

He walked up the side of the bed and Porter turned to look at him. There was a shaky vibration to his head movements, as though he were in the back of a truck driving along a dirt track. Blake had seen this before with his grandmother. It wasn't due to muscle weakness in the neck, it was the sign of a stroke, or some other brain injury.

"Hey buddy, how you doin'?"

Porter stared at him blankly, head twitching.

A screen on the wall displayed his vital signs. The pulse rate increased as Blake looked at it. Porter's whole body shook now, his teeth clenched. It lasted only seconds, but it seemed to stretch out for several minutes. Finally, Porter seemed to relax and a light returned to his eyes that might have been recognition.

"Brake?"

Blake smiled. Close enough.

"I'm here, Sam. Can you move? We've come to bust you out, man."

"They said you'd come, but I didn't believe them."

Porter's voice was slurred, like he'd been drinking.

"Who did?"

"Cops."

Adrenaline slammed into his body. He glanced at the door, the only way in or out of the room. If the cops knew he'd arrived, it would be a simple task to contain him. He had a small amount of ammunition and a limited field of fire. They might have Sara already.

"You gotta go."

Blake looked at his friend. He'd known him for 20 years.

"I can't leave you like this."

Porter closed his eyes. "I don't want you to."

There'd be no walking Porter out the front door on top of a gurney. No squeal of tires as the three of them tore out the parking lot to freedom. Porter was done and he knew it. Blake reached into his pocket and pulled out his knife. The blade had a lock that clicked into place, but he knew how to open it to prevent the click. He looked at his friend's chest as it rose and fell, trying to picture where his heart was, as he lined up the blade. He thrust sharply down and blood surged up over the knife, coating his hands. A siren wailed from the machine on the wall. The traces were flat and red, the pulse 0.

The door slammed open behind him and the cop stood there, his mouth hanging open. Blake swung around to face him and blood ran off his hand onto the floor. Time seemed to slow down. The cop went for the gun on his belt. A leather strap held it in place and he struggled to free it. By the time he pulled the piece free, Blake was halfway across the floor with the knife in his hand. A bullet flew past his head, then another. He dropped to his knees and slid across the floor and thrust the blade up under the cop's chin, into his brain.

The cop crashed onto the floor next to him.

Blake got to his feet. People were shouting and screaming down the hall. The cat was out the bag, things were about to get interesting. Sara walked into the room and had to step over the pool of blood spreading out around the cop's head.

"Jesus, Aidan. I just spent five minutes talking to that guy."

Blake wiped his knife clean on the bed sheet and returned it to his pocket.

"You talked to him, he talked to your tits."

"Believe me, I'm used to it."

"No doubt."

"You're a jackass, have I ever told you that?"

"All the time. Listen, get his radio, we need to get the hell out of here. This whole thing was a setup from the get-go and I'm pretty sure everyone heard those gunshots."

He noticed the cop's 9mm under the chair in the corner and he picked it up. You can never have too many guns. Sound erupted from the radio.

Shots fired! Shots fired!

Fourth floor, northeast corner.

Garret, report. What's your status?

She passed him the radio and they made for the door.

"Did Sam feel anything?"

"Not a thing. Come on, we gotta book."

THIRTY

Blake glanced into the hallway, bracing himself for another shot. It was empty, but it wouldn't be for long. He walked out the room and set off at a fast pace. After a short distance, he stopped and doubled back to the door to wipe down the handle. He had to be careful, he couldn't risk leaving anything behind. He would've worn gloves if his disguise didn't prevent it. He ran back to where Sara stood waiting. He was off-plan; that stupid cop and his gun, he'd screwed everything up. This should've been a simple in-out operation. He cursed himself for not injecting an air bubble into the IV. An air bubble would've allowed them to escape before Porter got the bad news. It would've looked like he'd died of natural causes, it would've been perfect.

Instead, he'd sprung Cabot's trap like an idiot.

Blake paused at the corner of the hallway and the main corridor to look back at Sara. She'd re-buttoned her shirt and pinned her hair up in a ponytail. Her face was serious, her mouth a grim straight line. She had her right arm behind her, ready to draw the pistol tucked into the back of her pants. She was hardcore, but this wasn't her scene, it was his. He nodded, silently asking if she was ready. She nodded and he stepped out into the main corridor.

"ON YOUR KNEES!"

It was the young detective. He had his gun drawn in a two handed grip, feet shoulder width apart. Blake put his hands up. The other cop had missed, but this guy wouldn't. He knew the type, down the gun range once or twice a week.

"I'm a doctor!"

"GET DOWN!"

The detective was on his own, but backup would arrive soon. Blake got on his knees, his eyes fixed on the cop. The floor was hard and bending his legs caused pain to soar from the stab wound.

"Interlace your fingers behind your head."

The cop was closer now, less than twenty feet. His voice was raised, but he wasn't shouting now. He was relaxing, in control. It was exactly what Blake wanted.

"Listen," Blake said. "It was that woman I was with. She went crazy, she has a gun. She killed the policeman and I think she's going to kill the patient. You have to hurry."

He saw the detective's face change. A frown flickering across his smooth forehead; a quick glance to the left. Part of him was believing it. Interesting. They must know a woman is involved, it was the only thing that made sense. The moment passed.

"Nice try, asshole, but I can hear the alarm from the heart monitor. The patient's dead. Now lie on the motherfucking floor and face the wall."

Blake smiled and glanced over the cop's shoulder.

"You know, she really does have a gun. At this range, I'll be picking your brain out my teeth for the next week. Now lower your weapon."

"Face down on the floor, now!"

Sara pressed her gun into the back of the detective's head.

"Can I shoot this pig yet, hon?"

The detective closed his eyes and sighed, his gun lowering to the ground. When his eyes opened again, Blake was standing in front of him with a big smile. He reached out and took the cop's pistol, his eyes locked on the younger man's face.

"Don't worry, my friend. We're not going to kill you, not if you do what you're told. Can you do that for me?"

"Why should I believe you? You killed Garret."

Blake nodded. "He gave me no choice. It was him or me. I trust you're smarter than that. I've done what I came here to do, all I want is to leave. You let that happen, I got no problem with you. Okay?"

"Okay."

Above them, a speaker crackled into life.

Code silver, code silver. Clear all public spaces. This is not a drill.

Blake smiled as he pocketed the cop's gun. Code silver, eh.

"You got handcuffs?"

"I only have zip ties. Right jacket pocket."

Blake reached into the man's pocket and pulled them out. Two thick plastic ties, overlapping, already formed into a circle ready for use.

"Stand against the wall and put your hands behind your back. Press your forehead right up against the concrete."

The detective glanced at Sara, then did as he was told. If he was looking for some sign of weakness in her eyes, he didn't find it. She held her gun against his head as Blake pulled both ties tight around his wrists. He knew it was possible to break out of plastic ties using the leverage of your arms, so he fastened them below the man's watch where the leverage was weakest and where the veins were more exposed. When he was done, he spun the man back around so that he could see his face.

"What's your name?"

"Barnes."

The detective's face was tight, his eyes flicking between them. It was the face of someone who expected to die. Blake didn't want that. Men that thought that were liable to be unpredictable and make sudden, desperate moves. Moves that exposed themselves and everyone else to danger, because they felt they had nothing to lose.

"Here's how it is, Barnes. If I intended to kill you, you'd be dead already. It would've been quicker than tying you up and having this conversation. Agreed?"

Barnes nodded, his eyes wide.

"All right," Blake said. "Let's take a walk."

He grabbed the detective by his elbow and dragged him along the corridor toward the stairs. Barnes moved easily alongside him. If he resisted, or moved too slowly, he risked falling face-first onto the floor with no way to break his fall. He glanced at the detective.

"You a college boy, Barnes?"

"Yeah."

"What's it like working for a moron?"

"Why don't you ask her," Barnes said.

Blake smiled. "I like your style, kid."

Up ahead he saw the doors to the stairs.

He thought about the police. They'd set a perimeter around the building and block exits. That would eat into their manpower and cost them time. Even if there were a lot of them, they'd be thinly spread securing a building this size. If they went floor by floor, room by room, it could potentially take them hours to find him; and that assumed they didn't go into the ventilation or some other crawl space. The police he'd seen so far were standard cops, what Cabot needed was a SWAT team. Since this whole thing was a trap, he had to assume the lieutenant had people lined up. They'd already be briefed and it would just be a matter of following the agreed plan. Getting into position.

He pushed the detective against the wall and waited until Sara covered him with her gun. Blake drew the Glock with his right hand, and standing to one side of the doorway, used his left to push open the stair door. He ducked his head around the jamb, then pulled it back. All clear. He heard boots coming up the stairs. A couple of guys, moving fast. The closer mechanism pulled the door softly closed again.

"You're wasting your time," Barnes said. "This place is in lockdown. Let me take you in, it's your only chance. They'll kill you for what you did to Garret."

194

Blake turned to the cop as if noticing him for the first time.

"Here's what I need you to do. She's going to hold the radio up to your mouth and you're going to say that you chased me down to the third floor and need backup. Make it believable and you live, otherwise you die. No special codes, just the message. We clear?"

"Yeah."

He pressed the Glock against the detective's forehead.

"One more thing. Do *not* mention my friend here. Not a word. You talk about her, or say *they,* or imply plural in some other way and I'll spray your brains against the wall before your mouth stops moving. You chased a single man, that's all."

Barnes swallowed. "Okay."

Sara held up the radio and keyed the mike. She nodded.

"All units, this is Barnes. Suspect now on the third floor, heading east. I'm in pursuit and in need of assistance. Suspect is heavily armed and extremely dangerous, approach with caution. I say again, third floor. Barnes out."

Blake smiled. "That wasn't half bad."

He put the gun in his pocket, then pulled the detective away from the wall and forced him onto the floor. The plastic ties prevented the younger man from fighting back. Blake stood over him and reached back into the white coat.

"Please, I did what you asked. I've got a kid."

"I've not forgotten," Blake said.

He hit Barnes across the temple with the rubber bone. It was a light blow but the detective dropped to the floor and lay motionless, his arms twisted awkwardly behind his back, his face pitched forward onto the floor. Blake went through the doors into the stairwell and looked down. A lot more boots coming up. He caught glimpses as they made turns at the corners; he saw vests, assault rifles, and shotguns. Cabot had a tactical team in place after all. They were pouring up the stairs and out onto the third floor. Fifteen, twenty guys easy. He glanced at Sara. Her mouth was open and she was breathing heavily. Blake had never seen her nervous before, but this wasn't exactly how he'd wanted the day to go himself. He leaned in, and they kissed. It was fierce, their lips smashed together like two cars in a head-on collision.

When they broke apart, he looked into her eyes.

"Relax," he said. "I got this, okay?"

She nodded.

Blake looked over the stairwell. The cops had stopped coming up, it looked clear. He started worked his way down, his body hugging the outside wall in case anyone looked up and saw them. Sara picked up what he was doing and did the same. She had no training, but she learned fast.

195

At the half landing, he paused and glanced down to the second floor exit. A female cop stood there holding a 9mm. Her body faced toward him, but her head and arm were turned sideways, at the stair door. She was aiming her gun low at the floor. It was the stance of someone nervous about shooting one of their own by mistake. After a moment, he realized it was the officer he'd flirted with earlier at the elevator. She now wore a bullet-proof vest and a helmet. The vest had an SCPD patch across the front. Cabot had called in a few markers. Still, they had to be stretched thin if they'd left her all alone.

He pocketed Barnes' automatic and leaned around the corner.

"Hey, miss!"

Her whole body snapped around, weapon aimed at his head.

"It's okay, I'm a doctor."

She seemed to recognize him, and lowered her gun.

"You can't be here, sir. We have a situation."

"Can we keep going down?" Blake said. "I need to treat my patient and I'm locked out of critical care. She needs painkillers."

The cop looked back and forth between him and the stair door.

"I guess so."

Blake stood from his crouched position and waved Sara over. She put her arm around his neck, and he put his arm around her waist, as if he were helping her to walk. The last time the cop saw them, Sara had been in a wheelchair. As they came down the stairs, the cop ignored them. She was there to guard the door, she couldn't afford to be distracted. As they passed, her head turned toward him. Her eyes had a smile in them, a sparkle.

She liked him.

"Thank you," he said. "Be careful."

She didn't reply, but her cheeks colored. They were past her now, but he kept his arm around Sara and their uneven shuffling gate. They had to keep the descent sounding the same in case the cop heard their step pattern change and became suspicious. It might occur to her later that they hadn't made that sound as they'd approached, but that would be her problem. Nobody covered the next door and they exited the stairs onto the second floor. The corridor was empty; the code silver had cleared everyone out.

"I notice you didn't hit *her* over the head," Sara said.

"She was wearing a helmet."

He looked around, orientating himself with the layout of the building then set off, fast, along the corridor. Sara had to half-jog to keep up with him.

"Admit it," she said. "You thought she was cute."

"There's no winning with you, is there?"

"You got that right, mister."

They fell into an awkward silence. The cop had looked good with the riot gear on and her gun out, but she was no Sara. He hadn't thought she was the jealous type, but stress comes out in different ways. He came up to a nurses' station. It was abandoned like everything else, but someone had left so quickly they'd knocked over their chair. He felt the presence of people everywhere, just out of sight, hiding. Waiting for the all-clear. Sara lagged behind. From her facial expression, he got the feeling this was deliberate, a protest.

"You know, it's not going to take them long to realize we're not on the third floor and if they talk to my girlfriend back there, someone might work it out."

"Keep going smart guy. Maybe you'll wake up dead."

"You're so damn hot when you're angry."

At the end of the corridor he opened a door into wide, brightly lit room. A heavyset woman lay sleeping on a bed. There was an outside chance she was pregnant, but he'd been wrong about such things before. People were all sorts of shapes, and more were her shape than his. Beside her was a long rectangular window.

"What are we doing here, Aidan?"

Blake turned to face Sara.

"Like that detective said, it's a lockdown. No one in or out."

"That doesn't answer my question."

"No," he said. "I suppose it doesn't."

He walked over to the window and looked down.

A platform extended out beneath them over the hospital's entrance. It wasn't exactly how he'd pictured it. The drop was greater than he anticipated, between fifteen and twenty feet. Beyond the platform were lines of police vehicles, their strobes flashing. There were so many of them, it looked like the Fourth of July. Blake found himself thinking about Thorne. His old friend's mind worked on a different level to his; Thorne saw options and alternatives he couldn't. Blake knew his strength *was* his strength, but it was also his weakness. Because he could physically dominate people, he relied on brute force to solve all his problems. This situation called for something else, one of Thorne's ideas.

Blake turned to face Sara and his face split in half with a grin.

Over her shoulder, in the hallway, he saw a sprinkler head sticking out the ceiling. It was perfect. Hospitals feared two things more than any other; fire, and explosions. Evacuating a building like this was a logistical nightmare. Patients could not be easily moved, and there weren't enough people to move them safely. Were they even allowed to use the elevator?

Sara frowned. "What you smiling at?"

"I just had an idea," he said.

Her head tilted back, her chin sticking out.

"No kidding. I guess this is why I never see you smile."

The problem was it would be obvious to everyone that a fire alarm was no more than his escape plan. He was going to have to sell it as the real deal. He placed the detective's Glock and the dog bone on the table in front of the sleeping woman and began to take off the doctor's white coat. The disguise had served its purpose.

"See if you can find cleaning supplies. Something flammable."

Sara nodded slowly, understanding. He dropped the lab coat onto a chair next to the bed, knowing that when he turned back to the door, Sara would be gone. She liked being involved, but she didn't like being told what to do. He supposed they had that in common. It had been a mistake to bring her, he'd endangered her for no reason. It would've been more difficult without her, but there would've been a way if he'd thought about it long enough. He pulled the scrub top off over his head, dumped it on top of the coat, then took off the scrub pants.

He needed to think clearly, free from irritation.

The woman on the bed was going to be a problem. There was no chance at all that she'd sleep through what he had planned. He considered using the dog bone on her while Sara was out the room, but dismissed the idea. Sara had a point, it wasn't right hitting women, particularly if they were asleep. This is how it was when they fought, he'd resent what she said, then realize later she was right. He saw the bed had wheels at the head end. He lifted the foot of the bed up carefully and pulled. The bed was heavy, but it rolled easily enough along the floor. He continued to roll the bed across the room and through the doorway. Out in the corridor, he pushed it in front of the stair doors and wedged it into the space so that it blocked the doorway. If Cabot's men decided to come this way, it might buy them vital extra time.

Sara pushing a cleaning cart toward him.

"I wasn't sure what to bring, so brought everything."

"Perfect."

Back inside the room, he took a steel bucket off the cart and put the doctor's scrubs into it. They took up quite a lot of space, so he pressed them down with his shoe and put the lab coat on top. Might as well get rid of DNA evidence. He looked through the bottles of industrial cleaner and solvent on the cart. He hadn't heard of any of them, but judging by the labels they all appeared to be flammable. He poured a gallon container over the clothing, making sure there was an even spread. The fumes rose up into his face, making him cough. When he was through, he took out his knife and cut the plastic bottle into strips.

"What're you doing?"

"Burning plastic creates thick smoke and makes the fire last longer."

"Nice," she said. "You learn that in the Marines?"

198

"Inglewood."

He laid the strips of plastic out over the lab coat, like chicken on a caesar salad. Seeing the bottle lid, he threw that in too. He considered adding the lids from all the other bottles. The plastic used to make lids created the best smoke, but they burned poorly. He decided what he had was enough, he couldn't risk the fire being smothered by its own smoke. The hotter the fire, the better the smoke would rise and be seen. Blake stood up, his head swimming from the fumes, then carried the bucket out into the hall. If he put it right out in the open, the sprinklers would put it out long before any fire crews showed up. It would also be easy to extinguish using a fire blanket, something well within the grasp of hospital staff.

He pressed the button for the elevator.

"Where are we going?"

He turned to her. "Nowhere."

The doors slid open. It was empty.

"Okay," he said. "Hold the doors for me."

He got in and looked up at the escape hatch in the ceiling. He flipped it open with one hand and lifted the bucket over his head and through the hatch. Above his head it became heavy and difficult to position. His hands shook as they moved the bucket. The door began to close and Sara stopped them and they opened again. He took a paper napkin out his pocket and lit it with his Zippo. The doors closed and chimed as they once again met with Sara's hand. The elevator was beginning to get pissed off. He tossed the lit napkin into the bucket and heard the fire *woof* into life. The elevator shaft was lit by flickering orange flames. He closed the hatch and stepped off the elevator. The doors closed, though it didn't move as no buttons had been pressed. Soon, smoke would begin pouring out through the doors on the floor above, where the cops were.

"You want to do the honors with the sprinklers?"

Sara smiled. "Hell, yeah."

He threw her his Zippo and she caught it one handed.

"Move fast or you'll get really wet."

She looked at him, deadpan.

"That never bothered you before."

He laughed and turned, so he was walking backward down the corridor away from her. He wanted to increase his distance from the cone of water. She had no idea what was coming. She stood on her toes, right arm extended, and held the lighter's flame under the sprinkler. It took about ten seconds to go off, and maybe another two for her to cross the floor to where he stood, but it was all it took to soak through her top and make it transparent.

"Oh my god, that was intense."

Blake said nothing. She looked fantastic. He wondered if there'd be a way to replicate this look another time when he was better placed to do something about it.

She frowned. "Why's the alarm not ringing?"

"Some of these systems take up to 40 seconds."

He'd only just finished speaking when the alarm rang. It was deafening.

"Or less," he continued.

They ran back to the room. He pulled a fire axe off the wall as he passed it. The axe was light and well balanced. It had a chopping blade, and a pointed end. It was the point he needed. They walked into the room and he crossed the floor to the window. He stood side-on to the glass and took a couple of practice half swings with the axe, like he was warming up for a baseball pitch. He swung for real with all his strength. The window exploded in every direction, hitting him with a blast of air and fragmented glass. Behind him, the door to the room slammed shut like a gunshot.

"Jesus!" he said.

His hands were covered in small cuts, and he felt some on his face as well. He checked to see if Sara was okay and saw only anger. He turned away without comment. Any conversation that started now would end in an argument, he knew that much. The rush of air through the opening continued, buffeting him and creating a strange sound inside the room. He used the chopping edge of the axe to clean up the edges of the window frame, then leaned out through the opening and looked down.

The platform looked farther away than ever.

Sara came over and stood next to him.

"Aidan, I'm sorry but there's no way."

Rage was building inside him. Not because she was wrong, but because he knew she was right. He'd gone to all this effort, and it was for nothing. This was his backup plan, and he didn't have another. The drop was survivable, he was certain of it, but it would certainly break both their legs. Maybe worse. Some falls, you could lose your legs altogether. He'd rather go out in a hail of bullets, than down that route. Over the top of the fire alarm, he now heard the sound of fire trucks. Sirens and honking horns. They'd be here any minute, whatever he was going to do, he had to do it quickly. Blake sighed. If only there was some way to get closer to the platform before they dropped, the rest would take care of itself.

A smile spread across his face.

"Have you seen *Die Hard*?"

THIRTY-ONE

Cabot stood looking through the smashed hospital window into the far distance. He'd been standing in the same position for several minutes. At first, he'd been trying to think of anything positive to come out of the situation, but it soon became clear that there was nothing. The whole thing was an unmitigated disaster, and there was no way of putting any of it in a good light. It had probably already hit the news. He imagined Thorne sitting with his feet up, laughing at the television, all his worries over. Then his thoughts turned to Mancuso, the SAC of the FBI field office in San Francisco. There'd be another long telephone call, not just pushing for a seat at the table, but for complete control.

Is this room where my career ends?

"You've really screwed the pooch this time, Victor."

He turned to see Sheriff Carson standing behind him.

Between them, running across the width of the room, was a fire hose. It ran from the hall, through the door and out the window. It was painfully obvious what had happened, yet he hadn't foreseen it as an escape route.

"Let me explain."

Carson held up his hand to cut him off.

"There's no need, I saw it on television. That woman delayed you and your men in the lobby with her legal nonsense and you were unable to respond in time. Then, while you were searching the building, the Fire Department breached your lockdown and allowed those responsible to escape. Is that about right?"

It was like music entering Cabot's ears.

"That's it exactly!"

The crow's feet around the sheriff's eyes deepened, his eyes narrowing.

"I'm not an idiot, Victor. I'm just making sure we're both on the same page. The last thing the Sheriff's Office needs is a string of litigation stretching into infinity, which is precisely what we can expect if the truth comes out. Some heat is inevitable, no doubt about it, but we should be

OK so long as we keep roughly to the script."

Cabot nodded. A whitewash was in both their interests. He hadn't considered the legal implications of his botched operation, but it was a fair point. It seemed like these days you could trip on a sidewalk and sue some poor sap for a million dollars.

"I'll make sure our ducks are in a row."

"This needs a light touch, Victor. The press are already sniffing around."

With Carson, there was always an extra comment tossed in at the end like a live grenade. A comment that seemed to be there to remind him who was boss, but which added no new information. He clenched his teeth.

"I *got* it."

"Cabot, I want you to know that I never liked this sting idea of yours. It's not the kind of operation I want under my command. I'll admit, I was curious to see how it would play out. I decided that if it went to shit I could use it as an opportunity to pass this investigation to Miller and move you into his spot at patrol. But we're in a dead zone right now. You bungled this thing so spectacularly that my hands are tied. If I drop you, it looks like I'm admitting we screwed up. To cover your mistakes, I have to keep you on the case, isn't that hilarious?"

Cabot stared at the sheriff and said nothing.

"That's right," Carson continued. "It's *not*. So let me be clear, you got until Monday morning, then you're *done*. That will be enough distance from this farce that it'll appear coincidental to even the softest liberal media types. I'm sure I'll be able to come up with some *other* reason for the change in command, your mistakes pile up by the day."

Cabot pointed his finger at the other man's chest.

"This is *bullshit*. We nearly closed the case today and you know it. If we'd dropped the net on these two clowns the whole thing would've been over. Let's be honest, you *hoped* this would fall apart, it was the only reason you approved it. This is about damaging my reputation ahead of the election. It's no secret I'm planning to run for sheriff, I know you know so you can drop the act."

Carson smiled unpleasantly.

"You have your story, Lieutenant, I have mine."

"Son of a bitch."

"That's the spirit. Now, if you don't mind, I have other matters to deal with that don't require me to look at your face." The sheriff turned and walked away from him toward the door, before turning back. "Oh yeah, I need you to notify Garret's wife before the press release his name. She's a teacher over at Gault Elementary. Get it done in the next twenty minutes, I doubt we can keep the lid on his name any longer than that."

THIRTY-TWO

The trees glowed where light burst in along the edge of the tree line. Thorne checked his watch and smiled. They'd made good time; five miles in thirty five minutes and he didn't feel tired. They entered the clearing with the fallen tree and slowed to a fast walk. The area marked the middle of their run and they typically took a break here before heading back. It was the farthest point from the mansion, and the place where they had the most privacy. The surrounding woodland masked the area on three sides, with the fourth giving a view out over the Pacific. She'd told him once that Ashcroft had never been out this far, and he had no reason to doubt her. Knowing what he had to do, he couldn't think of a better place.

She'd been here often enough that a path had been worn into the ground. In the forest, that path had been wide enough for them to run side by side. It was relatively dark in there and the ground was dry. Nothing much grew between the trees, so the path had widened out over time. The clearing was a different story, the path was narrow and only wide enough for them to travel single file. It didn't seem right to walk on the grass next to this path so he walked behind her. He was a gentleman, he always let her go first.

"Stop looking at my ass," she said.

"I wasn't."

"Yes you were."

"I'm not looking, I'm staring."

Lauren glanced over her shoulder.

"Oh," she said. "My mistake."

When they reached the tree he took off the backpack he was wearing and passed her a bottle of water. She took a long pull from the bottle, her head tilted way back. Her throat pumped up and down as she swallowed. The hairs on his arms stood on end. He turned away from her and looked out to sea.

"It's gorgeous, isn't it? I always meant to come when the sun was setting, but the trees make the journey too dark and Jimmy thinks lions come out at night."

Thorne turned back toward her. "*Lions?*"

"Mountain lions...cougars."

"You ever see any?"

"No," she said, passing the water. "But I've seen their poop."

He wasn't thirsty but drank anyway. Maybe some of her spit was in there, he thought. When he finished, Lauren was stretching her legs. Her right foot up against the tree trunk and she was thrusting forward with the other leg. She was warming up, preparing for the second half of their run. He returned the empty bottle to the backpack and set it carefully next to the tree. Ashcroft's gun was in there, wrapped in a piece of fabric. He hadn't put it there and it didn't give him much comfort. Lauren swapped feet and began thrusting again. He needed to get this done, but he didn't know how to launch into it. She stopped stretching and made a circular movement with her hips, first clockwise, then anti-clockwise.

She glanced at him, then at the backpack on the ground.

"You not getting ready?"

"We need to talk."

She smiled. "Haven't we been talking?"

"I wanted to tell you first, alone."

Her smile faded. "You're leaving, aren't you?"

"It's been three weeks. I have to go."

She sagged before his eyes.

"But those lunatics are still out there. You said it yourself, they'll keep coming until they get what they want. Who will protect me if not you?"

"You need professional security, Lauren. At least five or six guys. James can easily afford it. I'm just a second-rate actor who was in the right place. We got lucky before, I surprised them. Next time they'd be ready for me, they'd take me out with the first shot."

The haunted look returned to her face. It made him feel bad, but he knew that as long as he was here, she'd never be able to move on from the attack. Part of the reason she felt safe with him was because he reminded her of the moment they first met. He would always terrify her as much as he reassured her. He was part of her problem, whether she knew it or not.

"Please, Chris. Just one more week. After that, we'll be in D.C. and everything will return to the way it was. I don't trust anyone else."

"You know this isn't about what I want. I need to go back and deal with the fire investigation. I can't hide up here pretending it didn't happen. When they finally release Kate's body..." He stopped and hung his head. The rage was there again. It was unbearable, as if a nuclear bomb was exploding in his chest and he had to contain its blast. In the days since Kate had died, he'd pictured his hands around Blake's neck many, many times. He was going to kill Blake, he had no doubt about that. He would finish what he started in that hotel bar and nothing would stop him. Lauren put her hand on his arm and squeezed. She was right in front of him now, their running shoes were touching. He took a deep breath and let it out slowly. "I have to arrange Kate's funeral, her mother shouldn't have to do that. She's dead and it's my fault."

There were tears on Lauren's face.

"It's my fault too, isn't it? They did it because you saved me."

"That's not your fault."

She was quiet for a moment, before she spoke again.

"When are you leaving?"

"Tomorrow."

She gasped like he'd punched her in the stomach.

"You can't, not tomorrow." Her eyes ranged about desperately. "That's before Jimmy's birthday! Say you'll stay for that, you're practically the guest of honor."

Thorne had expected this, even allowed for it. She needed time to prepare herself for his absence, hell, maybe they both did. The party was in two days' time, he could give her that. As long as the painting was in play, the Ashcrofts would remain a target. It dawned on him that Blake knew about the birthday party, it was the reason the painting was out the gallery in the first place. Whatever was going to happen, would happen in the next two days. After the party, Blake wouldn't know for sure they still had the painting. Time was running out for him, and that wasn't going to be a good thing for everyone else.

"All right," he said. "I'll stay for the party but that's it, okay?"

Lauren wiped tears away with the back of her hand and nodded.

There was a subtext that had nothing to do with Blake.

Whatever had been building between them, neither of them wanted it to end. He'd assumed his feelings for her had started the night he caught her in the swimming pool; or maybe even as early as the hospital room, but now he knew different. They'd started the moment he first saw her picture online. Something had awakened inside him, something primal, and it was this spark that had made him betray Blake and everything that followed. But it was almost over now. Soon, he'd be leaving and no matter what they might say as he left, he knew they would never see each other again. It would be like death.

Her eyes were closed, but tears still ran down her cheeks.

She was falling apart. He had to say something and make it right with her, but what could he say that wouldn't make everything worse? He didn't like that he was hurting her, but it felt strangely good to know she'd miss him. There was nothing left for him in L.A., not even a home. If there was a way to stay here and be with Lauren, he would. But it wasn't going to happen, it couldn't happen. A dream can only exist as long as you are asleep; sooner or later, you have to wake up. It's the waking up that makes a dream special.

Without thinking, he reached out and placed his hands on her hips. They were perfect, like part of a sports car. The front of her hip bones rose up in smooth curves then sank below the surface as he slid his hands up to the taut, bare skin of her waist. He'd wanted to touch her like this every time he'd seen her in her work-out top. Her bare, golden skin, the muscle tone...it drove him crazy. After a moment, she exhaled a long, jagged breath. He looked up and met her gaze. Her eyes were cooked, gone. She pushed forward so their bodies were pressed together.

Something close to a shiver went down his spine, something amazing.

She looked into his eyes. A rose tint had spread across her cheeks and her lips were swollen and parted. Lauren's eyes dipped to stare at his mouth. It was all the permission he needed. He kissed her. She wrapped her arms around him and clung on as though she feared the kiss would end too soon. Behind her, his hands slid down her back, down the ridges of muscle to her ass. She took this as an invitation to jump on him and wrap her legs around his waist. He wasn't expecting it, and they fell onto the soft grass and rolled over several times. When they stopped, she was on top of him and they were laughing.

"Am I really that heavy?" she asked.

"Give me a break, I was shot in the gut."

"Ooo," she said, in a high voice, "I was shot in the gut!"

"Is that how I sound?"

Lauren gazed into his eyes, amused. Teasing him, daring him. There was still the silvery trace of tears on her cheeks, but her face was transformed. She looked alive, electric. When they'd fallen, her hair had gotten all messed up and the sun lit it up, made it look like feathers. He wanted to run his hands through it, feel that blonde hair sliding between his fingers. It seemed to capture the sunlight itself. He could fix it for her, so it was all back in place. Perhaps tuck some behind her ear, the way she liked it. But Thorne did nothing. He knew he wouldn't fix her hair. Not now, not with her lying on top of him. If he touched her again in even the slightest way, her hair stood to get messed up a lot more than it was already. They'd gone too far. She was married and he considered her husband a friend. That should mean something, it shouldn't just be empty words.

She sat upright and drew her knees up on either side of his rib cage. Her legs were doubled over and he could clearly see the swell of her thigh muscles beneath her hands. Lauren looked casually around the clearing, then back down at him. The message was clear. *We are alone.* She smiled at him and he found himself smiling back.

Her ass was against his groin, the warmth and pressure of it pinned him to the ground. After a moment, she adjusted her position on top of him to give him more space, then lowered herself back down. Thorne was losing control and he knew it. They were on a roller-coaster that was about to nose over the top of the track and race down the other side. They should stop before they did something unforgivable, something they couldn't take back. The more he thought about leaving and never seeing her again, the clearer it became for him.

He was in love with her.

Thorne let out a deep breath; a mixture of sadness and relief.

"Am I hurting you?"

"No, it's just...I realized something is all."

Lauren raised an eyebrow. "What's that?"

"You know," he said, "some things are better left unsaid."

"I disagree. I've been waiting to hear you to say it for weeks."

"I think we're talking about different things."

She rolled onto the ground next to him and stared at the sky.

"We're definitely talking about the same thing, Thorne."

"And...you?"

"Are you serious? You want me to say it after you refused?"

"I mean do you feel the same way, or am I a sad joke?"

She propped herself up on her elbow and looked into his eyes.

"I feel you in my ovaries, Chris. How's that?"

"That's...that's just great."

"I'm inside you."

"Yeah. I guess you are," he said.

"No, really. I donated blood at the hospital."

"That's a weird thing to know, Lauren, but thank you."

Thorne got to his feet and arched his back. He was expecting a flash of pain from his injuries, but there was nothing. Not even the usual crunching pops of his spine lining up, which had become wearily familiar over the last couple of years. He felt good. When he looked down at Lauren he noticed she was staring at the front of his workout pants. Yeah, he felt *really* good. After a beat, she glanced up and smiled sheepishly. She raised her hand and he reached down and pulled her upright. It brought her into the previous kissing position and he immediately stepped backward to give her space. There was a flicker of disappointment on her face but she hid it as quickly as it appeared. He wasn't sure he'd be strong enough a second time around to deny what they both seemed to want.

"So," she said, her tone businesslike. "What now?"

"This doesn't change anything, Lauren."

"Are you kidding me? This changes everything."

"I still have to leave."

"I know."

He frowned. "Then what's different?"

"Isn't it obvious? I'm coming with you."

"But James, all this…"

Thorne spread his arms to indicate everything around them.

Lauren sighed. "Jimmy will barely notice I'm gone. I'm an accessory to him, a clutch purse and nothing more. When he's in the Senate I hardly see him. I never wanted to move to D.C. and become a politician's wife. Going to fundraisers and charity functions, it's not me. Then there's the age thing. When we go to a restaurant people look at me like I'm a whore, I can see it on their faces. I didn't marry him for his money, but that's what people think. He was funny, he treated me right, that's all it was. Sure money doesn't hurt, but I'm tired of the judgement in people's eyes. Why should I have to explain myself to anyone? I wasn't cut out for this; I'm a valley girl and that will never change."

"Lauren, I don't know. I really don't."

"He doesn't love me, Chris. But *you* do."

"Jesus!" he said, then laughed. This was the worst break-up ever.

She stepped closer, then closer again. Her face filled his view, it was quite beautiful. At that moment, nothing else existed but her face and those lips. He debated the merits of kissing her again. He knew he'd made a mistake kissing her before, but he couldn't honestly say he regretted it. Mistakes were like that; you didn't always regret them.

"Hey," she said softly.

He'd wanted to believe he wasn't one of those guys. Guys that took what wasn't theirs to take. But the whole time he'd known it was a lie. He *was* one of those guys. Kate Bloom hadn't been single when they first slept together, she'd been dating a producer on the show. He hadn't let that stop him then, and it had turned out to be the best decision of his life.

"Hey," she said again, a little more forcefully.

It hadn't worked out so well for the other guy. He left the show shortly after, but not before he'd taken some time to practice his golf swing on Thorne's car. He suspected the producer had since then been working against him within the studio to get the show canceled. Perhaps, ultimately succeeding.

"Goddammit, Thorne! Say something."

His eyes came into focus.

"We should head back to the house."

She sighed. "Not about the house, wing nut. About us."

"I'm sorry, Lauren. I'm not that guy anymore."

Her face changed in a split second.

"You think I *belong* to him, is that it?"

"You're married, that still means something."

"I'm talking about leaving him, Chris. Getting a divorce."

He looked at the ground and nodded. It had been different with Kate, she hadn't been married and had only been dating for a couple of months. He'd convinced himself that the producer would quickly get over his setback and find someone else. Producers never seemed to struggle getting beautiful dates. Lauren was married, had been for close to ten years and had a husband that was very much in love with her. If Thorne went along with her plan, Ashcroft would be destroyed. His run for president, his standing within the party, the community. Everything would be wiped out. A man that had let him stay in his home, and become his friend. Kate would be disgusted with him for even thinking about it.

Thorne looked back up, his jaw set.

"We should head back to the house."

THIRTY-THREE

Thorne drove fast, the car's cabin filling with the dull roar of the Maserati at high revs. It was a truly beautiful sound. He was becoming intimately familiar with the roads in the county, of the curves, and the speed he could take them. A speed far higher than the posted limit. He had no destination but the next turn, the next press of the gas pedal. You drive fast enough, it's all you can think about. He drove up the 17 to Los Gatos, down the 9 toward Santa Cruz, then crossing over to rejoin Glen Canyon Road. He noticed little, instead calculating the optimum break points, maximum speed through upcoming curves, and the best way to pass other traffic. He slowed as he approached Ashcroft's mansion once again. Just short of the turn, he pulled the car over and parked. A second or two passed, then it hit him in the gut.

Kate's dead.

It had been right there all along, bubbling under the surface. His conversation with Lauren had brought it all back. The guilt, the rage. He hadn't been there for Kate, he'd been here, falling in love with another man's wife. Thorne opened the door and got out, holding the side of the car for balance. Waves of nausea passed over him, but there was nothing inside to bring up. The OxyContin had seen to that. He closed his eyes and concentrated on his breathing. In through his nose, out through his mouth. The air was fresh and pure. The trees around him had a sharp scent like a freshly squeezed lime.

No matter how fast he drove, or where he went, the truth would be just the same. Kate was gone and there was nothing he could do about it. He heard a horn blast, followed by the suction of a vehicle whipping past him. There'd be time to mourn her later, for now he had other things to deal with that required his full concentration.

He opened his eyes and looked around.

He'd stopped where Blake had parked his van the day he'd seen it from the forest path. He walked around the front of the Maserati and bent down to study the verge. The grass here was all but gone, the earth turned to mud by the tracks of tires coming and going. Some tracks overlapped, others cut across from the side. He had no idea about tread type, but the tire widths were consistent with coming from a single vehicle over a period of time. He stood facing the forest. Lauren's running path weaved around trees, the earth worn down over time. There was no artificial surface or straight lines to catch the eye and it took him a long time to see it. He moved closer to see if it became more visible. It did not, but the sun was low overhead and at a different time of day that situation could change.

He felt something springy under his shoe.

The property boundary fence.

It lay flat along the ground for fifteen feet in both directions. He could see that the nearest post was rotten and would've broken easily. The weight of the post would act as a lever against the base with a single result, what he saw in front of him. He supposed other sections of fence around the perimeter might also be down, but the proximity to where Blake parked and Lauren's path bothered him. It seemed unlikely that the two events could be unrelated, yet it realistically made no difference. The fence was old and had not been designed with security in mind. At best, it marked a property line and kept forest animals within from wandering onto the highway. Thorne got back in the car and sat there for a moment, his hands resting lightly on the wheel.

There were two possible causes.

Option one. As he'd discovered, the vans used by television networks were similar in size to Blake's. When he had first arrived at the mansion, reporters had camped out here for close on a week. This verge would have offered a good spot to cover the entrance, just as it had for Blake. It was also easy to imagine the fence becoming damaged by vans reverse-turning to head back into Santa Cruz.

Option two. Blake had been here multiple times and had deliberately damaged the fence in order to make some future breach easier. When he thought about it, the fact that the path wasn't obvious from the road gave him little comfort. If Blake had spent time here, eventually he would've needed to relieve himself and the forest offered privacy. From there, it wasn't hard to imagine him stumbling across the path and seeing it as a perfect method of entry, just as he had.

Thorne started the car and was about to rejoin the asphalt again when four trucks rolled past in convoy. The trucks slowed to a walking pace then swung across the narrow road using both lanes and in through Ashcroft's gate. The sides of the vehicles were decorated with logos for a catering and corporate events company in Santa Cruz. He shook his head. This, he supposed, was how millionaires prepared for their fiftieth birthday party. He tagged the Maserati onto the end of the line and followed the last truck in through the gate.

*

Thorne stood next to the Ashcrofts in front of the mansion as a crew of people worked to transform the mansion into what appeared to be a Christmas cake. A short man in a tuxedo bustled around giving orders, while carrying out a separate conversation via a cell phone headset. Instead of punching the man repeatedly in the face, Thorne accepted a glass of Scotch that James Ashcroft held out for him. He'd noticed that since he'd stopped using Fentanyl, he'd started drinking alcohol again. He took a sip. The glass had three fingers of whisky and no ice. The senator was a no-ice guy. It tasted a lot like a cigar had been put out in it, if there was a good way of that happening.

"Not bad," he said, nodding.

"It's 40 years old. I couldn't find one that was 50."

Thorne studied the contents of his glass. When he was born it had already been in a barrel for four years. He couldn't imagine what difference all that time could make, except for the price the senator paid for it. He looked back at Ashcroft.

"James, can I have a word in private?"

"Of course."

Thorne noticed Lauren glaring at him. He didn't know which she disliked more, the idea that she was being excluded, or the idea that he and James might be friends. They walked away from the house onto the large area of grass that was spread out before it. He was keen to get down to business and the senator walked slower than an old lady with a cane.

"Look, I may be out of line here," Thorne said, "but I wish you'd warned me you were having all these people here today. There's like thirty people crawling all over your house doing God-knows-what. It's a security nightmare."

Ashcroft smiled.

"You've nothing to worry about, I've used these guys for years."

"How many people know about your birthday party?"

"Most of the county probably know about it from previous years' press coverage. If it's been covered by the national press this year then you're talking millions."

"Christ, OK. Now some of those people will also know that you always use the same catering company, right?"

Ashcroft seemed to think about this.

"You're suggesting the clown gang might have *infiltrated* the catering company and are here now, is that right?"

"James, if they were here we'd already be dead. That's the truth. I'm

212

saying we need to be smart. I think we can assume the gang know about this party. They'll also know you return to Washington some time after it, and that their time is running out."

"What do you suggest?"

"Tonight at the party, have two armed guards at the gate and six more around the building. The two at the gate are for show. It tells them you have security, that you're not some sitting duck. The goal is to dissuade them from attacking in the first place."

"I can't do that, Chris. My whole platform is anti-gun. It would end my candidacy."

"Then have the guards dress like Secret Service. It makes you look presidential and still sends the gang a message. It's not just your safety here, it's your friends as well."

Ashcroft nodded. "I hate this, but I'll do it."

"When *do* you guys go back to Washington?"

"I haven't decided. Usually I leave a couple of days after my birthday. Lauren stays on here for almost another month, before following me over in time for Christmas."

"James, there's no way. You can't leave Lauren here alone."

"I realize that. She spoke about visiting friends in L.A. this year but I'm not sure." Ashcroft paused, a new light in his eyes. "The two of you should go together in your car. She feels safe with you around and she hates flying. What do you think? It's perfect, no?"

"Uh, sure."

"Good, then it's settled."

Ashcroft couldn't see what was happening, but he could. Lauren wasn't giving up. She was engineering a situation that would allow them to spend this period before the holidays together. He drank from his glass to hide as much of his face as possible. She might meet a few of her friends, take some pictures with them, get a few stories to make it sound good, but most of the time she would spend with him.

Sensing their conversation was at an end, the senator turned and they walked back toward the house together. Thorne was relieved to see that Lauren was gone from her spot out front. She thought they could sneak around and not get noticed, but that was ridiculous after the rolling TV coverage they'd had. It seemed to him like the press had already got wind of the potential for romance between them. He needed to disentangle himself from Lauren and her husband as soon as possible. He couldn't imagine having her stashed in some hotel room while he went to Kate's funeral. The idea of it offended him. He was crazy about her, sure, but it needed to stop while it could be stopped.

As with his burned deal with Blake, he didn't want anyone to get hurt.

He'd convince her to go to Washington with her husband. She'd be safer there anyway. He and Blake had unfinished business and he was certain his old friend would find him and make him pay. There was no personal animosity between Blake and the Ashcrofts, so it was unlikely he would pursue them across the country to settle some imagined score.

His cell phone rang, derailing his thought process. He dug his cell out his pocket and in what was becoming an automated manner, hung up without answering. The number wasn't one he recognized and he wasn't in the mood for what he was certain would be a prank call. An increasing number of people seemed to know his number, he would have to change it. Before he could turn the device off, it rang again. Whoever it was, they were persistent. He looked at the display. The caller had an 818 prefix. That made the caller from North Hollywood, Burbank, Studio City, somewhere around there. This was the problem with calls, he thought, there was always the chance they could be important. A lot of industry people drew their water up there. He decided to answer.

To be an actor you had to also be, at heart, an optimist.

"Don't hang up."

A woman's voice. Quick, familiar.

"Who *is* this?"

"Jocelyn Cooper, KCAL 9."

It was the reporter that had been riding Cabot's ass about the shoot-out, the one he'd spoken to at the marina. His heart sink; it wasn't a job offer after all. His instinct was to hang up again and avoid any calls from her in the future, but he decided to hear her out. He'd liked her reports, her style. She was smart and could be a useful ally, or a powerful enemy depending on how this went. It never hurt to have more friends.

"Are you still there?"

"Yeah," he said.

"All right, we need to talk."

"I can't give interviews, it's a condition of the immunity deal."

"This won't be an interview. There will be no cameras, no mikes, no crew. Nothing like that. Just me and you." She paused, waiting for him to respond, but he said nothing. It wasn't clear to him what this could be if not an interview. Her voice came back again, her tone harder, more threatening. "I've got something you want to see Mr Thorne, make no mistake."

He sighed. Just what he needed, another problem.

"When?"

"Tomorrow. I'm at the *Dream Inn*, it's right down on the beach. Come around 8 a.m. I'll meet you in the lobby."

"Fine."

She paused for a moment.

"I hope you'll be more communicative than this when we meet, Mr

214

Thorne. Grunting one word answers isn't going to cut it. We have things to discuss."

"What do you expect from me? I'm an actor without a script. A glass of water has more personality."

She laughed, then began to cough. He was funny, but not that funny. He disconnected the call before the coughing ended. She hadn't said what the meeting was about, but he had to accept that it wasn't going to be good news. His knowledge of her so far was based solely on several short segments on the news, but he knew she was dangerous. He made sure to turn off his phone before anyone else called him. He'd know soon enough what she had, and what she wanted. Until then, he had other things to worry about.

THIRTY-FOUR

This time it was just Thorne on his own. Blake watched him move through the trees, careful to stay hidden from his old friend. Thorne was later than usual today and he wasn't running, though he was still wearing those ridiculous running pants. If it were anyone else, Blake would've brushed this time change aside, but he *knew* Thorne. Knew how he liked to structure his day. He'd been doing it since before the Corps. Something was going on. Either Thorne suspected what he was up to, or he was just taking precautions before the party.

It didn't matter to Blake, it all worked to his benefit.

The sling was gone from Thorne's arm, which hung awkwardly at his hip as if only partly connected. The news networks had covered his injuries in great detail. Whatever threat he'd been before, that was over now. The wound to his shoulder alone likely guaranteed him victory over the actor in any unarmed conflict. A single heavy blow to this area would be enough to wipe him out. But all this had been the case the last time they'd met when Thorne had attacked him with the knife. You could never write someone off, take their abilities for granted. As soon as you did that, you lost.

Thorne was close now, moving to his position. Sticking to the path as it twisted through the trees toward the highway. He could hear Thorne breathing but didn't risk taking a look. Not long now. He squatted down slightly, ready to pounce.

This time, *he'd* have the element of surprise.

The actor walked past at a fast pace. Thorne's head started to turn toward him, perhaps sensing his presence, but it was too late. Blake flew through the air at him and they collided and rolled on the forest floor. Thorne was disorientated and Blake managed to punch him four times to the head before he reacted and fought back. By then, his nose was bleeding profusely across his face, and Blake had him pinned to the ground. His weight was too much for Thorne to overcome, so he concentrated on landing blows to Blake's face and neck. Thorne was strong, but his swing was limited and his arm weak. Blake leaned forward.

"Brother, you gotta learn which battles to fight and which to let go."

Thorne screwed up his face, his teeth clenched together. He'd never stop fighting, not until he was dead. Blake respected that. He looked for Sara, this was her cue. To his surprise, Thorne brought his fist down hard on his leg wound, causing his body to contract in agony. He then lifted his knee fast into Blake's groin and a white hot flash of pain went up his body. Thorne flipped him over and scrambled to his feet before kicking him in the stomach. It was a major impact, and it spun him around. Blake got on his hands and knees, his body ready to vomit. He turned to look up at Thorne and saw he was lined up to kick him in the face. He was going to finish him. Finally, he saw Sara behind Thorne. She stepped forward and touched her Taser to the actor's neck. He immediately collapsed to the ground. She sank down next to him and held it against his neck again. One second. Two seconds. Three seconds. Blake could hear the crackle of electricity.

"That's enough," Blake said.

She ignored him and kept it going. *Click, click, click.* It had to be at least ten seconds now. Thorne's arms and legs were as stiff as the trees around them.

"Sara! Goddammit, we need him alive."

She stopped and looked up. There was a sad expression on her face. Thorne had beaten him before her eyes, forcing her to rescue him. He sighed. She could think what she wanted. The man had punched him in a stab wound and kneed him in the balls. She didn't know what that was like, she couldn't. He got to his feet using his hand on one knee to steady himself. Nausea surged like a tide through his battered body. Thorne lay still and unmoving on the forest floor. That wouldn't last either, he thought. They had to move quickly.

"You got the cable ties?"

Sara seemed to emerge from the spell she was under and nodded. She pulled Thorne's arms behind his back and slipped the cable ties around his wrists. Blake approached, ready to assist. Thorne's face was pressed into the ground, but his right eye locked onto him, the only part of his body he could control. They'd decided to use two interlocking ties like the cop at the hospital. When the second tie was secured, Blake knelt down in front of Thorne so they could see each other properly.

"Sorry about this old man. I knew you wouldn't agree if I just asked nicely."

The muscles in Thorne's jaw were clearly defined through his cheeks. He couldn't reply, not yet. The electricity had clenched his muscles and it would take a while longer for them to relax back to normal. He smiled and buddy-slapped Thorne on his wounded shoulder.

217

Back in the van, Blake drove carefully at the posted limit. No point getting pulled over by a cop with a chip on his shoulder. He had a spot picked out in his mind, a place off the road less than a mile away where they could be left alone. It was a parking lot made out of dirt in among the trees where you could go to walk dogs or whatever else. If things didn't work out the way he hoped, it would give him options.

"What's this *old man* shit?"

Blake looked back over his shoulder. Sara was in the back with Thorne. He sat against the side of the van, next to the wheel. She stood over him, one hand braced against the roof, the other holding the Taser.

"Why don't you ask him?"

"I'm asking *you.*"

Thorne nodded.

"Blake found out I was born twenty three minutes before him. Same hospital. He thinks it's funny to call me old. Sometimes he throws *brother* in too, like we're twins or something."

"It means he likes you, Thorne. Don't you know that?"

Blake's eyes stayed on the actor a moment longer waiting for a reply, but none came. It was true, or had been once. They'd been brothers long before they'd joined the Corps, the only family either of them really had. They'd looked out for each other when they were growing up. Alone they would have been picked off, vulnerable to other street kids, but together they survived. Despite everything that had happened, he knew he'd be sad when he put a bullet through Thorne's head. The man had probably been his only true friend his whole life and there would never be another. Blake spoke without turning his head.

"I want you to know something. This ain't the end, you feel me? All I want is for you to fix up the gear, tell me what to do with it. After that, you leave town. You and me, we got history and that means something. If you're sticking around to protect your friends, there's no need. I got no interest in hurting them either. Fact is, it would bring too much heat. Maybe you convince them to go out on their stupid boat, make it easier for everyone. Empty house. We go in take the picture and go. How's that sound?"

Again Thorne said nothing. It was obvious he didn't believe him and Blake couldn't blame him. There was no trust left, Sara had blown it away with that fire. That Kate Bloom thing had gotten out of control. Well, so be it. The motherfucker had stabbed him in the leg and given him a limp that might be permanent. Why should he offer Thorne words of comfort? Why should he try to make anything easier for him?

Blake noticed cars were backed up behind them, snaking through the bends together. It was that kind of road, only the brave or the insane passed other vehicles. He put on his turn signal and pulled into the end of a road junction so they could pass. He waited until they were clear and out of sight before rejoining the highway.

No sense advertising where they were headed.

The parking lot was at the end of a short dirt track. No signs marked the entrance, which possibly explained why it hadn't been packed with tourists like others he'd seen. Blake swung off the highway and drove slowly over the uneven surface. The trees pressed in close on either side, their branches brushing the sides of the van. When he saw a place like this, all he could think was *good place to dump a body*. Instinct told him that something was wrong. Something was different to when he'd been here before. Sure enough, as they rounded the curve he saw a man, a woman, and a young girl standing next to a Volvo. The man was in the process of pulling a mountain bike off a roof rack and all three turned to look at the van. Blake lifted his right hand off the wheel in a half-hearted wave. The man smiled weakly in acknowledgment, before speaking quickly to his wife.

The family left along the trail, into the trees. It was clear that this Volvo-man knew he and the van didn't belong here. The man set off with his cycling helmet still hanging on his handlebars. He didn't want to wait the extra seconds required to put it on. Blake turned to see Thorne standing behind him, watching them leave. It was perfect. This family gave him some missing leverage, that little girl in particular. He smiled and it seemed to him as though Thorne understood. Leaving the engine running, he swung open the driver's door and stepped down onto the hard, baked earth. He drew his Glock and slid back the side door. Thorne was right there in front of him, less than three feet away. The actor's eyes glanced briefly at the gun, then back up to his eyes. He'd know that any change in the dynamic was an opportunity for him, Blake had to be careful.

"Back up, I'm coming in."

Thorne backed wordlessly away from him, but he didn't get far because of the narrow bench Blake had set up down the opposite side of the van. He put his hands down and gripped the edge of the wood. For the first time, Blake noticed that the cable ties were gone. Thorne was good. He'd have to be careful. The gap at the door was tight, made worse by Thorne's height and long arms. If he was quick, Thorne could grab him around the neck and use him as a shield, preventing Sara from firing. He stepped into the van and moved quickly past Thorne to the back, where Sara stood in a low squat, two-handed firing position.

Thorne looked casually through the open side door, calculating the odds. Two steps to freedom. It was an obvious move, but he could still rely on a half second lag before they would react and fire. If they wanted him to complete the job enough, maybe they wouldn't fire at all but hope to re-capture him. To Blake, Thorne was completely transparent. He'd known him for too long to be surprised by anything.

"You wouldn't make it," Blake said. "Not even if one of our guns jammed."

Thorne turned to him, his face calm. Bored.

"It's funny. You assholes have the guns, but it's like you're afraid of me."

"I guess it seems that way. We were waiting a while and drank a bunch of Red Bull while we waited. I can practically see the future here."

"What was that bullshit fight about when you have guns?"

"When I pictured our little meeting in my head, all I saw was you charging me down. Forcing me to shoot. If things were the other way around and I saw you appear in front of me with a gun, I'd figure that you were there to kill me. I wanted to subdue you first, then tell you what I wanted. If I wanted you dead I could've made that happen a dozen times over by now, you must realize that."

"Right," Thorne said. "How are your balls?"

"They've been better. That was a bitch move, brother."

Blake spoke to Sara without taking his eyes off Thorne.

"How about you give us some space, babe."

"Sure you can manage this big guy on your own?"

Blake felt his cheeks redden. "Yeah."

She stared at him for several long seconds, her eyes burning. Sara wasn't military, she had no concept of chain of command. Either they were equal in everything, or he was an asshole. In hindsight, it probably also explained the string of jobs she'd had that lasted less than a week. After a moment, she nodded and backed out the rear door out of sight.

Thorne turned from her to look at him.

"You know she's a Section 8, right? Soon as you get the twelve mill she's going to kill your sorry ass and take the money. The way I picture it, she'll wait until you're asleep then carve you up like a Thanksgiving turkey. First thing you'll know about it, she'll be straddling you naked and covered in blood as the knife plunges repeatedly into your chest."

Blake tightened his hand around the pistol.

"You want to be careful what you say about my girl, Thorne."

"I can see that you've thought about it. The woman's bat shit crazy, but you don't care. Maybe it's love. Maybe when you fuck it's like breaking in a wild horse. Who knows?" Thorne paused to smile. "It must be something real special."

Blake didn't know what he hated more; the fact that Thorne had assessed Sara Dawson so accurately, or the fact that he'd made him smile.

Breaking in a wild horse, I like that. Kind of why we're here, isn't it? The painting of that mental horse. Let's skip all the bullshit and get down to business. How about it? I got the stuff you asked for. I'd rather be gone before that family comes back here with their bicycles and their questions.

Things could work out badly for them if that happened and I know you don't want that."

The actor's body seemed to inflate like he was preparing to launch himself across the floor at him, but it lasted only a second. There'd be only one winner in this fight, there was too much space between them. In a head-on assault, Blake could empty the entire magazine into Thorne before he could reach his position. Attacking him was suicide. Thorne let out a slow breath, then nodded. He'd do what he was told right up to the moment he thought he could escape, or he could take him out.

Thorne opened the first case and took out the defibrillator.

He watched Thorne work at the makeshift bench. The task seemed to relax him, removing him from his immediate situation and into the world of electronics. His face calm, his hands steady. Blake could almost forget that any tension existed between them. The light was poor, even with the side door open and a small lamp turned on. The actor removed the paddles from one of the defibrillators and attached a computer lead. The interior filled with the smell of hot solder.

"So what's the plan?" Blake asked.

Thorne continued to work as he spoke.

"Ashcroft's security system is high end, but it runs through the same server as his home network. This creates a hardware link between the ethernet ports in every room, and the cameras protecting the painting. I'm almost certain he's forgotten about the wired network, everything's wireless these days. Phones, tablets, laptops...nobody uses ethernet anymore. One of the first things he did was give me the Wi-Fi password so I could get online." Thorne paused to blow on a solder connection. "Anyway, *the plan* is to use this defibrillator to simulate a lightning strike on his network which will blow the internal fuse in his router. The cameras will be undamaged, but no recording will take place."

Blake grinned. "Nice."

Thorne seemed to finish what he was working on and sat back on the cheap office chair. It creaked dramatically under his weight. Blake frowned.

"Why'd you ask for four of these if you only needed one?"

Throne sighed, like he was dealing with a child.

"This one is for the router, these *other* ones are for mains power. You'll need the juice from all three to knock out the power breaker. If I knew where the isolator switches were located it would be a different story, but I've not seen anything like that and there's only so much sneaking around I can do without looking suspicious."

"Okay."

"Anyway, once the power is out you have 90 seconds to cut the phone line before the system resets. There's a pole out on the highway. Take that out, and the alarm can't call for help. Do *not* cut the phone line first."

221

"What difference does it make?"

"The system is connected in real time to the alarm company via satellite internet. If you cut the phone line first, it can still raise the alarm. The landline is a failsafe; SOS calls only, no live data. Since the first defibrillator takes out the router, the alarm can't do shit when you take out the phone line."

Blake thought about this for a moment.

"Why doesn't the alarm use the landline when we hit the router?"

"The Ashcrofts aren't in the property most of the year. Eight months of the year, they're in D.C. The alarm is smart enough to recognize certain events, like a lightning strike or a power outage as being no cause for concern. The phone line on its own would also be fine because the live alarm data from the satellite would still show everything was OK; but if you're on camera holding a cutting disc then that's not going to hold up. Everything has to be in the right order to look natural."

Blake nodded. This wasn't his field, but what Thorne said made sense. When he didn't say any more, the actor resumed his work on the remaining defibrillators.

The hunched-over position had caused Thorne to sweat through his T-shirt, making it cling to his body. Blake could see his muscles flexing through the thin cotton material as he moved. Thorne was larger than he'd previously thought, possibly even a match for his own build. He fed this into his own calculations. Thorne was four inches taller than him. In a fist fight, Thorne would be able to hit him two inches farther away. It wasn't much, but at the same distance Thorne could hit him with more power. He'd had a taste of that in the hotel bar, and that was only for *threatening* Kate.

Blake thought back on the earlier fight. He'd caught Thorne by surprise and landed some brutal blows before the actor had a chance to hit back. Despite this, Thorne had still managed to gain the upper hand. Without Sara, the fight might have had a very different ending. The relaxed man he saw in front of him was an illusion. Thorne was waiting for an opportunity to kill him. Without thinking about it, the Glock moved to aim center mass.

"You know you can't shoot me with that thing, right?"

Thorne missed nothing.

"I told you, brother. This ain't where it ends."

"I know what you *told* me. I just don't like having a gun aimed at my chest while I'm trying to work. It's distracting."

"You've had worse."

Thorne swung around in the chair.

"Look, Blake, aim it at the goddam floor or you can do the rest of this yourself. I'm not going to be blown away because you've sneezed. In case

222

it's not obvious to you, the plan requires me to walk these things in through Ashcroft's front door and set them up. If I'm dead, so are your chances of getting the twelve million."

Blake swore silently to himself.

When Thorne had laid out the plan there'd been a niggle at the back of his head, but he hadn't put his finger on what it was. Blake had to hand it to him. Thorne had devised a plan that needed him to be alive until the end. But that didn't work for him, he had his own plans.

He lowered the pistol toward the floor of the van.

"How's this buddy? You like this better?"

"Why don't you just eat it? Save me the trouble later on."

Blake smiled. After everything that had happened, he still liked Thorne.

THIRTY-FIVE

Thorne sat on the edge of his bed staring into Lauren's eyes. She had a bowl of warm water on her lap and she was using it to clean up his face with cotton balls. Her proximity forced him to spread his legs, which was all the more uncomfortable since James Ashcroft stood in the doorway watching.

"You're sure it was the man from the mall?" Ashcroft asked.

"A hundred percent."

They'd already changed into their party clothes. Ashcroft a tuxedo, Lauren a blue-black evening dress with too much material in some areas, and not nearly enough in others. It seemed to Thorne that women's clothing fell into two groups; the type that hid the owner's body, and the type that exaggerated it. All of Lauren's clothes were from the latter group. She wet another cotton ball and he tried not to stare at her cleavage.

"We need to tell Victor about this immediately."

Thorne's eyes zipped back to Ashcroft.

"*Cabot?* No way. You know he's trying to frame me, right? To him, this will be everything he wants to hear."

"You can describe these people to him, he needs that information."

"James, it happened so quickly. I don't have much to add to the description I already gave him from the time at the mall. All you think about in a fight is not getting hit and how to hit the other guy. You register pain and little else."

"Why do you suppose they let you live?"

Lauren turned sharply to her husband. "Jimmy!"

"No," Thorne said, "it's a fair question. The honest answer is I don't know. The man was having problems breathing after our fight and probably wanted to get out of there."

Lauren leaned closer and lay her forearm on his thigh for support. He could feel the warmth of it through the cotton of his running pants. It was both casual and intimate at the same time. Her back hid it from her husband, so it was unlikely to be accidental. All he knew, was that he was increasingly enjoying it and that soon it may become obvious.

"Lauren, it'll wash off in the shower."

"I hate that this happened. I want to help."

"It's fine. I've been in fights before, this is no different."

Ashcroft sighed. "You think I should I cancel the party?"

"No. If anything, this has bought us time. Whatever they were planning is out the window now they've lost the element of surprise. Did you arrange the security we spoke about?"

"Yes. Eight men. Four are outside already, another four are arriving later."

"Good."

"I hope you don't mind," Ashcroft said, "but we got you a tux for the party. A lot of people are going to want to meet you and shake your hand. You're the man of the hour."

Thorne was silent for several seconds.

"There a free bar at this party?"

Ashcroft smiled. "Of course."

*

After he showered, Thorne found a card envelope sitting on the table in front of the mirror. It was about the same size as his laptop with a bulge in the middle the thickness of a Gideon Bible. Three words were handwritten on the outside.

Just in case.

Thorne sighed. He knew what was inside the envelope without opening it, and it was no Bible. Ashcroft had hired eight men, but this envelope told him everything. He picked it up and felt the contents move between his fingers. The envelope wasn't sealed, the flap had just been folded inside. He reversed the flap and tilted the opening at his palm. The Smith & Wesson slid grip-first into his hand. He stared at it for a moment. Every gun he'd ever held had eventually been fired at another human being. Ashcroft treated him like a friend, but this made him feel cheap and disposable.

He'd almost died for the man once, wasn't that enough?

Almost immediately, the anger passed.

The senator didn't know the full story of his afternoon with Blake, only what he'd told him to explain his physical appearance. As far as Ashcroft knew, there'd been a brutal fight on his own property that pointed to a further attack. An attack *he'd* warned him about. But now Blake had the modified defibrillators Thorne thought it was unlikely. Aidan Blake was unpredictable, but he always chose an easy option if there was one. He was

225

lazy, it was who he was. If he planned to hit the party, Blake would've killed him.

He sighed and tucked the pistol into the back of his pants.

Just in case.

He caught sight of himself in the mirror. The tuxedo made him look like a maître d' at an upscale restaurant. Or at least, a maître d' who had recently had his ass handed to him. He smiled and tried to make it look genuine. Holding this on his face all night was going to hurt. He'd been to his share of terrible parties, but none like this. Lauren had admitted that most of the guests were north of 70, some closer to 90. Millionaires and billionaires who could later be called upon to finance Ashcroft's candidacy. Fewer than a quarter of the guests were real friends.

Thorne left the room and almost immediately came across an old couple standing looking at the Picasso. They jumped at the sight of him, then seemed to relax. He could tell they planned to start talking to him, but he was altogether too sober for that so nodded and slid quickly past before they got a word out.

The entrance hall was packed with people dressed like they were at a wedding, something enhanced by the over-the-top decorations that hung suspended from the ceiling. In the corner of the room, an Asian man in a white suit sat playing a piano. Thorne wasn't certain, but it sounded like the man was doing Barry Manilow covers.

"It's like being in God's waiting room, isn't it?"

He turned and saw Lauren standing next to him. She passed him a glass of Scotch that was so full he had to take a drink to prevent any from spilling.

"Thanks," he said.

"Come on," Lauren said, "let's go upstairs."

They moved through the guests to the stairs. Everyone turned to stare at him. Some smiled, but most did not. They knew who he was, what he'd done. He'd saved one of their own kind but it wasn't enough. He wasn't rich and he didn't belong here. Lauren led the way. She was two steps in front of him but he could still look at the back of her head due to their height difference. Her ears stuck out, he realized. She tucked her hair in behind them to disguise it, but they clearly stuck out.

Even her flaws were perfect.

There were more guests upstairs, though the thick carpeting made it quieter. The library had close to 20 people in it, including Ashcroft himself. They were all men and most were smoking cigars. The senator was talking and the guests had gathered around to listen. Lauren kept walking and disappeared into the master bedroom at the end of the corridor. He checked they were alone, before following her in. She waved him into the bathroom with a lit joint already in her hand. She wasn't wasting any time.

"I hope you're not planning on going out the window," he said.

"Not in this dress."

She sat on the edge of the bath, then patted the space next to her. He closed the door behind him and turned the lock. Lauren tilted her head over, an eyebrow raised. It was hard to place what she was thinking but he didn't want anyone walking in on them in the bathroom together, even if all they were doing was smoking a joint. She moved closer so her leg pressed against his and held out her hand so that he could take the joint.

"Do you know how many people you have kissed in your life, Chris? Proper kisses, not a niece's cheek, or something."

"Not off the top of my head."

"I keep a count, I like knowing."

Thorne said nothing and stared at the Scotch in his glass.

Earlier in the day he'd decided not to take his OxyContin, knowing that alcohol was likely to be an unavoidable feature of the party. Combining the two had some pretty terrible potential side effects, including death. The pain in his abdomen and shoulder was intolerable, and it was getting worse by the second.

"Forty six."

He nodded and blew smoke from the joint out his mouth. It seemed like a good number, a believable number.

"Why are you telling me this?"

"None of them felt like the kiss you gave me this morning."

Again he said nothing.

"I know you felt it too, Chris."

His eyes slid down to her mouth. Her lips were full and juicy. He could hear her breathing. There was a jagged shake to it as the air moved in and out of her lungs.

"Lauren, you can't say these things to me."

"Because I'm married?"

"Because I like it."

She smiled, and it made him feel sad.

"You ever worry James might actually become president?"

"All the time," she said, her face souring.

A silence fell between them. It'd been a mistake to mention her husband while they were alone together. Thorne felt no buzz developing at all and when she went to pass the joint back for the third time he shook his head.

"He asked me to drive you to L.A."

"And?"

"I said yes, what else could I say?"

This time, Lauren remained silent.

"Does he really not see what you're doing?"

"He sees what he wants to see. Everybody does."

"I won't split you guys up, I refuse."

"It's a little late to be a gentleman."

He took a mouthful of Scotch and ran it around his mouth. It was a fine drink, but it was nowhere near as good as oxycodone.

"You know, I think maybe it's never too late."

"If it matters to you, I could break up with him then we could get together a month later. No one would accuse you of anything."

She wasn't getting it. He didn't care what other people thought. He'd know the truth for himself. Perhaps he'd been that guy in the past, but he'd changed.

"Things are already different between us, you must feel it."

"Don't say that," she said.

He stood and walked to the door, before looking back.

"I don't know what would have to change for me to see things as clearly as you. It's not that I don't want to, I just don't think I can."

He gave her a moment to reply, but when she said nothing he turned the lock and opened the door. Angry, raised voices flew through the gap. He reached behind his back and drew the 1911 from under the tux. Lauren gasped as she saw the weapon.

"Stay here," he said. "You hear any gunshots, go out the goddamn window and stay out there until I come back."

He charged through the master bedroom and down the corridor. The sound was coming from the library. There was something off about the sound. The anger had shifted and he could make out a single voice. *Ashcroft's.* He barreled into the room and saw the senator standing on top of the pool table at the end of the room. The crowd parted around him due to his size and speed, then began to scatter further seeing the gun in his hand. He scanned the room for Blake and Sara, but they weren't there. It was just Ashcroft and his guests. Blood rushed to his face as he realized his mistake. The man had just been giving a speech. He lowered the gun and held up his left hand.

"Sorry! It sounded like the world was ending in here."

There was a long pause followed by a single, booming laugh. It was a laugh he'd heard before and Thorne turned toward Ashcroft. He was almost doubled-over and he was using his hand on his knee to support himself. Next to the senator's feet were two bottles of Scotch. One of them was empty and lay on its side, the other full. Ashcroft was drunk, maybe they all were. He saw Lauren appear in the doorway.

"It's OK, everyone," Ashcroft said, his laughter finally in check. "This, my friends, is my very own guardian angel. You've probably all seen what he did for Lauren and me. We owe him our lives. At that terrible moment I froze up, but Chris here, he was a real action hero. He placed his life on the line for two people he'd never met before. The man didn't even know who I was! Now, I won't deny it, I was insulted by that. But then, maybe if he'd known who I was he would've let things play out, eh?"

There was a ripple of polite laughter from the guests, who were still recovering from their own recent experience with a gunman.

"Chris, come over here! A round of applause everyone."

Thorne returned the pistol to the small of his back and moved toward Ashcroft with a thin, embarrassed smile on his face. The guests here were younger than the ones he'd seen downstairs, closer to the age of Ashcroft himself. These then, must be the ones that were real friends. He reached the front and nodded at Ashcroft who leaned over to smile at him.

The senator tipped forward drunkenly, before catching himself and taking a step back from the edge. Ashcroft laughed and took another step back. The heel of his shoe caught the raised edge of the pool table and fell backward onto the floor. The room fell silent. Thorne rushed around the table and saw Ashcroft spread out on the parquet floor, eyes staring straight up. Other guests gathered around. Lauren pushed through the crowd beside him and stared at her husband. Between their bodies, her hand found his and gripped it tight.

Ashcroft jerked upright. "Gotcha!"

A big cheesy smile was spread across his face, his hands held wide. Relieved laughter spread around the room, followed by chants of *Ash-croft! Ash-croft! Ash-croft!* Thorne and Lauren were pushed aside and James Ashcroft was pulled to his feet. Two of the bigger guests got on either side of the senator and lifted him so he was sitting between their shoulders, then carried him around the room like a match-winning quarterback while the chanting continued. Thorne turned away and his eyes connected with Lauren's.

His own disappointment written on her face.

He walked over to the window and looked out, down at the driveway where Cabot had parked that day. A makeshift parking lot had appeared on the grass and some very expensive vehicles were parked on it. The whole area was lit up by floodlights, the lights designed to give Blake no place to hide. Two of Ashcroft's security drones stood out front.

Lauren's reflection appeared on the glass next to his.

He knew she'd come over, the look they'd exchanged was too heavy to ignore. She spoke softly so she wasn't overheard.

"Is that what it's going to take for us to be together?"

"Maybe," he said. "But that's not what happened."

She sighed. "No."

He touched the glass with the tips of his fingers.

"Not this time, anyway."

Lauren stared at his reflection, her mouth open.

He'd wanted to shock her and it appeared he'd succeeded. She needed to wake up. He left her standing there and walked back to the pool table, where he picked up the full bottle of Scotch. The chanting had stopped now, but the volume of conversation in the room was as loud as any sports bar he'd ever been in. There was a buzz around the room, as if the people in it had witnessed a miracle. When everything calmed down again, the senator might come looking for him. Thorne was through being the man's guardian angel for the night. He was no more than a trained monkey to these people, and now perhaps, the source of future jokes.

He glanced at the bottle in his hand as he descended the staircase. It was one of Ashcroft's expensive bottles. He retraced his steps back through the mansion. Eight people stood in front of the Picasso this time, none looked like they wanted a conversation with him.

Finally, things were looking up.

THIRTY-SIX

Thorne walked into the *Dream Inn* at just after eight a.m. A handful of people were milling about, and a small line had formed at reception. He looked around for the reporter. His height made this a quick process: she wasn't there. He walked over to a seated area to wait for her, but didn't sit down. A young Asian woman sat in a curved crimson seat with two small children. Behind them loomed a huge photograph of surfers walking along a beach carrying their boards. He liked the picture and immediately thought how well it would go in his apartment. Several seconds passed before he remembered the fire. The apartment was gone, and Kate along with it. He felt sick. Every time he remembered, it was a body blow like no other. It didn't seem real, and he didn't think it would until he stood before the building and saw it with his own eyes. Thorne glanced at his watch. It was now ten after eight and there was still no sign of Jocelyn Cooper. He decided to check his cell phone and see if she'd left any messages.

"Mr Thornhill?"

He looked up from the screen. A smartly dressed man stood in front of him.

"Huh?"

"Mr Roger Thornhill?"

He had a feeling that was him. "Yes?"

"I have a message for you."

The man held out an envelope and Thorne took it. This would be Jocelyn canceling their meeting, he supposed. Some breaking news that required her attention elsewhere. The man was still standing there, a thin smile on his face. *Right*. Thorne fished around in his pocket and gave him five dollars. The note disappeared and the man nodded his thanks, already turning to go.

"Just a second," Thorne said. "How did you recognize me?"

"The lady said you were over 6 feet tall and would be wearing sunglasses."

Thorne smiled. "Thanks."

"No problem, sir."

The man stalked off, his hands clasped behind his back. Thorne slid his finger under the flap of the envelope and tore it open. A single folded sheet of paper lay inside.

I'm in 516. Come on up!
Eve

He lifted both the note and the envelope up to his face. It confirmed his first thought: it smelled of perfume. It wasn't a subtle smell. Either she'd left the paper and envelopes lying near where she applied her perfume, or else she'd applied it to the paper directly. He held it up to his nose again and inhaled. Unless he was mistaken, it was *La vie est belle*, the same perfume Kate used. When he lowered the paper, he noticed the woman and both her children were watching him closely. He wondered if he'd sighed or even sworn out loud, either seemed possible. He put the envelope into his pocket and headed for the elevator.

It sat waiting for him, doors open. He got on and hit 5. Nothing happened, so he reached out and hit button again to hurry things up. Now he was here he wanted this over, whatever it was. Finally the doors closed and he was on his way. He took off his sunglasses and put them in his pocket. He didn't want the journalist to know how accurately she'd described him to the man downstairs. As the doors opened on the fifth floor, his mind returned to Jocelyn's message. She'd become playful. For the first time since her call, he questioned why she wanted to meet him. If she'd discovered his involvement, wouldn't she reveal this live on camera? Whatever she had, she'd been sitting on it since yesterday at the earliest.

He knocked on her door, and while he waited for her to answer, he got out his cell phone again and muted it. He didn't want Lauren calling him asking where he was, because he wasn't sure how he would answer her question. There were two main reasons for this and one was so ugly he couldn't bear to think about it. As the screen went blank, he registered the numbers contained in small red balloons over two of the apps. It appeared he had 164 new text messages and 23 new voicemail messages. Something major was going on. The door opened a short distance and Jocelyn Cooper looked around it. A white towel was wrapped around her hair and it rose up like a beehive on top of her head.

She smiled. "You got my message."

"Roger Thornhill, that's cute. *North by Northwest*, Alfred Hitchcock. A decent movie, getting a little dated now though." He frowned. "That's how you see me? A helpless patsy being manipulated by everyone?"

Her eyes seemed to sparkle.

"Oh, you seem like a very *capable* patsy, Mr Thorne."

She pushed her head through the gap and looked up and down the corridor. He found himself doing the same, as if infected by her paranoia. There was no one coming. When he turned back, the door was wide open and he saw her fully for the first time. She was wearing a cream colored robe with a rich, glossy surface like satin or silk. It stopped short of her knees and was tied loosely by a belt. The front bunched out toward him, allowing him an extensive view of her cleavage.

He locked his eyes on hers. "Am I early or late?"

She studied his flustered expression, amused.

"You tell me. A minute ago I was in the shower."

He shifted awkwardly.

"Maybe I should come back another time."

Her face split into a goofy grin. She wasn't wearing any makeup and it suited her. It was the kind of natural girl-next-door look he'd always liked. She appeared to be a totally different person to the one he was familiar with from TV.

"I'm not going to eat you, I'm running late, is all." Her eyes moved up and down his body, assessing him. "Wow, you're bigger than I was expecting. Like a horse or something!"

She laughed to herself, then turned and walked into her room, leaving the door open. He hesitated for a moment, before stepping inside. *A horse.* He'd never been compared to an animal before. His mind churned. Ashcroft's painting was of a horse. Had she traced him back to the heist? He moved into a living area with a sofa and a table. Despite the hour, the room was dark and a couple of table lamps had been turned on. Jocelyn had gone toward the bedroom and stood silhouetted against a window that filled the end wall. She removed the towel from around her head and shook her hair loose before turning to face him. She was small, not much over five feet. Her hair looked wild. It spoke of danger, of passion. He realized he was staring at her, but he couldn't seem to help himself.

"Give me a minute," she said. "I'll be right with you."

"Sure," he said, still staring.

She noticed the way he was looking at her.

"My hair goes curly if I don't dry it quick enough."

Thorne nodded. She sat on a yellow chair in front of a desk and began to dry her hair with a hairdryer. It was a strangely intimate domestic scene and he couldn't help thinking again about Kate and what had happened to her. He took off his jacket and laid it over the back of the sofa, then sat next to it. He looked around the small room to distract himself from thinking about the fire. The hotel's retro theme continued here too, with rich pastel colors and pale cream walls. A photograph of a fairground wheel hung on the wall. On the table in front of him, was a thick book with a man's face on the cover. Hair everywhere, a patch over one eye. It was a face he now recognized; one of Santa Cruz's most famous sons, the late surfer and sportswear industrialist, Jack O'Neill.

After a couple of minutes, the whoosh of air stopped and his head turned automatically toward the silence. He should say something to her, now that she'd be able to hear him again. Something that might defuse the tension between them. He wished he'd thought of something while he'd been waiting. Before he could think of anything, she walked past the bedroom doorway. She was naked. He turned his head away and stared at the opposite wall like he was being paid for it. Music started to play softly from the next room. Something pop, a female artist he didn't know.

"Do I embarrass you, Chris?"

She was several feet away now, facing into a storage closet and flicking casually through clothes on hangers. She was still naked.

"What the hell, lady? We don't even know each other."

She nodded, as if understanding something.

"My skin color bothers you, that it?"

"That is *not* it, and I resent the implication."

"I know that, Thorne. Jesus Christ. I'm fucking with you."

"Do people still use that expression?"

She laughed. "Probably not. I'm bringing it back."

A moment passed before she spoke again.

"You know she's married, right?"

"Who?"

"Lauren Ashcroft. Isn't she the reason we're both here?"

Thorne stood. This meeting was over; the woman was a flake.

"You don't know what you're talking about," he said.

"Sure I do. You can't bring yourself to look at me. Even my *brother* would've looked at me, I'm not exactly gross. You're in love with her."

He sighed. What harm did it do?

"I thought I was, I don't know. The shoot-out made us close, we went through something together. I know it can't go anywhere I'm not stupid." He turned to her. "That's why you asked me here? You're going to ridicule me on television?"

"Of course not, but it does explain a few things."

"Not everything I do has an explanation, Jocelyn."

She made a face. "It's *Coop*. Nobody calls me that other name."

"Put your clothes on, Coop, or I'm leaving."

"Okay."

She turned back to the closet and began looking through the hangars again.

When he'd started to leave, he'd moved closer to the exit; but he had also moved closer to her. As they'd spoken he'd continued to move closer, as if on a fishing line. He was too close, and she was too damn naked. She took a bra out the closet and he looked away as she put it on. After she fastened the clips, her hand swung out and appeared to accidentally brush across the front of his pants. A smile curled the corners of her eyes and mouth. He sighed and walked past her, toward the bedroom. He'd go out onto the balcony and allow her to finish dressing. It was as far as he could get from her without leaving the hotel suite. She was pushing him, testing his boundaries; just as she did with Cabot. It was a power play, and he wasn't going to stand for it.

The air in the bedroom was saturated by the smell of her body, her soaps, and her perfume. The mixture was intoxicating. He glanced toward the bed. The covers were all messed up, and the pillow still had the impression of her head on it. She'd got up in a hurry, just like she'd said. All the same, her note could easily have asked him to wait in the lobby or the bar. There was no reason for him to be here unless she wanted it. Unless there was something she could only do here and not in public. As he approached the window, he saw her reflected on the glass. She'd turned to watch him leave. Her shoulders had sagged and her arms hung down by her sides. The hair on the back of his neck stood on end. He'd seen something private, something real. If she really was playing him, she was one of the best.

He slid open the balcony door and stepped out into the cool air.

The view was amazing, he could look out across the beach, the wharf, and the deep blue water of Monterey Bay. He leaned against the railing and looked down at the people on the beach below. The summer season had been and gone but there were still people down there. Perhaps some of them, like Jocelyn, had been brought here by the shoot-out. There was still a sizable media presence in town, all waiting for the next shoe to drop; all of them sensing the story wasn't over. He suspected they wouldn't have much longer to wait.

Jocelyn came out onto the balcony and leaned against the rail.

"Hey," she said.

"Hey," he said back, still looking out over the bay.

"My hideous body is all covered up if you want to come back inside."

He nodded slowly, not knowing if she was even watching him.

"Thank god. I thought for sure my breakfast was going to come back up."

She laughed and punched him on the arm. "Bastard!"

Thorne smiled. He sensed they had a similar sense of humor. He turned to look at her and saw almost exactly what he expected. She was wearing high heels, navy slacks and a loose white blouse. It was what she wore on camera; smart, professional. Her hair was still down, however, and it was a lot longer than he expected. She wore it so it was directed down one side of her neck, with the ends stopping above her heart. Thorne moved as though to pass behind her on the narrow balcony. She turned with him, so they were facing one another. He stopped and put his fingertips on the rail on either side of her. A light touch. If she didn't like it, she could brush past him. Intimate, but not controlling. Jocelyn looked up into his eyes, uncertain. Her back was arched, her ass pressed against the guardrail. Her eyes sparkled again. The two of them were closer than at any time before. She was wearing the perfume. It filled his nose with every breath and if he closed his eyes, it would be easy to let himself believe he was with Kate. She could see the desire in his eyes, he wasn't hiding it anymore. He thought she'd been playing a game with him when he arrived, but he wasn't so sure anymore.

"You said that you had something I needed to see."

"Yes."

He glanced down, at her body, then back up.

"Did I already see it?"

She smiled. "No, something else. But you're not going to like it."

"I see," he said. "Are we going to stop being friends?"

"Maybe."

He gazed at her, as if memorizing every detail. She had an angelic face, with a delicate bone structure and a rounded chin. Her mouth looked like a ribbon tied into a bow and he longed to kiss it. On impulse, he raised his left hand and slid it down under the collar of her blouse and let it rest on the bare skin of her shoulder, up near her neck. She took a deep breath, her eyes dancing nervously. This crossed the line. This wasn't in the same *time zone* as the line. His thumb rested just above her collarbone, near her carotid artery. He felt the acceleration of her heart. He couldn't tell if she was excited, or afraid. Sometimes, the two were the same. It would be the simplest thing in the world for him to tip her over the rail. One sharp push. The fall would kill her, but would take less than two seconds. She'd be confused, disorientated; she might hit the ground before she realized what happened. It would be clean, painless.

They could look for Roger Thornhill all they liked, they'd never find him.

"You've started to grow on me, Coop. I'd hate if I never saw you again."

"That's not the impression you gave me back there."

"All right, let's you and me start over. We'll go inside and you can tell me what this is all about, then we'll take it from there."

"Fine, but you got the wrong idea about me, Thorne."

"Shhh, don't spoil it."

He got a flash of the goofball smile again, before she got it under control. She wanted to be serious, because she was about to brace him with something difficult. *Playful Coop* was being parked now that it was time to get to business. He understood that, he'd done much the same when he'd channeled some of his fictional character's traits during both the robbery attempt, and the shoot-out. Jake Vasco feared nothing. He followed her back into the bedroom. The music was no longer playing. She sat in the chair she'd used before and opened a laptop that lay on the desk in front of her. It was a top of the line MacBook Pro, a distant cousin of his own laptop. A document was open on screen and she hurriedly closed it before he could see what it said. It looked like one of his scripts for *Night Passenger*: a fat double-spaced column in the middle of the page. Perhaps her next news report.

She glanced over her shoulder at him.

"Okay, this all starts with that security footage."

"I don't want to look at that," he said.

She raised an eyebrow. "You've never watched it before?"

"I've seen it more times than I want to, I'm sure everyone has."

"I need to play it, Chris. If you like, I can mute the sound."

He sighed, then nodded. She clicked on the browser icon and Chrome opened with the page already on it. There was an image frozen on screen of him from above, lying on the ground with his head in Lauren's lap. A large amount of blood covered his clothing and more still had pooled on the asphalt beneath them. It was difficult to believe from looking at this image that he wasn't dead and he found it hard to look at himself this way. He knew this was the last frame of the video, it wasn't where she'd chosen to stop it. She clicked the mute key, then hit replay. It was the same thing they kept showing on TV, he could describe it in his sleep. Around the one third's mark, she pressed pause and looked at him.

"The video has five different camera angles. Four of them are mall security, but not this one," she said, pressing the screen. The colors shifted under her fingernail, desperate to escape. "This one is different, it comes from the dash cam of a vehicle in the parking lot. Only a single instance from this camera appears, this one right here."

"So what?"

"Well," she said, "I assumed whoever made this video was somehow involved with the official security staff at the mall. I mean, how else would they get this footage?"

Thorne nodded. The extra angle, combined with the access to the official security feeds created a problem.

"A cop," he said. "The same one who had the dash cam."

"*Bingo.*"

He sat heavily on the end of her bed.

"You're telling me there was a goddam cop there the entire time, and he did nothing to help me? He just sat in his car and filmed it?"

"Yeah, I didn't think you'd like that. For what it's worth, he didn't do nothing. He called in backup; he called in the helicopter. You'd certainly be dead without him."

Thorne rubbed the back of his neck in frustration. The cop would've been on the other side of Blake and the others, there would've been nowhere for them to hide. Cabot hadn't mentioned anything about this man, either to him, or in any press conference. It was probably a source of embarrassment that this officer sat it out inside his car, while a civilian had stepped up and saved the day. Thorne took a deep breath and let it out slowly. The cop would have shot at him too, there would've been no way for him to tell them all apart. He would have looked like just another shooter, and the one that had Lauren.

"A cop was there and he uploaded this to the internet. So what?"

"Actually he didn't, his son did. I contacted him through his username *dimebag69*. He was more than willing to meet up when I explained who I was."

"I'm sure. Did he get the same routine I got with the robe?"

Her face seemed to collapse.

"I guess I deserve that, but no he didn't."

He'd hurt her feelings and it surprised him how bad he felt.

"Hey," he said. "I'm sorry, okay? Please carry on."

She nodded. "I met this kid in Starbucks. His real name is Angelo Caruso. He was all worked up about the footage. At the time, the clip had been watched over 300 million times and he hadn't received a cent of advertising money. He claimed Google stole it, citing a breach of their terms and conditions. He was bummed out, he thought he had a Zapruder movie on his hands. I let him go on about it for several minutes before I steered him back to the content of the video.

"I told him I was interested in seeing the entirety of the footage from the dash cam, I didn't need the other feeds. He admitted it wasn't a great angle or he would've used more of it. Sensing blood in the water and feeling a little sorry for him, I said I'd buy the footage off him for $200. It was all the money I had with me. Anyway, his eyes lit up. It wasn't the type of money he'd hoped for, but it was better than nothing. I made him sign a network release form to tie him in and make it a legal contract. I wanted the exclusive, I said, so if the footage turned up elsewhere he could expect to find himself in court. He didn't care, he thought he was selling me a lemon. He transferred the footage onto my thumb drive right there in Starbucks, then took the money and ran. Almost literally."

Thorne couldn't see where this was going, or where it connected to him. There had to be something from this angle that the other cameras had missed. Not being part of the mall's security system, Cabot and his deputies hadn't seen it. They'd look at the original, unedited recordings, not this clip.

Was it possible that they didn't know about the dash cam footage? He glanced at the view counter and saw it was now at 630 million. He blinked. The number had almost doubled since he'd last looked. People couldn't get enough of him being shot.

"All right," he said. "Show me."

"It's easy to miss, I don't blame the kid for not seeing it. You're going to want to come closer than that."

He got up off the bed and looked around. There were no other chairs. He stood behind her and leaned down close, so that he was looking over her shoulder. Again her perfume entered his nose, his lungs. It was making him crazy. She minimized her browser and played the dash cam video that was sitting in a window underneath. There was no preceding movement of the vehicle getting into position, the footage started from the same angle they'd already seen. He watched it all unfold once again. It seemed the same, and he could see why the kid hadn't used much of it. The angle was low, and faced a little too far to the left. Additionally, there were several static marks that were probably squashed bugs on the vehicle's windshield.

The clip ended and he shook his head.

"I didn't see it," he said.

"I told you. Let me play it again. This time, don't look at what you're doing, look at what happens behind you."

She started the clip again. This time, he saw it immediately. He saw Foster rise up like a mountain behind him, huge and out of focus. His left hand across his gaping throat, slick with blood. The giant staggered toward his position with something shiny in his free hand. The screwdriver. A puff of red rose up out of his chest, then another. Foster collapsed backward and didn't rise again. The clip continued to play, but he didn't ask her to stop it, nor did he need to re-watch it to know who'd fired the shots.

"From where I'm sitting, it looks like one of those guys saved you. The one in that *Doors* T-shirt. The same one you have that weird *Point Break* stand off with later on, where neither of you takes the shot. That part never made sense before, but now it's starting to look like something else. Part of a pattern."

She was onto him. How long would it be before she had the full picture? Not too long, he suspected. Jocelyn Cooper was smart, and wasn't constrained by procedure or jurisdiction like Cabot. He straightened up and walked over to the window. On it's own, the footage wasn't much. As far as investigators would be able to tell, the shots Blake had fired at Foster could be dismissed as accidental. In the military, it was known as friendly fire, or blue-on-blue. In a shoot-out like this, in a confined area, it wouldn't be that surprising. He sensed, though, that there was more to come. If he went the wrong way with her now, she wouldn't believe him when it mattered. He had to draw her out and see what else she knew.

Without turning around he spoke again.

"Why am I here? Are you coming after me?"

"I'm giving you a chance I wouldn't give other people. In case it isn't obvious, I like you a lot. I have a huge respect for what you did and I have a lot personally invested in this story. You are the best thing that's happened in news for a very long time, and I don't want that to turn to shit the way everything always does. There is no limit where you could go with this, and I want to be part of that. I want a deal. Exclusives, now and forever. You're worth more to me a hero than you are as a criminal.

"I see you becoming a movie star, then maybe entering politics like your friend Ashcroft. You could be president yourself one day, you realize that? You have everything people want from a leader; a hero with a military background, good on camera, attractive, not to mention charisma out the wahoo. It's all there for you. But here's the thing. I know you know who this man is, you're connected somehow. The only chance you have is to get out in front of this and control the story. If this comes out the wrong way, no one will to listen. Trust me, I know what I'm talking about."

He sighed. To hear her talk about him as a force for good depressed him. She didn't know him at all. He turned to face her.

"I know you mean well, but there's no getting out in front of this. It's not like announcing I smoked pot in college, or that I banged some intern on my office desk."

"You've got to give me more than that. What kind of journalist would I be if I backed away from a story? What's your endgame here? Do you even have one? For whatever reason, Cabot hates you and wants to see you in prison. The man's an idiot, but he's motivated. If he's digging in the right spot, even by accident, he might find something incriminating."

Thorne nodded. "That's a chance I'm going to have to take."

He walked past her into the living area and picked up his jacket. Time to go. Jocelyn watched him silently from the bedroom. He'd given her nothing. She'd continue to investigate his link with Blake, but without knowing his name that would be difficult. Thorne put his jacket on then pulled down on the lapels so that it sat correctly across his broad shoulders.

"Was the fire at your apartment really an accident?"

Her question was like a knife in his heart.

"I wish you hadn't asked me that, Coop."

"It was payback for what happened at the mall, wasn't it?"

Anger flared within him. Forgetting his shoulder wound, he reached his right arm straight out and pointed at her.

"Say that shit on-air and they'll kill you."

Her eyes dropped to the floor. He thought he'd frightened her, but to his surprise she walked over, slid her hands in under his jacket, and held him tight. It felt good. Words could never compare with the power of touch. He allowed himself to accept it and after only a few seconds, felt no awkwardness. He listened to her breathing into his chest. Thorne supposed he'd just admitted knowing the people involved and that he was in some way to blame for what happened to Kate. He'd grown strangely fond of Jocelyn in their short time together and he didn't want anything bad to happen to her. He drew back, out of their embrace. He'd been away too long already, he needed to get back to the mansion.

"There's only one solution to this, surely you can see that?"

She studied his face closely.

"You plan to kill all of them."

He nodded and she shrank away from him.

"Did…did you kill the one in hospital?"

"No, although I did go up there that day. I told myself I was only going to speak to him, but I doubt that's what would've happened. Anyway, when I got there the place was surrounded by police cruisers and fire trucks. It was already done." Thorne stopped. He was losing her. "These are very bad people, Coop. Do not judge me on this. I would never have killed that cop, surely you know that? You can see the difference."

"How many are left?"

"Two."

"You think you can do that? Murder two people in cold blood? I don't think that's who you are. Before, you were defending the Ashcrofts. Your motives were pure. You put their safety above your own. You are a warrior, Thorne, not a serial killer."

He nodded. "You might be right about that."

"That's why you can trust me," she said. "I *know* you."

He wasn't sure he followed that logic at all. To his mind, this made her more dangerous. If he failed to keep her sweet, she could pull the pin on him at any time. She was also forgetting something important. He might be no murderer, but he could defend himself when it came to it. He'd never had any problems doing that, not since he was a kid.

"Your deal, the exclusives; I'll think about it."

"Don't think too long, Thorne."

"Chris," he said.

"Okay."

"I gotta go," he said, glancing at her mouth.

"What would happen if you stayed?"

"I think my car would get towed."

She smiled. "Damn right. That thing would get pounded."

He laughed. Her sense of humor was perfect. She walked in front of him, toward the exit. She moved slowly, and kept looking back at him over her shoulder. His height meant he was used to walking quickly. At this speed, he had to keep looking down to see where to place his feet. His eyes repeatedly passed over her ass and each time they did so, he remembered the view she'd provided him earlier. He'd taken in a lot more than he'd let himself believe. They were at the door now. She put herself in front of the handle, preventing him from leaving.

"You're not going to stop investigating me are you?"

"No."

"I guess I'd be disappointed in you if you did."

"If I call you again, will you answer?"

"I don't know; does that go both ways?"

Her eyes lit up. "Of course."

"Then, sure."

They stared silently at each other for several seconds.

She was still blocking him.

Again, his eyes dipped to look at her mouth.

"Chris, there's something I need you to do before you go."

THIRTY-SEVEN

It was almost nine thirty when Thorne got back in his car. He'd been away from the mansion for over two and a half hours. Assuming Blake hadn't killed them, the Ashcrofts would be losing their shit. He should've left a note saying he'd be back later; even a vague promise was better than none at all. Lauren might think he'd decided to leave without saying goodbye. Even the idea of it tempted him, just drive off and leave it all behind. He'd done his part hadn't he? He didn't owe the Ashcrofts a damn thing. He'd warned them and they'd chosen to do nothing. Whatever happened next was on their own heads, his conscience was clear.

Up ahead, he saw the coffee place Lauren had taken him to before and without thinking, swung the Maserati into a spot out front. A good strong coffee was exactly what he needed, get his focus back. Then he'd be ready to face Lauren and finalize things there. He wasn't one to run away from an awkward moment. It was time to leave, he could see that now. Los Angeles wouldn't wait any longer. The line at the counter was short and soon he was back out on the street with a steaming Americano.

Traffic was slow, and he was able to comfortably drive holding the cup in one hand, taking sips every now and then. The coffee stung his lip. He glanced in the rearview mirror and saw his lower lip was swollen.

Jocelyn Cooper had bitten him.

As Thorne turned off Cedar onto Laurel, he noticed something white flickering under one of the Maserati's wipers. The windshield had a dark tinted band at the edge of the glass and only a small amount of the object stuck up above it. He squinted to try and make it out. Too small to be a parking ticket, he thought. Looked like a business card. He'd had that before in L.A., people would walk along a street and stick their card under every wiper. Realtors and gardeners mostly, one time, a naked housekeeper. He almost smiled thinking about it, but he knew this wasn't going to be someone wanting a job. Not this time. He parked in front of a 7-Eleven, popped the driver's door and with his leg still inside the vehicle, reached across the glass and pulled the object out. He recognized it immediately. It was the security pass from the art gallery, with the ink cross in the upper left hand corner.

Two words were written across the middle in precise capitals.

WATCH IT

Thorne looked around, his heart beating fast in his chest. *Blake.* He almost expected the man to be standing beside him, a gun pointed at his head. But of course there was nothing, just people going about their day. The card had to have been under the wiper for several minutes before he noticed it, Blake was long gone. He could've put it there when he was at the hotel, or while he was getting his coffee, it didn't really matter. He got back inside the car, slammed the door and swore. Blake was never going away. Despite the risks of being identified from the footage and the mugshots Cabot had hung all around town, the man was going nowhere. The truth was, nobody ran from a $12 million payday, no matter what. He looked again at the card. Blake was a man of few words, that was for sure. It was a warning, pure and simple.

Blake planned to make another run at the painting and wanted him not to interfere. He'd hit the truck tomorrow, take the Picasso as it returned to the gallery. Blake had reversed his own truck heist plan. If looking the other way was all it took to get Blake off his back, it'd be worth it. The painting was nothing to him, it never had been. All he cared about was Lauren. So long as Blake posed no threat to her he could have the painting and the twelve million dollars.

He tossed the card onto the passenger seat and sighed.

There was another message here. He'd been followed again, and this time he hadn't noticed the tail. It seemed impossible to him that anyone could do this given the mansion's isolation, but he hadn't exactly been on top of his game the last couple of days and the Maserati was far from inconspicuous. If he'd wanted to, Blake could've killed him. An old tan station wagon pulled into a space next to Thorne. He found himself looking blankly at the driver, his mind a million miles away. The driver was wearing a cowboy hat and he remembered the Texan, Stockton. Somehow, he'd managed to forget all about him. He hadn't been at the kidnapping, or if he had, hadn't had a clear shot.

Thorne backed the car out of the space and swung out onto Chestnut.

He cursed himself for remembering Stockton, just thinking about him made his skin crawl. There was no defense against a sniper, they could hit you from any direction, at any time. All they needed was line of sight. Stockton could choose a spot then sit back and wait for him to enter his kill zone. The Texan could shoot him from a mile away and he'd never know what hit him. He turned the problem over. No. The fight in the woods had been more Blake's style. Hands on, brutal, and immediate. The

244

two of them had unfinished business. Blake would never have someone else take him out, he'd want to do it himself.

In a strange way, Thorne found this comforting.

At Lincoln, an SCPD cruiser pulled out in front of him and Thorne eased back on the gas to let a gap build between them. No point looking for trouble. He took the ramp onto PCH, his head turning to watch the police car continue along Chestnut. As he swung back to face the highway, he caught sight of the security card on the passenger seat. It looked different. It had turned over when it landed and he saw the back of the plastic for the first time. There was a strip of duct tape on it. Thorne frowned. He hadn't thought to turn it over, he thought the card *was* the message. With the Maserati now merged into its lane, he reached for the card and ran his fingertips over the duct tape. There were two distinct bumps in the tape, one rectangular, the other circular.

Blake had sent him something.

Holding the steering wheel and the corner of the card with his left hand, he forced his right thumb nail under the corner of the tape and peeled it back. Something small and silver dropped on the floor between his legs and rolled out of sight. He glanced down to try and find it, but it had disappeared. For now, it would have to wait. Thorne turned his attention back to the duct tape and continued to peel, slower now. More careful. He only had to peel a small section to know what lay beneath: an SD memory card.

His stomach lurched. *Watch it.*

It wasn't a warning at all, it was a video.

"Lauren," he said.

Blake had finally done it. While he'd been with Jocelyn, or on his way to her hotel room, Lauren was being kidnapped. This memory card was the proof of life. He called her cell phone. The dial tone went on and on, amplified by the car's built-in comms unit.

"Answer, goddammit!"

He braced for Blake to pick up. If his old friend really did have her, and he was growing more and more certain of it, then it followed that he had her cell too. She took the phone everywhere, Ashcroft had even joked about it. The dial tone stopped and Lauren's whispery voice poured out the speakers.

Hi! I'm busy right now, you know what to do.

He canceled the call and pressed the gas pedal to the floor. The car surged forward, his back sinking into the soft leather seat. There was something bad on that memory card, something unspeakable. He didn't want to see it but he knew he had to watch. Whatever it was, it might not be too late. There was still time to save her, he had to believe that. Why would Blake send a video if it were already too late? To torment him? He drove faster than he'd ever driven before, weaving in and out of traffic. Soon he was off the highway and onto the road that twisted its way north, into the pines.

It took eighteen minutes to reach Ashcroft's mansion. From the outside, there was no sign of anything unusual. Lauren's car was parked out front where it always was, next to the senator's SUV. He realized that this didn't surprise him at all. They would've grabbed her in the woods while she was running. It was the perfect spot for a kidnapping for the same reason she liked it there: total privacy. Blake hadn't been after him that day; it was Lauren he'd been waiting for. It was so obvious to him now. Lauren gave Blake leverage.

He slotted the Maserati in next to its twin on the far side of the doorway, rucking up an angry tide in the small stones as he braked. A cloud of dust floated on ahead of the car like a ghost and he watched it pass before he got out. Only now was he able to look down into the car's footwell and see what had dropped out from under the duct tape.

A nickel.

You make it sound like you're picking up a nickel someone dropped on the sidewalk.

Blake had taken his line to heart, it amused him. Since then, it had become a private code referring to the painting's acquisition. What it meant here was not clear to him. He slammed the car door and ran into the house. The front door was unlocked. The front door was never unlocked. He went straight for his room, his feet echoing off the cold stone walls as he ran. The place was like a museum. In his room, he opened his laptop and sat down. The memory card contained two files: a movie, and a text document. Thinking it might give him advanced warning about the content of the movie, he opened the document first.

Daryl's parking lot, highway 9. 2 am. Bring painting. NO COPS.

Of course. Blake wasn't taking another run at the painting. He was.

Thorne moved the cursor over the video file and hesitated, his finger hovering over the touchpad. The movie was named you_did_this. The preview image was black. He sucked his swollen lip and double tapped the button. The screen went dark. He clicked play. Unlit concrete or asphalt, blurred as the camera zipped upward. An empty street. Early morning, somewhere abandoned and industrial. A single dim light shone in the corner of the frame. Out of the darkness, a figure approached wearing black clothing and a gorilla mask. The mask was covered in long hair that fanned out across the owner's chest and shoulders. The camera turned to follow, revealing the squat shape of the Audi sedan. The figure walked to the rear of the car and popped the trunk. Light spilled out from within, causing the focus to jump briefly before sharpening. A muted sound started up inside the trunk. Thorne had heard the sound several times

246

before, in Iraq. It was the sound of someone screaming with their mouth taped shut.

The figure looked down into the trunk, angled its head, then abruptly punched whoever was inside. The sound stopped. The figure bent over and reached into the car with both arms and dragged the occupant's body until it was in an upright position against the side wall of the trunk. A blood-soaked white pillowcase was tied around the neck with a belt, and a bed sheet had been wrapped around the body like an Egyptian mummy. Thorne didn't want to accept it, but the body was the right size to be Lauren Ashcroft. The figure turned toward the camera as if to set up a selfie, then twisted and again punched the covered head, causing it to snap back and lie over at an angle. Thorne swore, his own hands balling up into fists in front of him. Off-camera Blake said *All right, that's enough. Get that bitch outta there.* The figure nodded, a small gesture almost hidden by the mask. Despite the small size of Lauren's body, the figure struggled to get her out and Blake had to reach into shot and help lift her over the lip of the trunk and down onto the asphalt. She lay in her worm-like cocoon, silent and unmoving. Her feet were bare and deathly pale. The light inside the trunk illuminated her body and Blake walked around it to get a better angle. As he did so, Thorne saw the motorcycle boots the gorilla figure was wearing.

Sara.

Well, that figured. He hadn't pegged Stockton as a puncher of defenseless women. The camera jerked to one side then back again, before moving toward Sara who reached out and took it. The view snapped around and Thorne found himself looking at Blake who was again wearing his clown mask. It was a grim reminder of the botched kidnapping and it still bore some of Porter's blood. Blake reached down and picked up Lauren like she was a gym bag and flipped her up over his shoulder in a single movement. Her body sagged inside the sheets at what must have been her hips and a low moan issued from the pillowcase. Blake set off quickly, leaving Sara behind with the camera. Lauren's weight accentuated his limp, his right leg noticeably dragging on the backswing. There was the sound of the trunk closing and then Sara followed along behind Blake.

The screen was dark again, the image pixelated and blurred.

Thorne glanced at the progress bar; he was already halfway through the movie. He considered stopping it where it was. If he saw them kill Lauren he didn't know what he'd do. He didn't know if he could take them killing someone else he cared about and know he was responsible. He sighed. It was no use, he had to know. One way or another, the remaining four and a half minutes would probably determine how the remainder of his life played out. On screen, Blake opened the door of a large building and stepped inside. A blueish-white light shone up ahead. It flowed around the shifting bulk of his body and appeared to pulse like a living thing. Sara moved to one side and the scene opened out. They were in an old factory or warehouse. A single office chair was set up in the center of an open space, surrounded by a circle of LED storm lanterns.

Next to the chair was a chainsaw.

Thorne gripped his head tight in both hands. Not a chainsaw. He'd seen a lot of bad things, but he couldn't watch someone do that to Lauren, that was too much. Sara was moving again. For the first time, Thorne noticed there a tripod on the floor in front of the chair and the view moved toward it. She clipped the camera to it, leaving him with a static view of the chair, then she walked into shot. Blake lowered Lauren's sheet-wrapped body onto the floor and pulled something from his jacket pocket. Thorne heard the distinctive click-click-click sound of a box-cutter blade being pushed out. *Help me get this shit offa her,* Blake said, then, after a beat. *Yeah, that's it.* His arm lifted up to free a large section of sheeting. The cutting and tearing continued for several more seconds before Blake lifted Lauren up and over to the chair. His wide back blocked the view to the camera, with only her arms protruding. Thorne frowned. Before his thoughts could crystalize, they too were hidden, this time by Sara. *Tape her wrists and ankles to the chair,* Blake said. He'd backed up toward the camera to give her space, filling the frame with his ass. When he moved aside the camera focus drifted back to the seat. Thorne gasped.

Kate Bloom was strapped into the chair.

Her head moved unsteadily from side to side, her eyes blinking against the light from the lanterns. Above her left ear, her blonde hair was matted down with blood. Her face was heavily bruised and her nose had bled over her taped mouth to her chin. She appeared dizzy, with little idea of what was happening. She was wearing his *Top Gun* T-shirt. The movie was one of her favorites and she'd given him the T-shirt at the beginning of their relationship. Later, when it became old and faded, she'd refused to throw it out and instead kept it under her pillow. She wore it at night when they were apart and, as far as he could tell, sprayed his aftershave on it. The T-shirt came down past her hips and almost covered the white briefs she wore underneath.

Thorne felt sick. He could see it so clearly in his mind. They'd come for her while she was asleep, when she was least able to defend herself. Perhaps waking up with the pillowcase already tied over her head and the sheet being wound around her body. She'd stood no chance at all, no one would in that situation. Blake emerged out of the darkness behind Kate and rested his hands on her shoulders. She stiffened visibly, his touch surprising her. He leaned forward and thrust his left arm through the neck hole of the T-shirt and casually groped her breasts. Thorne clenched his teeth, his fury uncontrollable. Kate looked straight at the camera; her face flat, showing nothing. It would've taken a lot of self control for her to do that. Thorne had never been more proud. Getting no reaction, and apparently bored, Blake withdrew his arm and began to run his fingers roughly through her hair. She tried not to react to this either, but she flinched as he pulled back hair that blood had dried through. He gathered up the ends of her hair behind her head and fixed it into a tight ponytail with a rubber band.

Blake stroked her exposed neck, his masked face hovering close.

Sara picked up the chainsaw and pulled the starter. It took three pulls to start, then roared into life. Kate's eyes locked on the chainsaw. Sara walked behind Kate, who twisted her head first one way, then the other trying to see what was happening. Sara stayed there, in the blind spot, revving the chainsaw over and over. After several fruitless seconds, Kate stopped trying to see Sara and instead stared at Blake. Sara held the chainsaw out flat so that the spinning teeth were an inch from Kate's neck. Half an inch. The teeth edged closer and closer. Kate closed her eyes and tears rolled down both cheeks. Thorne had a hand over his mouth. He could no longer see a gap between the spinning teeth and her skin, they blurred into each other.

Then, abruptly, the chainsaw was gone and its engine silent.

Blake detached the camera from the tripod and moved in tight on Kate's face. Her eyes opened and she looked into the lens. It was no longer the look she had directed at Blake moments earlier. It was pure, loving. She knew who would see the recording, this look was for him. A message. Thorne could feel her inside him, squeezing his heart. She still loved him, he was certain of it. The camera drifted down to her right leg. Thorne glanced at the progress bar. Nine seconds left. The picture became shaky. He thought Blake was hunting for the stop button when his fist slammed down, leaving an ice pick buried in Kate's calf. The image of the handle sticking out her leg froze on screen as the clip came to an end.

"Motherfucker!" Thorne shouted, jumping to his feet.

Without thinking, he turned and punched the mirror, destroying it. Pain shot up his arm, but it wasn't enough to cut through the rage and frustration. He roared. The sound didn't seem to be part of him, it was as if a creature were escaping from his body that could no longer be contained. When he was done he slumped back in the chair, exhausted. He put his head in his hands and concentrated on his breathing. *Kate's alive*, he thought, *focus on that*. Before watching the video he would've given anything to know this simple fact, but now he needed more. Something had happened to him when she'd looked into the camera that last time. He'd realized, finally, what she meant to him, and what he'd lost.

"Chris."

His head jerked around.

James Ashcroft stood in the doorway. He was white as a sheet.

"How long have you been standing there?" Thorne asked.

"Long enough."

"You saw the video?"

"I saw."

Thorne sighed. "That's too bad."

"What do they want, Chris?"

"Same thing they've always wanted. The painting."

"I thought so. What are you going to do?"

"I'm giving it to them. They have Kate."

Ashcroft was silent for a moment. "All right."

"Just like that?"

"Don't get me wrong. That painting means a lot to me, but it's not worth any of this crazy shit. Besides, I think we both know that if you don't give them the Picasso now, it'll only be a matter of time before Lauren is sitting in that chair and I'm faced with the same decision. First we rescue your girlfriend, then, and only then, will we worry about the painting."

"Thanks, man."

"Do me a favor. Don't tell Lauren about that video, she's freaked out enough as it is. She thought you'd gone back to L.A., she went crazy. I had to give her an Ambien."

"Sorry."

Ashcroft paused in the doorway, looking him up and down.

"Clean yourself up before you join us. You're a mess."

THIRTY-EIGHT

It was over an hour before Thorne remembered the activity on his cell phone he'd noticed outside Jocelyn Cooper's hotel room. He looked at the text messages first, on the basis that he could deal with them faster than voice messages. There were now 182, according to the balloon over the app. He opened it up and looked at the list of names or numbers. There were 19 different senders and he recognized almost all of them. Friends, co-workers, even a couple of neighbors from his apartment building. Their messages were predictably trite, but supportive. There were 32 messages from his agent, a woman called Carli Stahl, who landed him the role on *Night Passenger* before apparently losing his number.

That left two unknowns.

The first claimed to be from an executive at Marvel Studios telling him to check his goddamn messages. The second, with remarkably similar wording, was from a Detective Burrows of the Santa Monica Police Department. No part of Thorne believed that Marvel were interested in him as an actor. It was a prank call, just like many others he'd had before. Pranksters only seemed to know the name of one movie studio, which made it a lot easier to screen them out. He had no idea at all how genuine Marvel executives got anyone to answer their calls. That left the cop. He sighed. Like he needed another cop in his life. Thorne decided to skip tracking down the right voice message and just call the detective direct. The call was answered on the third ring.

"Burrows."

"This is Christopher Thorne returning your call."

"You're a hard man to get hold of, Mr Thorne."

"I don't have much to say to anyone anymore, Detective."

"I have good news and bad news on that front. Are you sitting down?"

*

Thorne parked on Beach Street, just down the road from Jocelyn Cooper's hotel. It was only a matter of hours since he'd been there, and everything had changed. After five minutes, he saw her appear in the car's tiny door mirror. Her hair was pinned up in a bun like it was when she was on TV. He wondered if she'd been on-air again since he last saw her. Anything was possible; Blake's murder of the deputy and Cabot's star witness, followed by his dramatic escape from the hospital had re-energized the story. Once again, people wanted updates. The news cycle was relentless and required constant feeding, and Blake was only too willing to provide. Jocelyn drew level with the car and he popped open the door and stepped out onto the sidewalk next to her. She looked up at him and smiled.

"Wow, nice car."

"A gift from Senator Ashcroft for saving his life."

"*Awkward.*"

Thorne nodded. He clicked the remote and the doors locked. Jocelyn's face fell as she realized she wasn't getting into the car, but that was too bad. He didn't want the smell of her perfume lingering around for Lauren to notice, he had enough problems. A gap appeared in the traffic and they crossed over to the beach side of the street. They walked a short distance in silence until they reached the boardwalk, where he stopped and leaned on the rail and looked out to sea. It brought his head close to hers in a way that looked natural to passers-by. Jocelyn studied him, her face caught between confusion and amusement. She looked good. There was something between them like an electrical charge. It was the reason he'd asked to meet here and not back at the hotel.

"Coop, I'm not exactly sure what happened this morning."

"You don't remember, or you don't understand?"

He sighed. "I guess the latter."

"It's simple, Chris. You fucked me."

Thorne flinched. "That wasn't what I meant."

"What then?"

"Who does that? We just met."

"This is pretty much how it is in L.A. now. Nobody has time to meet people socially, go on dates, to the movies, all that. You like someone, you take the chance immediately because you might not see that person again. I give so much of myself to my career, I'm not going to give up on the stuff that makes life worth living. Does your heart need a movie and a pizza to know what it wants, or does it just know?"

"I've been out of the game a long time."

"I did *not* get that impression."

Thorne felt his face go red and looked out to sea to hide it.

"Hey," she said. "Where are you? You know it's what I wanted."

"I know that, Coop."

His mood darkened as he remembered why he was here. He straightened up and turned toward her. She was so small, her head had to tilt way back just to see his face.

Jocelyn ran the tip of her index finger down his forehead.

"This isn't a happy face, Thorne. Are we about to have a conversation where you tell me this was a big mistake and it will never happen again?"

"It's not like that. Things got complicated after I left."

She sighed. "Just say it, man."

"It's Kate. She's still alive."

"Jesus."

"Yeah."

"So who died in that fire?"

"Elizabeth Warner, Kate's stunt double on the show. They were friends, I guess she was staying the night. It wasn't that unusual, she lived in Riverside and would often crash at ours after a night out." Thorne paused as he remembered the murdered woman's face. "Beth did the stunts that were too dangerous for Kate to do herself. They were really nothing alike, but with the right clothes and make-up she passed for Kate in a mid shot. I guess she was the right age, sex, and height for the person they expected to find in the apartment. Obviously the fire delayed identification."

Jocelyn nodded. "I'm with you."

He looked down. She'd put her hand on top of his and curled her fingers around into the palm. It felt good.

"Look," he said, "I don't know where you and I stand, I didn't call you about that. I just wanted to give you the heads-up. The L.A. County Coroner is releasing this at 3 o'clock, so if you want the scoop you'll have to hustle."

Her face brightened.

"You're taking my deal?"

"I haven't had a chance to think about it."

"Chris, if Kate wasn't in the fire, where's she been all this time?"

"You know the answer to that as well as I do."

"*They* took her?"

"You can't say that, and there's no way you can explain it if you do. The Santa Monica PD have issued a warrant for her arrest. She's a person of interest now, not a victim. They think she killed her friend and set the fire as a forensic countermeasure. They think she's a murderer. I need you to make this right, Coop. I can't let them poison her name when they should be trying to find her."

Jocelyn said nothing. Either because she was thinking things over, or because she disagreed with his assessment.

"Look," he said. "I'll do whatever you want. The deal, anything. She's *not* a killer."

"I believe you. It's just you said she's alive, then that the police are looking for her. You *knew* they'd taken her, which means they've already sent you a video."

"I don't have time for this. They're threatening to cut her head off with a goddamn chainsaw. Are you going to help me or not?"

She squeezed his hand.

"I got this."

THIRTY-NINE

Thorne found Ashcroft in the kitchen holding a mug of coffee. They nodded at one another across the room. Another mug of coffee was on the breakfast bar, and Thorne sat silently behind it. He was wired already, he didn't need any help from caffeine. He put his hands around the mug to warm his hands. The air crackled with things they weren't talking about. Ever since he and Lauren had revealed their feelings for each other, all but the most transitory moments spent with James Ashcroft felt awkward and endless. The senator wasn't drinking his coffee either and after a minute he put it down on the counter in front of him.

"All right," Ashcroft said. "Let's do this."

Thorne stood and followed him out the room and down the hall. When Ashcroft got to the painting next to the Picasso, he stopped and stood in front of it. He ran his fingernail under the edge of the frame and the painting flipped out of the wall on a hinge. Behind it was a gray screen the size of a tablet computer. Ashcroft put his hand flat against the glass. A light passed over it and a small green LED came on. There was a heavy mechanical clunk, and the wooden panel on the wall between the two paintings popped out at an angle. Thorne smiled. A secret door. Ashcroft pulled the edge and it swung slowly open, like the door of a vault. A light came on and they walked inside. The space was about half the size of Thorne's bedroom. There was a bookcase along one wall, a floor lamp, and a wingback leather chair straight out of a Sherlock Holmes movie. Against the other wall, was a small table with a wooden shipping case laid on top.

Ashcroft saw him staring at the chair.

"Lauren doesn't know about this room. I come here sometimes to have time to myself. I read, sleep, whatever I feel like. Never any work; that's the point I guess. I've not been here much since I got into the senate, I spend most of my time now in D.C."

Behind Ashcroft, he saw the edge of the door frame. The wall was six inch thick reinforced concrete, with a multi-point lock, and a milled stainless steel edge. It really was a vault. The man was married to a homecoming queen two decades younger than he was, and this was how he liked to spend time: in a sterile crypt, breathing chemical-flavored air through a vent in the wall.

"So it's a panic room, for hiding from your wife?"

"It's weird when you say it out loud, isn't it?"

"No," Thorne said, amused. "It's perfect."

Ashcroft smiled and nodded, clearly pleased by Thorne's reaction. After a beat the smile faltered as he remembered why they were here. The senator moved over to the wall beside the door. A rectangle was cut into the smooth concrete, and next to it was a keypad. They were on the other side of the Picasso. Ashcroft punched in four numbers to disable the alarm system, released two catches and the rectangle came out the wall with the painting attached. He lifted the painting off with one hand and passed it to Thorne. It was small and light, yet it felt strangely heavy. It made him uneasy to hold something so valuable and so fragile.

He looked up and found Ashcroft watching him.

"There's something to it, isn't there? A weight, like it knows its own value."

He nodded, then lay it on the shipping case before he broke it.

"The two of us," Ashcroft continued, "are probably the first two people to touch that painting without gloves in at least 25 years."

"I don't know what to say to that."

"We live in a strange world, Chris."

"You got that right."

Ashcroft picked up something that had been leaning against the wall. It was another painting. This had to be one that hung there while the Picasso was on show in Los Angeles. Thorne hadn't thought about it, but a man like Ashcroft wouldn't want an empty space on his wall for 11 months of the year, not even if most of that time was spent in Washington. Ashcroft attached the new painting to the rectangle, fitted the panel back through the wall, and punched in the code to arm the system.

Thorne stepped out into the hallway and let Ashcroft pack the Picasso into the shipping case. The mood had changed. It changed the second they'd touched the painting. Neither of them wanted to give it to Blake. Thorne didn't much like the picture, but he knew it was important, that it deserved respect. He glanced at his watch again. They had to go. Inside the room, Ashcroft had finished screwing the lid down. He stood in front of it running his fingertips over the rough wooden surface, like a silent prayer.

They closed up the secret room and walked out the building. The senator's Range Rover had a split tailgate, and he held the painting while Ashcroft opened both doors, then slid the Picasso into the trunk.

"What will you tell Lauren when she sees it's gone?"

"I doubt she'll notice. The Hopper's there more often than the Picasso anyway. Art's not her thing anymore; she'd rather be running or swimming. If I'm being honest, I rarely have time to look those paintings myself. Something I have come to understand about owning art, is that it's there for the benefit of other people."

Thorne bristled. It was offensive to him that anyone should have so much money that they could afford to treat hundred million dollar paintings like a piece of wallpaper. He watched Ashcroft fold up the lower tailgate and activate the electronic close for the top. They stood back as the large door powered shut.

It looked like Ashcroft was going to say something else; but nothing came. Instead, he sighed and they climbed wordlessly into the SUV. The interior was cold and Thorne felt the leather sucking the heat from his back. Ashcroft reversed slowly out the space and then took off down the drive. He knew what was bothering Ashcroft, it wasn't rocket science. He was remembering his last encounter with Blake at the mall.

Thorne watched the road go past. At night, it all looked the same. The blur of trees caught in the headlights, the twists and turns. Normally, he hated being a passenger but tonight he wanted to plan for what was coming without concerning himself with directions. As much as he appreciated the senator's help, there was something about it that didn't ring true. He'd agreed to the swap far too easily. The video had shaken him, Thorne had seen it on his face, but that could only explain so much. A hundred million dollars was a hundred million dollars, no matter who you were. It demanded a certain level of care, yet he appeared to have little concern for the safety of his painting. He knew Ashcroft's actions could be explained by a belief he was doing the right thing, or the fear that Lauren would be taken next; but neither of these explained everything to his satisfaction.

They were nearly there, just another couple of minutes.

Now that he thought about it, something else was bothering him. At no time had Ashcroft suggested calling the police or the FBI. Don't politicians usually have connections at law enforcement agencies they can reach out to for help? It felt like he was missing something important, and the last time he'd had the same feeling he'd been sitting next to Blake. Perhaps he'd lived too long in Los Angeles, but in his experience, this kind of thing never happened. There was always a personal angle that drove one person to help another. It had been greed and guilt that had got him here, and it would be fear and anger that would get him out. You always knew where you stood with people that were in it for themselves.

He saw light roughly a quarter mile ahead of them. The roadhouse. He looked at his watch: 01:30. They were exactly half an hour early, just the way he wanted. Never operate to someone else's timetable, always be early.

He had to assume that Blake would also be early, preparing for his own part in the drama.

"OK," Thorne said. "This is close enough. I'll walk from here."

Ashcroft pulled the SUV to the side of the road.

"You sure about this?"

"Yeah. We need to keep our options open, at least at the beginning. He won't expect me to be on foot, he can't prepare for it. You remember what I said? Give me a couple of minutes to get into place then park where you can see me."

"I remember," Ashcroft said.

"If this turns sour, get the hell out and don't look back."

"It's too bad that gun went missing."

"As long as they have Kate, it makes no difference."

"Of course."

Thorne opened the door to get out, paused, then pulled it closed again. He couldn't do it. He couldn't continue to pretend to be someone he wasn't. He was no hero, he wasn't even a nice guy. In all the ways that mattered, he was still a stranger to Ashcroft and it wasn't right to let him go through with this without knowing the truth, no matter how ugly.

"James, there's something I have to tell you. Something hard. It's about the gang that attacked you and Lauren." Thorne stopped, then forced himself to continue. "I knew them. I was one of them, before they decided to become kidnappers."

Ashcroft didn't respond, he kept looking through the windshield as if he hadn't heard, or didn't want to hear. Finally, he turned to Thorne, the skin around his eyes creased as if amused by some private joke.

"There's nothing to worry about, Chris. We're cool."

"You knew, didn't you?"

Ashcroft shrugged, the smile still on his face.

"I figured it out. I mean, why else would you have been there? It made no sense that someone with exactly the right skills would be there by accident. I appreciate you telling me, but how you came to be there is less important to me than what you did once you were. You risked your life for us, that's all there is to say."

Thorne sighed. Nothing had changed, the guilt remained. It ate into him, hollowing him out from the inside like some terrible parasite. He supposed he'd wanted Ashcroft to go crazy, to shout at him for all he was worth, even hit him. It was what he deserved.

"You're wrong about that. I didn't risk my life for either of you, I just didn't think about it. The two are not the same."

"Cabot tells me you slept in your rental car for three nights before saving us. You can't expect me to believe that in all that time, you didn't once think about what could happen to you. I will never believe that. What you did was amazing, it meant something."

Thorne looked down at his lap and nodded. He couldn't explain himself to someone like Ashcroft, who had never served. He knew the nod would be misinterpreted as agreement, but that was probably for the best. Swinging the door open again, he stepped out onto the dirt next to the highway. The SUV's interior light came on and he saw Ashcroft clearly for the first time in nearly half an hour. He looked older than he remembered.

"James? Thank you."

"You're welcome."

Thorne closed the door and jogged toward the roadhouse. The highway was deserted, so he ran down the asphalt between Ashcroft's headlights until the darkness swallowed him. The air was in the low fifties and he liked the feeling of it moving over his face. He was in no hurry, but it was late and exercise invigorated him. Blake would already be there waiting for him, he was certain. He would've spent time familiarizing himself with the location and with exfiltration routes in case anything went wrong.

As he got within a hundred yards of the roadhouse, he slowed to a fast walk. He didn't want to arrive breathless or overlook something. *Daryl's* was busier than he expected. A small parking lot out front had spaces for eight vehicles, all of which were full. Three men and a woman stood in the doorway smoking. The men wore a lot of denim, the woman not too much of anything. He avoided eye contact as he approached hoping they might return the favor, but it was no use, their conversation stopped and he felt them turn to watch him pass. He'd hoped to avoid being seen at the site of the swap but there wasn't much he could do about it now. A gas station sat next door and the two businesses were joined by a common apron that allowed vehicles to go from one to the other without rejoining the highway. A narrow access road ran down the side of the roadhouse, past overflowing dumpsters to the main customer parking lot. Lights covered in wire cages guided his way. The lot was large and was lined on both sides by trees, and in the middle by a dirty cinder block wall.

He saw Blake immediately, standing right in the middle of the lot. He was alone.

"Where's the goddamn painting, Thorne?"

He walked toward Blake, anger increasing with every step. He felt pumped-up, ready for another fight. It took all he had not to fly at Blake and tear him apart.

"Where's Kate?"

"She's here. *Close.* I just got to give the word, you know?"

Blake's eyes flicked to the left as he spoke and Thorne pretended not to notice. Was this a tell, or a misdirect? He fought the urge to look until there was an opportunity to make it look natural. Blake had played him too many times already.

259

"Then maybe you should give that word because you aren't getting shit until I see her. This is a swap, pure and simple."

Blake's lips rippled with anger.

"Be careful, my friend. I hold all the cards here."

"I disagree," Thorne said. "I have the painting now. The only way you get the money is through me. I say that makes us about even, don't you?"

Blake threw his hands up, his thick fingers gripping his head tight. The muscles in his arms filled the space that formed in the triangle on each side of his neck. His lips were peeled back and his teeth bit hard together to keep from screaming. After a second he reached around the back of his jeans and pulled out a Glock.

The pistol sat between them, aimed it at Thorne's gut.

"Keep pushing me, man, see what happens."

Thorne glanced at the gun. It was within his reach. Rage was causing Blake make basic mistakes. Despite the threat of being shot, it felt good to finally be getting the upper hand. All the same, he needed to make a gesture to keep things moving forward. It was time to see if Ashcroft had fulfilled his end of the deal.

"Tell you what, Aidan, I'll make the first move and maybe we can get this show on the road. What do you say?"

"Sure."

"I need to raise my hand, OK?"

Blake nodded and Thorne held his hand up.

Behind him, the headlights of Ashcroft's SUV snapped on.

The lights caught Blake right in the face. He raised his free hand to shield his eyes, his head turning away from the blinding light. After a beat, his startled expression changed and a smile spread across his face. *The painting's here, and now I know where it is.* Thorne could almost hear his old friend's thoughts as they tumbled through his head. All he needed to do was keep the painting in play until he got Kate back. Thorne dropped his arm again and the lights went out. He turned, as if to look at the Range Rover and quickly scanned the parking lot to his right. In the shadows he saw the familiar black van parked up under the spreading arms of a Douglas fir. None of the lights dotted around the lot cast any light on it, although he was sure if he looked hard enough, he'd discover a smashed bulb somewhere nearby. He made meaningless circular gesture with his hand in case Blake wondered why he'd turned around. To his surprise, Ashcroft started the Range Rover and revved the engine once. Thorne smiled to himself. It was a good idea. Now that they'd revealed the painting's location it made a lot of sense to be ready to move quickly. For a senator, Ashcroft was proving himself to be a capable wingman.

He turned as the Glock was lowered toward the ground.

Blake was looking past him and squinting at the SUV.

"Who you got as backup, Thorne? Is that *Ashcroft?*"

The Range Rover was distinctive even in the poor light of the parking lot and it should've occurred to him that Blake would recognize the SUV from the shoot-out. It was a stupid mistake, because if Blake thought long enough about it he'd realize that his leverage didn't stop with Kate.

"Make the call, asshole."

Blake was fast. Too fast. Thorne didn't see the fist flashing around until it was too late. He twisted to one side but it was no use, the base of the Glock clipped his head with a force that dropped him to his knees. He felt the cut open and blood start to weep out. The pain was sharp but not dangerous. There was no darkening at the edge of his vision, no nausea. He stared up at Blake, fury burning in his eyes. His anger was real, but he couldn't help but feel pleased at the same time. It was exactly the kind of over reaction he'd hoped for, designed to keep Blake in the moment and not have his thoughts drifting to other scenarios, like plans that didn't need Kate to be alive. Thorne touched his head then looked down at his fingers. In the light of the moon, his blood appeared almost black. He ran his thumb across his fingertips. The blood felt thin and watery, like store-brand cola.

The cut would need to be stitched.

"You got some mouth on you, Thorne."

He got to his feet and spat on the ground.

"Your old man used to tell me the same thing at Boy Scouts."

Blake shook his head in disbelief, then laughed.

"Shit, brother. You're crazy."

"You don't get to call me *brother* after what you've pulled."

Blake smirked. After a beat, his cell phone rang. It was on silent, but Thorne could hear it vibrating right through his pocket. Blake swapped the gun to his left hand and held the device up to his head. His features turned ugly, his eyes narrowing at Thorne. He grunted and returned the handset to his pocket, the Glock pointing again at Thorne's chest.

"Lift up your shirt." Blake said. "C'mon, man, lift it up!"

"What?"

"Do it, Thorne, or I'll shoot you in the face."

Blake was repeatedly glancing to his left and when Thorne looked over his shoulder he saw a sheriff's cruiser rolling slowly down the side of the gas station. The headlights were off and the engine silent. It was coasting, not under power. Trying not to be noticed. As the vehicle passed under the last light of the gas station, Thorne could see Cabot behind the wheel. He was looking straight at them.

"You think I'm wired?"

Thorne angled himself so that the lieutenant wouldn't see, and lifted the front of his shirt. The Glock, however, remained between them. It was now out of his reach and Blake had a crazed look on his face that wasn't going away.

"What's under all that tape?" Blake said.

"Wounds, from when you and your friends tried to kill me."

Blake shook his head. "You set me up."

"Stay cool. This isn't me, I don't know why he's here. Perhaps this has nothing to do with us. Don't blow the twelve mill, you're almost there. All I want is Kate, you know that. I would never put her life in that idiot's hands."

"You expect me to believe this is a coincidence?"

The muscles on Blake's arm were flexing and his fist jabbed forward to emphasize what he was saying. Thorne watched the jerky movements of the pistol in alarm. Blake's finger was on the trigger. It wouldn't take much for the gun to go off and blow out the back of his spine. The problem was, Blake was right. The odds of Cabot showing up for any other reason, were zero. Less than zero. Thorne had a sinking feeling in the pit of his stomach. He didn't want to accept it, but there was a single obvious explanation. Ashcroft had sold him out. The senator *had* reached out to someone in law enforcement after all, Lieutenant Cabot. It explained both his earlier behavior and his willingness to use the painting. He knew it was never in any danger. The only mistake he'd made, was trusting the cop not to arrive early and screw up the exchange.

He needed an explanation for Blake, something reasonable.

"I guess he followed me here. The man's been on my ass from day one, so it wouldn't surprise me."

"That's some pretty weak bullshit, Thorne."

A resigned calm settled over him. He'd more than used up his allowance of fight-or-flight with Blake, it was time to go all in with one last dice roll.

"You know, I feel bad that after all this time I've never once asked how your sister is getting on without that operation. Andrea, wasn't it? I'm wondering; will you tell her you shot the one person capable of making her operation happen, or will you choose to say nothing as she slowly rots on that hospital bed?"

Blake leaned forward, his eyes bulging out his head.

"As soon as that cop leaves, I'm going to end you and that blonde bitch. Maybe I'll kill her first and make you watch. I could really spin it out, make it something special. Then, when I'm finally finished with you, I'm going to just take the painting from Ashcroft. I don't need you for shit."

Thorne smiled. Sometimes, nothing riled a man up as much as a good smile at the wrong moment. But that wasn't why he was smiling. There was a clarity to Blake's anger that couldn't be denied. Thorne believed him when he said he'd kill Kate, he could see it in his eyes. He'd pushed Blake too far, but the threat to her life meant she was alive. He could still save her. There'd been nothing on the video to indicate when it had been made, it could've been a week old. Part of him feared that Blake had killed her shortly after making the video and that the swap was a sham. He was also pleased to note that rage had brought the Glock back into range. It probably wouldn't be possible for him to snatch the pistol from Blake's muscular hand, but he could certainly steer it away from his body for that first shot, and that was all the chance he needed.

"Since you mention it," Thorne said, "I added a small amount of ANFO to the inside of the shipping case. Enough to destroy the painting, along with any dreams you may have of playing a piano. I'm the only person that knows how to disable it, which I am not going to tell you until me, Kate, and Ashcroft are all clear. Consider it insurance."

"Not. Another. Word," Blake hissed.

There was something close to insanity carved into Aidan Blake's face and, for now, Thorne thought it wise to stay silent and let him calm down. There'd been no time to rig the painting with explosive, he hadn't even thought of it before it came out his mouth. The irony was how little difference it made if he had or hadn't, Blake couldn't risk opening the case without knowing how to do so safely. It was the perfect bluff.

A door opened and closed several times behind them, followed by the tumbling bass of male voices. Half a dozen men, possibly more. Mid twenties to early thirties, he thought. Not drunk, but getting there. The roadhouse was closing up for the night. It would now be after 2 a.m. Thorne resisted the urge to break eye contact with Blake and instead cast his mind back to when he arrived. There'd been five vehicles in the parking lot, excluding Ashcroft's Range Rover and the black van. Three behind him and two behind Blake. For any of them to leave, Cabot would have to move his cruiser which blocked the narrow strip of asphalt leading to the highway. Either his problems were all over, or they were about to get a lot worse.

Thorne spoke softly, calmly.

"*Aidan.* We're about to be overrun, put the piece away."

The shift in tone caught Blake off guard and he appeared to deflate as if he'd let out a deep breath. His shoulders dropped and the arm holding the pistol lowered to the ground once more. He sighed, then tucked the Glock into the back of his pants.

"This ain't over, Thorne."

"Yeah, it is. I'm sick of your shit, Blake. I came here willing to give you exactly what you want and that hasn't changed. I have nothing to do with Cabot showing up. In case you've forgotten, that cop is bad news for me as well. Now, either you trust me for five more minutes and become a millionaire, or shoot me and get nothing. Your choice."

Blake appeared to think it over, then nodded.

"There ain't much trust left in the world, brother."

With Blake's pistol stowed away, Thorne risked glancing around the parking lot. He counted five men and three women. None of the men was over five eight, and none of them looked like they'd picked up much more than a beer for the duration of their life. They were no threat; he and Blake could take them apart without breaking into a sweat. He recognized two of the men from the front door. They shuffled toward him now, heads down. They were half in the bag, and neither of them had any business being behind a steering wheel. Cars were starting all around them. This might be his only opportunity to leave the parking lot alive. With everyone gone, Blake could do what he liked.

The lights of Cabot's cruiser flickered into life. The lieutenant had blown it by staying in his car. If he'd parked around front and approached on foot they'd never have seen him. He could've pulled off the arrest of his career. Instead, he'd stayed in his warm car, sitting on his fat ass. He was a buffoon, and Thorne felt nothing but contempt for him. Cabot reached his arm out behind the passenger head restraint, looked back through the rear window, and reversed his car along the narrow access road. At the gas station he turned to face onto the road and sat there waiting. Thorne noticed Blake was watching the same shit show he was.

"That's right, asshole, nothing to see here. Move along."

"What if he stays there?" Thorne asked.

"Then you and me conclude our business someplace else."

There was a hard edge in his voice that Thorne didn't like. Blake was losing it. This job was taking far longer than he'd allowed for and things had gone wrong from the start. Thorne knew what that was like, how it could drive you close to madness. An apparently quick job that never seems to end. The pay-off that never gets any closer. Blake would take any shortcut he could to make it end and get his life back on track.

The last two cars were leaving the lot, slowly making their way around the corner and up the access road. They drove one behind the other, with the one in front driving particularly slowly. The driver of the rear car was riding the brake and Thorne had to screw up his eyes at the brightness of the tail lights. His night vision was burned out and when the cars cleared the road it took him a moment to realize that Cabot's cruiser was also gone. He could see the cars lights moving through the darkness of the trees.

"Seems like your buddy deserted you, Thorne."

He turned back toward Blake. His face showed no sign of irony.

"You can't be serious?"

Blake punched him hard in the guts, doubling him over. While he was pitched forward, Blake hit him again across the top of his head with the

264

butt of his Glock. He fell face-down on the asphalt, his vision swimming.

"*That's* for what you said about my sister."

Thorne scrambled to his knees, but Blake was ready for him and pressed the barrel of his pistol against his forehead, his other hand on Thorne's shoulder, holding him in place.

"Not so fast, Thorne. How about you stay right there?"

"Fuck you, Blake, and fuck your sister. We had a deal."

Blake nodded. "We did. We *had* a deal, but as we were standing here talking I realized something. After you and me went our separate ways, you'd still be out there floating around. You'd still know everything that happened and without the pay-off there'd be nothing to stop you talking to the cops. That makes you a loose end, and that's a problem."

"Aren't you forgetting something, Blake?"

"No, I don't think I am."

"The explosive I put in the case. You kill me, and that painting might as well not exist. You'll never see a dime of that money."

"I've been thinking about that too, my friend. I know how smart you are, smart enough to make up that stuff about the explosive. I got to admit, you had me going there for a minute. But I see it now for what it is. Bullshit. You had no time to set that up."

"And you're going to risk your life on that assumption?"

Blake smiled. "No. I'm going to risk Kate Bloom's."

"You bastard."

"We're both bastards, I'm just better prepared. If there actually is any explosive you better tell me now, or Kate will pay the price."

"What's the difference? You'll kill her anyway."

Blake sighed. "I was angry, all right? I don't need to kill her. She doesn't know who we are, or why she was taken. But that's beside the point. I know there's no explosive, you would've given it up immediately at even the idea it would hurt her."

Thorne's eyes dipped down to the ground. He was out of options. This was where his story ended, in a roadhouse parking lot.

"I want you to know that I'm going to miss these little chats of ours, Thorne. Not to mention your sense of humor. You do make me laugh sometimes. It's too bad things didn't work out the way I'd planned, but I guess not everyone is cut out for this life."

"I can't decide which is worse; being shot in the head, or listening to your endless Bond-villain speeches."

"Goodbye, Thorne."

Blake lifted his hand off Thorne's shoulder and straightened his arm. Thorne felt the pistol press harder and harder against his head. He knew what it meant. Nobody liked getting brains on their sleeve. This was it. Behind them, the Range Rover's lights snapped on high beams. The SUV was already moving, accelerating hard toward them. Blake turned, his gun swinging with his head. Thorne jumped out of the path of the SUV. As he landed, he heard a shot from Blake's Glock and when his head whipped around, saw the tank-like vehicle flash past. He expected Ashcroft to stop so he could get in but it kept going, continuing to accelerate right up to the moment it plowed into the concrete wall, causing the rear wheels to pop up off the asphalt with the force of the impact.

He turned back to Blake. Half of his face was covered by blood, and his left leg was folded underneath him at an impossible angle. His teeth were biting together in pain, and he was staring grimly at the Glock which lay in the space between them. Thorne scrambled forward on all fours, not wanting to waste time standing and then squatting down to get the weapon. He was three feet away from it when Sara appeared on a motorcycle. Before she stopped, she pulled a MAC-10 machine pistol from inside her jacket and aimed it one handed at his chest. He sat back and raised his hands in surrender. Sara glanced quickly at the SUV. Somehow, the vehicle's engine was still running, and it was making a terrific noise. He watched her hands carefully, waiting for an opportunity. The stock of the pistol was closed. He doubted she had the skill necessary to control the pistol one handed without it. That probably wouldn't matter too much, not at this range. The MAC-10 was a messy beast, and it would shred him.

"Help him up," she said. "Get him on the bike."

Thorne nodded and got to his feet. Sara was crazy, but she needed his help. As soon as that situation changed, he'd be right back to being a loose end. Next to him, Blake rolled onto his back. His left leg was bent sideways at the knee. It was a bad dislocation, not a break. He could fix it for him, but he had no desire to do so. The longer it went untreated, the more pain Blake would be in and the longer it would take him to recover. But there wouldn't be any recovery, not if he had anything to do with it. He grabbed Blake's left arm and got him upright, then put the arm over his shoulder and walked him toward Sara. While he'd been dealing with Blake, she'd turned the motorcycle around and pulled forward, ready to leave. It increased the distance between her and Blake's discarded gun. She was good. He'd never be able to reach it before they left the parking lot. So be it. The sooner they were gone, the better. All he could think about now was Kate. The motorcycle sank down as Blake sat on it, and she had to stow the pistol to balance his uneven weight with both hands. Sara took off as soon as Blake's hands were around her waist.

He hurried toward the van, dreading what he might find. If Blake believed he was getting the painting tonight, what more use would he have for Kate? She'd seen their faces, she could identify them. That made her disposable to Blake, a means to an end and no more. Thorne touched the hood with the palm of his hand as he walked past. The metal was cold; the van hadn't moved in a long time. He continued around the side and saw the foot-long dent above the back wheel arch. It was definitely Blake's van. He pulled on the side door handle. It was unlocked and the door slid open along its track and bounced on the end stop.

Kate was not inside.

FORTY

Thorne ran toward the Range Rover. The impact had caused the front of the SUV to crumple up like paper against the wall. Despite the scale of the damage, the engine continued to roar, sending a thick plume of black smoke into the night sky. There was no sign of Ashcroft nearby, he had to still be inside the vehicle. As Thorne drew level with the driver's door, his fears were confirmed. The senator sat staring at the smashed windshield with his hands on the wheel as if he was still driving. Aside from a cut on the side of his face, he appeared uninjured. A gray blob sat in James Ashcroft's lap like a half-empty pillowcase. The airbag. It had saved his life, but its sudden deployment had clearly stunned him.

Thorne pulled on the door handle, but nothing happened. It was jammed.

There was a series of loud bangs, followed by the shrieking of metal-on-metal grinding. The engine was fixing to tear itself apart. He ran around to the other side of the SUV and tried the handle. It was no use; the collision had twisted the chassis, pushing the alignment out on the doors. He would need to force his way in. He tried the tailgate and it opened with ease.

The painting lay across the floor in its wooden case.

A hundred million dollars, right in front of him. He'd known it was there, but the sight of it caused a space to form in his mind. All he needed to do was pick it up and walk away. He pushed the thought aside and dug around for the tire iron. Back at the driver's door, he rammed it between the door frame and the support pillar. He pushed it away from his body as he pulled on the door handle. The metal started to buckle. Thorne gritted his teeth and gave it all he had. The pain from his shoulder wound burned like a hot knife, but he kept on going. After several seconds, he spun around and the tire iron fell on the asphalt. When he looked he saw the door handle had come off in his hand, tethered by an umbilical of wires.

The lever was too short, he'd never get the door open in time.

He needed a pry bar at least, perhaps cutting tools.

Nausea swept over him, and he coughed violently. He leaned forward and put his hand on one knee to steady himself. The acrid smoke was in his lungs and his eyes were streaming. It was difficult to breathe. He wouldn't be able to stand here much longer. If he couldn't get Ashcroft out, he'd have to leave or risk passing out. There was a popping sound from the engine bay, followed by the sound of liquid splashing onto the ground. The heat from the front of the car was critical. He rapped on the glass with his fist and Ashcroft looked up at him.

"Look away from the glass!" Thorne shouted.

The senator nodded and turned toward the passenger seat and Thorne drove the tire iron through the window. The glass sprayed inward in hundreds of pieces, covering the senator's head and shoulders. He ran the tool around the frame, removing the remaining fragments of glass. When he stopped, Ashcroft twisted back around and his suit jacket opened. There was a large blood stain on Ashcroft's shirt.

"James, I'm not going to lie to you, this is going to hurt. I have to pull you out through the window. Lean forward so I can get my arm around your back. Do you understand?"

Ashcroft frowned. "I think I've been shot."

"Lean forward, can you do that buddy?"

"Sure."

Thorne got his hand under Ashcroft's left arm and pushed it around his back. He curled his fingers into a C shape and hooked it on the fingers of his other hand and pulled. Ashcroft screamed, but Thorne kept on pulling and twisting until he got him out through the window. He carried Ashcroft across the parking lot to Blake's van and propped him against the back wheel, his head resting on the tire. Now that he was safely away from the SUV, Thorne took out his cell phone and dialed 911. He gave them their location and impressed upon the operator that the senator had been shot and urgently needed help. After he finished the call, he looked down at Ashcroft.

"I'll be right back."

He double timed it back to the Range Rover. The entire front of it was now on fire and he felt the heat of the flames on his face from twenty feet away. He slowed to a fast walk, his senses on alert. His training made him cautious and want to slow down but this was no IED and time was against him. It was quieter now, the engine having finally stopped. Around him was the unmistakable smell of gasoline. The tailgate was still open so he reached in and grabbed the painting and ran back to the van. He'd heard that gas tanks only exploded into fireballs in Hollywood movies but he didn't want to put it to the test.

Ashcroft shook his head when he saw what he was holding.

"You should've let it burn, it's been nothing but bad luck."

"That may be true, but I still need it."

Ashcroft said nothing.

When he'd been shot, Lauren had talked to him and held his hand until help arrived. He didn't remember too much about it, but he was certain it had kept him going somehow, kept him fighting to survive. He wished she was here now for her husband, but she wasn't. Ashcroft's crazy stunt had saved his life and he couldn't let him die because of it. He sat facing the senator so they were looking into each other's eyes. All he needed to do was keep the man talking and try not stare at the dark stain spreading across his pale blue shirt. He felt anger and resentment welling up inside him. Nobody had saved his life before and he didn't much like the way it felt. It was a debt he could never pay back.

"I don't understand," Thorne said. "Why would you do something like that after what I told you? I'm not a good guy."

Ashcroft smiled grimly, his teeth smeared with blood.

"Because I owed you."

"You owe me nothing, man."

"Chris, there's something I need to tell you, too. I'd planned on telling you the day I gave you the car, but the right moment never presented itself. You were so happy, I didn't want to ruin it. I should've though, I can see that now." Ashcroft shook his head. "This situation spun out of control so quickly, there was just no way to make it stop."

Thorne groaned. He should've seen this coming.

"The whole thing was your idea. *You're* the buyer."

"It was a simple plan," Ashcroft said. "No one was supposed to get hurt."

Blake's words coming out of Ashcroft's mouth.

"The gang have no idea who you are?"

"I kept it anonymous so I couldn't be blackmailed later."

Thorne nodded. It was the smart play, Blake would certainly have seen the opportunity to make more money once he learned Ashcroft's identity.

"How much is it insured for?"

"One hundred twenty million, double what I paid for it. The truth is, I need the money. You might think I'm rich, but running for president is an expensive business. Donors prefer to support candidates who look like they don't need their money. Needing funds makes you weak, like you're a loser. That's what's wrong with this damn country, you're either a winner or a loser. I want to change that, to heal this divided nation. The campaign doesn't start until next year, but without the insurance money I'll be bankrupt by Christmas."

"I see that, James, but why a robbery? Why not sell it?"

Ashcroft nodded, like he expected the question.

"I'm almost certain the painting was stolen by the Nazis. Picasso wasn't one of their favorites, but it's the most obvious explanation. Perhaps a thief took advantage of the chaos I don't know. I've been buying documentation from the time and destroying it, but it's only a matter of time until something gets digitized and put online for everyone to see." Ashcroft paused, his face pinched with pain. "I couldn't risk selling the painting at auction. The provenance paperwork wouldn't stand up to the scrutiny they have now. The ownership covering '33 to '45 is clearly bogus and it doesn't take a genius to figure out why. I wouldn't see a dime from the sale and my reputation would be in ruins."

"Were you actually going to pay those clowns to get the painting back? It seems to me that you could pay them nothing and still get your insurance money."

"I thought of that," Ashcroft said. "But if I didn't pay them, I knew they'd try to sell it to someone else. Perhaps direct to my insurance company, it's happened before. An insurer would rather pay a thief a fraction of its value, than pay it all to the owner. I couldn't risk the painting being recovered, I'd be back where I started. The money's all in place when it comes to it."

They sat in silence for a while, each of them lost in thought. It was hard for Thorne to accept that, in his own way, James Ashcroft worried about going broke. It seemed like a bad joke, and yet it made him like Ashcroft all the more. He was rich, but he was prepared to lose it all to become president so that he could help the poor.

In the distance, Thorne heard the chopping blades of a helicopter. Most likely, the same one he'd been in. To his ear, the helicopter was five minutes out. Ashcroft looked in a bad way. He wasn't convinced the senator was going to last long enough for the paramedics to save him.

This was the reality of being shot; once was usually enough.

He heard a siren and saw red and blue strobes cutting through the trees. It was moving fast, and would be with him in less than a minute. Thorne knew it wouldn't be an ambulance. They were in the middle of nowhere; the closest first responder was Cabot. He looked back at Ashcroft. His face was the color of wet cement. Thorne crouched over him and, supporting the senator's neck, laid him out flat on the asphalt. He shouldn't have propped him up, he realized, it would have accelerated his blood loss.

He smiled at his friend and made it look good.

"Stay with me, Jimmy. They're coming."

"You called me Jimmy."

Ashcroft's voice was little more than a whisper. A butterfly flapping its wings. Thorne leaned in close so that his ear was an inch from the senator's lips. Cabot's siren was almost on top of him now, and he didn't want to miss a word.

"Tell Lauren I'm sorry. Tell her -"

271

He waited for a couple of seconds, but there was no more. He looked at Ashcroft's face, then looked away. He'd known what he was going to see. Twice before he'd been with someone when they'd died. It never got any easier.

His eyes slid across to the case containing the painting.

FORTY-ONE

A bad feeling gnawed at Cabot's insides as he drove back to the roadhouse. He should never have left. He'd known it was a mistake even as he drove away, but it seemed pointless to stay as long as Thorne knew he was there. Once he'd been made, it was game over. He'd been tired and embarrassed at his own blunder but public safety was his primary function and he'd chosen to ignore that when his illegal surveillance had been discovered.

He cut the final corner, swinging his cruiser across the gas station apron and down the side of the roadhouse he'd left less than ten minutes earlier. The side access road was no longer in semi-darkness, flickering orange flames lit his way past overflowing dumpsters and broken wooden pallets. He turned into the parking lot and slammed on the brakes. Thorne was on his knees, crouching over a man's lifeless body. *Ashcroft*. Cabot threw open his door and from a standing position behind it, drew his weapon.

"Show me your hands!"

Thorne slowly held up his hands and turned toward him. His eyes narrowed as they came into line with the headlights of the Taurus. His left sleeve was dark with blood.

"This isn't what it looks like, Cabot."

"Is he dead?"

"Yes."

"You son of a bitch!"

His finger flexed against the trigger. He could do it. Put a bullet through the actor's head. It would be so easy, no one else was here. His word would be official record, nobody would challenge it, not now. Not with the senator dead. Cabot came out from behind the door and walked carefully toward Thorne's position. He kept his pistol aimed center mass. He was taking no chances, he'd seen that video enough times. The man was deadly.

"Think about it," Thorne said. "Why would I risk my life saving him before, only to shoot him here less than a month later? Why would I call 911?"

Cabot ignored him. It wasn't for him to work out why a criminal did something, only that they did it. Working out motivation could help you catch someone, but once he'd caught a suspect, it bored him. In his experience, most crimes only made sense to the person that committed them and you could twist your mind in a knot trying to figure out their reasoning. In any case, it was perfectly obvious why Thorne had called 911 - because the actor knew he could be placed at the scene by him and others.

He closed up the final few feet in silence, still thinking through whether to take him in alive, or kill him. Whatever he decided, he didn't have much time, he could hear a helicopter approaching. The air ambulance. Witnesses were about to appear. They couldn't save Ashcroft but their presence could once again save Thorne. Without thinking about it, he transferred his pistol to his left hand and punched Thorne with his right, knocking him backward onto the asphalt. Pain surged up his arm from his fist and he shook his arm several times to try and shake it off. He'd used the full power of his arm from an elevated position and he'd hit bone.

Thorne remained on the ground where he'd fallen.

"All right, son, get up. Quit the act."

Thorne stood slowly, first to his knees as before, then rising up to his full height. It seemed to Cabot as though the man was taller than ever, perhaps a whole six inches taller than he was. Instinctively, he took a step back and a trace of a smile moved across Thorne's lips. With his left hand, Cabot fished a dog-eared card out of his back pocket and he read the words printed on it, his eyes twitching nervously between the card and the former Marine.

"You are under arrest for the murder of James Ashcroft. You have the right to remain silent. Anything you say can and will be used against you in a court of law. You have the right to have an attorney present during questioning. If you cannot afford an attorney, one will be appointed for you. Do you understand these rights I have explained to you?"

Thorne sighed. "Yes."

"Having these rights in mind, do you have anything to say to me now?"

"Go suck a dick, Cabot."

Now it was his turn to smile.

"Hands behind your back, smart guy."

"No."

"Excuse me?"

"I can't. My shoulder injury won't allow it."

The helicopter passed slowly overhead then moved away from the burning SUV and over the roof of the roadhouse and out of sight. This was a complication Cabot didn't need. He wanted Thorne locked down before anyone else arrived. He couldn't afford to be distracted and risk

274

Thorne getting away.

"All right, fine. Let's speed this up. Hands out front, no funny business. If I even *think* you're making a break for it, I'm just going to shoot you, OK?"

Thorne nodded.

Behind him, he heard the helicopter engine wind down. It must've landed on the highway in front of the bar. The road was empty and it was probably the only landing spot for miles. He pulled out his handcuffs and paused, sensing danger. Cabot wet his lips. He couldn't put the handcuffs on Thorne and maintain the aim with his weapon. For the first time, he wished Barnes was with him to provide cover.

"Toss me the cuffs and I'll put them on."

The actor's voice was calm, reasonable. People could get that way when they realized that it was all over. For some, being caught was a relief. In any case, Thorne's suggestion seemed like the best option, so he threw him the cuffs and watched him closely. It was procedure to cuff suspects behind their back for a reason, he'd have to be careful with Thorne. The cuffs clicked shut around one wrist, then the other. It was no trick.

Tension immediately started to leave his body.

"Into the back of my car."

Two medics appeared around the side of his Ford. They glanced at him then across at Thorne. Seeing enough, they turned their attention to the figure on the ground. They ran over to Ashcroft, a folded up stretcher hanging between them. They slowed to a walk before reaching the senator, they knew the score without touching him. Cabot caught movement out the corner of his eye. Thorne had done something, his hands were moving quickly down in front of his chest, both moving together, still handcuffed.

"What was that?"

"Relax, Cabot. I scratched my head. I had an itch."

He waved the actor over to his car with his gun. "Let's go, hero."

Thorne turned and walked in front of him toward the cruiser. His shoulders were down, his swagger gone. Just the same, Cabot hung back, his automatic aimed at the man's kidneys. It embarrassed him how much Thorne still intimidated him, even with the advantage of a gun and handcuffs. He knew logically that he was in no danger but he couldn't seem to get past it. His mind skipped ahead, thinking about his Taurus. It was the next danger point, he'd have to open the rear door and load Thorne into the back. He'd have the actor stand to the right of the door so he could watch him as he opened it. Until Thorne was safely locked inside, he could take nothing for granted. He smiled to himself, imagining the solid clump of the door shutting and seeing Thorne's sad face through the glass. It would be a sweet moment, one he'd started to believe might not happen.

As they came up to the rear of the car, Thorne appeared to stumble and fell awkwardly on the asphalt with a loud grunt. Cabot laughed. If this was Thorne's play he was wasting his time. This was no accidental trip. It was a clumsy, half-hearted move and made him appear foolish to Cabot. For the first time since they'd met, he felt superior. This scrabbling about on the ground, this was the last moves of a desperate man. All it needed now, he thought, was for the actor to try throwing dirt in his eyes as an escape plan. This was lame, and it lifted his spirits. He noticed both medics had turned to stare at him, their interest in Ashcroft apparently at an end. Cabot made a show of his hands as if to say *nothing to do with me,* though the smile that was still on his face probably made this a tough sell. It was likely that the medics would recognize both of them from the rolling news coverage and had probably worked out what had gone down here. It also seemed likely, given recent history, that they wouldn't believe Thorne was guilty. No matter. The evidence would tell a different story.

"Come on Thorne, this shit's gettin' old."

"I can't get up...the handcuffs."

He sighed and glanced again at the medics. They were still watching. It had been inappropriate for him to laugh so close to where a man had been murdered, he saw that now. He couldn't help it, not even when the dead man had been his friend. It was a release from stress, and from knowing he'd finally nailed the actor. He wanted to kick Thorne a couple of times to see if that helped him remember how to stand up. He holstered his weapon. He was taking a chance, but he believed the presence of the medics would prevent Thorne taking action against him, just as it had prevented him taking action against the actor. Cabot reached down and grabbed Thorne's left elbow and pulled on it. The younger man was heavy and rose slowly at first, then with a jolt, snapped up to full height little more than a foot away from him. He felt movement against his firearm and spun sideways, automatically drawing his weapon again. His heart thumped wildly in his chest. Thorne stared back impassively.

"Jesus Christ. What now, Cabot?"

He felt his face turn red. Had he imagined it?

"Against the car, hands on the roof and spread your legs."

Thorne shook his head and wordlessly did as he was told. Cabot performed a thorough pat down. He was limited by only having his left hand free so the process took longer than usual. He found no trace of a gun or other weapon. The actor was carrying only a cell phone and a car key fob, which he took and placed on the roof of the Taurus. This done, he made Thorne stand to one side, just as he'd planned. Cabot fixed his gaze on him while he blindly felt for the door handle beside him. He pulled it open and stepped to one side again, still covering Thorne with his firearm. The actor's face was blank and emotionless as he looked into the darkened rear of the cruiser. After a beat, he stepped forward and folded himself down onto the back seat. He sat still, eyes front, until Cabot slammed the door closed on him. To his disappointment, it wasn't as he had imagined. It was too dark to see inside, he saw only a reflection of the flames that still licked at the burned-out husk of the SUV behind him.

Cabot returned his firearm to his holster.

Tension had been building within him ever since he'd started to tail Ashcroft. He'd followed him for miles without headlights, only dropping back where street lights and houses would have revealed his position. There was a dull ache from his jaw muscles from clenching his teeth, soon, he knew, it would become a headache that would last all the next day.

He bagged up Thorne's personal items and dropped them into the front passenger seat, then used the car's radio to call it in. Now that the arrest had been made, he decided to call Barnes at home from his cell. If he was to make the arrest stick he'd need the younger man's assistance. The detective's voice was thick with sleep. He gave no reaction to his news and simply stated he'd be about an hour. Out front, Cabot heard the helicopter engine start and he turned to watch as it rose over the roadhouse heading south east, back to Gilroy.

For a short while he had the scene to himself.

He looked around the parking lot. Ashcroft still lay where he'd first seen him. Now that Thorne was contained, he walked over and stood next to his old friend for the first time. A lot of blood had leaked out underneath the senator and he had to be careful where he placed his shoes. He pulled on evidence gloves as he ran his eyes quickly over the body. From a quick pass, it was obvious the medics had performed no medical procedures beyond checking for a pulse. His shirt remained fastened, a blood stain just off center marking where the damage was done. Cabot took a pen flashlight from his jacket pocket and aimed the beam at the area of his chest. The wound was small, the width of his smallest finger. He directed the flashlight up to Ashcroft's face. His eyes were open, but there was nothing in them.

Cabot looked away, directing his attention to his surroundings. If there was anything to be found, he wanted to be the one to find it. He turned his head and flashlight together, sweeping carefully across the cracked asphalt of the parking lot. He worked in a grid, never trying to take in too much of the scene at once. After a minute, he found a single shell casing. A 9mm. It had come to rest up on its end, like a rocket ready to be sent into space. Using his cell phone, he took photographs of it from several angles. These were for his own record and would not be used in evidence. When he was done, he took a business card from his wallet, folded it in half and positioned it near the shell casing to act as a marker. He then used a stack of loose coins to prop the card up and prevent it from blowing away. He resumed his search and looked for another five minutes but found nothing else.

The gun used to shoot Ashcroft was not here.

He sighed. Getting a conviction without the murder weapon wouldn't be straightforward, but he wasn't worried. Thorne had simply disposed of it before he arrived. No doubt thrown into the woods that surrounded the roadhouse, or tucked into one of the dumpsters around the side. Thorne couldn't have gone far to hide it, the window of his own departure and return put this at no more than ten minutes. By first light, half the Sheriff's Office would be combing the area for it. That firearm would be found sooner or later. He yawned and decided to wait for backup to arrive from inside his warm cruiser. He couldn't leave until the crime scene had been secured. He resisted the temptation to step over Ashcroft's body and instead walked around it. As he did so, the beam of his flashlight came to rest on the vehicle behind the senator's head.

A black van.

A smile worked its way up the side of his face, like his flesh was slowly tearing. It was the same goddamn van he'd been looking for, he'd swear on it. Despite being the only other vehicle in the lot apart from Ashcroft's SUV and his own Taurus, he'd completely failed to register it. Somehow, it receded into the shadows under a pine tree, unwilling to be seen. In his mind, a delicious possibility presented itself: what if there was a fingerprint of Thorne's *inside* the vehicle, somewhere he couldn't explain. He'd gotten nowhere near it during the attempted kidnapping, the security footage proved that. It would represent an undeniable link between the actor and the original attempted abduction of the Ashcrofts. With that, the immunity deal would be over and Thorne would be on the hook for three more counts of murder one and whatever they could pin on him for the shooting of Samuel Porter.

He walked back to the cruiser, a new spring in his step.

Thorne was *done*.

FORTY-TWO

It was cold in the back of Cabot's cruiser and Thorne felt it seep slowly into his bones. He had watched the lieutenant blunder around the parking lot pretending to be a cop, first with disdain, then with growing alarm. Could it really be that the one thing he wasn't guilty of would be the thing that would bring him down? He could be placed at the scene beforehand, he was standing over Ashcroft's body when the lieutenant arrived, and he was covered in the senator's blood. It didn't look good for him.

Thorne thought through possible courses of action.

First of all, naming Blake as the shooter. On the face of it, this was a no-brainer. If he *wasn't* the shooter but *was* at the scene, his only option was to say someone else pulled the trigger. This had the advantage of being the truth, not to mention getting the police to look in the right direction. With the right names, photographs would quickly follow and a proper manhunt would begin.

Only, he couldn't do that.

If he gave them up, Kate was as good as dead. Blake would kill her, then disappear. He'd *have* to kill her, he couldn't leave any witnesses. But Aidan Blake was no D.B. Cooper. They'd catch him quickly, probably inside of a week. With decent photographs, correct ID, and a personal background, most manhunts ended in one of two ways. Assuming he was still alive, Blake would reveal his own role as one of the gang members. He would implicate him in the murder of the cop at the art gallery and the former guard. It occurred to him that there was an official link between them from his defense of Blake at his court martial. It probably wasn't a standard search, but a good investigator could turn up documented proof and it would be impossible for him to deny a pre-existing friendship.

He could do nothing to protect Kate while in police custody. Within hours, Blake would hear he was being questioned by police and would assume the worst. The only thing he could think of to do to save Kate, was to admit that he'd killed Ashcroft. The news of his arrest would be followed immediately by the revelation that he'd already confessed to the crime, leaving Blake no reason to kill Kate before he skipped town. This relied on Blake doing the right thing and of him hearing the news before he made his decision to leave. Once he released Kate, Blake would know that there'd be nothing to prevent him from recanting his confession and pointing the cops in the right direction.

Thorne looked through the glass into the darkness outside.

A patrol vehicle arrived to secure the crime scene and Cabot laid it all out for the two deputies. After several minutes, Cabot got into the car and they were underway, headed back toward Santa Cruz.

"Well, Thorne. It's just you and me in here. We got some time before we get back to headquarters. You have anything to say to me?"

He looked at Cabot in the rearview mirror. The lieutenant's head was angled toward the middle of the windshield, his eyes flipped up to watch him. Thorne supposed that modern police cruisers were equipped with the facility to record conversations held inside them. There'd be a switch somewhere on the dashboard, next to the other police upgrades. He didn't know for sure, because it had never come up on his show. The fact that he'd been read his rights made anything he might say admissible in court.

Thorne nodded. "Yeah, I got something to say."

Cabot looked at him hopefully in the mirror.

"What's that?"

"Your car smells like ass."

The lieutenant's face soured.

"That's a smell you'll have to get used to where you're going."

Light from somewhere was landing on Cabot's eyes. A reflection of the car's headlights, or the instrument panel. It gave them a strange shiny appearance, like he was possessed. There was no way he was going to confess to this joker, no way. He'd made his play. It wasn't much, but it was something. All they had was circumstantial. In the grand scheme of things, perhaps this was for the best. Cabot had wanted to arrest him from the beginning; now that he had, he'd have to produce evidence or release him. One way or another, this party was about to end.

"I'll tell you something for free, Cabot. By lunchtime tomorrow, there'll be a line of federal vehicles parked outside your building and you'll be back in charge of wife beaters and purse-snatchers. All you're doing right now is giving me a ride back into town."

Cabot sighed and returned his eyes to the road.

Rain was falling by the time they arrived at the Sheriff's Office. It was thick and heavy, the kind that bounced back up off the asphalt in a shimmering blur. It had rained like this several times since he'd been in Santa Cruz, but it felt different as he sat in the back of Cabot's cruiser. He thought of Ashcroft lying on the ground and wondered if one of the cops would think to cover him. Their friendship had been brief and filled with betrayal, but he'd grown to like the senator. It was a matter of days since he'd joked about his death with Lauren. He was ashamed that the words had come out his mouth and he wished now he could take them back.

In front of him Cabot sighed again, then stepped out into the rain. It appeared that he'd hoped to wait out the weather and had given up. He walked around the back of the cruiser and opened the door. The lieutenant's mouth was pulled back as if in a smile, but there was no humor there, just teeth. It wasn't hard to understand; his friend was dead and the man thought he was responsible. Cabot held a clear plastic bag, which he pulled down over both Thorne's handcuffed hands. The bag was deep and swallowed his forearms. He knew it was to preserve gunshot residue evidence, but Cabot was going to be disappointed.

Thorne stuck his right leg out onto the asphalt and managed to balance against the door frame as he dragged his wounded left leg out. Cabot grabbed him roughly by his elbow and walked him quickly toward the building. The rain lashed against them as they covered the short distance to the entrance. Inside, the building was quiet. He could see a few lights and computer screens lit up, but only a couple of people. It was early morning, and word of his arrest had yet to draw other cops in. He supposed that some who were on duty were now involved in locking down the crime scene. Cabot led him to an interview room and pushed him into a chair. He removed the plastic bag then re-handcuffed him through a bar on the table in front of him. The position pulled painfully on his shoulder injury, but he said nothing and instead stared blankly up at the lieutenant.

"All right, how about you tell me what happened?"

"I'm not saying shit to you without a lawyer."

Cabot's nostrils flared.

"That's not what innocent people say, Thorne. If you want me to believe you're not guilty, you're going to have to convince me. I got to tell you, this silent routine works fine for me. Saying nothing is like admitting you did it."

It was true, he couldn't give them nothing. He needed to clear himself without giving them Blake. Obstruction only stood to lengthen his stay in custody and both Lauren and Kate were at risk. Cabot had seen him talking to Blake in the parking lot beforehand, as had many of the patrons. The lieutenant could hardly act surprised if he told them about another man being there, all the evidence would support it. Thorne hunched forward in his seat to take the pressure off his shoulder.

"That other cop, the young guy. I'll talk to him."

"Detective Barnes?"

Thorne could tell he'd struck a nerve. There was friction of some kind between the two cops, perhaps envy. The detective was going places, the lieutenant was not.

"Yeah."

"A man's dead. I have to tell his wife that her husband's not coming home and you're sitting there playing games. You need to wake up, Thorne. The time for bullshit has passed."

Thorne said nothing.

Cabot leaned over him, his jaw thrust forward like he was tonguing a piece of steak out of his front teeth. The lieutenant's desire to inflict pain on him was obvious. Thorne knew he had to walk a fine line while they were alone together. People died in police custody all the time, and he had no plans to be one of them.

After a beat, Cabot stepped back, over to the doorway.

"Since you've been so co-operative, I've got a real treat in store for you. I'm going to make some calls and with a bit of luck you won't have too long to wait. Might even be done before I get back. A sign of things to come."

Cabot winked at him in way he didn't much care for, then pulled the door closed. Although he listened for it, he couldn't hear if the door was locked or simply shut. In the heel of his right shoe was a thin piece of metal from an old watch strap. He'd used it on *Night Passenger* to escape from a pair of handcuffs back in season two and he'd gotten into the habit of carrying it around. It had become something of a party piece. He could get out the cuffs if he wanted to, but then what? Escape would certainly make him look guilty. He needed to relax, let Cabot make a fool of himself and get the man off his back for good.

After a while, a heavyset man opened the door and stood before him. Though time moved slowly inside the room, he estimated no more than half an hour had passed outside it. The man was wearing a paper suit and latex gloves that extended up over his forearms. He carried an aluminum flight case in one hand and a roll of plastic in the other. Thorne suspected his day was about to take a bad turn. Cabot's 'special treat' had arrived. The man set his equipment down on the floor and sat on the chair opposite.

"I'm here to collect physical evidence regarding the death of James Ashcroft. Do you consent to this search?"

"What happens if I don't?"

The man nodded. "Not much. I make a note of your objection, then get a couple of deputies to help me perform it anyway. I assume that was a hypothetical question?"

Thorne sighed. "Let's get this over with."

"All right." The man unsnapped his case and began to pull gear out. "Let's get those handcuffs off. We don't need those, do we?"

After he'd removed the handcuffs, the tech photographed Thorne's hands with a close up lens and a ring flash. His hands were pretty beat up,

282

he realized, particularly his right from the time he'd driven it through Lauren's dressing table mirror. This done, the technician set the camera aside, and opened a small plastic case. He peeled off a cover and pressed a disc into the webbing of Thorne's right hand between thumb and forefinger. The disc was sticky and the man lifted it up and down across the area, spreading out across the back of his hand until the disc lost adhesion. He sealed the tester into a container, then began the process again on Thorne's left hand.

"You're wasting your time, I didn't fire the gun."

The man spoke without lifting his eyes.

"I never waste my time, Mr Thorne. If you're innocent and I can prove that, I will gladly do so. There's no justice if the wrong person is convicted."

"Too bad Cabot doesn't have that attitude. He damn near busted my head open before he arrested me. It probably needs stitched."

The man was sealing the second wand into its protective enclosure and his hands froze and his eyes flipped up to look at him.

"Lieutenant Cabot assaulted you?"

"With his gun."

"Tilt your head forward."

Thorne did so and felt the man's gloved fingers moving through his hair. The pain in his scalp returned as the movement started a fresh bleed. The technician swore quietly to himself. He felt no guilt doing this to Cabot, as far as he was concerned it made them square. The cut on his head would've been discovered anyway and this allowed him to control its meaning, made it work for him.

"I'm going to photograph your injury. When we're done here, I'll arrange to have someone come deal with it. You might, as you say, need stitches."

When the man was through he stood and unrolled the plastic sheeting across the floor next to the table. It was obvious to Thorne what was going to happen next, it had been clear to him from the moment he'd seen the plastic.

"Stand here and remove all your clothes. Place your clothing into this bag, and your footwear into this bag."

Thorne clenched his teeth, then walked over to where the other man stood holding two bags. This was Blake's fault. From a certain point of view, it was Adolf Hitler's. Because of the Nazis and a painting, he was on the hook for a murder. He took off his shoes and dropped them into the first bag. There went his handcuff pick. To his surprise, he felt more vulnerable knowing the small piece of metal was gone. It might've been a futile gesture, but it was something they didn't know about, something he could use to escape. The first bag was taken away and sealed. He stripped down mechanically, without thinking where he was and his circumstance. He had lost his fear about what other men thought of him naked when he was in boot camp and, like Kate, had appeared in various states of undress on national TV. If this was what Cabot had actioned against him he wasn't going to see what he wanted on any video playback. Before too long, he'd removed everything. The cold floor sucked the heat out of his body straight through the plastic. He looked at the man in front of him who was staring at the marks on his chest and the bandages.

"I'm not removing my bandages. If you need to see under them, you can have a medic remove them and replace them with new dressings when you're done."

The tech considered this for a moment before nodding.

"OK, we can come back to that if necessary."

The man fetched a second camera which he set up on a tripod in front of him.

"Just a couple more pictures. Keep as still as possible."

Thorne said nothing. He'd seen pictures of famous killers as research for his show and every one of them looked like the killer they were. He made his face calm, with no trace of emotion. Anger was a natural reaction under the circumstances, but angry pictures didn't go down well in court. The tech took multiple pictures using filters over the lens. UV/IR shots. *Night Passenger* had explored latent evidence recovery pretty extensively during its five year run. Different wavelengths of light revealed things not visible to the naked eye or normal lighting. He told himself to relax. They'd find nothing beyond Ashcroft's blood on his hand and clothes that were the result of dragging him from his car.

After photographing him from the waist up, the technician changed lenses and shot Thorne's arms, face, and chest from no more than a foot away. When he was finished, the man stepped back, broke down his equipment and returned it to his flight case.

"Unfortunately, Mr Thorne, we're not quite through. There's one more thing I'm required to do. The lieutenant was very clear on this, it's not up to me."

The man was holding a tube of lubricant.

FORTY-THREE

Blake lay on the floor of their motel room staring at the ceiling. He'd sweated through his clothes on the ride back from the roadhouse and the pain was incredible. His leg looked bad. Down to the knee was fine, after that, not so much. The knee joint appeared to be twice normal size and barely fitted inside his jeans. Below the knee, his leg was pulled out and twisted around so that his foot pointed to three o'clock.

Using the thumb and forefinger of his right hand, he twisted the top off a quart of vodka and leaned over sideways to take a couple of mouthfuls. The liquor surged out the bottle and made him cough. He lay back on the floor. The pain was exhausting. Sara leaned over him holding a knife, her face in some distant place.

"You sure about this?"

"I can get another pair of jeans, Jesus Christ."

She hummed to herself, as if to a crying baby.

It was true that he hadn't changed the jeans after Thorne had stabbed him. He'd leaked over a pint of blood into them and he'd simply washed them out and hung them up to dry. Good jeans were hard to find and often took months' of wear to get right.

She moved down his body and began cutting through the denim. The pressure immediately came off his skin, which had become hot and highly sensitive. He propped himself up on his elbow and watched his distorted leg appear through the fabric. Sara stopped after about twelve inches, which was about as much as she could do without cutting him. She put the knife down, then, using both hands, tore the material up and over the knee joint. She sat back on her heels and stared at his leg.

"Fuck me, Aidan. That's gross!"

She wasn't wrong. His leg had become inflated and his skin discolored as if by a huge bruise. The tibia and the fibula had rotated at the knee joint and the patella, or knee cap, had been pulled right off the center onto the side of the joint. He looked back at Sara who was pale and breathing rapidly through her mouth.

"You all right?" he asked.

"Just peachy."

"You know, it's actually a lot better than I thought."

Sara laughed. "It *is?*"

"I thought for sure a bone would be sticking out."

She said nothing. Blake picked up the bottle of vodka again and took another long pull. He'd never had his leg pop out before, so he had no idea what was in store when it got put back in. He figured it didn't hurt to be prepared, though he guessed the vodka would make little difference. When he put the bottle down again he saw he was already half way through it, the most vodka he'd ever drunk in his life. He hated it.

"What now?" she asked.

He drew his left foot sideways back toward him as far as he could and with his knee as close to the floor as possible. It wasn't a comfortable position and only served to accentuate the crazy angle of his other leg.

"OK," he said. "Brace your right foot against my knee, put your left against the bed frame. Then it's simple. You pull my leg as hard as you can and twist it. Hopefully it snaps back into place."

She lined herself up on the floor, her legs on either side of his knee.

"You want me to take off my boot?"

As ever, she was wearing heavy motorcycle boots.

"That would be fantastic," he said.

While he waited for her to get her boot off, he finished the vodka. He didn't feel drunk, not even slightly. He'd hoped it would've been enough to dial the volume down, but if anything, it had the opposite effect. His senses appeared sharper, the pain, stronger.

Sara was looking at him. "You ready?"

"As I'll ever be," he said.

She licked her lips. "After three?"

"Fuck that. Just do it."

She pulled hard on his leg and tried to twist it. He felt bones grating against each other. He yelled through gritted teeth.

"Stop! Stop! Stop!"

She released her grip and looked up.

"What's wrong?"

"You can't turn it straight away, you got to pull it out first. You can drive a stick shift, right? You gotta push the clutch all the way in before you change gears. It's like that. Pull the bones apart and they'll slip past each other. Otherwise, you're grinding them together."

She nodded and got back into position.

"Wait," he said. "I think you were right before. Do it after three. It will focus our energy and breathing."

They counted down together.

"One."

"Two."

"Three."

She pulled hard on his leg, harder than before. He felt it move, it was working. He worked his hand down next to his knee, his fingers pressing the bone into position. Almost there. He tried to relax his muscles, willing the joint to open. His eyes flipped over to hers. She was maxed-out. She couldn't keep it going much longer, and next time she'd be weaker. His voice cut through the air.

"NOW!"

She twisted his foot hard to the left and he felt the bones bounce across each other and *thunk* into place. It was both a feeling and a sound he could hear. His knee cap waited a moment on the side of his leg, then seemed to scurry into place under the skin, like a mouse moving under a carpet. Sara fell back onto her ass then hurriedly got to her feet and ran for the bathroom. He lay back on the carpet and listened to her vomit into the toilet.

FORTY-FOUR

Thorne awoke with his head pressed against the interview table, a fat finger tapping on the wood in front of his face. *Tap, tap, tap.* The fingernails were thick and yellow and were surprisingly loud to his sleepy ears. He straightened up and saw Cabot standing over him, a strange smile pulling at his lips.

"They say only the guilty sleep, Thorne. And you, you were out like a light."

Thorne yawned and didn't bother to cover his mouth.

"I guess your little stunt isn't working."

"My *stunt?*"

"I'm not a school kid, Cabot. You left me here to make me sweat. It tells me you've got nothing, which I already knew because I didn't do it. You arrested me over four hours ago and you've not asked me question one. The maximum you can hold me is twenty four hours, after that, you have to charge me or release me. So are you here to continue this charade, or are you here to release me?"

"Oh, we're going to *continue this charade*, don't you worry."

The young detective bent down next to Cabot.

"L-T, can I have a word?"

Cabot sighed then went out into the corridor with Barnes. He heard the detective speak before the door closed.

"You actually arrested him?"

There was incredulity in Barnes' voice, he couldn't hold it back. It seemed to be genuine to Thorne, though he couldn't discount the scene being staged for his benefit to set up a good cop, bad cop routine. By saying he'd speak to Barnes, he had opened himself up to such a cliched trick but he felt that the younger detective had actually listened to him before and he had few other options. The two deputies came back in, Cabot sat opposite him, while Barnes remained standing. This was not exactly what he'd had in mind. The lieutenant made a show of leafing through his notepad, a good twenty or thirty pages like he was trying to find something. Thorne knew he was meant to see this as the amount of evidence built up against him, but it was nothing but a cheap trick.

"*Cabot*," Thorne said, sharply. "Tick, tock."

The lieutenant put this notepad down and placed his hands flat on the table on either side. There was a tremor to his hands before they touched down. Anger.

"OK, smart guy. Let's hear your account of the night, from the top."

Cabot was getting him to nail down his story. If he changed anything later or missed something important out, it could be made to look bad for him at trial. He'd had plenty of time to think about it and he decided to tell it almost straight. He rolled it all out for them, omitting only the reason for the night time drive, the presence of the painting, and the identity of the man with the gun, who he described as a drunk from the roadhouse.

When he finished the two cops looked less than convinced.

"So you're saying that someone else did it and ran away?"

He looked up at Barnes, disappointed.

"I guess I am."

Cabot continued in the same skeptical manner.

"Leaving you covered in his blood, standing over his dead body."

"I carried him out of the car, then tried to stop the bleeding. Of course I had his blood on my hands and clothes. If I shot him myself, why would I have *any* of his blood on me?"

Cabot leaned in, across the table.

"Say we believe you, Thorne. Why did you just let this *mystery man*, this drunk as you tell it, escape. We've seen what you can do on that video tape. You're an action hero. Why didn't you catch him and bring him to justice?"

Thorne sighed.

"Because I was pulling a friend out of a burning vehicle at the time."

"Of course you were."

"You were there beforehand, Cabot. You saw the man. Are you going to pretend he doesn't exist now because it doesn't fit your agenda?"

"I have an agenda?'

Cabot was smirking. Thorne lifted his eyes to Barnes.

"Look at his dash cam if you don't believe me."

He saw a small nod.

"All right," Barnes said. "Describe the shooter to me."

Thorne thought about Blake. His description couldn't line up or they'd be on to it.

"He's white. Five ten. Dark hair. Mid 30s. Maybe 190 pounds."

Cabot snorted.

"Congratulations, Thorne. You just described every man in that roadhouse."

Thorne ignored him, kept his eyes on Barnes.

"What was he wearing?"

"Blue jeans, black canvas jacket. Boots."

Barnes pulled a chair over from against the wall, flipped it around and sat on it so the back was in front of his chest.

"You said the man approached you and was immediately aggressive."

"That's right."

Thorne saw a problem in his story as soon as he said the words. If they were in the car talking the drunk would never have seen them. Not unless the interior light was on, and since they weren't teenagers on a date, that could be pretty much ruled out.

"You were already outside the vehicle?"

"Yes."

Barnes was sharp. Perhaps he should've left it to Cabot after all.

"I see. Why were you in this parking lot in the middle of nowhere at two a.m.?"

"No reason at all. Like I said before, it'd been a long day and we just went for a drive. It was a spontaneous thing. We stopped there because it was far enough and we were going to head back afterward. It was our turnaround."

"You stopped to use the rest room, is that it?"

Thorne's eye was drawn to a sticker on the wall behind Barnes.

"No. To have a cigar."

"You left the vehicle to smoke a cigar?"

"The smell is difficult to remove. Lauren doesn't like it."

The deputy nodded, like it was making sense now.

"Where was Senator Ashcroft when the man first appeared?"

Cabot glanced sharply at Barnes.

"Standing right next to me. We were talking when this guy walked up with an attitude. I suggested to James that he go back to his SUV while I dealt with it. I figured the man recognized me from the news or from my TV show, and wanted to take a swing at me. It's happened before. I wasn't worried, he was smaller than me and was clearly intoxicated." He shrugged. "I didn't know he was armed."

"You said before Ashcroft was in the SUV."

"And he was, except at the very beginning. I didn't think it was important."

"This is ridiculous," Cabot cut in. "Admit it. There *was* no drunk. *You* fired the shot."

"You're saying that I risked my life to save him at the mall so that I could shoot him a couple of weeks later. That makes more sense to you, does it?"

"We haven't got to the bottom of the shoot-out yet, Thorne. But we will. We're close. I'm sure that black van will contain all kinds of interesting evidence."

Thorne said nothing. He'd said too much already.

"Since you mention the TV show," Cabot continued, "We called some of your coworkers last week. Want to take a guess what they had to say about you?"

Thorne took a deep breath and let it out slowly. He had a damn good idea what they said. That he'd been in a fight with a man matching the description of the lead gunman just days before the attack on the Ashcrofts, and that he'd tried to kill him right there in the bar. It would tie him to Blake, at least as much as Coop's video footage.

"I imagine they said I'm a great guy and a pleasure to work with."

The lieutenant scowled. "In fact, that's almost exactly what they said."

Thorne laughed. He'd had his ups and downs with the cast and crew over the years, but when it came right down to it, they were a loyal bunch. He noticed that neither of the deputies appreciated his laughter, which made it harder to stop.

"I apologize. Please carry on."

"You laugh, but I've not told the funny part yet. Detective Barnes spoke to forty-two coworkers of yours, past and present. Took him nearly a day, running down those names and numbers. They said you are a good guy, you work hard, train hard - some even said you've a great sense of humor. I got to say, that surprised me, you don't strike me as the funny type."

"What's your point? Being popular isn't a crime."

Cabot shook his head, as if he was dealing with a fool. "You're not getting it. Forty-two people said the same thing about you. The same words and phrases appear over and over again. That only happens when a story's been arranged beforehand. They're lying to protect you, which means you have something to hide."

Thorne had to stop himself from smiling. The studio had brushed everything under the carpet, possibly floating the idea of a movie version of the show that was reported in the news as a way to keep everyone sweet.

"That's an interesting theory, Lieutenant."

"Those people might be in your pocket now, Thorne, but I guarantee you that when I get them in here and start talking about aiding and abetting a murder suspect, you're going to hear a different story come out."

"Who did I murder again? I keep forgetting."

Cabot stood abruptly, his chair falling over backward.

"Don't push me, Thorne!"

"You going to hit me with your gun again?"

"*What?*"

Thorne tilted his head forward and parted his hair.

"This ringin' any bells for you, Cabot?"

"Jesus, boss. What did you do?"

Thorne could tell from Barnes' face that he believed it. Cabot, meanwhile, appeared frozen between surprise and guilt. He *had* hit him on the top of his head, just not with any gun. There was more there, crawling under the skin. He'd *wanted* to do more, but there'd been no time. The paramedics had arrived, pinning him down. He thought of the lieutenant's dash cam footage. It had been dark in that parking lot with Blake, but by the time Cabot returned there'd been the light from Ashcroft's burning SUV.

Would the footage reveal if Cabot's hand had been empty?

"Boss? Say something."

There was a knock on the door and another deputy came in. When he saw Thorne he flashed a smile. The lieutenant looked up.

"What is it, Summersby?"

"Thorne's lawyer's here. She's demanding to see him immediately."

"His *lawyer?*" Cabot swung around. "When did you call a lawyer?"

Thorne smiled. Lauren. She hadn't believed the lieutenant's lies. Cabot must've told her he'd been arrested, or else she'd figured it out from his absence. He sat back in his seat and relaxed. He'd been against going the lawyer route but now that it had happened, he knew it was the right way to go. Cabot could keep him bottled up here for hours and all the while Kate was out there with Blake who had to be close to cutting and running. An exchange for the painting was the only thing keeping her alive, and that ended as soon as they announced he was arrested. He looked up from the table and found the three cops were watching him, waiting for an answer.

"GET ME MY LAWYER!"

The sudden volume of his voice in the small room knocked them back and the third cop, Summersby, scuttled away without a word from the lieutenant.

"Finally we see your true colors."

Cabot sounded weak and it looked like he heard the defeat in his own voice, because he flinched after he spoke.

292

FORTY-FIVE

Thorne heard the lawyer before he saw her. She spoke fast and left no gaps where she could be interrupted. He found himself wondering how she could talk and breathe at the same time. He tracked her progress through the building and up to the door of the interview room. It opened and Barnes stood there with a red face next to the lawyer. She wore an immaculate navy-black pant suit with a white shirt with the first three buttons undone and what appeared to be a man's tie with a large square knot pulled halfway down. She had a strong masculine look to her face and it appeared she'd decided to accentuate it, rather than soften it. She strode into the room and thrust her hand out toward him.

"Nicky Kaplan, pleased to meet you."

He shook her hand. It was a solid grip, like she frequently spent time gripping the pommel of a mechanical bull in sports bars. Her eye contact was one hundred percent as their hands moved up and down. She was assessing him. The shake ended and she placed a briefcase down on the floor. As she bent down, her pants rode up revealing boots with a thick Cuban heel, like those worn by Stockton. It wasn't the only resemblance either, the open-necked shirt was practically his wardrobe.

She turned to Barnes who stood in the doorway watching.

"Are you still here? Piss off."

Barnes shook his head and left, closing the door behind him.

"He's actually the friendly one," Thorne said.

"Don't you believe it. Give me the old, fat lion any day of the week." She walked to the door and looked at the switches next to it, then up at the camera. She pressed a switch and nodded to herself. "Okay, we have the place to ourselves."

She sat in Cabot's seat, took her cell phone out and placed it on the table between them. Thorne glanced at the screen and saw a voice recorder display. She stated her name, his name, their location and the date.

"I record all my interviews, Mr Thorne. Nothing personal. I don't take notes anymore, waste of time. I can't read my own handwriting."

"Are you married?"

She raised her eyebrow.

"You don't waste any time, do you. Yes, why do you ask?"

"What was your surname before?"

Her eyes narrowed, amusement fading.

"*Kaplan*. This isn't the 1950s."

"Sorry, it's been a long night. You reminded me of someone when you came in. I thought maybe you were related."

"A friend of yours?"

"No, he's an asshole."

Thorne smiled and Nicky Kaplan smiled back.

"Maybe he *is* related after all. How about you tell me everything that happened tonight, followed by anything you think is relevant, like the way they've treated you."

He gave her the same version he gave the cops, he saw no point telling her about Blake and the painting. It sounded ridiculous to his own ear now, but she listened and nodded without comment. He guessed that true stories often did sound stupid, unlike events in his TV show, where one thing always built to another with no dead spots. Fiction had become his touchstone for truth and he thought he had a pretty good ear for what sounded believable. The only part of his story she reacted to, was Cabot striking him during the arrest. Here, she interrupted his story to examine his injury.

When he finished, there was a different light in her eyes. She stopped the voice recorder and put her phone back into her pocket. He could tell that she was preparing what to say to Cabot, or someone higher up the food chain.

"I need to get out of here. How long is this going to take?"

"Mr Thorne, if you're still here in 20 minutes I'll be very surprised."

His stay lasted maybe half that, with most of the time taken up by a nurse sowing two stitches into his scalp. He'd really thrown Cabot under the bus with this head wound business but he couldn't say that he was sorry about it.

After the nurse left, his lawyer came back and stood in the doorway.

"How about it, Thorne? You ready to blow this dump?"

"Very much so."

"Come on. I have a husband and a labrador to get home to."

Thorne nodded and got to his feet. Barnes was waiting in the corridor with a sour look on his face. They set off along the corridor, Barnes on his right and Nicky Kaplan on his left. The sheriff's deputy had the lethargic motion of someone rousted out of their bed just as they were getting to the good part, while his lawyer strode purposefully along the corridor, apparently unfazed by the early hour. Lieutenant Cabot, meanwhile, was nowhere to be seen. The big man would be keeping his head down, embarrassed as to the way things had gone.

He turned to Nicky Kaplan.

"So the charges are dropped?"

"For now. They'll continue to process evidence taken tonight, including evidence from your hands and clothes, but I don't think you'll hear any more about it. Their own tests will exonerate you."

Thorne nodded, although he wasn't so sure. Getting him released gave the cops more time to investigate him. The 24 hour limit effectively disappeared. Her timely intervention removed the mistake Cabot made arresting him. The speed of his release suggested that the Sheriff's Office had deliberately not fought to retain him in custody. Now, they could pour over Blake's van off the clock and find whatever they needed.

"Cabot took my car keys and cell phone, can I get them back?"

"You'll have to come back for them later," Barnes said.

At the front, the detective peeled off to unlock the door.

Thorne's eyes went past Barnes to movement outside.

Two figures stood in the darkness staring at him. Since neither held a cigarette, it was fair to assume they were waiting for him. A curved platform projected out over the entrance like a large thumbnail and the figures were taking limited shelter underneath it from the rain which continued to fall. He knew instinctively that neither figure was Lauren.

"Stay local, Thorne. We wouldn't like it if we had to come look for you."

Thorne grunted but said nothing.

"If you need to speak to my client you can contact me at my office. Any other contact will be considered harassment and grounds for civil action."

Barnes wasn't listening to the lawyer, he didn't even look at her. His eyes were fixed on Thorne with an expression that was hard to read. It was the same flat expression people got looking at a television. Blank and emotionless. He'd always sensed that the deputy believed his account of the shoot-out, but the presence of the lawyer now had cost him that.

"Do yourself a favor, Detective. Check Cabot's gun."

The gaze dipped. "Already underway."

Nicky Kaplan was trying to put herself between them, with little luck.

"Don't say anything else, Mr Thorne. It's what he wants."

A smile appeared on Barnes' face and he stepped aside. The lawyer took the opportunity to guide Thorne swiftly out through the door with her hand resting on the small of his back. In front of them, the two waiting figures lunged forward. A man and a woman. A bright light snapped on and Thorne squinted his eyes. A TV crew, he should've guessed. The smaller figure came forward and some of the light lit her face.

Jocelyn Cooper.

"Christopher Thorne, can you tell us what has happened?"

To his surprise, he noticed his lawyer shrinking back and not closing down the interview. This was his opportunity to reassure Blake, tell him everything was fine and that he hadn't named him. There was no need for him to hurt Kate, the deal was still on the table.

Thorne looked into the camera. He hadn't prepared anything, but he knew how he wanted himself to appear. Sincere, upset, haunted even. He knew what to think about to produce the right effect on his face. How to speak.

"Late last night, I went for a drive with Senator Ashcroft. We stopped at a roadhouse, where I became involved in an argument with an unknown man who recognized me from TV. The man had been drinking heavily and for some reason picked me out for special treatment. I suggested he go home and sleep it off, at which point he pulled a gun and pointed it at my head. James Ashcroft, seated in his SUV behind us, saw what was about to happen and drove directly at the man to save me. The drunk fired a shot through the windshield, before being thrown up in the air by the vehicle. The SUV then crashed into a wall and burst into flames. When I looked around, the drunk had fled the scene. I pulled the senator from the wreckage and moved him a safe distance away but it was for nothing. The senator had been hit."

Coop paused for a moment, uncertain.

"Are you saying that Senator Ashcroft is dead?"

The microphone came back over, pointed at him.

It hadn't occurred to him that they wouldn't know.

"Yes."

Jocelyn Cooper appeared to be stunned by this revelation and the microphone continued to point at him, so he spoke again.

"By the time the air ambulance arrived, it was too late. He was gone. James Ashcroft saved my life without a thought for his own."

He saw a look go across Coop's face as she realized what everything meant.

"*Then* what happened?"

"Then Lieutenant Cabot arrested me for the senator's murder."

"Why did he arrest you?"

"You'd have to ask him that. He's been pursuing a vendetta against me since we first met." Thorne paused, thinking again about Ashcroft's last moments. "I don't want to talk anymore about the lieutenant or the things he's done to me, they don't compare to the loss of a man I considered a friend. A man who would've made a great president one day."

He glanced at Nicky Kaplan and she came forward.

"My client has been released without charge, however this is still an active case with the Santa Cruz County Sheriff's Office and we must be mindful of their ongoing investigation. Our thoughts and prayers are with the senator's wife at this very difficult time."

As if it had been arranged, he and the lawyer walked out of shot and Jocelyn Cooper took their place in front of the camera. The reporter spoke for another couple of minutes wrapping things up but Thorne didn't care to listen to it. He was tired to the bone. Nicky Kaplan handed him her business card and said she'd be in touch, then walked out to a huge beast of a Mercedes-Benz and climbed inside. She sat there with the interior light still on and made a quick call on her cell phone before starting the engine, reverse-turning and driving away. His eyes moved over the near-empty parking lot looking for Lauren's car, but it wasn't there.

He recalled the short distance Nicky Kaplan had put between them when Coop had asked her question and he understood what it meant. Jocelyn Cooper had arranged his lawyer, it was never Lauren. His heart sank. He wondered where he would go now. The thought that Lauren had been behind it had sustained him, because it meant she believed in him. That they were OK. Now this feeling had been ripped away. Assuming she wasn't in an Ambien-powered sleep, she might be hating him right now. Believing Cabot's bullshit. For sure, he couldn't go back to the mansion now, not while there was any doubt over what had happened in the roadhouse parking lot.

He followed Coop and the cameraman back to their van because he had nowhere else to go, and because the constant rain blocked his ability to think of much else. He was wearing a jumpsuit provided by the Sheriff's Office and was carrying no money or identification. They reached the van and Coop turned to look at him.

"I'm sorry we ambushed you, Chris. The footage has to look real on TV. If Nicky told you who called her it wouldn't have looked right. I didn't know he died, I'm sorry. I only heard you'd been arrested. I thought it was connected to the shoot-out at the mall."

He remained silent, but his face hid nothing from her.

"You thought someone else was out here, didn't you?"

Someone else.

She was being discreet in front of the cameraman and he appreciated it.

"I suppose I was."

They climbed into the van. It had a long bench seat across the front and he sat in the middle position with Coop next to the passenger door. The cameraman opened the side door and climbed in with his equipment. There was no divider, he could look right into the back. It was almost identical to Blake's van.

"How'd you hear about my arrest anyway?"

"I have a source inside the Sheriff's Office, keeps me up-to-date with

Cabot's blundering investigation." Coop lowered her voice so the cameraman wouldn't hear. "Kinda surprised you didn't call me yourself, actually."

Thorne stared at the windshield, at the rain covered glass.

"I had other things on my mind."

They said nothing for a moment. It wasn't hard, the cameraman was crashing about behind them, setting up the uplink to the television station. The senator's death was a major scoop, as was his arrest and subsequent release. The story had to go out before other networks got wind of it. Thorne guessed that if any editing took place it took place at the other end. The cameraman was seated in back now and talking quietly into a pair of headphones with a microphone bar. They had a moment of privacy. He turned to Jocelyn and saw her big eyes looking back like a pair of headlights.

"This isn't what I wanted," he said. "You know that, right?"

"I know."

"What do I do? Do I go to her? She'll be all alone."

Coop shook her head. "Nicky told me there's a deputy looking after her."

"I guess that makes sense. They won't want me there, that's for sure."

"You're coming back with us, Chris. The *Inn*'s sold-out, but I have a super comfy sofa in my suite. Or there's one in Brad's if you prefer, though I can't promise he'll be a gentleman."

There was warmth and humor in her voice, but it was impossible for him to feel it, or to smile. Instead, he felt like a snake that has swallowed its prey whole and has to lie for days slowly digesting it. Only, he'd swallowed a large, cold stone. He could feel it inside him, weighing him down. James Ashcroft was dead, and it was entirely his fault. He may not have fired the shot, but he may as well have. Without a word, Thorne tilted his head over until it rested on her shoulder and closed his eyes.

Within seconds, he fell asleep.

FORTY-SIX

Soft pop music played nearby. Thorne turned over in bed, his eyes tightening against the bright light of a window. All that kind of music sounded the same to him. Meaningless lyrics, sung in the same way, produced in the same way. It wouldn't be long before it was all computer generated. A moment passed before he stirred again. He could smell coffee and some kind of pastry. It almost obscured Kate's perfume. His eyes snapped open and a familiar room appeared around him. Jocelyn Cooper's bedroom at the *Dream Inn*. He swung his head around, taking in the room. There was no sign of her. A large cup of black coffee sat on the night stand, along with a cruller. As if on cue, his stomach growled.

Thorne picked up the coffee and drank from it. It was strong and at the perfect temperature. He drained half the cup and felt his brain come alive. The coffee flowed like electricity through it, turning everything on. A bunch of cut scenes came back to him. Sharing a bottle of Scotch with Coop. Talking for what seemed like hours. Finally, when it was time to call it a day, things had taken a predictable turn.

Thorne sighed. He didn't know who he was anymore.

A business card was stuck to the base of the coffee cup. He peeled it off and saw there was a handwritten message on it.

Gone to get you some new clothes, back in half an hour.
Eve x

Coop was using her *North by Northwest* name again. She thought it was clever. Maybe it was, he wasn't sure. He stared for a beat at the kiss she'd added to the end of the message. He'd noticed that some women added kisses to the end of messages all the time and that it meant nothing. It might indicate that they were friends. Is that what this kiss was, or was it something else? He flipped the card over. *Nikolai Kaplan, attorney at law*. No wonder she went by Nicky, he thought. He picked up the cruller and bit it in half. Another bite later it was gone, followed shortly after by the coffee.

Thorne sat all the way up and put his feet on the floor.

He'd betrayed Kate. There was no other way of putting it. When he'd believed her to be dead it was different, but he couldn't say that this time around. He put his head in his hands and ran his fingers back and forth through his hair. He stood and walked toward the shower. Showers helped him think. As he passed the living area, he was surprised to see Jocelyn Cooper sitting there with a newspaper spread out before her on the low table. She was smartly dressed, had her hair pinned up in a bun and wore a pair of dark framed glasses on her face. She looked up and smiled, quickly removing the glasses.

"There's something strangely familiar about this."

Thorne felt his face redden.

"Your note said you were out."

"I was, two hours ago. It's nearly one in the afternoon. I let you sleep, looked like you needed it. Go shower, we'll talk after."

He nodded then went into the bathroom and removed his dressings. They served no real purpose anyway, the wounds were all closed. It was getting to the point where he could look at himself again without hating what he saw. He had it easy, a lot of vets couldn't hide their injuries with a shirt and a pair of pants.

After the shower, he set out the clothes she'd bought him on the end of the bed while she stood in the doorway watching. Apparently, they were the kind of friends that saw each other naked. Thorne found he didn't care, at least not with her. He could feel her gaze move over his battered body. She showed no disgust at the scars and wounds. The clothes were from Gap and not his style, but they sure beat wearing a police jumpsuit. He dressed quickly and without comment. Everything fitted perfectly, except for some running shoes which were a size too small. When he was done, he noticed another bag, under the first. He looked inside and saw she'd also bought a baseball cap and sunglasses.

He held them up.

"What are these for?"

"This doesn't work if we're seen together."

"Great. Another woman embarrassed to be seen with me."

She flashed the goofy smile and he felt it inside him, like the tug of a fish hook. It was the kind of smile you could make room for in your life. He put on the cap and sunglasses and walked over so that he stood directly in front of her. She looked at him, her eyes narrowed. He was certain that he looked ridiculous. A label still hung from the leg of the sunglasses, it fluttered in a breeze from the open balcony door.

"I don't know if I thanked you for arranging that lawyer."

"I didn't do it for you, Chris."

She was a bad liar. He lent forward and kissed her forehead.

"Thank you anyway."

She smiled then tilted her head up, her mouth slightly open. He kissed her on the mouth. Coop was a hot little thing, and a fire seemed to burn below the surface. It was a trait that reminded him of Kate, but not at all of Lauren Ashcroft. Lauren had ice water in her veins. She didn't feel things in the same way. The kiss ended and her goofy smile was back.

"Your face," she said.

"What about it?"

"I like it."

Thorne nodded somberly. "A lot of people do."

Her face twisted, but the smile came back.

"That must be awful for you."

He took off the baseball cap and sunglasses then walked over to the end of the bed and dumped them on it. He stood like that for a beat with his back to her.

"How'd you feel about giving me a ride back to Ashcroft's mansion?"

"Conflicted," she said.

He turned to her.

"We can't do this again, you know that. I'm the story."

"You won't be the story forever."

He nodded.

"I can't give you an answer to that. Lauren needs my support and Kate is still being held by the gang. I can't make long term plans. I could be dead tomorrow."

"Fine. But just so you know, it's not going to be easy to get in. I've been up there already today. There's a police guard on the gate and all the main network news stations are back."

"There's another way in."

FORTY-SEVEN

Cabot sat at his desk with his chair tilted way back, his feet crossed on top of the blond wood. His legs were short and it had taken a couple of minutes to find a position that worked for him. The angle flattened out his whole body so that his head almost disappeared behind the tips of his shoes. It wasn't exactly comfortable, but his hope was that the sheriff would walk in and decide to make good on his threat of full suspension rather than this desk-bound version. After years of sitting at his desk, he needed to be out there asking questions and leading from the front. He also had no interest in solving a hit-and-run case, their only active investigation now that the mall shooting and Ashcroft's murder had been taken from them. On full suspension, he'd be free to conduct his own enquiry and take it where it needed to go without interference.

He reached down and picked an orange out of a sack that sat next to his chair and methodically began to peel it. There were no papers on his desk, just piles and piles of discarded orange skin. He liked to get not just the peel off, but every trace of pith underneath until he had a slice of clean fruit. He took his time, he had nothing else to do all day and it helped take his mind off Thorne.

This is what the sheriff wants, he thought, for him to look weak in front of everyone in the department. That's the real reason he was being kept around. If he'd been sent home until the farce with his sidearm was straightened out, it would be seen as mere procedure. This was political, this was *personal*. It was a year before the election, but Carson was an opportunist and he'd seen the perfect time to strike.

There was a knock on the door and Barnes stuck his head in.

"Got a minute, boss?"

"My whole week has opened right up, Detective."

Cabot saw him take in the mass of orange peel, the feet on the desk, and the half dozen coffee cups scattered about. It appeared to be almost too much for him. Barnes liked things neat and tidy with everything in its right place. He smiled uncomfortably and sat on the seat opposite. The detective looked around the room as if it was his first time inside it. His face was tight, his lips pressed shut. Cabot continued to eat, slurping noisily to annoy the younger man. Finally, Barnes cleared his throat and made eye contact with him.

"I need to know if it's true, boss. One way or the other."

"You want to know if *what's* true, Barnes? I'm not a goddam mind-reader."

The detective stared at the floor.

"If you beat Thorne with your gun."

"Jesus, Mason. No."

Barnes continued to stare at the floor.

"I guess I'd understand it, the way you found him over Ashcroft's body. I wouldn't say anything if you told me. I owe you, you've been good to me since I've been here."

Cabot sighed.

"Did that dick Carson put you up to this?"

Barnes shook his head as if to brush this comment off.

"I need to hear you say it."

"I *have* said it. I didn't fucking do it. I punched him, OK? I admitted that. But I didn't pistol whip him. You can't see it on the dash cam video, but I swapped my firearm to my left hand. Which is why I'm sitting here with busted up knuckles. Thorne framed me. He's destroyed my life, my career, my whole reputation. *This* is what I'll be remembered for, and I didn't do it. If you don't believe me you can piss off, I got nothin' else to say to you."

Barnes smiled, his features relaxing. "I believe you."

He supposed he'd given Barnes no reason to trust him. His position on Thorne had been static since day one and it wasn't such a stretch. Hadn't he thought about killing the actor before the medics appeared? Hadn't he thought of killing him every minute since he was released? Cabot swung his feet onto the floor and pulled his chair forward so he could rest his elbows on the desk.

"What about everyone out there?"

"Some think you did it, some don't. Probably an even split."

He decided to change the conversation.

"I had a call this morning from a detective investigating the fire at Thorne's condo that killed Elizabeth Warner." Cabot paused for a beat, his gaze steady on Barnes' face looking for a reaction. "He wanted to know if I thought Thorne could be behind it."

"You're kidding me."

"Turns out, Kate Bloom has a two million dollar life insurance policy. He's the only listed beneficiary. Her own mother wouldn't see a penny."

303

Barnes was silent for a moment.

"Even still, there's no way."

Cabot nodded. "I know it. If I know one thing about Thorne, it's that he didn't burn that poor woman alive. I had to give the son of a bitch a glowing character reference."

"Where do you suppose Kate Bloom is now?"

"That's the big question, isn't it? There's been no activity on her credit cards, cell phone, or social media. None of her family or friends have seen her. It's like she vanished into thin air."

"I don't like the timing of it."

"Me neither," Cabot said.

He glanced down and saw his hands resting on the desk in front of him. The first three fingers on each hand were heavily stained from peeling oranges. His eyes flipped back up to Barnes and then at the closed blinds behind his head. He'd shut himself away in his office, hiding from the world and the squad room. Carson had benched him like a junior league baseball player and he was playing his role of sulking teen perfectly. He wondered what he'd do differently if he really had beaten Thorne. Not much. For sure, the sheriff had zero motivation to clear his name. Carson would use this as leverage to make him retire with the understanding he didn't run for sheriff. As long as he played ball, there'd be no consequences. He could almost hear him say it. Carson would leave him in this office for a few more days to soften him up, then make the pitch. Retire with his pension intact, or face investigation, loss of pension, and possibly time in prison.

Cabot let out a sigh.

"You ever play Sudoku, Barnes?"

"Nah, that's an old man's game."

"Oh no, you want to check it out. For example, this situation right now it reminds me of the way a Sudoku game can go if you make a simple mistake. You don't notice it at first, but that first error multiplies as you keep playing. In order to make that wrong number work, other wrong numbers go in and sometimes it looks like there's no mistake at all. The grid is almost complete, only there's a couple of numbers that don't fit..."

Cabot's voice trailed off.

"Yes, boss?"

"Well, it's like an investigation. You think you're on to something and it turns out to be nothing. You were walking in a dark wood, but by the time you realize you made a mistake you can no longer see the path to get back."

Barnes was nodding. "I see that, but how does this apply to Thorne? I never thought he was involved."

"*That* is your wrong number."

After Barnes left, Cabot decided to go over the text of Thorne's immunity deal with the DA and look for space to maneuver. The document was written in the form of tortured English favored by the law profession. He'd skimmed it once before, but had largely relied on Barnes to provide the *CliffsNotes* version. The document could've been summed up in a single paragraph but had instead been spread across 78 densely populated pages. The extra padding seemed to remove clarity, rather than add it.

He read the document twice and although he didn't consider himself a slow reader, it took him nearly two hours. He found little in it to cheer him up. Thorne's immunity was total. As it stood, he could not be pursued for the deaths of Lucas Foster, Ricky Martinez, Taylor Lynch, or the wounding of Samuel Porter. A clause had even been added to cover Porter dying from his injury, and Thorne was protected for that too.

The immunity deal was based on a variation of self-defense known as *defense of others*, a law that was less than black and white in its implementation. Thorne made the first move, usually a barrier to this form of defense but his military training had been cited in foreseeing danger, a privilege normally only extended to law enforcement officers. The fact that he hadn't been armed at the time and had put his own life in danger wrapped things up nicely for the DA. There was no mention in the document of who Ashcroft was, but Cabot knew it had been a critical component. Had Thorne killed four people to save the life of someone selling hot dogs, he would currently be in a cell awaiting trial. Ashcroft had pulled strings to get this pushed through and the DA had been a willing participant.

Cabot sat back and let his head rest against the chair.

It was like Barnes had originally said; Thorne was bulletproof. Overturning the immunity would require nothing short of a miracle. Some fact would have to materially alter the terms that had framed the deal. His original plan had been to link the actor to those he'd killed. But he saw now that personal involvement would not be the knockout blow he'd assumed. Thorne lying would open him up to arrest and trial, but everything else would stay the same. A jury would swallow up his charm, his heroics, and his pretty boy looks. Prosecuting Thorne for the shoot-out was pointless and a judge at pre-trial would know it.

That left Ashcroft's death, Thorne had no immunity for that. His failed arrest and the false assault charge would make things difficult, but not impossible. Unless he was careful, he'd be open to harassment charges that would only reinforce the legitimacy of the assault claim. Cabot remembered the 9mm shell casing, standing up on its end. The pistol had still not been located, despite a full search of the area.

Where had Thorne hidden the gun?

He stood sharply. He needed another coffee, get his old brain to find the piece he was missing. He opened his office door and found Summersby walking toward him, picking chocolate out of his front teeth with his finger.

"Hey, Lieutenant. Thompson said we got company, that we should go outside."

"Could that kid be any more vague?"

"You coming, sir?"

Word had got around and half the department was out front looking down the street. Six black Suburbans in convoy. He watched as they lined up in front of his building and a line of doors opened at almost the same time. Close to thirty suited figures emerged. It was exactly what Thorne predicted in the back of his cruiser.

Cabot shook his head.

"Your tax dollars at work. The federal government is here."

FORTY-EIGHT

The limo stopped and the driver opened the door. Thorne got out and felt the gaze of hundreds of people immediately fall upon him. It was like stepping onto a vast set, cameras rolling. He turned and reached into the back of the vehicle. Lauren Ashcroft's hand gripped his tight and he helped her out. He'd instinctively offered his right hand and was now supporting her weight on his wounded shoulder. He kept his face flat and pushed the pain into the back of his mind. He put his arm around Lauren's waist and moved her to one side so the driver could close the door.

The cemetery lay on a strip of land between the San Lorenzo River, the Cabrillo Highway, and the top of Ocean Street. Surprisingly little traffic noise filtered down from the highway, no more than tape hiss from an old audio cassette. Thorne guessed it was normally a calm and restful place to visit, but today it was crawling with people.

His eyes moved along the vehicles parked up on Ocean.

The TV networks were back in force. He counted five large trucks and two vans, satellite dishes already deployed. Lauren's arrival had probably triggered a live broadcast. Another serving of death for the American people. He looked for any sign of Jocelyn Cooper, but soon abandoned his search. Her size made her too hard to see. He continued his scan of the vehicles. There were a lot of cops, both back up on the road and dotted throughout the cemetery. Their SUVs and cruisers bore the branding of the Police Department, the Sheriff's Office, and the CHP. At the edge of his vision, almost out of sight, were two unmarked black Suburbans fitted with tinted glass.

Thorne felt his chest tighten.

The sheriff had finally pulled the pin and brought in the FBI.

He couldn't say he was surprised. Cabot had made no progress with the investigation and by passing it to the feds the sheriff had effectively washed his hands of the whole business. Thorne's eyes moved through the crowd with a new interest. The one place FBI agents truly blended in, was at a funeral. He picked out four likely targets, three men and a woman, all with the same blank face and dark sunglasses. Their heads moved slowly around like surveillance cameras, back and forth. All except for the woman, who stared directly at him.

Lauren pressed her body against him like a cat, her face right up against the thin felt of his jacket. He could feel her breath pushing through the material and the cotton shirt underneath. It wasn't until the limousine pulled away, that he realized she was weeping.

He took a deep breath and let it slowly out.

This was not part of his skill set. *Strong silent type*, that's what he was. He had that shit locked down. Calm exterior, glacial eyes, the whole bit. But to sell that, people knew you were bearing some burden inside, otherwise it could be mistaken for *heartless bastard*. Thorne wondered if it was appropriate for him to be here at all, since everyone knew about Cabot's failed arrest and were probably wondering if he'd done it.

He gave Lauren a squeeze to let her know he was right there with her. The crying slowed, the jags of sobbing becoming further and further apart.

In front of them a wizened old piece of jerky waved them through the crowd of people into the chapel where James Ashcroft's service was to take place. Thorne nodded and with his arm still around Lauren's waist, guided her toward the building. The other mourners parted to make way for them, their gaze shifting between Lauren and up to him and back. As they walked through the entrance, Lauren's head flopped over and came to rest on his shoulder. The strong independent woman he'd come to know so well was sitting this one out.

He got Lauren seated and sat next to her. She immediately twisted around, like she was turning over in bed, and put both of her arms around his right arm. Hugging it tight against her body. The angle of her upper torso forced her legs apart, the hem of her black dress rising up over the smooth curves of her thighs. He saw Jerky staring at her honey-gold legs, like a deer frozen in headlights. Thorne reached his hand across into his line of vision and snapped his fingers. The man blinked and shook his head as he walked off.

"Lauren," he said softly. "Your dress is a little high."

She mumbled a reply, but he didn't catch it.

"What was that?"

Lauren lifted her head out of his neck, which was already hot from her breath. Her face was crumpled like she'd slept on it in a funny position and her eyes were bloodshot.

"I *said*, since when were my legs a problem for you?"

He winced. Her voice this time was loud enough for those filing into the row behind to hear. Thorne glanced up and saw a woman in her 70s with her mouth open in a big O. He kept his voice low, hoping to draw down the energy of her response.

"Never, Lauren. But this is hardly the time or the place. Agreed?"

Her face twisted.

"Leave me alone. I don't care anymore."

Her head went back into the crook of his neck and he heard her crying. Thorne stared stoically forward at the front of the chapel. The place was filling up fast. As with the senator's birthday party, there were a lot of old people present. Late eighties, early nineties. *Hardly worth their time going home,* he thought. After a moment, Lauren's hand drifted to the hem of her dress, tugging it down.

The arrival of the FBI was bad news and he couldn't help thinking it was time for him to leave Santa Cruz before Blake pulled him into a hole he couldn't get out of. *And yet.* His mind clicked back into the rut he'd found himself in since he got here. Blake held all the cards. He had Kate, he could just as easily take Lauren, and if Blake was arrested, he'd give him up to the cops in a plea-bargain. The painting was gone and the chances were pretty good that Blake wouldn't believe him if he said it was out of reach. No, he thought. It was essential that Blake didn't find out about the loss of the painting, it was his only leverage.

As he waited for the service to begin, he continued to be preoccupied by the painting, which he realized had ended up costing Ashcroft his life. Owning anything above a certain value put a target on your back, that was the truth. You could protect valuable items with sensors and bullet-proof glass, but could you protect yourself? At some point, everyone had to leave their homes and venture out in public. The rich were the physical representation of everything they owned back home and everything they had in the bank. Kidnapping was routine in Latin America and Southeast Asia, and it was coming to the USA. These days, you could get jacked for the watch on your wrist, the cell phone in your pocket, or the sneakers on your feet. Nobody was safe, not even the rich.

Somewhere, bagpipes played and they all stood.

He recalled a conversation with the senator, made over drinks, about some distant relative being Scottish. Thorne suspected that if Ashcroft had liked Sake instead of Scotch, he would've told everyone he was Japanese. Nevertheless, he stared down at a spot on the floor ten feet in front of him. Bagpipes made him think only of death or defeat and reminded him of other funerals he'd attended by people who also considered themselves of either Scots or Irish descent.

Ashcroft was carried past by four men, his coffin wrapped in the stars and stripes. The men lowered the coffin onto a stand at the front, paused for a second, then retreated off to the side. The mourners all sat back down and Jerky began to speak. His voice was old and dusty like the inside of a drawer in some museum, and about as interesting. Thorne tuned it out.

Nobody ever said that the strong silent type had to listen.

Thorne pondered the fate of the missing picture.

He'd hid it inside Blake's van, which had then been taken away by the Sheriff's Office. Thorne was certain they hadn't found it, however, as Cabot would certainly have used it as evidence against him. The painting spoke to motive and tied him to the gang and their activities. He'd put the painting, together with the Glock Blake used to fire the fatal shot, behind the panel of the van's sliding door. They had probably stripped the van bare by now, but they'd probably done so with the side door open, hiding the space from view.

Around him, people began to sing.

His day was getting worse by the second.

FORTY-NINE

Cabot was in a foul mood as he followed the other cars back to the Ashcroft mansion. Lauren's behavior at the graveside made his blood boil. At times he felt like he'd been watching two teenagers on a first date. Holding hands. Hugging. Her cheek, wet with tears, pressed against his. Her chicken wing arms fluttering against his back as they lowered her husband into the soil. Cabot gripped the cruiser's steering wheel tight. *Thorne.* The man was the Devil. He had everybody fooled. But not him. He was immune to the charm. As far as he was concerned, charm was just another form of bullshit. Facts, that's what he believed in, and the facts in this case didn't add up. Somehow, the man was involved in both the kidnapping and the fatal shooting of Ashcroft. It was the only thing that made sense and he was more determined than ever to prove it.

Next to him, Barnes stirred.

"You think he's banging her, boss?"

Cabot sighed. "Certainly looks that way."

"Wouldn't mind hitting that myself. She has an ass like a peach."

"Jesus, Barnes! She was my friend's wife."

The deputy nodded, a smile still on his face.

"You suppose the relationship started before or after he was dead?"

It was a good question, and one Cabot hadn't thought to consider. He couldn't believe it. His anger and petty jealousy had prevented him from seeing what was, potentially, right in front of him. Could it really be so simple? He glanced at Barnes.

"Say they were having an affair before, what changes?"

Barnes shrugged. "Not much. It gives Thorne motive but we already cleared him."

"I'm not sure we did."

"Oh man! I can't hear this again. *It's not Thorne.*"

Cabot gritted his teeth. Why was he the only one that saw it? They already knew he was a killer, why was the idea that he could kill one more person too much for anyone to believe?

"So you're saying it gets us nothing?"

"Not unless *she* shot the old man," Barnes said. "A relationship gives her motive too. Lauren Ashcroft was never tested for gunshot residue, never asked for an alibi. If you think about it, her motive is far greater than his. I mean, dollars to doughnuts the senator had a prenup limiting how much money she'd get in the event of a divorce. Perhaps nothing at all if she was unfaithful. Now, with him dead, she inherits everything. Hundreds of millions, that's how much that little cupcake's worth now."

Cabot's head was about to explode.

"That's ridiculous! Lauren couldn't hold a Big Mac in those arms without it shaking, never mind fire a 9mm automatic."

"My point is you never checked her out. It's reasonable doubt. If you ever got Thorne to trial, his defense would be there was a more obvious suspect that was never investigated. His lawyer would use your friendship with the Ashcrofts against you and say you were too close. A conflict of interest. The case would be thrown out."

Barnes might be right about that. He could see angles lawyers might use because that's how they trained cops now. Barnes was part of the new breed; aggressive, educated, and career-focused. Cabot was a dinosaur and he knew it. A top lawyer would tear him apart in minutes. Portray him as a pathetic old fool who'd fallen in love with the victim's wife, like a detective in a movie. He'd be discredited, the punchline to a thousand jokes in bars across America. Was it really possible that his single-minded pursuit of Thorne could be the very thing that would get the actor off the hook? Even imagining it was too much for him.

The law is a goddamned ass, he thought.

When he spoke again there was genuine sadness in his voice.

"Sounds like you don't think we'll ever catch his killer."

"I know you don't want to hear this, but James Ashcroft was not universally liked. His views on gun control were well known and a lot of folks take their Second Amendment rights seriously. The potential suspect pool in this case is huge and our chances of catching someone remote. Everyone that hated him had both the means and motive to kill him."

Cabot had heard variations of this idea articulated several times by different people in his department during the investigation and it frustrated him to hear it again from Barnes. He'd thought the detective was smarter than this, believing in what he saw as the crime version of Santa Claus, but apparently not.

"I guess it's possible, but I don't buy it. What you're saying is that the shoot-out at the mall was nothing more than a coincidence. I don't believe in coincidence, never have. The two events are linked and that link is Thorne. He was at both locations and is in this up to his neck. Either he fired the shot, or he knows who did and I aim to find out which it is."

The traffic had ground to a halt and was now advancing in slow, regular chunks. It was obvious why; the front of the line had hit the turn into Ashcroft's property and the cars were being stopped at a security cordon. Cabot wondered if there would be room for all the people. Not a problem they'd have when he died, he supposed.

"Let me ask you something," Barnes said. "If you'd just killed someone and gotten away with it, would you then go to that person's funeral and hug the victim's widow in front of hundreds of people?"

"No."

"So why would Thorne?"

"Because this is a game to him. It amuses him.

Barnes sighed and shook his head.

"Well, one thing's for damn sure, the press were eating it up. Every time they touched each other I could hear their cameras going crazy. The two of them dry-humping will be all over the news and it will go viral online. There's probably a hashtag for it already."

Cabot swore. He'd managed to forget all about the press. Those cockroaches would dine on this for another week. The senator would be lucky to get mentioned at his own funeral. Thorne had given them exactly what they wanted, whether he knew it or not.

They were almost at the Ashcroft property now. He saw two CHP officers standing guard at the gates. They were stopping each car and speaking to the drivers. Identification. One held a clipboard, the other a Remington 870 pump-action shotgun. As he approached them, he rolled down his window but was waved straight through without a word. He drove the cruiser down Ashcroft's driveway toward the mansion. Parked cars lined the road and more still were parked up on an area of grass in front of the building. A trooper waved him into a space there and he killed the engine. Before he could open his door, a long black sedan pulled in next to them and two men with brush cuts and earpieces emerged. One of them stared at him through the glass and showed him the palm of his hand, telling him to remain where he was while a woman in her 70s was helped out the rear of the car.

"Who's she?" Barnes asked.

"Gillian Braxton. California's other senator."

"I didn't know senators got protection."

"Yeah," Cabot said. "Me neither. Folks in DC must be getting twitchy."

"Unless I'm mistaken, we're in for a real treat."

Cabot turned to the detective. "We won't be here long."

"Why *are* we here exactly?"

"To pay our respects."

Barnes looked at him knowingly. "Right."

Inside the mansion it was standing room only. The great and the good were all there, Ashcroft's friends and enemies alike. Guests had been screened coming in, so the only security inside the building were Braxton's Secret Service drones. As far as Cabot was concerned, it was as close to perfect as he could've hoped.

"Hey, kid, stay here will ya? I got to hit the head and cut some cable."

"I did *not* need to know that," Barnes said, his face screwed up in disgust.

Cabot moved through the crowd toward the back of the room. Nobody paid him any attention, they knew who he was and didn't care. To them, he was little more than a worm. He'd probably known the senator the longest of anyone there, but he hadn't been part of the inner circle for a long time. If he was honest with himself, he'd kept the friendship going long after it had faded to nothing. His faux pas with Lauren had been the last straw, but their relationship had become increasingly formal before that night. In a perverse way, Ashcroft needed him more now he was dead than he ever did when he was alive. He'd come through for Jimmy one last time, he thought, when his killer was dead or in handcuffs.

At the back of the room a staircase rose up on one side, and a corridor lead off on the other. He took the corridor. He was alone now, everyone was there to see the golden couple, not roam the building. It'd been a long time since he had last been this way, but he knew where he was going. The mansion had half a dozen bedrooms, but only two were on the first floor. One of those rooms would give him what he wanted, he was certain of it. The corridor made a sharp right and Cabot saw the first of the two doors. It wasn't fully closed, a thin wedge of light shone around the edge. He raised his hand so his fingertips touched the surface of the wood, took a deep breath and pushed. The door swung open.

In front of him was Thorne's wheelchair.

Bingo.

He glanced up and down the corridor, then stepped inside.

The room was small compared to other parts of the building, but that hadn't stopped the Ashcrofts from installing a huge bed. It had to be at least a king-size and it fitted the room like a tongue fits a mouth. To the right of the bed, a pale wooden dresser was pressed against the wall, while on the left was a nightstand. Cabot took the left side as it offered his ample frame the most space. He sat on the edge of the bed near the pillows, facing the wall. He breathed slowly with his hands on his knees, imagining he was Thorne. Did the actor lose sleep over the men he'd killed, or was it all just a half-remembered dream? Sitting on the bed made him realize how tired he was and how easily he could fall asleep if he lay down. He looked at the carpet between his feet. It was so thick he could feel it pushing against the thin leather soles of his formal shoes. He leaned forward and ran his fingers through it like a child, fascinated by the thickness of the pile.

He noticed two parallel marks in the carpet, the silvery kind of fibers brushed the wrong way. Drag marks. They extended down the side of the bed and stopped within three feet of the wheelchair. Cabot turned his head away as soon as he realized what they meant, but he started to feel doubt creep into his thoughts anyway. Plans went wrong for everyone, he told himself. Even bad people. Just because Thorne had been injured didn't mean he wasn't involved, or that he deserved special treatment. Cabot reached into his pocket and pulled out a pair of blue nitrile gloves. The color made it easier to see particulate evidence against the material than the traditional white latex gloves, and they were also a damn sight more comfortable to wear.

He directed his attention to the nightstand.

It was a simple shaker-style unit, the kind that looked like the top drawer was missing. A metal lamp sat on top, its angular shade aimed at a glass of water and a two inch high plastic bottle with a child-proof lid. He picked up the bottle and read the label. *OxyContin.* Cabot shook the container; not too many left. He considered stealing the painkillers to mess with Thorne, but couldn't do it. There were some lines he wouldn't cross, no matter how much he was provoked. He put the pills back and picked up a thin novel that lay on the shelf underneath. Its spine was heavily creased and, judging by the cover, it looked like it had been folded in half lengthwise to fit in a pocket. *The High Window* by Raymond Chandler. He had no time for fiction, why spend hours of your life reading a bunch of lies? Did people really have nothing better to do? He flipped through the pages, hoping some piece of evidence might fall out, but there was nothing inside; not even a fold of paper to mark a page. For all he knew, it wasn't even Thorne's book. He put it back and pulled open the drawer underneath. Four white cartons lay inside, next to a wad of scrunched-up foil packets. Fentanyl patches. Cabot sighed as he flashed back to his wife's final days. The drug was 100 times stronger than morphine, and she'd needed it all. She'd lurched from one patch to the next like a junkie, her eyes coming alive only when a fresh patch was opened.

Since the shoot-out at the mall, he'd allowed himself to think of Thorne's injuries as superficial, and the initial use of the wheelchair as no more than a legal requirement by a hospital keen to prevent litigation. But the evidence within the room did not support this. Instead, it pointed to the actor being far more seriously wounded than he let on. There were many reasons why a person might do this, and perhaps what he'd taken for guilt was in fact something more honest. Pride.

The last drawer held a light pink sheer material that had been folded up. He could see thin straps on top, he ran his finger underneath them, they felt weightless. A nightdress. Lauren had slept here. He lifted the nightdress, still folded, up to his face and breathed it in. Laundry detergent. Lauren had slept in this room at some time, but not recently. She'd given it up for Thorne, and had forgotten to move the dress. He was about to put it back when he noticed there was something else in the drawer, it lay diagonally across the bottom and filled it from corner to corner. A hunting knife. Cabot smiled, this was more like it. He lay the nightdress on his knees and picked up the knife and pulled it out of its nylon sheath. It was heavy and felt good in his hands, even with the gloves on. Perhaps *because* of it. The knife handle looked new, but already there were scuff marks along the blade as if it had been scrubbed with steel wool.

Reluctantly, he put it all back.

The knife meant nothing. Thorne had obviously picked it up for protection. It wasn't illegal, and he couldn't say that he'd do otherwise in the same position. Thorne would want a gun too, but given their beliefs, the Ashcrofts might have prevented him bringing a gun into their house. Would that change now, with Jimmy dead? He drummed his gloved fingertips on his legs. Thorne was arming himself. What implications did this have for the case? Perhaps the gunshot that hit Ashcroft was meant for the actor, just like he claimed. He stood and walked back toward the door.

Opposite the bed was a small dressing table with a tilting oval mirror. At least, there'd been a mirror there at some point, now there were only broken shards left hanging in the frame. Some of the broken glass still lay on top of the table, the silvered backing made it sparkle like diamonds. In the center of the frame was a large dent. It didn't take a genius to figure out what had happened; Thorne had punched the mirror and destroyed it. Something had upset him, but what?

There were two drawers on the right hand side of the desk. He pulled out the top drawer. Medical tape, fresh dressings, scissors, iodine, and a styptic pencil. He tried the bottom drawer. A slim leather wallet, car keys, a basic cell phone, and a laptop computer. He flipped open the wallet, knowing what he'd find inside. It was the fake FBI ID from his TV show. *Special Agent Jake Vasco.* A younger Christopher Thorne stared impassively up at him. He was a little more chiseled, a little more hopeful. Cabot tossed the wallet back in the drawer. There wasn't going to be anything here, he could see that now. It'd been a long shot at best that Thorne might hang on to something incriminating but people did it all the time, they couldn't help themselves. They kept things to help them remember what they'd done, even if what they'd done was monstrous. Everything here was new, or else he'd seen it before at the hospital. What he needed was something that predated the attack at the shopping mall, something that would shake Thorne's shaggy dog story apart. Then he smiled. He knew where to look.

He knew *exactly* where to look.

FIFTY

When Cabot and Barnes emerged from the mansion, it was to enter a bewildering scene. Cars had continued to park long after they arrived and every possible space had been filled. It explained the crush of people inside, which seemed to have almost doubled since they arrived. He set off for the cruiser at a fast clip, weaving between bumpers of other vehicles. After the first batch of cars had parked, a more random and panicked approach had set in as mourners kept on coming. He realized they might be blocked in and unable to leave, a process that could take hours to resolve. Two helicopters hovered overhead. The news channels couldn't get enough of Thorne. At this rate, they'd be giving the actor Ashcroft's spot on the presidential nomination.

Barnes trailed behind, clearly angry.

"You want to tell me what the fuck happened back there?"

Cabot sighed. He'd sensed this coming for the last forty minutes, the question had burned within the detective as they stood in line to pay their respects to Lauren. Cabot reached the cruiser and stood next to the driver's door waiting for Barnes to catch up. He didn't much like the younger man's tone, or where the conversation seemed to be headed, and he hoped to get it out the way before they got inside the vehicle.

"If you have something to say, just say it."

"I'm not your partner, but you need to keep me in the loop with what you're doing so we can back each other up. This isn't a Laurel and Hardy sketch, we have to be professional."

Cabot put both hands on the roof of the car.

"Am I *Hardy* in this scenario? I'm a fat clown, is that what you're saying?"

"What? No! I meant–"

"Listen, Barnes. I don't have to explain myself to you. I go where the evidence takes me, wherever that is, whatever it takes. If you're bored with this case I can put Summersby on it, maybe he'll have some fresh ideas."

Barnes rocked back on his heels like he'd been punched.

"I know you have a personal stake in this, but this is my ass too. You do some cowboy stunt it's going to look like I'm in on it even if I know nothing. It could destroy my career. The best chance of closing this case is by working together, not with me on the outside."

Cabot withdrew his hands from the car's roof and stepped back, his eyes still fixed on the detective. Barnes was a pushy little shit, but he was a better cop than he'd ever be and he found it useful to bounce ideas off him.

"All right. But you better not screw me over."

"I want the same as you."

"Nothing comes from nothing, Barnes. Remember that."

The inside of the car was a furnace and heat from the seats immediately soaked through his cheap polyester suit pants and began to cook his legs. Cabot squirmed uncomfortably and punched up the AC, only to have the cabin fill with a smell like old sneakers. He'd have to get something done about that, but he never seemed to remember. He eased the car out, the steering wheel over at hard lock, and drove as close as possible to a Lexus in front of him. It took three cuts to get out the space and a minute more to navigate the maze of automobiles parked on Ashcroft's lawn and drive. A Highway Patrol Interceptor blocked the entrance and he was forced to stop and wait for it to be moved.

Barnes turned to him, a smile already on his face.

"There's a rumor going around that Summersby was rejected by L.A. County Sanitation for a Dead Animal Collection job before he joined the department. That true?"

Cabot laughed. It was perfect, he could totally picture it.

"I hadn't heard that, but it's believable. He's such a lazy asshole. As near as I can tell, he's trying to solve that hit-and-run case without leaving his desk."

"I know it."

In front of them, the state SUV rolled forward and Cabot lifted his hand off the wheel in thanks before pulling out onto the blacktop, and back toward town. His mood had improved dramatically. He'd noticed in the past that Mason Barnes had a way of calming him, effortlessly winning him around whenever they'd disagreed. A joke, an observation; the kid sure had his moments and he seemed to be able to call them up at will. It made him easier to tolerate than other detectives, but it also hinted at emerging political skills that could cause him problems in the future. He glanced over and saw Barnes, still smiling, take his cell phone out his pants pocket and start typing onto the screen. The clock on the dash told him it was after six. He thought about what he planned to do, then about the conversation they'd just had and decided this might be a good test.

"I gotta make a quick stop on the way back, you mind?"

"Go for it," Barnes said without lifting his head.

"Only take a couple of minutes."

The road had few other vehicles on it, but he drove well down on the speed limit anyway. It relaxed him, knowing the safe speeds all the different corners could take, preferring to slow naturally where he could and only braking where he had to. It was how his father had driven, and he was starting to get the same way. It took him about half an hour to reach the edge of town and another ten before he got to the mall and he didn't think Barnes had looked up more than twice from his cell phone in all that time. He pulled into the parking lot and stopped within ten feet of the blood-red Toyota Camry that filled his dreams. The sudden stop made Barnes' head snap up, a frown instantly forming on his face.

"What are we doing here? Whose car is this?"

"It's Thorne's rental."

Barnes sighed. "Of course it is."

"My gut tells me he's jerking us around."

"That much, I already knew."

Cabot pulled the blue nitrile gloves out of his pants pocket and removed them from the bag he used to carry them. The bag prevented the gloves from picking up dust and fiber contamination from inside his pocket, and from becoming damaged and worn. He felt Barnes watching him, judging him. Taking evidence gloves to the a funeral of a friend. It was wrong, no question, but you couldn't pick and choose when you were a cop. He pulled the gloves on and opened the door. As he approached the vehicle, he noticed the rear windows were partially misted on the inside. Leaning forward, he cupped his hands on either side of his head to mask out reflections. It looked like garbage had been tipped onto the back seat. Cabot took the keys he'd borrowed from Thorne's drawer, blipped the remote and opened the rear door. He immediately took a step back, as if to let someone out.

"Shit, that's ripe," he said.

After a ten-count he ducked back in through the door. He took a pen from his jacket pocket and used it to move items around.

"Let's see," he said. "Beer cans, coffee cups and fast food."

"You don't think…"

Cabot froze. "What?"

"You don't think Thorne's a cop do you?"

"That's not funny, Barnes."

"Sure it is. I'm always hilarious when I'm party to illegal searches."

"If you're afraid to get your hands dirty to solve a case, you're more than welcome to go wait in the car like a little pussy. I promise not to plant any evidence in your absence."

319

"You're a disgrace to the uniform, sir, but I'm not going anywhere."

Cabot smiled. "Glad to hear it."

He returned to his search, his hand moving about on the floor. As Barnes said, it was an illegal search and if he did find something, using it in court would be impossible. He'd have to orchestrate a reason to have Thorne's car searched officially and rediscover the evidence. At present, no such justification existed and finding some might not be easy. The situation was messy at best and relied heavily on Barnes playing ball, something that was not a given. One of the things he disliked most about the detective was his boy scout attitude in relation to following the letter of the law. In time, Barnes would learn how fruitless that attitude was, but for now it stood to get in the way of his investigation.

"I think we have a winner on the dead body smell," he said, holding up a bag. "Burritos, half-eaten. What kind of person leaves half-eaten burritos in the back of a hot car?"

"The kind that leaves in a hurry to save the lives of two strangers?"

Cabot eyeballed him from inside the car.

"You've got a real hard on for this guy, don't you Barnes?"

"The question is, why don't you? He's a hero."

"We'll see about that."

He picked up a thick woolen blanket that was stuffed under the front passenger seat. They were sold locally in one of the stores, he recognized the pattern. He unfolded it carefully at arm's length to prevent contamination. Nothing fell out and there were no blood stains, it was just a blanket. Cabot dropped it on the floor without re-folding it. There was nothing significant in the car at all. He wasn't sure what he'd expected to find, but it was hard not to be disappointed. Thorne had flown up from Los Angeles, hired a car and then spent three days eating takeout and a mixture of beer and coffee. It didn't sound like a vacation to him, but what was it? He reversed out the door and stood there, staring at the mess.

"What does all this look like to you, Barnes? First impression."

"Like he spent a lot of time in his car. Maybe even slept in it."

Cabot nodded. "Right. Which would explain why we found no evidence of him booked into any accommodation, he spent the whole time in the car. Why?"

"Maybe he was moving about and wasn't too bothered about where he slept. A road trip. He used to be a Marine, could be he got used to sleeping in tight spots. He told us he and his girlfriend had broken up, that he just wanted time to himself."

Cabot tilted his head from one side to the other. It cracked. He'd been in the car for two minutes and it had given him a crick in his neck.

"What height would you say Thorne is?"

Barnes thought for a moment. "Six three? Six four?"

"I don't think anyone that tall can sleep in a car and not be bothered about it."

"Okay, maybe not. What does that prove?"

"Not much," Cabot admitted.

He slammed the rear door, his mood souring again.

All he had on Thorne so far was borderline vagrancy and some open container violations, hardly the smoking gun he wanted. If he hoped to nail the actor for anything it would need to be good. The public loved their new hero, and if today's performance was anything to go by, so did Lauren Ashcroft. If it came to it, he knew she'd protect Thorne with the best criminal defense lawyers her money could buy, she'd figure she owed him.

Cabot opened the driver's door and sat behind the wheel. He sat there looking straight ahead for several moments. There was something off with what he was seeing but he couldn't put his finger on it. He turned his head one way, then the other. Driver's door, windshield, passenger door. Sometimes you had to change your view to see what was right in front of you. He did two full passes before he had it: not what *was* there, but what *wasn't*. The outside of the car was filthy; mud coated the side and rear windows, but the windshield was immaculate. Not just by wipers, the whole area of glass was clean from corner to corner. No dead spots, no bugs. It was so clean it looked like there was no glass there at all. A cloth lay in the passenger side footwell next to a green plastic bottle with a spray head. He leaned down and flipped the bottle over. Glass cleaner.

"Hey, Barnes," Cabot said. "Suppose Thorne knew in advance something was going down, what would be different?"

"He'd call the cops?"

"Would he? What if he couldn't?"

"Why couldn't he?" Barnes asked.

"Are you kidding me with this shit? I'm just saying *supposing*."

"All right, say Thorne knew. Perhaps he was somewhere he shouldn't have been and overheard the plan to attack the senator. He can't reveal how he knows what he knows, but he can't stand back and do nothing. The threat is real, but if he calls it in anonymously it might be dismissed. Just another random threat to a public official, one of thousands every year. He can't risk doing nothing, he'd feel guilty the rest of his life if something happened. How am I doing so far?"

"Sounds good," Cabot said, nodding.

"Okay, he knows the target, perhaps even where the kidnapping will take place, so he camps out here in his rental car and waits for the gang to show." He paused for a moment, before continuing. "Then, armed only with a can of Coke and a screwdriver, saves the lives of two of your friends. The man should be in prison, he's a monster."

"Don't be a dick, Barnes."

321

"It doesn't track for me. If he knew of the danger ahead of time, why wasn't he better prepared? He'd be armed to the teeth, surely. Wouldn't you be, in that position? The way it went down seems more spur of the moment. He saw something, he reacted."

That much was certainly true. What the hell had Thorne been thinking?

"Nevertheless, say I'm right. Say he knew about the planned kidnapping and thought it would happen here. Put everything else to one side and..." Cabot stopped mid-sentence, a new thought occurring to him. "Actually, how about this. Take a look around the lot and let me know if you can find a *single* better parking spot than this one for observing the crime scene, because I don't think there is one."

Barnes shook his head and wandered off.

Cabot knew the detective thought he was obsessed, but there was nothing much he could do about that. The truth was, it wouldn't be long before Barnes had his job. He had the skills, he had the sheriff's ear, and, most of all, he had the desire. A case as high profile as this one was once in a lifetime and it would swing it either way. Cabot needed to solve the case, and solve it on his own. He couldn't let Barnes get even partial credit or, ultimately, he was finished. They'd move him out of Investigations and put him in Patrol. He couldn't have that. Patrol was where they put you on the way up, or the way out.

He leaned across and opened the glove box and arranged the contents on the passenger seat next to him for closer study. Cabot sighed. Rental papers, maps, a cell phone charging cord, and a Mars bar. Squat, that's what this was, squat. The only person committing a crime here was him. He put the bar of chocolate to one side and put everything else back where it was. The sun, low on the horizon now, broke through a bank of clouds and filled the small cabin of the car. He could feel the heat of it through the glass even with the door open. But soon, the sun would sink below the horizon and the car would be plunged into twilight. It would get cold pretty rapidly after that, he thought.

Thorne would've needed that blanket.

Cabot opened the candy bar and began eating. What did Thorne think about as he sat here? He glanced up and saw two pale yellow elastic bands wrapped around the sun visor. They were spaced roughly three inches apart and were centered in his vision as he faced forward. He ran his fingertip over one of the bands and found it hard and cracked like an elephant's knee. He pushed the visor down and a smile spread across his face.

Pinned under the bands, was a photograph of Lauren Ashcroft.

"Fuck me."

Barnes called out. "You say something, boss?"

He thought for a moment. This picture was exactly what he'd been searching for since his interview with Thorne. It proved there was a link

322

between the actor and the kidnapping attempt. He'd be totally vindicated. But the moment of triumph would be brief and all eyes would turn on Thorne. At that point, he'd lose his advantage. Carson had already passed the case to the feds just to sink his run for sheriff. He'd be a footnote in the investigation, a witness that wasn't called. Nobody would remember he was involved in the case, never mind that he cracked it. For now at least, it would be best to keep this to himself.

"Nothing," he said. "Never mind."

Barnes muttered something and continued down the lot.

Cabot reached up and removed the picture from the visor. It was thin, low quality paper, the kind printed out from a computer. The sides had been cut with a pair of blunt scissors and the blades had chewed at the surface of the picture causing it to wrinkle along the edge. The left hand side, however, was smooth having been folded instead of cut. Thorne had run something repeatedly over the crease so that it was as flat as possible. A fingernail maybe. The fold had cropped off part of Lauren's right shoulder and a third of her arm down to the elbow. There was only one reason he could think of to fold at that particular point: to hide a person standing next to her. He pushed the remainder of the candy bar into his mouth and threw the wrapper over his shoulder into the back of the car. With both hands now free, he unfolded the paper and felt his mood darken.

James Ashcroft's face looked out at him full of health, humor and promise.

One way or another, he'd make Thorne pay.

FIFTY-ONE

The wake dragged on and on. Thorne longed to slip away but Lauren seemed to be increasingly reliant on him for support, both mental and physical. He'd seen Cabot enter the mansion, before pushing through the crowd and out of sight. The lieutenant had been gone for almost ten minutes, and he'd lay money on him spending all that time searching through his belongings. After close to an hour, Cabot and the other deputy appeared in front of him as they took their turn to speak briefly to Lauren. The lieutenant avoided his eye but the younger cop, Barnes, had stared at him with undisguised interest and a thin, knowing smile.

It was obvious what the cops thought, he would've thought the same thing in their position. They thought he and Lauren were an item due to the way she had hung onto him at the graveside. A relationship with Lauren gave him motive to kill Ashcroft, a motive more believable than a random altercation with a drunk he'd just met. The two deputies didn't appear to be the only ones either. Everyone who came to give Lauren their condolences had performed a near identical eye slide from her face up to his and back as they spoke. Something was going on between the two of them, and everyone saw it. He let out a slow breath.

They could think what they liked.

There was nothing going on between him and Lauren.

He scanned what remained of the crowd and saw there were less than 20 people left. Soon, he and Lauren would be on their own, a prospect that he was less than thrilled about. To take his mind off it, he thought about Cabot again. There'd been something new on the lieutenant's face when he'd stood in front of him, something he hadn't seen there before. He could be wrong, but it looked like hope. Whatever it was, it had to be something he'd found in his bedroom. A lead. The people around them could be here for another hour, it was like they didn't want to leave her alone with him.

Thorne leaned in close to Lauren's ear.

"I need to take care of something."

She looked up, eyes wide.

"You're leaving?"

Her voice faltered as she said it. He decided to keep it light.

"Too much caffeine."

Her cheeks darkened and she gave a small nod.

Thorne made his way toward the back of the room where there was more space. His limp was back from having stood for so long without moving. He recognized some of the people from the birthday party. A couple smiled at him, but most did not. Either assuming he was involved somehow in Ashcroft's death, or remembering the scene he'd created with the pistol. Finally, he was past them and walking down the square pipe of the art gallery. He fought the urge to run, he'd only damage his leg.

The bedroom door was fully closed.

He'd stopped fully closing the door after the first week. He felt safe here, and the room became stuffy due to a lack of natural ventilation. He pushed the door open and studied the room, sweeping his head around slowly. Nothing stood out. He walked in and glanced over at the bed. There was an imprint on the left hand side. Cabot had sat while he'd gone through his belongings in the nightstand. He'd then left his ass-print through incompetence, or as a special message to him. Thorne went over and took out the bottom drawer. The hunting knife was still there. He looked around the room. There was so little of his in here and most of it had already been documented by Barnes at the hospital.

He walked over to the dressing table and sat down in the chair.

He went through the drawers. Pulling one open, shuffling around, moving to the next one. He assumed he'd notice what was wrong immediately, but he was mistaken. It all appeared to be there. Laptop, burner cell phone, fake ID, charger cables. Thorne went back to the first drawer and took everything out, spreading it across the desk in front of him. It looked fine. He put it all back and moved to the next drawer. Nothing changed. The result was the same, everything was there.

He sighed. It was harder to notice something missing, than it was to find something you were looking for, or something that shouldn't be there.

Thorne opened his laptop.

He'd saved this for last, because he knew it was the most likely location for evidence against him. Even a blockhead like Cabot could find something incriminating in his search history. Items about Lauren and James Ashcroft. The dates of those searches preceded the shoot-out, which would undo his immunity deal with the DA. Perhaps he'd found the video of Kate. It wouldn't be hard to find, he'd put it in a folder on his desktop.

He opened Console, a diagnostic app that logged processes running since startup. The list was long and mostly meaningless to him, but there was a time noted against each item. He scrolled down past the startup he'd just initiated, to the previous activation. It was from ten past midnight. Thorne let out a long breath. Cabot hadn't looked here. Computers were obviously not one of the lieutenant's strengths, but they would be someone's. He opened his browser and cleared his internet cache back to the beginning of time. He then logged into his Google dashboard and cleared all activity stored on Google's servers. No doubt the FBI could bring it back, but it was something. He closed the lid and let his hands rest on top of it, his eyes straight ahead at the broken mirror.

He had no idea what Cabot's lead was, or how to counter it.

FIFTY-TWO

Kate Bloom watched them carefully as they entered the small office. Something about her had changed, but Blake couldn't put his finger on it. No matter. He could see that the cable ties around her wrists remained in place, holding her arms to those of the chair. He moved in close and stood looking down at her. Her face angled up, her green eyes darting between him and Sara Dawson behind him. The person he'd seen in Pasadena was gone. The effortless beauty and confidence, wiped out. Blood smeared her face and matted down her hair in black clots. He dropped the greasy paper sack he was carrying onto the desk next to her. A bad smell was coming off the sack, but her eyes were drawn to it anyway. She hadn't eaten anything in 48 hours, and he knew what that was like. He reached out and removed the strip of cotton that was tied around her head and threaded through her teeth. Underneath, her lips were swollen and split, her mouth hanging open. He could hear her breathing through it. She flexed her jaw then ran her tongue around her teeth and gums.

Her eyes were pinned on his. Fierce. Strong.

That's what was different about her. Kate Bloom was a survivor. Something dark and ancient had risen up inside her and assumed control.

"You must be hungry," he said.

She said nothing.

"There are four quarter pounders in that sack, complete with fries and soda. They're all yours if you answer my questions right."

Kate shot a glance at the paper bag.

"All right," he continued, pulling up a second chair. "Now, this is really important. I don't want you to just give me the answers you think I want. I'm not going to be angry with you, okay?"

Kate nodded.

"You and Thorne. *Chris*. Are you guys in a good place?"

She shook her head.

"We had a fight. I've not seen him since."

This much, he knew.

"What was the fight about?"

"I broke up with him."

Blake swore loudly. Kate stiffened, her eyes wide.

When he'd watched them arguing in the hotel bar, he'd seen only passion. He didn't see a couple breaking up, he didn't see an explosive ending. He'd seen something of his own relationship with Sara and he'd smiled. It had made him feel close to his old friend, that they liked the same thing in a woman. Someone that didn't take any shit.

He took out a small knife and held it between them.

"I apologize," he said. "I promised I wasn't going to get mad."

He thrust the blade toward her, making her scream. She pulled her arm back in a defensive pose, then stared at it as she registered that he'd cut the cable tie. He tore open the paper sack and held out one of the burgers and she reluctantly took it. She paused with it in her hand, her face less than thrilled by the reality of the food. The moment passed, and she bit deep into the limp, lukewarm meat. Her hand shook with hunger.

"How's that?"

She swallowed the mouthful half-eaten. "Disgusting."

She took another huge bite, undeterred.

"Let's continue. Were you seeing someone else?"

She shook her head, but her eyes dipped to the floor.

"*But?*"

She shrugged.

"When I broke up with him, he never asked. I think he automatically assumed I was and didn't want to know any details. Things hadn't been right between us for a while and he probably took this as the reason why. I should've told him the truth, but his assumption made it easier for both of us. I knew he'd never stop trying to win me back as long as he thought I was available. I didn't want that, I'd made my decision."

Blake stood and rubbed the back of his neck in frustration.

This was his problem. It had been his problem all along.

She continued to eat. Her first burger down, Kate Bloom began to work her way through a bag of fries. She ate quickly, either from hunger or because she feared he'd take the food away before she was finished. She started on another burger.

"How long were you and Thorne in a relationship?"

"Five years, nearly six."

"Do you think he's still in love with you?"

"Yes."

He liked her confidence, but she hadn't seen what happened at the funeral. Thorne and the Ashcroft woman had practically made out in front of the mourners, the cops, and the long lenses of the nation's news networks. The whole of America knew Thorne was banging Lauren Ashcroft, except for his old girlfriend.

"How long do you think he'll feel that way?"

"*Chris?* Forever. He'd die for me."

Sara spoke up.

"Why would you give up on a man like that?"

"Because I forgot what my life was like without him."

Sara shook her head. "That kind of love? It's once in a lifetime."

A silence fell over them and Kate went back to eating. The girl could sure pack it away. She was onto a fresh burger, which would make it her third. Her right arm was steady now as the hunger shakes passed. She looked brighter too, with more color in her face. He wondered if she'd given any thought to how this conversation might affect her life expectancy. She'd all but told him she was of little value to him as a hostage. Did she think he'd let her go?

Blake sighed. Lauren Ashcroft was now a very wealthy woman, or would be soon enough. If Thorne played his cards right, his money problems were over. He recalled how the two of them had interacted in the coffee store. She'd touched his hand, her puppy dog eyes locked onto his. It had been right there all along. Thorne had been working the long con and by shooting the old man he'd only made things easier for him. Instead of having to convince Lauren to leave her husband and take half his money, she'd get all of it guilt-free.

Thorne had no need for deals and paintings, nor for the exposure involved in pulling off a robbery while the FBI sniffed around. The actor could just sit back and let things play out. But he couldn't. Sooner or later, he and Sara were going to get caught. The whole county was looking for them and with the level of media interest, he wasn't sure how far away they'd have to be before they were safe. He made a mental list of the options open to him.

Send Thorne one of Kate's fingers, tell him the whole hand's next.

Kidnap Lauren Ashcroft, repeat his threat.

Give up on the painting and the deal, go back to L.A.

Find another way to the painting.

It wasn't a long list, now that he came to think about it. Four options, two still requiring Thorne's assistance, and one ending in failure. He couldn't face walking away with nothing now. Would Sara stay with him if he did that? Not likely. Yet any option that relied upon Thorne's help seemed doomed to fail. There was a time when the actor was willing to do what he was told, but he sensed that time had come and gone. There'd been too much bad blood between them for any plan to work. That left one option.

The Picasso would normally have returned to the gallery by now.

Ashcroft's death had caused that timeline to slip, but after a tasteful period had elapsed the gallery was certain to enquire when the picture would return. Once back in the gallery, he was out of options. Thorne's original plan to hit the security truck wasn't bad, but he had no idea when that transport might take place. He'd need a schedule, a route, and the company that the Ashcrofts used. Without that information, it was no plan at all.

But why wait for it to be in a security truck, in a remote place? It was already there. He'd seen the Ashcrofts home through the trees. No armed guards, no dogs, no neighbors. Sure there was an alarm, but it would be no more than background music buried in the woods like it was. He wouldn't need to break any locks either, the place was practically made from glass. Blake smiled to himself. All along he'd believed that Thorne increased his chances of success and minimized the threat of being caught, but the reality was the reverse. He had proven to be a serious obstacle. His mind, his tactical skills; not working with him, but against him. If he was going to get the painting on his own, he had to also take Thorne out first.

It was time to say goodbye.

Kate Bloom looked up, into his eyes.

FIFTY-THREE

Thorne was in a drugstore when Coop called. It was noisy inside so he went out onto the sidewalk. She said that with Ashcroft dead and buried, the network were pulling them out. The story was over. She wanted to see him again before she left, that they had unfinished business. Coop didn't state what that business was, but he had an idea and agreed to meet. Behind him, he heard the sound of a vehicle accelerating hard and he turned sharply toward it. A large black SUV hurtled toward him, it's front tire mounting the curb and skidding to a halt alongside him. Four men in suits sprang out and surrounded him. FBI agents.

One of them gestured at the vehicle.

"Step inside, Mr Thorne."

He glanced into the dark interior.

"There's been a mistake, I didn't order an Uber."

"It's better for everyone if you get in voluntarily."

Thorne looked up and saw Blake ten feet back with his arm folded across his chest, his hand up in his armpit. The two exchanged a look, before Thorne stepped into the SUV. The four suits packed themselves in around him and the vehicle pulled away, pushing itself into the stream of traffic. They rode in silence, the men around him pretending he didn't exist. His mind returned to the pick up point and Blake. He knew exactly what had been about to happen. Another five or ten seconds, and his brains might have been all over the sidewalk. A trip hazard for the unlucky tourist. He took off his sunglasses and looked at the suited figures around him. His would-be saviors. He should have seen this move of Blake's coming, but he hadn't. If Blake had decided to get rid of him, that meant he no longer needed him. What did that mean for Kate? Was she still alive?

After several minutes, they came to a halt and got out. He looked around and saw the Sheriff's Office. Great. His favorite place. The suits surrounded him, like a presidential detail, and walked him up to the building. There were five of them, including the driver of the SUV. None over six feet tall, but lean and serious-looking. Another agent stood inside the doorway, waiting. Their eyes connected.

"This way, Mr Thorne."

The man walked in front of him. He had a natural swagger that twisted his shoulders from side to side as he walked. Cops and admin staff turned to watch as they walked past. Some stood to get a better view. The agent looked over his shoulder.

"We've taken over some offices here and a couple more at the CHP building down in Aptos. Wherever we go, we're standing on someone else's toes, getting in their shit."

Thorne gave him his cheesy Jake Vasco grin.

"Are you going to be the good cop?"

The man laughed and faced forward.

"We're the FBI, we're all good."

He was led into a small office at the side of the building. A man stood staring out the window, his hands folded behind his back like they were cuffed. Thorne glanced around the room. A large table sat in the middle of the room, two chairs on one side, one on the other. Between the two chairs, at the rear wall, sat a video camera mounted on a tripod, it's red LED already burning. That made the single seat his, he supposed. The man at the window now faced him. He was in his mid to late fifties and his face looked like it could hold a pint of water.

"Take a seat, Mr Thorne."

He sat on the single seat, which creaked under his weight.

There were five men in the room, all staring at him. Thorne sensed they were trying to intimidate him, but they were wasting their time. He was an actor, being stared at was his job. Somewhere in the room he heard a clock ticking. He listened to it, letting the slow beat enter his body. It relaxed him. He imagined his heart slowing, the two beats synchronizing. His breathing slowed, becoming deeper, more spaced out. Opposite him on the table were two folders, one about two inches thick, the other closer to four. The larger one had a cell phone on top of it, holding it shut.

The old man came over and stood behind him.

"Sapperstein, Johnson; take a walk fellas."

Two of the suits filed out the room. The old man sat down in the chair behind the folders and studied him. His face was grizzled like a cowboy, but he had kind eyes.

"You look tired, Thorne. You want a coffee? A Coke?"

"I'm fine."

The old man turned to the good cop agent.

"Get the man a Coke."

The suit nodded and left the room. Thorne stared at a casually dressed man at the back of the room. He wore jeans and a blood-red hooded sweatshirt with UCSC printed on the front. The sweatshirt was large, but he had little doubt that it covered a muscular frame. His hair was short and black like the coat of a labrador. Thorne placed him as ex-military.

"Thank you for coming here today."

"It didn't seem like I had a choice. You sent five armed men."

"I thought if I sent five I'd get at least two of them back."

Thorne smiled.

"This going to take long? I got things to do."

The agent stared at him with a level gaze.

"I've been doing a little light reading." He said, putting his hand on the thicker folder. "This is your service record, I had it printed out. I'm kind of analogue. Things mean more to me when they're on something I can touch with my hands. I'll be honest, I've never read a record like this in my life. You're a hero."

Thorne said nothing. He knew roughly what the file would contain. His eyes moved over the jumbled edges, trying to imagine what they were. After action reports, commendations, a breakdown of his tactical skills and training, medals. Then there'd be the history of disobedience, the official reprimands, and time spent in the brig. He'd amassed a serious paper trail during his time with the Marines. He wondered if the file also included his deposition for Blake's court-martial, and if that explained why he was here now. It wouldn't take the FBI long to notice the similarities between archive pictures of Aidan Blake and the wanted picture Cabot had all over town.

The door opened and the agent returned with the Coke, which he set on the table in front of him. The metal was beaded with condensation. It looked good. Ice-cold, the way he liked it. The agent sat in the other chair, his body half turned so he could see him and the old man with the smallest turn of his head. The old man cleared his throat.

"I suppose we should introduce ourselves. I'm Supervisory Special Agent Mancuso, the SAC of the Bureau's San Francisco Field Office, Special Agent Corrigan here you've already met, and lastly, this gentleman behind us is Mr Teece from another agency."

"Detailed *and* vague, I like it."

"As you may know, we've taken over the investigation of the shoot-out at the mall, the fatal shooting of Senator Ashcroft at the roadhouse and, additionally, I have some people looking into Lieutenant Cabot on criminal assault charges against yourself."

"I already said I'm not pressing charges. Cabot found me covered in blood next to his friend's body, any one of us might have reacted the same way. I don't hold it against him."

"Well, that's not how it works, and I'll tell you why. Suppose every reported abuse by a law enforcement officer could simply be withdrawn, then you'd have a situation where the victim could be threatened until they withdraw their complaint. The abuse would continue and other people would be effected. There always has to be an investigation."

There'd be no taking back the assault claim, not without exposing himself to some new charge. He nodded that he understood. Cabot had been a pain in his ass from day one, but he was only doing his job and he appeared to be the only cop close to the truth.

"Look, I already gave the deputies my statement, it's all there."

Mancuso smiled.

"No offense to the locals, but we operate to a different code."

Thorne had no doubt about that. A code that, he was sure, knew it's ass from its elbow. He looked at the three men, from one face to another. The two agents he understood, but the presence of the shadowy third figure stuck out. *Teece*. What the hell kind of name was that? Was it real, or fake? *Another agency*. CIA? No matter how much he turned it over in his head, he just couldn't make the pieces fit together.

"Do I need my lawyer?"

"An interesting question. From our point of view, we're taking a statement, following procedure. We noticed you only invoked your right to legal representation after you were assaulted and assumed you'd be happy to work with us as a neutral third party. Do you feel that you might incriminate yourself in some way?"

Thorne sighed. No matter how much they pretended to be different, they were all the same. The presence of a lawyer always changed the mood music. He'd burned his bridges with Barnes because of the lawyer, he should try and keep the FBI sweet.

"Fine. Ask your questions. I got nothing to hide."

Mancuso nodded and opened the smaller folder. He took from it a handful of eight by ten color photographs and lay four of them across the table in front of him. They were morgue pictures of Sam Porter, Taylor Lynch, Lucas Foster, and Ricky Martinez. He'd never met Martinez, and only knew his name thanks to media coverage of the shoot-out.

"You recognize these men?"

"I guess they're the men I killed."

"You guess?"

"They didn't look like this last time I saw them."

Mancuso nodded again.

"And do you recognize them?"

"Is this an Abbott and Costello sketch?"

The agent didn't respond. Instead, he laid out another four photographs, on top of the previous set. Pictures of the men alive. This time around, Porter and Lynch were wearing desert pattern camouflage; Foster a motor pool jumpsuit. Martinez wore only baggy shorts down to

334

his knees, while the rest of his body was covered in tattoos.

"How about now?"

"Right. Three Marines. Cabot said something about that to me before. Still, I don't recognize them. Doesn't mean I never met them, I just don't remember. There are a lot of Marines and ex-Marines out there, we don't all know each other." He leaned forward and pointed at Foster. "This guy here? That's not a face you'd forget, am I right?"

Mancuso was watching him closely. They were testing him. He had never met Lynch and Foster before he'd walked into that bungalow in Culver City, but he'd known Porter since before he could shave. Could they prove that somehow?

"Take a good look," Corrigan said.

Thorne sighed.

"You already know who they are, it was in the news."

Mancuso spread his hands apart, a gesture of honesty.

"We're looking for the leader. Cabot thought it likely he was also a Marine and that's how all these people were connected. We don't disagree with this assessment. It was a long shot, but we hoped that if you recognized them you might be able to point us toward likely candidates for the leader or even remember who he is."

"Wouldn't that be a huge coincidence?"

"Ah, coincidence," Corrigan said, wistfully. "You mean like a team of ex-Marines being stopped by another ex-Marine? These men served in the same locations as you, Thorne, in the same unit. I'm not sure *coincidence* quite covers this."

Thorne forced himself to stay silent for a moment to let his anger fade.

"Look, I don't recognize them. Nor did I recognize the two that got away. My memory isn't the best, but I *am* good with faces. I never hung out with anyone from the motor pool, and this guy here looks like a goddamn pedophile. None of them were EOD, I know that much. There's not a lot of mixing in the Corps, you stay with your own people. Ask Teece, I'm sure he served. The man's got Ranger written all over his face."

At the back of the room he saw Teece smile.

Mancuso turned to Corrigan and exchanged a look.

"All right, Thorne, let's go back to that day in the mall."

It was now over a month since the shoot-out and many of the details had become fuzzy. When Cabot had interviewed him, it was still fresh in his mind and he'd already gone through it once already with Barnes. He had also known Cabot was coming and had time to prepare.

As he gave his account of the shoot-out, it came to him that he'd done nothing about his rental car. He'd forgotten all about it. The thought made him pause, and to hide it, he drank from the can of Coke. The Chinese-American deputy had fetched his backpack out the car's trunk for him while he'd lain in hospital, but she'd returned the key, he was certain of it. He put the can back down on the table in front of him. Everything from the hospital had been brought back to the mansion and stuffed into the dresser drawers and the nightstand.

But there'd been no key there after Cabot had made his visit.

It gave him a sick feeling in his stomach.

This was what Cabot had on him.

He finished up his story in a mechanical manner. It was no longer something he'd experienced, as much as a scene from a movie he'd watched. He felt no emotion. He'd lived it once and it had lasted only a couple of minutes. But he'd seen the video many times and his own point of view was fading from his memory to be replaced by the security footage.

Mancuso and Corrigan went over his account for a quarter of an hour before moving on to the death of the senator. He supposed they'd already seen a copy of Cabot's interview, not to mention the shoot-out video from the internet. On top of that, much of what he was telling them was already in the public domain, covered by rolling news updates. When you arrived this late to the party, there was no new juicy detail to get your teeth into, just cold coffee at the bottom of someone else's mug.

They spent close to an hour on the death of Ashcroft and his arrest and assault by Cabot. The questions were simple enough, designed to make him remember more detail, rather than establish his guilt or innocence. As during the shoot-out section, neither agent took any notes. He had the feeling that they were taking part in some kind of charade. They'd brought him in to make a statement and had asked no difficult questions at all. Perhaps, they didn't suspect him of anything and were just, as Mancuso had said, following procedure. Finally, the two agents glanced at each other and nodded.

"Mr Teece, cut the feed."

Teece reached out and turned off the camera. Thorne frowned. The word *feed* caught his attention. This wasn't just a recording, they were transmitting it somewhere. Someone was watching. In the next room, or farther away? Mancuso leaned forward.

"How would you characterize your relationship with Lauren Ashcroft?"

"We're friends. I guess quite close."

"*Intimate?*"

"No."

"I find that hard to believe."

"We went through something bad together, a bond forms. That's it."

"At the funeral, you appeared to be much more than friends. She was holding your hand and hugging you almost the entire time. You looked like you'd done it before."

"Haven't you heard? Funerals are the new Tinder."

Teece laughed.

"I don't know what that means, Mr Thorne."

"I know how it looked, okay? But she was falling apart. She loved her husband and she's pretty isolated up here. I don't think she has any friends of her own anymore, she left them all behind to be a senator's wife. I was all she had."

"Still, with her husband out the way the two of you can do what you want."

Anger boiled over inside him and he didn't bother to hide it.

"You know what I am to her? I'm a reminder of the worst days in her life. If you think that's an attractive proposition to a woman, then you don't know much. I certainly did not kill James Ashcroft to be with her, he and I had become friends. The man gave me a Maserati."

Mancuso's eyebrows shot up.

"That's quite a gift." Mancuso began to tidy the desk in front of him, putting everything back in their folders. "In fact, we do *not* think you are responsible for the death of the senator. Lieutenant Cabot's own dash cam footage clearly shows you in some kind of argument with another man, obviously this man you mention in your statement. Sadly the resolution and lighting is not good enough for a positive ID. I would also assume that a man of your skills would find an easier way of killing the senator than by shooting him through his windshield as he drove toward you."

Despite knowing he'd done nothing to the senator, it was nonetheless a relief to hear that the FBI didn't consider him a suspect.

"So what was all that shit about me and Lauren?"

Mancuso looked blankly back at him.

"When was the last time you were in touch with Kate Bloom?"

Thorne sat back in his seat. Hearing her name from the agent's mouth stunned him. Had Blake killed her? He couldn't lose her again, he wouldn't survive.

"I don't know. Before I came up here. She broke up with me."

Corrigan's eyes lit up. "She broke up with you and nobody's seen her since?"

"Jesus. You make it sound like I dissolved her in acid."

"You're right at the center of everything, aren't you?"

Thorne stared at the two agents. If she was still alive, Kate's best chance was for him to come clean, lay the whole thing out in front of the FBI. They had the people, the technology to find her. To track Blake down. The right word from him could unlock it all, but only if they believed him. Revealing everything would make him hard to take seriously, as well as party to any number of crimes, including murder.

"I ask myself," Mancuso said, "how can one person be so close to all these different events and not be somehow connected? Doesn't that seem odd to you, Agent Corrigan?"

"Very much so. Suspicious even."

Opening up to the FBI would be a mistake.

He'd be arrested and Kate would be on her own.

"Are we done here?"

Mancuso smiled and slid a business card across the table at him, and tapped the center of it once with his index finger.

"If you think of anything, don't hesitate to contact me."

He reached out to take the card, but Mancuso held it in place.

"Don't go leaving town without telling me first, you hear?"

Thorne stood and the others did the same.

"Just a moment," Mancuso said, his face twisting. "I got a favor to ask. A friend of mine in the D.C. office is a fan of your show. He asked me to get a picture, you mind?"

He could hardly believe it. They had practically kidnapped him off the street and questioned him without charge for an hour and a half and now they wanted mementos. Nevertheless, it always made him feel good to hear about fans of the show and he liked how the agent had willingly made himself look foolish on behalf of a friend.

"All right, but I don't want anything turning up on Facebook."

Thorne stood in front of a wall with a map of the county pinned to it. Light from the window was coming in at a high angle and the Venetian blind cast a stripped diagonal shadow across the wall behind his head. It looked like a scene from a noir movie, which he thought was about perfect. Mancuso lifted his cell phone up in front of his face and Thorne heard the fake shutter sound as the old man took his picture. He liked the idea that an FBI agent was a fan of his show about an FBI agent. Maybe there was a compliment in there, a validation. The shutter sounded several more times.

The door closed and he noticed the two other men had left.

"What was all this really about? And don't tell me procedure."

The agent lowered the cell phone.

"You'll find out soon enough is my guess."

338

FIFTY-FOUR

Thorne stood in the mall parking lot next to his rental car. It was the first time he'd been back since the shoot-out and it felt like he was walking over his own grave. He reached out and tried the door handle. Locked. He sighed. He hadn't expected anything else, but it never hurt to try. He bent down to the glass and used his hand to shield the sun. It was a real mess in there, even more of a mess than he'd left it in.

Cabot had taken his keys and performed an illegal search.

Thorne sighed. It was a pattern of behavior he recognized. On his TV show, Jake Vasco had frequently done the same thing. He was a classic rebel, following nobody's rules but his own to get the bad guy. Now that he *was* the bad guy, he didn't find it half as amusing. There was only one thing in the car that could cause him problems and he could see from the angle of the sun visor that Cabot had found it.

He'd found it, and he'd removed it.

In order to use the picture against him, Cabot would have to return here ahead of a legal search and plant it. So he'd kept the car keys. He'd taken the evidence with him to protect it, but there was a huge flaw in his plan.

Thorne took out his cell phone and dialed a number.

"Enterprise, San Jose. Tracy speaking."

"I need to talk to someone about my rental."

"What's your name?"

Her tone was friendly, bright.

"Christopher Thorne."

"One moment, sir." He could hear keys being pressed, more than just typing in his name. The woman hummed to herself while she did this. "Okay, it seems we have been trying to contact you for several weeks. Your car was due back on the fourteenth of last month."

"I'm sorry. I was hospitalized in Santa Cruz and forgot about the car."

The line went silent for a moment.

"You're *that guy* that's been on the news?"

"Yes, ma'am. My situation here has changed and I'm hoping you might be able to collect the car for me. Unfortunately, I've lost the keys and I'm ashamed to admit that it's going to need a clean inside as well. Would you be able to get this straightened out for me, Tracy?"

"Could you hold for one moment please?"

"Sure."

This time there was no humming, he heard music. *California Dreamin'* by The Mamas and Papas. Whatever happened for the rest of the day, this song would be playing in his head. He hoped she wasn't going to transfer him to someone else, he didn't want to start over from the beginning. After almost two minutes, the woman came back.

"Where is the car at present?"

"The Capitola Mall parking lot."

He heard this being typed in.

"That's no problem. Do you have any personal effects inside the vehicle?"

"Nothing I need."

"Perfect. Okay, everything is all set. You will notice a return on your credit card within 3 working days representing an accrued daily fee and your original payment."

Thorne frowned.

"You're not charging me anything for the car?"

"That's correct."

"I don't understand."

The woman laughed.

"It's our special *hero* rate. Will there be anything else today?"

"That's it."

"Have a wonderful day, Mister Thorne."

He thanked her and disconnected.

Across the lot, Lauren stood next to his Maserati her face turned up toward the sky, arms folded on top of the roof. She was thirty feet away and wearing dark sunglasses, but he could tell she was upset. He'd tricked her into coming here, a place that was nothing but a nightmare for her, and she wasn't pleased with him.

One thing at a time.

Cabot had his incriminating picture of Lauren and her husband, but unless it was found inside his rental it meant nothing. The only thing that made it relevant, was when he'd printed it. Planting it somewhere else wasn't going to work. Thorne smiled as he walked toward Lauren. Her head dipped, coming down from the sky to look at his face. He kept on smiling, like it was a light with a brightness control he kept turning up. Her mouth was a flat line, but he didn't stop. He smiled all the way back, then stood across the roof from her, smiling straight into her face. Finally, she crumbled and laughed.

"Motherfucker," she said.

He nodded, and let the smile melt away.

"I just had an idea. Two, actually. Come on."

"Where are we going?"

"Shopping."

Lauren smiled. "Cool. What for?"

"A really cheap suit."

*

Thorne sat shirtless and sweating in the gym, fresh from another workout. The senator's rowing machine was kicking his ass. He'd only managed twenty five minutes before he'd been forced to stop. His shoulder felt like it had a hot poker twisting about in it. He stood and walked over to a corner unit set into the back wall and drank from a glass of water. The fingers of his right hand were starting to shake. He took a handful of roasted almonds and chewed on them while he made up his second protein shake of the day. He'd dropped ten pounds since he'd been in Santa Cruz and he didn't want to lose any more. Muscle mass had to be fed or it disappeared fast.

He finished mixing the shake and quickly knocked half of it back. It fell far short of delicious and he chased it down with another handful of nuts. The almonds were salted and the salt cut through the funky flavor of the drink. He turned and saw Lauren standing in the doorway. If he had to guess, he'd say she'd been there for several minutes. Her eyes followed the movement of his hand between the large cardboard drum of almonds and his mouth. Her face was screwed up, like she was disgusted.

"What gives with the almonds?"

"I was wounded once before, in Iraq. When I was in this field hospital, the guy next to me swore on almonds. Said they helped with the healing process." Thorne shrugged. "Might be a load of bunk, but there's no downside if he's wrong. I like them."

She stared at him blankly, like she hadn't been listening.

"Being at the mall today, it brought it all back."

Thorne nodded, but said nothing.

Taking her to the mall had been a mistake and he couldn't honestly say why he'd done it. He'd grown used to having her around and had involved her out of habit. Since Ashcroft died, Lauren had gone out of her way to avoid being on her own. Even when she was swimming laps in her pool, she liked him to be nearby on one of the loungers, or by the breakfast bar where he could see her. It didn't matter if she couldn't see him, knowing he

341

was there seemed to relax her and he'd gone along with it. But she wasn't relaxed now, she was building herself up to something. She had something to say but didn't know how to get there. Thorne finished the rest of his shake and put the glass down on the granite counter and wiped his mouth on the back of his hand.

"What is it that you think you know?"

"It was you they were after, wasn't it? Those fucking clowns."

Thorne shook his head. She almost had it.

"No. Actually, it's kind of worse."

"Chris, you need to tell me. I'm going out of my mind."

He sighed. This moment had been a long time coming.

"I wasn't there by chance in that mall. I knew those men were going to be there and what they had planned. I was there to stop them."

"I don't understand what you're telling me."

"I think you do. I think you've always known. It's time to say it out loud."

"That you were one of them?"

"Yes."

Her face distorted.

"I'm going to throw up."

"Let me explain."

"No, no, no! You don't get to explain. I want you to leave."

"Lauren, look at me."

"I can't! How could you do this to me? I trusted you completely. I *loved* you. And all this time you're-"

"I mean look at me and see what's happened to me. They shot me remember? I killed some of them. It's safe to say that I'm not on their side. I was being blackmailed."

She glared at him, unimpressed.

"Did you even think about going to the police?"

"Come with me. There's something you need to see. I promised James not to show you, but we're past that now. You need to know what's at stake."

There was something in her eyes he hadn't seen before. Fear. She nodded anyway, the corners of her mouth turned down. She didn't believe him, and she didn't believe that anything he showed her would change her opinion. He should've been straight with the Ashcrofts from the very beginning, even if that threatened his immunity deal. Right was right, he'd known that once. He led her to his room and opened his MacBook.

"I've done unforgivable things, Lauren, but I had no choice. The first time I saw this I thought it was you in this video. Next time, it might be. James thought that too, that's why he helped me. That's why he was there that night."

She was growing angry with his excuses, he could see it.

"*Chris-*"

He held up his hands in surrender.

"Watch first, judge later. OK?"

Thorne started the video, then stepped back and turned away.

He couldn't face watching it again. He'd seen it twice now and that was enough. He stood next to his bed with his head tilted back against the wall, staring at the ceiling. In truth, it made little difference if he watched or not, the sound told him exactly what was happening on screen. His brain filled in every awful detail. Blake's low voice, the slam of the car trunk, the awkward limping footsteps carrying Kate. He could see it all. The chainsaw roared into life and he gritted his teeth. He wanted to cover his ears, but it probably wouldn't be enough. Some part of it would get through.

He pictured Kate in his mind, as he had so many times since. The way she'd looked up into the camera near the end, the face she'd made for him. It showed love. It was a message to him. She knew who would get the tape, she'd seen Blake in that hotel bar. Perhaps she'd come to realize the fight she'd witnessed had been about trying to protect her.

He backtracked.

The Top Gun T-shirt.

If they'd made her get dressed, she would've been wearing more clothes. A semi-naked woman draws unwelcome attention. No. The T-shirt was what she'd been wearing in bed, he knew it in his gut. They surprised her, captured her either while she slept, or close to it. He was stupid not to see it immediately. It was the surprise of seeing her alive, he could think of nothing else. He almost smiled. She could've been wearing anything when they took her that night, but the only reason for wearing *that* T-shirt was because she missed him. It was such a personal item of clothing, there was little room for doubt.

Kate still had feelings for him; their relationship could be saved.

The video was short and soon came to an end.

Afterward, Lauren stood in front of him with tears running down her face. Her emotions were always close to the surface, but he knew it wasn't a meaningless affectation. It was always real for her, she felt everything. He knew that whatever had existed between them before Ashcroft died was now gone but she accepted his involvement. After a moment it was clear that she had no words for him, and she put her arms around him and gave him a hug.

FIFTY-FIVE

Blake sat on the end of the motel bed in boxer shorts, bending and straightening his leg while he lightly massaged the damaged thigh muscle with both hands. It was healing well, which was more than he could say for his knee, which kept drifting out of alignment. He cursed Ashcroft. He'd staved a finger once during a high school football game and it had taken nearly six months to heal. Is that what he could look forward to, six months of limping?

The burner phone on his nightstand lit up and began to ring.

He held it wordlessly to his ear.

"Let's meet."

Thorne's voice was flat, hostile.

"All right."

"Somewhere public. I don't want to get into something with you."

A buzzing sound started behind him.

Blake turned and saw Sara in her underwear with her foot on the toilet seat, shaving her leg. While she did this, she blew a large, pink bubble in gum. It was hard for him to imagine how she could be any more perfect. He waited for the bubble to burst and she sucked it back into her mouth, before speaking.

"Babe? You mind?"

Sara looked across with lidded eyes, reached out and slammed the door.

God, she was hot. He was going to marry that girl, he knew it.

"Where?"

"How about that coffee place where you ambushed me?"

Blake felt uneasy.

Until now, Thorne had communicated with him exclusively using text messages. By itself, a text message meant nothing. Anyone could have sent it. A voice call, on the other hand, was evidence. It could be recorded and played back in court. He thought about the FBI agents he'd witnessed surrounding Thorne the day before. Rescuing him. He couldn't see Thorne giving him up as long as he held Kate Bloom, but if he knew one thing for sure about his old friend, it was that his loyalty was highly fluid. If it looked like the FBI represented his best chance of getting Kate back alive, Thorne would throw him under the first bus that came along.

He thought about the coffee store.

The large picture window at the front would allow him to see inside before entering, but if it was as busy as last time, his view would be obscured by the line of people waiting to order. The store had a single entrance and exit, making it easy to box him inside. They could have agents posing as customers sitting at tables, even behind the counter.

The place was no use.

An idea came to him and he smiled.

"I got another idea. The mall."

"Are you high?"

"It's public. Lots of different ways in and out."

"I'm not going there ever again. Think of somewhere else."

Blake sighed. He supposed that was fair. Thorne had taken some punishment and didn't want to go back. Pity, it would've amused him to go back to the scene of the crime.

He wondered how long they'd been connected.

Were they tracing the call?

He scrambled to think of somewhere fast, somewhere he knew.

"All right. There's an Irish pub at Pacific and Walnut. *Rosie McCann's.* There's a bench out front on the sidewalk, be sitting on it at 13:00. If I see cops, feds, or anyone acting squirrelly, I'm out of there. You won't even see me."

"Whatever. McCann's at 1."

Thorne hung up. Blake sighed. He'd been about to tell the actor to bring some of his pain medication with him for his leg. He tossed the cell phone onto the bed next to him and turned toward the bathroom. Sara stood in front of it, watching him closely.

"Is it a trap?" she said.

"Probably. Hard to say."

"We're going anyway?"

"Yeah."

Sara moved closer until she was standing in front of him, her bare feet set wide apart. He could smell the natural musk of her body. She wasn't wearing deodorant and hadn't showered since the previous morning. Blake smiled. She stared at him for several long seconds while she chewed on her bottom lip. When she spoke, her voice was harder, more direct.

"Put your hands on me."

Blake reached out and held her hips, pulling her closer.

"No," she said. "Up here. Around my throat."

He stood.

*

Blake arrived with ten minutes to spare. He'd hoped to be a full half hour early so he could spot suspicious traffic movement in the streets around the bar, but there was no rushing Sara Dawson when she set her mind on something. He drove a slow circuit of the area, looking for spaces available on the street. There weren't many, though one was less than fifteen feet from the bar. Too close, he thought. He decided to park in a two level parking structure on Church Street. Before committing, he did another loop around the block. This time, instead of looking for parking spots, he pulled into a red zone in front of a fire hydrant and looked directly across at the entrance to the bar and the bench that sat to one side. A man sat on it, hunched over, elbows resting on his knees like he'd been there a while. He was wearing a baseball hat and sunglasses, despite sitting on the shaded side of the street.

Thorne, not wanting to be recognized.

Satisfied, Blake pulled away before his parking drew attention.

"Suppose this is a trap," Sara said, her voice trailing off.

"*Yeah?*"

"You should call him, say we're meeting some place else. Last minute change of plan, kind of thing. Doesn't have to be that far away. If it's a trap, there won't be time to move their people into different positions, or set up microphones or whatever."

Blake nodded.

"That's pretty good. I like it."

He took the burner cell out of his pocket and dialed Thorne one handed as he drove. It went straight to the network's answering service. Blake sighed and hung up, dumping the cell into a cup holder.

"His cell's off."

Sara made a face. "They don't want us moving the venue."

"Maybe," he said. "Or maybe it's just turned off."

She said nothing and they fell into silence with just the sound of the AC moving through the car's interior. What she didn't understand about men like them, was that they barely used phones to call anyone. Naturally it looked suspicious to her, but to him, not so much. Thorne assumed he was about to see him, so he'd turned off his cell. They came up to the Church Street junction and he made the turn. He was now a couple of minutes late for the meeting. Blake took the first level of the parking structure and found plenty of spaces. He reversed into one of them and turned the steering wheel hard over at the last second. If they had to leave in a hurry they could power out of the space without hitting the cars in the next row.

346

"Okay, here's what's going to happen," he said. "I need you to hang tight here. This meeting is just going to be Thorne and me."

"All right."

Blake almost laughed, he had anticipated an argument.

"I don't see this taking long, we're not exactly big pals anymore. I figure that if you don't hear from me in ten minutes you should assume it's gone to shit and you should drive back to the motel. If you still don't hear from me within a couple of hours you're going to need to clean house and get out."

He studied her closely in the low light to see if she understood what *clean house* meant. She looked down at her hands resting on her legs and nodded.

"Relax, it's not going to happen."

He opened the door and stepped out.

"Aidan?"

He bent down so he could look into her side of the cabin.

"He's not meeting to hand you the painting, is he?"

"No."

"So why are you going?"

Blake shrugged. "Because he asked."

"I thought you said we don't need him?"

"I don't have an answer for you."

He closed the car door and walked off toward the exit.

It *was* strange now he came to think about it. Thorne wasn't bringing the painting, not without a swap for Kate Bloom, so why were they meeting at all? He had been too busy questioning whether it was an FBI sting, to think about what else it could be. If it wasn't a set-up, he didn't know what it was.

He walked down Pacific Avenue, a cool wind blowing up from the sea. Unlike Thorne, he wore no sunglasses or cap and he felt like he was drawing looks from passing pedestrians. He crossed over, cutting between slow moving vehicles, to the shaded side of the street. He walked with his head tilted down, like he was looking at his feet. Blake knew from experience that the angle made the scar on his face less obvious, a detail that Cabot had thought to add to his wanted picture. After a moment, he noticed he was wearing the same *Doors* T-shirt he'd worn at the mall.

He was getting sloppy, making crazy mistakes. He should've disposed of the shirt immediately. He could even make out some specks of Porter's blood across the front.

He zipped up his warm-up jacket.

He was almost at Rosie McCann's, when a crowd of people burst out the bar's entrance laughing. Blake slowed his pace so they'd have time to get clear before he arrived. When a gap opened up he saw Thorne. The sunglasses were off and their eyes connected. The actor made a small movement of his head; left, right, center. The gap closed again. Was he shaking his head? Blake stopped and stood looking in the window of a store. Women's clothing. Slacks, dresses, sportswear. He glanced back at Thorne. The crowd had moved off and he could see him clearly. With his right hand, Thorne was scratching his neck with straight fingers, when he noticed Blake watching the scratch became a sideways chopping motion, like he was cutting his throat. Once, twice. He dropped his hand and tilted his head.

Abort.

Thorne was telling him to get out.

Blake turned and walked back the way he'd come. Not moving too quickly, not drawing attention to himself. He could hear his heart thumping in his ears. If Thorne had been trying to set him up with this meeting, he wouldn't warn him off at the last second, he'd want him caught. Blake stopped at another store window and used the glass to see if he was being pursued. Nobody stood out. The sidewalks were populated by the usual mix of older tourists and younger hipsters. If there'd been cops or FBI near Thorne, none of them had noticed him.

He moved off again, his ears straining for the sound of running feet or shouts from behind. As he crossed back over Pacific he risked glancing down the street to where Thorne had been seated. He was standing now, his height obvious even at this distance.

In front of him, were two men in suits.

Blake smiled. The meeting hadn't been a waste of time after all. Without saying a word, Thorne had proved who he was, and that he was no snitch. He could trust him again.

FIFTY-SIX

Cabot stood in Subway looking at the list of options above his head while a server glared at him. It was Saturday lunchtime, and the place was packed. Eventually, he told the teenager what he wanted and moved down the line to the register. He wasn't hungry, not even close, and the idea of eating what he'd just ordered was almost too much to think about. What he was, was hungover. He ordered a Gatorade and cookies, then paid. When he turned, he saw Mason Barnes standing watching him. He was wearing jeans and a sports jacket, and looked like he'd just stepped out of an Abercrombie and Fitch catalog. A large smile broke out on the younger man's face and they nodded at one another in greeting.

"I found you," Barnes said.

"Were you looking?"

"Yeah. I came from your house, this was the next place I tried."

"After my house, the mall is the next place you look for me?"

Barnes raised an eyebrow.

"I *am* a detective you know."

Cabot found an empty table and put his purchases on top of it. The last occupant's waste was still spread out across the surface and he had to push it aside to clear a space. Barnes sat next to him and laid a file folder he'd been carrying on the table. Cabot glanced at the folder, assessing it. Thin. No more than half a dozen sheets of paper inside.

"Did it occur to you to call my cell, Detective?"

Barnes smiled. "Where's the fun in that?"

Cabot picked up his sandwich and bit into it. Fun. He almost didn't know what that was anymore. He'd been thinking about how Thorne had framed him all morning and his mood had been darkening ever since. The man had ruined his life, there was no other way of saying it. He sighed. The bread of his sub was like a tree trunk and appeared to be designed for a human with bigger jaws and sharper teeth. He looked around the food court at the other patrons as he ate.

The older he got, the less he liked other people.

"You mind if I have a couple of cookies, L-T?"

"Knock yourself out."

The detective stared at him.

"Sorry, Mason, poor choice of words."

"That's all right."

They sat eating for several minutes without speaking, an easy silence between them. Finally, he forced down the last of his sub and drank some Gatorade.

He eyed the folder under the detective's hand.

"You got something for me?"

"Boss, there's something I have to tell you first."

Cabot held his hand up to cut him off. "It's Saturday, Mason. By Monday I might be out of a job or in county lockup. Call me Victor, OK?"

Barnes' face twisted uncomfortably. "OK."

"Unless you're here to take me in."

"No, never."

Cabot set his large cup down on the table in front of him.

"If it comes to it, Mason, I'd rather a friend took me in."

"The thing about that is, I might not be here."

There was something almost familiar about the detective's words, as if he'd heard them already. Perhaps he'd imagined this conversation so many times he was getting flashbacks.

"Let's hear it."

"I've been accepted by the Bureau. I leave for Quantico next week."

"Jesus. How long have you been working on this?"

"Nearly eight months. I never said anything because I thought it would go nowhere. When I found out, I asked the Sheriff and the Chief not to tell you so I could do that myself, but we've been so busy it kind of got away from me."

Cabot sighed. He'd frozen Barnes out of his investigation because he believed the detective was a threat and the whole time he'd been planning to leave anyway. Of course he was, a man as sharp as Mason Barnes wouldn't stay in a place like Santa Cruz.

Cabot put his hand across the table and Barnes shook it.

"Congratulations, Mason. You more than deserve it."

"Thanks."

There was an awkward moment as they let go of each other's hand and to cover it, Cabot took another long drink from his cup. He realized he had two differing views on Barnes; one where he was a rival, and another where he felt almost like a father to him. Now he knew Barnes wasn't staying, the threat vanished leaving him with bittersweet regret. For all his boy scout attitude, he was going to miss the younger man and not just for his natural

350

abilities as an investigator.

"So you're leaving me with *Summersby*? That's cold."

Barnes laughed.

"For that, I am sorry. Listen, I need a coffee, you want one?"

"Sure."

Barnes rose out his chair and set off, leaving the folder where it was on the table. Cabot stared at it. The longer it took him to get to the point, the more fascinated he became by whatever lay inside. Perhaps it wasn't related to the case at all, but was instead a form the FBI had given the detective for his superior officer to fill in. An evaluation, something like that. Was his leaving the only reason for chasing him down on a Saturday?

His mind returned to Thorne and the missing gun.

The Sheriff's Office had combed the area around that roadhouse and found no trace of the gun that had killed Ashcroft. The most likely explanation, was that the man he'd seen talking to Thorne had taken it with him as he fled the scene. It then followed that this man was the shooter, just as Thorne claimed. Cabot sighed. He didn't doubt people occasionally went into that roadhouse carrying a piece, but that one of them should shoot his friend, even by accident, was too much. Not with Thorne nearby. He had a better chance of winning the state lottery than of that coincidence playing out. It hit him after a couple of seconds.

The man Thorne was talking to, was Morrison.

A smile spread across his face.

Cabot recalled how the man in the parking lot had moved so that he was standing in line with Thorne, his body blocked by the actor's. It had happened so quickly that he'd only had a fleeting glimpse of him before he was hidden. He'd seen the same move so many times over the years that it almost didn't register. Criminals stepping to one side or turning away from the police. They couldn't stop themselves, it was like an instinct. He played the scene back in his head but could remember no new details. He cursed himself.

Out of habit, his eye had gone to Thorne first.

It didn't matter. Thorne had gone there to meet Morrison, he was certain of it. For all he knew, Thorne had *brought* James Ashcroft to that parking lot against his will and when everyone had left, Morrison had killed him in cold blood. Thorne knew who fired the shot and, for whatever reason, was protecting him. Cabot felt a buzz enter his system. The lack of physical evidence from the roadhouse had served to clear Thorne, but this was the missing piece. The shoot-out and the death of Ashcroft were linked after all.

He picked up the bag of cookies and found it almost empty. Two left. He cursed Barnes and ate them both, one after another. By the time he finished, a coffee appeared in front of him, along with another bag of cookies. The kid wasn't so bad after all.

"Thanks."

"You got it," Barnes said.

They sat and drank coffee in silence, working their way through the second bag of cookies. It came back to him that Thorne was untouchable. He couldn't prove Thorne knew Morrison, or that he met him in that parking lot. He no longer had access to his dash cam footage due to the investigation into his alleged assault of Thorne. Anything he did to pursue the actor could lead to a harassment charge, a charge the sheriff would use to force him out.

Barnes leaned back in his chair.

"When I worked in Oakland my partner had all these lame stories and jokes. It was the way he passed on advice, I guess. Lately, I've been thinking of one of his stories."

Cabot sighed. Barnes was really setting this one up.

"Yes, Mason, I am listening to you."

"Okay, so a cop sees a drunk on his hands and knees searching for something under a street light and asks what he's lost. The man says he lost his keys and they both look under the light. After a few minutes, the cop asks if he's sure he lost them here and the drunk replies, no, he lost them in the park. When the cop asks why he's searching here the drunk says, *this is where the light is.*"

Cabot nodded. He'd heard it before many years ago.

"What advice was your partner passing on with this story?"

"Look in the park."

"You're saying pursuing Thorne is like looking under the light?"

"Thorne isn't the key to this, you know that. He's protected. We find Morrison and Chelsea *then* we see if there's any involvement with Thorne. If there is, I will buy you a bottle of Scotch, I swear to god. But if there isn't, you still catch those responsible."

"Barnes, we already mined this for all it was worth. There are so many places to stay. Hotels, motels, Airbnb and whatever else. You had a list as long as your arm, and that assumed they hadn't broken into an unoccupied holiday place, or jacked a house and killed the owner. They could've been sleeping in their goddam van, there're plenty of places in the county where they could tuck themselves away. You said it yourself."

"I no longer believe that. People have neighbors, friends, dogs, alarms. The only place these people could come and go with a van and not be noticed is a motel. So I printed out a list of all motels within an hour's drive, then removed those within ten miles of Santa Cruz and Capitola. I figure anything too close is a waste of time. After what happened, they'd want a little distance between themselves and the crime scene. Then I thought, they probably don't want to be on the road too long and run the risk of being picked up by the CHP, so I eliminated motels over 40 minutes away. That leaves ten motels. Four north, six south."

"We checked motels at the beginning and it was a bust."

"As will the FBI, I'm sure. But neither have this." Barnes pulled a sheaf of paper from his folder. There was a head and shoulders charcoal sketch of a woman on the top sheet. "This is Chelsea, the way I remember from the hospital. My kid is quite the artist, we knocked this out last night. Nobody else has seen this. What I'm thinking, is that this Morrison character let his girl pay for the room and pick up the key while he hung back out of sight. It explains why nobody recognized his description or the later pictures of him on the news. I say we hit these motels tonight and show the sketch. What do you think?"

Cabot was disappointed. This was all Barnes had, and it was just a re-tread of a play they'd already made. No smoking gun on Thorne, in fact, no link at all to the actor. He took the sketch from Barnes to be polite and examined it closely. He was right about something, his kid was a damn good artist. When he looked up he saw that the sheet underneath also had a sketch on it, of a man with a circular scar on his face. It was horribly familiar and he had to swallow several times to clear his throat.

"This is Morrison?"

Barnes nodded, but said nothing.

"I met him."

"What do you mean you *met* him?"

"He bumped into me coming out of a coffee place in town. I called out to him for an apology but he kept on going like he had places to be. I shrugged it off."

"When was this?"

"About a week after the shoot-out."

"Damn."

"We could've had this wrapped up three weeks ago."

"You can't blame yourself for that, boss."

He nodded. "He must've done it on purpose. To amuse himself."

They both drank from their cups.

"All right. Suppose these assholes were hiding out at one of these motels, why would they still be there? If their goal was to kidnap Lauren and blackmail Jimmy, you got to say their plan ended with Ashcroft's death. Why stick around?"

Rather than defeat, he saw a glint in Barnes' eyes.

"Only one reason I can think of: to kill Thorne. Whether he was involved beforehand or not, it's his fault they aren't millionaires right now. Revenge is a strong motivator. If there *is* a prior connection then you can add betrayal on top."

He couldn't go after Thorne, not even unofficially, without getting into trouble. They'd been taken off the case and re-assigned, but the press conference to announce that wasn't until Monday morning. That left a small window where he could follow a lead on his own time. The FBI wouldn't like it, but if he managed to solve the case, they could suck it.

"What do you say, Lieutenant?"

FIFTY-SEVEN

Thorne tore off two long strips of duct tape and lay them side by side on top of the breakfast bar. He could hardly believe his bullshit play had actually worked. Lauren had followed Blake all the way back to his motel without a hitch. The timing of two businessmen in suits had really sold Blake the dummy. Thorne took the hunting knife sheath and pressed it into the mid-point of both strips, then used the tape to secure it to his right leg. The blade was long, stretching from his sock line to his upper calf. He pulled down the hem of his pants and inspected the result. The material bunched awkwardly around the handle, but he wasn't too worried about that. He was tall, people typically looked up, not down at his calf. Lauren padded silently across the room in bare feet. She had showered and changed into the loose cotton clothing she typically wore around the house at night.

Lauren looked at the kitchen counter.

"You made me a club sandwich? At eight o'clock at night?"

"I made us *both* club sandwiches but I ate mine while you were getting dressed. You were so long I nearly ate this one too."

"I won't lie to you, this is a little weird."

Lauren sat on the bar stool opposite him and began to eat. He watched her silently, memorizing her face. Even when she was sad, she was beautiful. Whatever happened tonight, the life he was living here would end. She paused to drink from an open can of Diet Coke he'd left on the counter.

"Listen," he said. "You're about 120 pounds, right?"

Her eyes narrowed. "128. Why?"

"No reason."

"Chris, you can't say shit like that to a woman."

"Sorry."

"I'm *tall*, okay?"

"I know that. How's the sandwich?"

She looked at him for a beat as if he was insane, before relaxing.

"It's awesome actually. I hadn't realized how hungry I was."

His eyes drifted over to the large windows. They were pitch black. Time was running out. When Lauren finished eating, he cleared a space on the counter in front of her and spread out a white cloth. Watching her closely, he took Ashcroft's Smith & Wesson 1911 out of his rear waistband and placed it in the center of the cloth. Her face froze.

"Funny story. I found this out in the driveway. Somebody had buried it in the stones like a dog buries a bone. Isn't that hilarious? I mean, there are crazy people out there who want us dead and our only weapon goes missing."

"I can explain," she said.

"Okay."

"Things were getting a little intense between you and me and I didn't think it was a good idea to have a gun lying around. So I hid it. Plus, if I hadn't, Victor would've found it and I'm not sure how easy it would've been to explain."

He had to give her that, Cabot was becoming a problem.

"So you hid the gun in case James found out about us?"

Her eyes slid across to the can of Coke in her hand. "Not exactly."

"You thought I was going to shoot him?"

"Honestly, I don't know. The day after the party I walked into his den and saw the gun sitting on his desk like he'd been playing with it. Maybe that meant something, maybe not. In any case, it made me remember our conversation from the night before. I told myself that you were trying to scare me off, but in truth, I could easily imagine you following through on it. I was nervous. I knew how a fight between the two of you would pan out, even if he started that fight holding the gun. I've seen what happens to men who try to shoot you."

There was no mystery. The gun was on the senator's desk because he'd put it there while the old man slept off his hangover. Lauren was just processing her guilt, and if it took her imagining him to be a monster, then so be it.

"Anyway," he said, his tone businesslike. "There's a pretty good chance we're going to need to use this thing and in this condition it's more likely to kill us."

He pulled on a pair of latex gloves and meshed his fingers together.

Gloves weren't normally part of his routine but he didn't want to leave fingerprints inside the gun where they couldn't be quickly wiped down. Agent Vasco, his fictional self, found a latent print inside a killer's gun in season 3 of *Night Passenger*. Instead of viewing it as a cop show *deus ex machina*, he decided to take it seriously.

Thorne picked up the pistol and ejected the magazine.

He was pleased to note that it came out smoothly, without sticking, or any kind of gritty noise. Ashcroft had told him that he'd bought ammunition, so he wasn't surprised to see fresh brass gleaming in the end of the magazine. He drew back the slide, clearing a round from the chamber and placed it to one side with the magazine. He turned the gun over in his hands, looking for damage. As best as he could tell, it was just dirty and scratched. His eyes were drawn again to the raw metal where the serial number had been removed. Whoever did it had known what they were doing. No lab geek was going to bring back any trace of that number using chemicals; looked like they'd used a grinding disk.

He began to field strip the pistol, laying each piece out on the cloth in the same way he'd always done in the Marines, with the slide at the top and the frame at the bottom. He could see the inside of the gun was even dirtier than the outside. The bushing, barrel and slide were visibly contaminated with what looked like mud from a riverbank. This furthered in his mind the idea that the gun had been tossed after a fatal shooting, probably thrown out of a moving vehicle as it crossed a bridge. If things worked out as he hoped, he might be doing the same thing in several hours' time.

He retrieved a bag of supplies from the counter behind him and emptied it out. Cleaning a weapon had always relaxed him, there was something about the repetitive mechanical actions involved that allowed his mind to take a back seat for a couple of minutes. He poured some solvent into a shot glass, dipped a .45 cleaning brush into it, and pushed it down the gun barrel. He did this several times, sending a fine mist onto some paper towels. It was black with dirt.

"There's something I don't understand," she said. "How did you find it?"

"I noticed that every time you got in or out of the car you'd glance down at the same spot of ground. Eventually, curiosity got the better of me."

She groaned.

"I couldn't help myself, it was like it was magnetic."

Thorne said nothing, his mind focused on the task at hand. The wadding cloth he was pushing out the end of the gun's barrel was like nothing he'd ever seen before, and he'd used truck-stop restrooms. He folded a fresh piece of cloth over the push rod and worked that one down the barrel, this time with far better results. He picked up a third piece of cloth. His preference was to continue until the cloth looked the same coming out as it did going in.

"Chris, I don't want you to kill for me okay? I would rather be dead than know I was the cause of another person's death. There's been too much already. I am grateful for what you've done for me, but it's enough now."

Thorne put down the barrel and looked up at her.

"What do you suggest? Nice words? A fruit basket?"

"We could let the police handle it."

It was as he had expected. She liked a bit of danger, but when it came to resolving their problems, when it came to *killing*, then she was against it.

"You have a good soul, Lauren, but these are bad people and they need to go away. I think we both know this won't be over until either we're dead or they're dead."

She said nothing, she couldn't admit what had to happen.

He finished cleaning and began to reassemble the pistol. Now that it was cleaned, it didn't look half bad. A little banged up, a checkered history and discarded after use...he could relate, he really could. He re-loaded the gun then, finally, took off the gloves. The tightness of the rubber was making his skin crawl. He looked up for the first time in several minutes and saw her eyes were half closed.

"I feel so tired," she said.

"Listen, there's no other way of saying this. I'm going to finish what I started at that mall. This ends tonight, one way or another. If it makes you feel any better about it, I'm not doing this for you."

"You're doing this for her."

"Yes I am."

"You love her, don't you?"

Thorne groaned.

"They're going to cut off her damn head, Lauren."

"I think I always knew. When I saw the two of you in that show, the way you looked at her...it was *real*. You never looked at me that way, not once. It's not Jimmy that's been between us this whole time, it's Kate."

"I can't have this conversation, I need to take care of this."

His reply, and the tone he delivered it, seemed to crush her.

"I'll come with you. I still owe you. I owe *her*."

"No."

"We make a good team, we look out for each other."

"I can't put you in that kind of danger."

Lauren stared at him, furious.

"What makes you think I won't come anyway? I know where you're going. It was me that followed him to that crummy motel in the first place, remember?"

Thorne nodded. "I thought you might say something like that. That's why I made sure you couldn't. You'll have to trust me when I say it's for the best. At least this way your conscience is clear."

Lauren swallowed.

"What did you do?"

"Isn't it obvious? I drugged your food."

She glanced at the empty plate. "Is that a joke?"

"Nothing sinister. I gave you some of my medication. It's very strong and without pain to keep you awake, you'll be asleep very quickly. I suggest you're not driving when it happens. Your throat is probably dry and scratchy already."

She could see the truth of it in his face.

"How could you do this to me?"

Thorne put his arm around her back and guided her from the breakfast bar over to the decking beside the pool.

"I can't deal with this and worry about you at the same time. Right here is the safest place for you to be, this place is a fortress. A woman got hurt once before because of me and I swear that's never going to happen again."

He eased her into one of the loungers facing the pool. He envied how effective the medication was on her. Tears ran down her face and he wiped them gently away with his thumbs and kissed her once on the mouth.

"Chris, stay with me."

"I have to go."

"Will I see you again?"

"I sure hope so."

FIFTY-EIGHT

Thorne arrived at the motel in Watsonville just after 10 p.m. He drove down the side of the single story structure, his eyes scanning the parking lot for Blake's sedan or Sara's motorcycle. Finding neither, he looped back and parked where his distinctive car couldn't be seen from the front desk. It had been too much to hope for that they'd be here waiting for him, he just hoped that they hadn't left altogether. He killed the engine and examined himself in the rearview mirror. The suit and tie weren't right, but the general public didn't take much in when it came to details like that. Acting was about projecting a character, and boy did he know this character. He got out and walked toward the reception, his heels ringing out like gunshots on the sidewalk. Inside his head he was changing over, becoming someone else. An old man sat at the front desk watching a television.

He pulled out the FBI ID which he flipped open in a practiced manner.

"Special Agent Jake Vasco, FBI. I need information on one of your guests."

The man was studying his face, eyes narrowed, trying to place it. He'd been recognized, Thorne could see it. He'd known this was a possibility, but there'd been no choice. He had to press on, before the man's brain could place him.

"*Sir?*" Thorne said, impatiently.

The man blinked, like he was coming out of a spell.

"What guest?"

"White female. Late 20s to early 30s. Long brown hair, pale white skin. Five foot seven, one hundred ten pounds. Athletic like a dancer. Is known to ride a motorcycle."

The man nodded. Sara was not someone you quickly forgot.

"Room thirty-four."

"I need to see it."

The man came out from behind his desk and they walked back the way he'd come. He had decided in advance that Sara represented the best target for identification because it was obvious to him that Blake would use her to deal with motel staff. The cops had never released any images of her because they didn't have any. Consequently, she could come and go as she pleased with no possibility of recognition. They reached room 34. The door was fitted with a modern plastic keycard slot, which the desk manager slid his master key in and out. A green LED pulsed briefly, his hand worked the lever and the door began to open. Thorne reached out and caught the edge of the powder blue door to prevent the other man seeing inside.

"That's fine," Thorne said. "I'll take it from here."

"I got to go in with you if you don't have a warrant."

"This ain't *Law and Order*, old man. Exigent circumstance. A woman's life is in danger."

The desk manager turned his head and spat a dark bolus of chewing tobacco and saliva onto the concrete before looking back up at Thorne. A fire burned in his eyes. It was an instinctive challenge to authority and dislike of the federal government. After a beat he nodded once, both hands half-raised in surrender.

"All right, son. Take it easy."

"Thank you for your cooperation, sir."

When the man had gone, he opened the door and stepped inside.

The room was similar to many he'd stayed in over the years. *Night Passenger* had operated on a small budget and often utilized motels such as this whenever they shot outside of L.A. His eyes moved quickly over the scene, taking it all in. It was a mess and there was plenty to see. Along the far wall were four heavy-looking flight cases. The defibrillators. Next to the door was one of the canvas bags Blake used to carry weapons, ready to be picked up before leaving. Nothing else seemed relevant. Take out boxes, items of clothing, and bottles of beer lay wherever they'd been discarded. He couldn't imagine the bag of weapons being left behind unless Blake planned to return for it. Thorne put on the latex gloves he'd purchased for cleaning Ashcroft's 1911 pistol.

He'd been dreading this moment and he wanted to be past it, however it turned out. He walked through the bedroom into the washroom and yanked open the shower curtain. Nothing. If Kate had been anywhere, it would've been at the bottom of the shower stall. Since she would also have been dead, he wasn't disappointed to find no trace of her. He realized he'd been holding his breath, afraid of what he might smell, and he let it out now in a ragged stream. This was a bolt-hole, where Blake kept his supplies and expected to sleep. The video footage showed somewhere industrial, somewhere unpopulated.

That's where Blake would be now, that's what he had to locate.

Back into the main room, the smell of Sara's cheap perfume was everywhere. It even cut through the sour smell of day-old convenience food. On one side of the bed, bloodstained dressings littered the floor. He squatted down to look at them, gingerly prodding them with his index finger. Some of the dressings had thick dark hairs protruding from the edges. These would be Blake's, from when he'd stabbed him. When he thought back on it, the timeline matched a little too closely with the abduction of Kate for his liking. It felt good taking action, but if he'd doomed Kate it would be too much to bear.

His eye was drawn to an iPad sitting on a low table, a thin white flex connecting it to a power socket. This was the first positive thing he'd found. Since Blake wouldn't have expected anyone else to see it, he likely hadn't gone to any lengths to hide anything. Google searches, open browser tabs, something like that. He picked up the tablet and sat on the edge of the bed, the flex trailing across the floor. The first thing he noticed was a Japanese anime sticker on the cover. A girl with huge eyes, a lollipop in her mouth and a sword up behind her head ready to swing. This suggested to him that the tablet belonged to Sara, not Blake. He sighed, but flipped open the cover anyway.

It didn't mean Blake hadn't used the device, or that it still might yield some clues. The display lit up and he was thankful that it was a home screen, not a lock screen. Thorne selected the browser icon. It showed a Street View picture of an intersection in Santa Cruz he didn't recognize. Three other tabs were open, one was the YouTube page with an image of himself frozen onscreen, and the other two were Google search results just as he'd hoped. The searches were for 'steakhouse in santa cruz' and 'motels near watsonville'. This told him nothing beyond the fact that even Blake had to eat and sleep. The only thing that surprised him was that the motel had been chosen for it's proximity to Watsonville. He'd assumed the motel had been chosen because it was located outside Santa Cruz and Capitola, where blurred images of his face were still to be found posted in stores next to cash registers.

Thorne thought about this for a moment.

Blake wouldn't want a long drive to wherever he'd hidden Kate, probably less than five miles. Assuming she was being kept in the same building as the one in the video, this narrowed his field of search still further. With no local knowledge of the area, however, it remained a lot of ground for him to cover, with little time to do it. He opened Facebook and Sara Dawson's profile appeared, confirming his assessment of the tablet's owner. Her feed was old, she hadn't posted anything or checked in anywhere in almost two months. Her posts before that time were exclusively pictures of herself, her motorcycle, and of leather boots with large zips and buckles.

He poked around on the tablet for a couple more minutes. Sara and

Blake communicated at length using *WhatsApp*, but their messages were of a pornographic nature and he gave up skimming them for clues very quickly. He sighed. His cell phone vibrated in his pocket. A text or an email, he could never tell the difference when his cell was on vibrate. Since he had seemingly hit a dead end, he pulled his phone out and glanced at the lock screen.

Two texts, one from Lauren, the other from Coop. It probably meant he'd lost service and had received both messages together now his connection had been restored. He could read the entirety of Lauren's message without unlocking his phone, it said *Everything OK?* She was worried about him. Coop's message was longer and had been clipped. *Hi, Chris. I have a bit of news that I thought you'd want to hear. My source inside the Santa Cruz Sheriff's Office has revealed that Lieutenant Cabot has now been...* He decided to read the rest later and slid the phone back into his pocket. A buzz was building inside him.

He'd had an idea.

Sara had three screens' worth of apps and he found what he wanted on the second. The app was called *Find My iPhone*. To his dismay, he was prompted to sign in, a feature he didn't remember from Kate's device. He swore. He had to get going, he'd been here too long already. Next to it on the screen was another app. *Find My Friends*. This app had no login feature and a list of people appeared before him. It shocked him to see his own email address on the list. He couldn't believe it, he'd never given Blake his personal cell number or email address, they'd always used the burner phones.

This is how they've been tracking me.

He remembered catching Sara holding his cell phone in the Culver City bungalow before the failed heist. She'd looked up at him, a flirty look on her face. *Sorry, is this yours? I thought it was Aidan's. They all look the same, don't they? You're even on the same network.* But it was no accident, he could see that now. She'd added him on this app and needed to authenticate it on his device. He hadn't questioned her story, not even after she handed his iPhone back unlocked, the home screen lit up. The flirty look had taken care of that. He recalled something else she'd said to him, way back at the beginning. *You're a lot like him you know.* And as much as he hated it, he knew it was true. His lock code was his date of birth, which was also Blake's. He'd made it impossibly easy for them, it disgusted him.

Judging from the list, every member of the gang had been tracked with the exception of Stockton who, presumably, was on Android. Being on the list would be impossible to explain, so he deleted his address. Until that moment, he'd done nothing during his search that Sara or Blake would notice, but he couldn't leave something this incriminating behind.

He clicked on Blake's entry and a map appeared with two dots on it.

One of them marked his current position, the second, Blake's. The two dots were less than a mile apart, he'd driven within a hundred yards of it on the way to the motel. He smiled. He'd planned to leave the tablet behind, but this changed things. He could use this app to track Blake right up to the last moment. If he left the tablet behind and Blake was gone when he arrived, he'd be right back to square one. He closed the cover and unplugged the charging cord, then set the device on his knee. It no longer mattered about hiding his visit from Blake, because now that Thorne knew where he was, he wouldn't be coming back. Eventually police would come here, but they'd find little to concern him.

He took a look at his watch. A little over an hour before Blake's deadline. He'd be able to get to the location well before midnight, it just wasn't clear to him what would happen once he got there. He didn't have the Picasso, there was only one play left. Thorne pulled out his cell phone again and opened Gmail. He'd saved an email to Mancuso in the drafts folder with the video of Kate already attached. He deleted a confession he'd started to write and instead entered only Blake's location. Thorne paused for a moment, uncertain, then tapped send. It was a long shot at best, the old man was probably asleep. He took one last look around the room, then stepped out into the night.

In the parking lot, somebody had parked a rusty pickup truck across the end of his Maserati, preventing him from leaving. There were only three other cars in the lot, all spaced out. The driver was not in the cab, or anywhere in sight. Thorne turned back to the motel's reception and saw a figure come out of the darkness, a gun in his hand.

Cabot.

"I follow a lead on the gang and find you. Interesting." An ugly smile broke out on the lieutenant's face. "Latex gloves, that's a nice touch."

Thorne said nothing. There was something off about the whole scene, beyond the gun that was pointing at him. For a start, Cabot was wearing street clothes. If he was investigating the gang, why the change of clothes? They weren't new either. 80s-era light blue jeans, plaid shirt, and heavy construction boots. He wished he'd taken the time to read Coop's message about Cabot. They stared at each other for a moment with open hostility. The lieutenant's smile had gone, but the face that had replaced it was no better.

"Get in the truck, sunshine. We're going for a little ride, you and me."

Thorne sighed. He had no time for more of Cabot's questioning, Blake was expecting to hear from him about the painting. Too long a delay would make him suspicious and the man had no shortage of reasons to distrust him. The only way would be to disable Cabot in some manner, and the distance between them was currently too great. Once they were inside the truck it would be a simple matter to overpower the cop with a choke hold and be back underway. He turned and walked toward the truck, already thinking through his moves. He still had Sara's iPad in his left hand, he'd have to be careful it didn't get damaged as he and Cabot fought. It occurred to him that once he was sitting in the passenger seat he'd be unable to draw Ashcroft's battered 1911 pistol that was tucked into the back of his pants. At that point, he'd be limited to what he could do with his hands and body.

The thought of taking action against a cop didn't sit right with him, but Kate Bloom was all he cared about now. Whatever the lieutenant had coming, he'd brought it on himself. As Cabot worked his way around the hood, Thorne dropped the computer tablet gently onto the floor of the truck to free up both hands. Cabot got in next to him, his gun still aimed at Thorne's chest. For the first time, he registered that the weapon was a revolver, not an automatic. It was a detail he found troubling and unlocked the true meaning of their ride. The gun would be untraceable, confiscated long ago from some street punk and kept for an occasion just like this. The barrel was enormous. He thought again about what Cabot was wearing.

Old clothes, the kind you might keep for painting projects around the house when you didn't want your regular clothes ruined.

"You going to kill me now, that it?"

Cabot fed a stick of gum into his mouth before answering.

"That's what I was thinking, yeah."

He found it hard to believe the lieutenant would really kill him, but the man's face was grim. It was a look he'd seen before, the look of someone who had an unpleasant task ahead of them, with no way out. Cabot started the truck and pulled away fast, his head flicking back and forth between Thorne and the windshield.

"I know what you're thinking, Thorne. You think you can grab the gun off me while I drive, but you're mistaken. At this range I don't have to aim, just squeeze the trigger."

Thorne turned and faced front, hoping to relax Cabot.

"Probably just as well," he said. "I'm guessing you have to sit down to pee."

Cabot laughed. It sounded like he hadn't laughed in a while and had forgotten how to do it. *Hack, hack, hack.* There was a desperate edge to it that Thorne found less than reassuring, like the man was about to lose control.

"I'll say this for you Thorne, you're pretty calm for a guy on the wrong end of a gun."

"This isn't the first time, doubt it'll be the last."

A silence fell between them. He regretted his comment, it had made both of them think ahead to what increasingly appeared to be his death. Out of the corner of his eye, he could see the revolver rock from side to

365

side in the lieutenant's fist as it rested on his fat thigh. One bad pothole, and Cabot would be hosing his kidneys out the bottom of his truck. To distract himself, he thought about Kate and the mess he'd gotten them into. If they survived, would she be able to forgive him? Could their relationship be repaired? He thought again of the look she'd directed into Blake's camera, the intense love he believed he had seen in her eyes. Whatever that was, it was worth saving.

Worth fighting for.

Cabot began to slow and pulled his truck over so that it bumped up off the asphalt onto the rough ground next to the highway. They'd been driving no more than ten minutes and were somewhere outside Watsonville. Thorne glanced around, but there was nothing to see. They were in the middle of nowhere. The truck headlights illuminated trees that came right up to the edge of the road. He turned back toward Cabot who had twisted around in his seat to face him directly. Watching him. The light in the truck was low, but he could see enough. The opportunity to overpower Cabot had not presented itself, and now it looked like his time had run out. He'd convinced himself the whole thing was a bluff by the lieutenant, but he'd driven *here*. This was a destination for Cabot, this wasn't nowhere. The only place it could be, was where he planned to shoot him and dispose of his body.

If this was a bluff by the lieutenant, he was taking it all the way to the end. Cabot twitched the revolver to the right.

"Out."

FIFTY-NINE

The revolver was getting heavy. Even resting it on his leg during the drive hadn't been enough to take the weight of it off his arm. It was a Colt Python with an eight inch barrel and it weighed almost 50 ounces. Cabot had carried a gun similar to this on his hip for close to thirty years, but when he'd changed to automatics there was no going back. His Glock 17 had a four and a half inch barrel, was just over 20 ounces and held fifty percent more ammunition. Freshly drawn, the Python had a pleasant weight, but that was fifteen minutes ago now and he could feel every inch of that eight inch barrel in the muscles on top of his arm. He smiled and again motioned the gun twice to the side.

Thorne reached behind his back and searched for the door catch. Their eyes locked together. The actor assumed it would make it harder to shoot him while he was making eye contact, but he was wrong about that. He was here to do a job, and that didn't stop because the man was looking at him. Finally, Thorne found the lever and pulled it, reversing out into the dark. Rather than go around the front of the truck, Cabot slid along the seat and followed Thorne out through the same door. He couldn't risk losing sight of him for a second.

Two cars approached and shot past them, almost as one. He had time only to step back against the truck, hiding his outline against the metal. A couple of kids racing each other, he thought. If they saw anything at all, they probably assumed Thorne had pulled over at the side of the road to take a leak or change a tire. All the same, he needed to get out of sight before there was any more traffic. With his left hand he fished around in his pocket and pulled out his personal flashlight, a Led Lenser unit capable of 1,000 lumen. He switched it on and Thorne flinched like he'd been hit in the face.

"Straight ahead. Into the trees."

"There's no path, Cabot."

"You'll manage. They're just branches."

They moved forward. Thorne was right, there was no path and without one it was slow going. The branches were wet and heavy, resisting every attempt for them to push through them. He wanted to rush things along, but he couldn't afford to get too close to the man in front. Another downside of an eight inch barrel, was that at close range it became easier for the other person to knock it aside and he didn't fancy his odds against the actor without it.

Thorne stopped and turned, unwilling to go any farther.

"Come off it Cabot, you can't expect me to believe you're a killer. I bet you've never fired a weapon at anyone before. It's not like shooting a target at the range."

"You're not the only one with military service, Thorne. I was in Nam. We got our hands pretty dirty, you know what I mean?"

Thorne looked around at where they were standing, as if seeing it fully for the first time. Wind whipped at his thin suit jacket and the bottom of his pants. It pleased Cabot to note that Thorne had lost his swagger and self confidence. Without a gun, he was no different to any other man.

The eye contact was back, Thorne looking wilder than ever.

"Look, if you were going to shoot me you'd have done it already, right? So how about you cut to the chase and tell me what you really want then take me back to my car, I got places to be. I don't have time for this cat and mouse bullshit."

He fired the revolver. The sound of the .357 cartridge was brutal in the silence and a flame seemed to follow the bullet out the end of the barrel as it disappeared over Thorne's head.

"Do I have your attention now? I haven't shot you yet because I want questions answered. If you answer them right, maybe I find a reason to keep you alive."

"I didn't kill your friend, man. I don't know how many times I have to say it or why it's so important to you that it was me that did it. You think I'm going to tell you a different story because you're pointing a gun at my head? Good luck."

"You think this is still about Ashcroft?"

"What else is there?"

"You *framed me*, Thorne. I'm on suspension and under investigation. I don't know how you did it, but somehow you planted your blood on my firearm. I can't lose my job because of you, I *won't*. Fortunately, there are any number of ways blood can get transferred and without your testimony, all this will go away. They'll have no choice but to reinstate me."

"Jesus Christ, Cabot. Your *job?* Are you kidding me? They're going to cut off my girlfriend's head with a chainsaw and you're worried about your goddamn job?"

His breath caught in his throat.

"What did you say?"

"They have Kate. The gang have been blackmailing me, trying to make me do what they want. They sent me a video. From the beginning I've known more than I was letting on, you were right about that, but not for the reason you thought. I couldn't risk her life by telling you the truth. They're going to kill her at midnight if I don't take them Ashcroft's painting, but I can't do that because you guys have that in lockup."

Cabot lowered the revolver.

He grudgingly admitted to himself that Thorne's story had the ring of truth to it and tied in with the mystery surrounding Kate Bloom. He could never square her disappearance with his investigation. For something to happen to her so close to the shoot-out and the death of Ashcroft was beyond coincidence.

"Jimmy saw this video, of Kate?"

"That's why he was there that night. He wanted to help."

The story was fitting together.

"Why you? What's your link to these people?"

Thorne sighed.

"I've known the leader since I was a kid, we grew up together in Los Angeles. We saw the National Guard on the streets during the riots in '92 and I guess it made an impression on us. We were ten years old and it was like a movie we couldn't stop talking about. They looked badass, and we wanted in on it. We signed up a couple of months before 9/11 and served in both Afghanistan and Iraq. But something happened to him over there, he became someone I didn't want to know. We fell out of touch until about a month ago, when he showed up recruiting old buddies from the Corps for some big score. When I heard what he had in mind I said no, but I ended up getting sucked in anyway. I knew what he was capable of and I thought that if I didn't stop him no one else would. It was like you said, I hoped to talk him around at that mall but I was tired and fell asleep in the rental. By the time I arrived there was no stopping it, only of changing the outcome."

Cabot nodded in satisfaction. *This* was what he wanted to hear. He'd been so close to the truth all along that it restored his faith in his abilities as an investigator. His mind moved on.

"How many of the gang are left?"

"Him and his crazy-ass girlfriend, the rest are dead."

The two from the hospital.

"What are their names?"

Thorne hesitated. It was the final betrayal, giving up his old friend.

"Aidan Blake and Sara Dawson."

Cabot ran their names though his brain, getting used to the flavor of them. It was always this way when he'd been using one of Barnes' aliases for any length of time. The names had a power, a way of sticking and becoming real for him in a way the actual names did not.

"And this man *Blake*, he's the one that killed Jimmy?"

"Yes."

That was enough for Cabot, he'd heard all he needed to know.

"Change of plan. Get back in the truck."

"You and me, we're good now?"

"Don't push it, Thorne. I'll help save your girlfriend, after that we go our separate ways."

The actor flashed his teeth at him. His composure, his swagger it was all back. It depressed Cabot, because it felt like it cost him something. It probably had, he thought. Without the threat of being shot, he had essentially ceded control to the younger man. He was taller and physically stronger, not to mention he had all the information on Aidan Blake. Where he was, what he looked like; Cabot was completely in the dark. Whether he liked it or not, he needed Thorne to close the case. As long as the actor thought he was on-side it left the door open to other possibilities. Like shooting him at the gang's hideout and claiming he was there when he arrived. Proving his long-running theory of Thorne's involvement would end any risk of the frame-up coming back to bite him.

They walked back toward the truck, the branches of the trees swiping at them again. Only minutes earlier he thought he'd be walking back on his own. He'd convinced himself he could shoot Thorne and leave him here in the trees to rot. Instead, he had a new mission, a new target. The man he was going to kill, now walking behind him unguarded. He wondered if the actor had played him, had *acted* his way out of the situation. Told him what he wanted to hear. It felt like it had been his idea to put the gun away, but he was beginning to wonder.

They reached the truck and he slid back behind the wheel.

He turned to Thorne. "Where are we going?"

"Watsonville."

He turned the key in the ignition. The engine turned slowly over, sounding tired, then stopped. A red light glowed on the dashboard with the symbol for the alternator. He groaned. He'd left the key in the ignition and the headlights on. The battery was flat. He turned off the headlights, the air conditioning, and unplugged a third-party GPS unit. There was nothing else to disable. They sat in the dark for a moment, his fingers drumming lightly on the worn leather steering wheel.

"It's dead, isn't it?"

His cheeks burned with embarrassment.

"Give me a moment, Thorne. I've not used it much lately."

"No doubt."

He turned the key again. Stronger this time, more purposeful. *Tick, tick,*

370

tick. He waited for it to catch, but again the red light came on and he turned the ignition off. If he had killed Thorne the way he'd planned, he would've been stuck here needing a boost right next to the crime scene. He gave it a full minute on the clock, then turned the key. This time he buried the throttle, all or nothing. The engine roared back into life and he kept the revs high, feeding as much juice back into the battery as he could. He put the truck in gear and swung it around, back toward Watsonville. When he hit thirty he turned on the headlights and seeing the way was clear, glanced at Thorne. He'd expected further comments about the truck, but Thorne had shaken it off and was looking down at a computer tablet on his knee. The screen lit up his face and judging by the expression, he looked worried. The actor then pulled out his cell phone and began to tap away on that.

"What are you doing?"

"I was tracking Blake's cell phone on this tablet."

Cabot wasn't good with technology, but he noted the use of past tense. "*Was?*"

"Yeah. The SIM card's either been removed from this tablet, or else it never had one. The app needs a connection to work and there's obviously no Wi-Fi here. I'm setting up a wireless network on my phone to use its data service. I'll get there, Cabot, this is my world." Thorne trailed off as he stopped typing. "OK. This will take a couple of seconds to load up."

Inside the dark cab the tablet's screen was bright and he had to squint his eyes to understand what it was displaying. A map with two markers. It wasn't hard to understand, one of them had to be them, the other, Blake.

"It's like a spy movie."

Thorne grunted, but said nothing. His comment likely marked him out as an old man, but the actor left it alone. Thorne was focused now, thinking about his girlfriend.

"There's something I could never understand about the shoot-out, maybe you can clarify it for me now."

"Sure."

"You arrived first, before Ashcroft, before the gang."

Thorne nodded. "How did I know they were going to be there?"

"*Exactly.*"

"When I was looking into the Ashcrofts, I found an article about them in the *LA Times*. James and Lauren met each other in that mall, and have been going back there every year on the same date. The date of the shoot-out. There was a big piece about it, how romantic it was, all that. Made me want to hurl, but some folks like that shit."

Cabot shook his head in amazement. Thorne was describing a side to Ashcroft he would never have recognized. Romantic, sentimental, and disarmingly honest to have shared all this with a reporter. It made a crazy kind sense for someone with an eye on the presidency, voters lapped this stuff up. Not Thorne, obviously, but a lot of people. It also answered a question that had bothered him from the start. Namely, what the hell had James Ashcroft been doing in that mall in the first place.

"Jesus."

"Only in America could a mall be considered romantic."

They said nothing for several minutes. He was driving at nearly sixty miles an hour, which was close to the vehicle's top speed. The back of the truck produced a lot of running noise and the cab had little in the way of sound insulation. The thrumming noise went through him like the heartbeat of a huge beast.

"You said before that we have a painting of Jimmy's in lockup. I don't know anything about any painting. How do we have it?"

"After the exchange at the roadhouse went south I had to hide the painting before you arrived. There wasn't a lot of time, so I put it in the gang's van. I didn't think you'd see the vehicle for what it was, but you did and you had it towed away."

"We went over that van with a microscope, there's no painting."

"Trust me, it's there."

Cabot was silent for a moment.

"Are you talking about Jimmy's Picasso?"

"Yeah, it's worth like a hundred and fifty million dollars. That's what Blake's been after. He was going to kidnap Lauren, then exchange her for the painting. As plans go, it was fool-proof. Perhaps it would've been better if I'd let him do it."

It was a fair point, and Cabot could see the logic behind it. Thorne's interference had caused a cascade of violence and death. Regardless, he didn't like the idea of the gang kidnapping Lauren and what they might've done to her before they returned her, assuming they did. Sometimes it was simpler for an abductor to kill the victim once their price had been met. In simple terms, they knew too much.

He decided to change the subject.

"What's with the suit?"

Thorne turned to look at him, his expression hard to read.

"I didn't have time to change."

"So if I go back to that motel, I won't hear a story about the FBI?"

"We're in this together now, Cabot. Remember that. There's no prize for stabbing me in the back. That cannon of yours will have left a bullet stuck in a tree back there that could be difficult to explain."

Thorne may not have been the person he'd taken him for, but the idea that they were partners didn't sit right with him. He'd invested time and energy into how he felt about the actor, and that didn't go away easily.

"At the moment our interests overlap, let's not pretend this is anything else."

372

"You know," Thorne said, "I asked James about you. What the deal was, why you were such a hardass. He told me that you wanted to be sheriff, said you'd wanted it for years but had been blocked by different people. Seems to me that rescuing a Hollywood actress, taking down the killer of a US Senator, and closing the biggest case in the county's history... I could be wrong, but you're going to be more than getting your shitty job back, right? Who will be better placed to be sheriff at the next election? Some no-dick pencil-pusher?"

"You're beginning to grow on me, Thorne."

SIXTY

They were almost there. Small residential properties gave way to huge warehouses that rose up like tombstones on both sides of the street, gray and anonymous. There was no traffic and the district had an isolated, end-of-the-world vibe. He could see why Blake had chosen it.

"This is it up here on the left," Thorne said, pointing through the windshield at a cold storage building. "I say we drive past to check for activity, then circle back."

"Agreed."

They turned their heads as the warehouse slid past.

A slender finger of light from a street light shone into the gap between the warehouse and the building next door. He saw Blake's sedan and, beyond it, the wheel of a motorcycle. He smiled grimly to himself. This was *definitely* the place. Once again, he had the element of surprise on his side and he hoped that would be enough. Cabot kept the speed slow and steady until they were clear, then hit the gas to complete the circuit around the block.

He realized that Cabot's truck made a perfect undercover vehicle. It was so old and run down it was almost invisible. Your eye saw it, then forgot all about it like it was a street sign or a fire hydrant. If Blake had seen it drive past he'd never think of him. The truck belonged here in a way the Maserati never could. Back to the start of the loop again, Cabot cut the ignition and they coasted to a stop, headlights off. It was the same move he'd done at the roadhouse and Thorne flashed back to that scene for a moment. If the lieutenant had thought to drive the truck that night instead of his police cruiser, he had no doubt Ashcroft would still be alive and Kate would already be safe. He pushed the thought aside.

Wishing on what could have been led nowhere useful and was little more than a prayer for losers. He needed to stay sharp and in the moment.

Thorne placed the tablet between them so they could both see it clearly. He was pleased to note that they were exactly where the pointer said they were. It was an encouraging sign, but it meant little. They were outside so their position would be calculated using GPS. Blake, on the other hand, was inside a concrete and steel building where the satellite signal couldn't penetrate. That left cellular network positioning, a system of triangulation based on cell masts. Compared to GPS it was a joke, with a potential inaccuracy of a quarter mile, depending on cell mast density. The vehicles outside indicated they were in the right place, but he couldn't rule out the possibility of Blake parking next to a neighboring building to backstop any search for him. There was nothing to be gained from mentioning any of this to Cabot, however, and plenty to be gained from keeping him in the dark.

He zoomed in on the warehouse until it filled the screen.

"Okay, Blake's here at this end of the building. They're not expecting company, so he'll just be cooling his heels waiting for my call. Kate is their only leverage so they'll want to keep her close, where they can see her. That creates a blind spot at the back. You enter there and work your way forward, while I go in here. If it all goes sideways and I'm discovered, he'll never expect me to have you as backup. You're my ace in the hole."

Cabot screwed up his face. He didn't enjoy taking direction.

"No, no, no. We should hit them both at once. I don't know if you've noticed, Thorne, but I'm not really set for squeezing through windows and sneaking about."

Thorne paused, thinking it over.

"Blake's not in this building legally, right? That means he has no key. I didn't see damage out front when we drove past, so I'm guessing he busted a lock off where it wouldn't draw the attention of passers-by. I figure this door is at the back next to the loading dock, he'd have time to work on it out of sight. That's how you get in."

"You think like a cop, Thorne."

Even from a joker like Cabot, this was high praise.

"Thanks."

"And once we're inside?"

"I draw Blake and the Dawson woman away from Kate, while you rescue her. Get her out of there, no matter what. Drive away and leave me, don't wait. I want to know she's safe."

"That's a shit plan."

"As soon as they realize she's expendable, they'll kill her. If my plan isn't heroic enough for you we can work out a better story later, but this is the way we're playing it."

"You know, it's too bad I never got to know the real you before now because you're actually a charming guy to be around."

Thorne said nothing. Cabot's attempt at humor either indicated a thawing in their relationship, or a sign of nerves. He flipped the tablet cover closed and tossed the device onto the floor next to his feet. Inside, he was changing again. Becoming Jake Vasco, the man with no fear. He didn't have any, because it wasn't in the script. Thorne reached behind him and pulled the S&W 1911 out of the back of his pants.

The lieutenant stiffened noticeably as he saw the weapon.

"How come you never drew that out in the woods?"

"Didn't think I needed to."

He let the pistol rest on his leg as if forgotten.

"Cabot, there's something I feel I should tell you before we go in there. In the spirit of us working together and all that."

"Yeah?"

"I'm not here to help you arrest people. If that's a problem you should stay here."

Cabot sat still for a moment, except for the slow mechanical chewing of his jaws. The gum must have lost it's flavor long ago, yet he continued to chomp on it. Finally, Cabot turned to him, his face almost entirely lost in the low light.

"You got nothing to worry about, Thorne. I'm not a cop tonight. You're here for Kate, I'm here for Jimmy. It's as simple as that."

"Just so we're clear, Kate's blonde, Sara's a brunette."

"Give me some credit, Thorne. I know exactly what your girlfriend looks like. They play two episodes of your show every night."

It was jarring for him to think about Cabot watching *Night Passenger*. Seeing Kate with her tastefully torn clothing, him saying all that corny wise-cracking dialogue.

"You've seen it? What do you think?"

"It's stupid and cheesy."

"Everyone's a goddamn critic, I swear."

"Tonight's the first time I missed it, so I set it to record."

Thorne smiled to himself in the dark. It would be interesting to see what numbers the show was getting with a prime time slot and the publicity rubbing off from the shoot-out.

Next to him, Cabot took out the revolver again. In his large hand it seemed perfectly proportioned, except for the barrel which seemed to go on forever. It was time. They nodded to each other and got out of the truck, closing the heavy doors as softly as possible. The adrenaline kicked in, his senses sharpening. They walked single file down the sidewalk, their left arms brushing the gray concrete wall of the building next to Blake's. Keeping the angle tight. He heard Cabot breathing through his mouth behind him like a team of attack dogs pulling against their leashes. The cop hadn't fought him too hard on a plan that gave him the lightest load to carry. He'd anticipated more resistance from Cabot, even if it was just for show. Perhaps the man hoped to keep his head down until the shooting stopped, then take care of whoever was left when the going was easy.

Thorne drew level with the edge of the first building, paused for a beat, flashed his head around the corner to take in the scene, then sucked it back around. No lookouts, no cameras. He jogged across the opening to the corner on the opposite side then turned to watch Cabot go down the side of the warehouse as planned. The man was in a half squat as he shuffled forward, like he was about to get on helicopter. Thorne shook his head. The lieutenant was so out of his depth it was pitiful. He moved on, toward his own entry point. The 1911 felt numb in his hand and it was difficult to tell how much was due to the glove, and how much was nerve damage from his shoulder wound. He tightened his grip on the pistol until he felt the latex begin to stretch between thumb and forefinger.

He'd lied to Cabot about where he planned to enter the warehouse. Given the imprecise nature of the tracking app without GPS or Wi-Fi, it was possible that Blake could be standing right next to Cabot as he made his breach. To preserve surprise, he had something a little more difficult in mind. He tucked his pistol back into his pants and removed his belt. The automatic moved a fraction, then held. He was next to a power line pole. It looked old and was made of wood. About ten feet up, were a sequence of staggered foot grips. Reaching straight up, his fingertips were less than eighteen inches from the bottom rung. He looped his belt around on itself and attached the buckle on the first hole from the end. He put both his arms through the loop and pushed it up over the top of his biceps. The leather band would ease the strain on his shoulder injury, but with his arms raised it cut across his face. It was the best he could do.

Thorne sank down and pushed off hard with both legs while arching his back and driving both arms forward above his head. His left hand bounced off the metal grip, but he managed to grab it again before he fell back down. His injured shoulder burned. He pulled himself up, transferring as much load as he could to his left arm as his right hand reached for the next step. He found it, then the next. It was brutal, and his chest heaved trying to get enough air down. Beads of sweat ran down his face. Finally he got his feet onto the steps and the weight came off his arms and shoulders. He moved effortlessly up the remaining steps, first drawing level, then eclipsing the height of the warehouse roof beside him.

The roof was flat but split across two heights.

The lower level next to him was connected by a ladder to a raised section that contained three boxy structures. One he made as an air conditioning plant, another a huge backup generator for the cold storage, and lastly the roof access itself. This was his way in. Thorne re-looped the belt so that it was now around the pole and back around a grip to form a handhold. In his head he began to count down from twenty, while taking long, deep breaths. He felt his heart slow and peace come over him. When he reached five he lowered himself on the top foot grip on the pole, bunching up his nearside leg to form a spring then he kicked off sideways with all his strength. For the briefest moment he felt himself flying through the air before landing in a diagonal roll across his back, left shoulder to right hip, and popping up on the other side in a one-knee squat. It was a landing he'd only successfully pulled off once before, during season one of *Night Passenger*. They'd done five takes that day, and they'd had to use his first as it was the only one he'd nailed.

He stood and walked to the edge of the building to look at what he'd just done. His eyes were wet with tears and he back handed them away. Ashcroft's pistol had dug deep into his skin next to his spine. The pain had been brief, but white-hot. Despite this, he couldn't stop smiling. The jump was one of the craziest things he'd ever done. No wires, no padded mats, no special suit. Pure technique.

His mind returned to Cabot.

He'd involved the lieutenant through necessity, but it was dangerous to have him anywhere near Blake. The story he'd told him was mostly true, but he'd been careful to omit any mention of the failed gallery heist. Blake's previous warning about conspiracy murder charges left no room for him to survive, he had to kill him plain and simple. If Cabot caught wind of the heist he'd have to die too, there was no other way. Directing the cop in through the back gave Kate two chances for rescue, but it was mostly about giving him time to wrap things up with Blake before the lieutenant arrived.

The sound of an approaching engine snapped him back into the moment and his eyes sought it out. A dark colored SUV appeared at the end of the block. It slowed to walking pace as it passed Cabot's truck then swung across the street and parked next to the power pole. Thorne dropped to his hands and knees, then shuffled forward until just the top of his head stuck out beyond the edge. Inside the vehicle he heard muffled male voices.

Keep going assholes.

This is not the place to stop.

He willed them to drive off, to do their drugs or whatever somewhere else. The engine of the SUV blipped high then cut out. Silence poured into the space it occupied. The driver door opened with a metallic pop. Light from inside spilled out across the concrete sidewalk and something there caught his eye. His belt.

Fuck.

The driver got out and stretched. He had a day-old buzzcut and wore a skin tight long sleeve black t-shirt over baggy track pants. His body suggested many hours spent in a gym, and many years taking steroids. Thorne wet his lips. This was bad, this was very bad. This wasn't a couple of guys looking for somewhere quiet to take drugs or hook up, this was reinforcements. Buzzcut gazed off down the street, bored. The passenger door opened and a man stepped out and walked around the front of the SUV. Even though he was wearing olive green alphas and a hard framed service cap, he recognized Jay Stockton immediately. The uniform was cut to fit him perfectly, so there was no disguising the shape of a weapon that was distorting the material around his left pectoral muscle. His head dipped, noticing the belt lying at his feet and Thorne pulled his head back fast before Stockton could look up.

Fuck, fuck, fuck.

SIXTY-ONE

Thorne walked across the roof then climbed the ladder to the higher level. He thought about Stockton and Buzzcut. His terrible rescue plan was getting worse by the second. It didn't seem possible that Blake could've anticipated his arrival here, more likely, this was part of his endgame for the next exchange. The first exchange hadn't gone so well for either side, but Blake had taken steps to improve his chances this time around. Sheer chance had allowed him to see these two extra players arriving. If he knew anything about combat, it was that it's better to know in advance you are out-gunned than to find out while engaging the enemy.

He reached the roof access door and tried the handle. As he expected, it was locked but he wasn't worried too much about that. He'd been on a few rooftops in his life, and he knew security was notoriously poor. Most doors weren't alarmed, often there was even a brick or some other weight there for holding it open while you had a smoke.

Using the glow from his cell phone, he analyzed the entrance.

The door was made from sheet steel and aside from patches of rust blistering through the paint, it was solid. Like other roof doors he'd seen, it was hung to open outward. This was likely a fire code regulation related to air pressure and backdrafts. If something went wrong, it would blow out, rather than be forced closed. It meant that the hinges were on the outside of the frame. He pocketed his cell phone, then pulled up his right pant leg and withdrew the hunting knife. Using the back of the blade, he worked it under the cap on the lower hinge pin, forcing it up with a see-sawing movement.

There was little weight on the bottom of the door and it took less than twenty seconds to remove. The top pin barely moved at all. After around a minute with little progress he stopped and stood back. This was taking too long. He couldn't let Cabot start anything before he was ready. Why couldn't the second pin have been as simple as the first? He smiled to himself. Of course. He picked up the first hinge pin and used it to push the other pin out from below. It was a different action, and he could put more strength into it. Once it began to move, he cleared the second pin in no time and it was a simple matter to pull on the edge, lift the door out sideways and prop it against the wall.

In front of him, a narrow metal staircase like a fire escape led down about fifteen feet at a near forty-five degree angle. He stepped through the doorway and cold air immediately soaked through his suit and filled his lungs. The metalwork was in poor condition and shifted noticeably under his weight. He moved slowly, careful to prevent his dress shoes slipping or ringing out on the steps. He came out on a mezzanine walkway that ran in a square around the outer edge of the building. Some kind of raised maintenance level. He leaned over a guardrail and saw a forest of pig carcasses hanging on wires in the darkness below.

It was freezing cold. Blake wouldn't want to spend time in this environment, he'd want to be somewhere warm and comfortable. Thorne thought again about where the tracking app had placed him inside the building. He turned his head to match the direction and saw a dim light pushing out into the void of dead animals. A manager's office maybe. It seemed like he'd worried about Blake's location for nothing.

He heard a door slam at the back of the building and his head snapped around.

Stockton and Buzzcut.

Another door slammed, the manager's office this time, and lights flickered on below him as Blake came out to investigate. He wondered about Cabot. The lieutenant might hear the activity and assume their plan was in play. He'd come forward to rescue Kate but instead of finding her alone, would be facing off against three heavily armed meatheads and a crazy woman capable of anything.

Thorne drew the automatic and crept along the metal deck toward where he'd seen the flash of light. If Kate was still alive, that's where she'd be. At the end of the mezzanine, stairs no wider than a ladder extended down to the floor. He took the steps two at a time, making the most of Blake's absence. The height difference came with a marked temperature shift and as he reached the warehouse floor his breath hung in the air front of his mouth. It was bitterly cold, and he had to clench his jaw muscles to prevent his teeth chattering together. He moved past the hanging pigs toward the structure at the end of the building.

The office pushed out from the wall and was roughly the size of a shipping container. It had a long window and a single doorway. The door was wide open. He imagined Blake blasting out of there, the door flying open as he marched off to see Stockton. Blake would be in a dark place having waited all night to hear from him and his mood was unlikely to improve now he was having to tell Stockton. The deadline had yet to pass but it had to be obvious to him by now that there would be no phone call, no trade for the painting and, by extension, no multi million dollar payout. Everything that had sustained Blake and kept him relatively grounded was evaporating with every second that passed.

He wondered if Sara Dawson was still inside the office. She knew about the gallery break-in, there was no room for her to survive, any more than there was for Blake. If she lived, he stood to spend the rest of his life in prison. He'd be damned if he'd allow it to destroy his life. It wouldn't bring anyone back. There was only one realistic choice and he'd known it for a while. He'd never killed a woman and didn't look forward to starting now.

Thorne kept low through the door, hiding himself behind two filing units then looked around the side and into the room. Kate sat slumped over on an office chair, her blonde hair covering her face. Her wrists secured to the chair arms, her ankles to the legs. His breath caught in his throat. It was impossible to tell if she was alive. There was no sign of Sara Dawson. He spoke softly, little more than a whisper.

"Kate!"

Her head twitched. *"Chris?"*

She flipped her head backward, forcing her hair to clear her eyes. Her face was pale and flecked with blood. Her left eye was bruised, her lip split. Thorne felt his chest tighten. Even now, like this, she was beautiful.

"Hi, honey."

He crossed the floor, careful to keep below the level of the office window. She wore tight jeans, sneakers and a shapeless hooded warm-up top. Clothes Sara had chosen. There was a blood stain on her right leg where Blake had stabbed her. A pulse of rage and guilt flowed through his system. It was almost exactly where he'd stabbed Blake and he knew this was no coincidence. He took off his right glove and held her hand. Tears began to roll down her face.

"Are you really here?"

"I need you to focus. We're not out of this yet."

She was looking him over.

"Why are you dressed like that?"

"Long story. The people that did this, where are they?"

"They just left. I wasn't sorry about it."

He nodded. It didn't matter, it was obvious to him where they were. They'd gone to meet Stockton and Buzzcut and before too long they'd be back here, the warehouse was too cold to go anywhere else. He pulled out the hunting knife and carefully cut the cable ties.

He considered leaving with Kate.

Thorne had no doubt the gang would kill Cabot, ending any danger to him from prosecution. The lieutenant was off book and below the radar, it would be a long time before anyone noticed he was missing. But that still left Blake, Sara, and Stockton that knew about his involvement. He could probably also add Buzzcut to this list. He rejected the idea. It was time to make a stand and get his life back and, as ironic as it seemed, Cabot might actually be able to help him.

"I've cut through your bindings. I don't have another gun to give you so you need to stay here and keep your head down. If you see an opportunity to get out, take it. There's a rusty truck parked down the street, the keys are on the center console."

Kate looked brighter, more focussed.

"Leave me the knife."

He nodded, then pulled up his pants leg, tore off the sheath and pushed the hunting knife into it before passing it to her. He locked eyes with her.

"If you need to use it, make sure it counts, okay? Hard and fast, no hesitation. As deep as you can go, as many times as you can. Don't let go of the handle. If you're not sure you can do that, hide it, you'll probably live longer."

"Thank you for coming for me."

"You never doubted that, did you?"

She said nothing.

"I love you, Kate."

"Jesus," she said. "*Now* you say it."

It wasn't the answer he wanted. He pulled the latex glove back on then turned and shuffled back toward the door, his head below the window. Maybe there was no way back for them after all. He didn't blame her after everything that had happened.

He squatted against the filing units that shielded him from the doorway, Ashcroft's Smith & Wesson in his fist. He had eight rounds in the magazine and one in the chamber. Two rounds each, with one left over. He didn't like those odds. He thought wistfully about the extra ammunition he'd left in the Maserati. Bloody Cabot. If it hadn't been for the cop, he would've had this done and dusted before Stockton even arrived.

He glanced around the corner into the warehouse. All clear. He took a deep breath like he was about to go under water, then spun out from around the corner of the unit and rushed forward into the warehouse. He moved to the right to form a flanking position so he could shoot at Blake and the others as they returned to the office. Pig carcasses passed on either side of him. As he neared the back of the building, he stopped and turned to face Blake's return path. The dead animals gave him cover, but they also limited his field of fire.

He took a fresh breath and felt the cold go deep into his body, spreading out fast from his lungs to his chest, arms, and legs. He'd hoped to get off at least the first shot with the warm office air still inside him, but it hadn't happened. Already his muscles were starting to shake. If Blake took too much longer to return, he'd be lucky to hit the side of a barn.

A door slammed at the back of the warehouse, followed by heavy footsteps. They grew louder and louder. There were no voices now, whatever Blake and Stockton had to say to each other had already been said. There was something businesslike about the footsteps. They had a purpose, like they weren't just going to the office to keep warm. Suddenly Thorne knew why Stockton was here, and it wasn't to help Blake deal with him or keep watch over the painting. Stockton didn't trust Blake to kill Kate. The whole operation had been a disaster and he was here to make sure nothing came back to bite him.

Thorne dropped down on his left knee and held the automatic in a two-handed grip, his elbows resting on his raised right knee. The gun barrel slightly raised, aimed center mass.

He'd only have the element of surprise once, he needed to make it count. They would walk into view from the right, so he'd fire from the left. He'd have a limited window to fire so programmed his brain with the target pattern. The seconds drew out, the footsteps almost on top of him until Blake and Buzzcut walked into his kill zone.

He began firing.

SIXTY-TWO

A pig carcass exploded next to Blake's face, spraying a jet of frozen meat out in front of him. His eyes began to turn as more flesh propelled itself toward him. It came to him as if in slow motion. *I'm being shot at.* The gunshots sounded like a distant firecracker inside the huge building. *Pop, pop, pop, pop.* His head swung around, trying to place the shooter. Instead, he saw the new muscle, Tate, collapse onto the floor next to him. He was screaming, his huge body doubled over in pain. Blake lunged behind the partially destroyed pig. It didn't provide much cover, but it hid his outline from whoever was firing and he'd take that over nothing.

He turned and saw Stockton standing opposite him, behind another pig. He'd drawn his pistol, and Blake did the same. The Texan indicated with his hand where the shoots came from and Blake nodded. He thought back over what he'd heard. A handgun, at a range of fifty to sixty feet. It was hard to be sure about distance when they were coming toward you. Four shots, with a split-second pause between the second and third. A two and two pattern. The shooter had attempted a double tap of two moving targets from the side.

Ambitious, but far from impossible.

"That you, Chris?"

Another shot whistled past his head.

"Looks like that shoulder injury is affecting your aim, brother."

There was no reply, but Blake knew it was him. Who else would come here to shoot him? Not cops or FBI. They'd at least pretend they wanted him alive. Surround the building, fire smoke canisters in through the windows, cut the power, something like that. Only one person wanted him dead this much. He looked at Tate writhing and screaming on the floor. The noise was getting on his nerves. It was like he was hearing one of the frozen animals as they were being slaughtered. He fired three rounds at Tate and the screaming stopped.

He looked up and saw Stockton glaring at him.

"That's not right, man."

His voice was low, but there was no mistaking the anger in it.

"I did him a favor. All he had to look forward to was pain."

"He's my wife's cousin."

Blake took a deep breath and let it out slowly. *Shit.*

"Which wife?"

"The first one."

"So…we're good?"

"You're an asshole, Blake."

He couldn't argue with that. People had been telling him the same thing his whole life. Over the years he'd learned to accept it and moved on. He knew one thing for sure; he hadn't asked Tate to be here and he didn't much care now he was gone. Tate had clearly been under Stockton's command and he wasn't sure what that meant for him. Most likely that the Texan planned on taking the painting for himself and would've used this beefcake to help him get it. Blake looked over Stockton's shoulder at Sara. She was staring at what remained of Tate on the floor. His wasn't the first dead body she'd seen, but from her zen-calm expression, it appeared she was getting used to it.

"All right, let's get this prick. Sara, you're with me; Stockton you stay here and stop the sneaky fuck from doubling back."

With Tate gone, the chain of command had become clear again. This was *his* op, regardless of the *costume* Stockton had chosen to wear. Sara walked over and joined him on the end of his row. He turned and looked down the next aisle. All clear. He moved forward, his Glock out in front of him, Sara following along behind. This move was easy to predict, they had to be careful. The one place Thorne was unlikely to be, was where he'd been firing from moments earlier. That location would be toast. He'd move to some new spot, perhaps one he'd already picked out for when they came back here to get him.

He thought about Thorne's ambush. The narrow space between rows had forced him to delay firing until the last second. If he'd fired at him in the middle of the aisle, he'd certainly have hit him. But Thorne had been greedy. He'd wanted to take out two of them at once, while their guard was down. That was Thorne all over, going into his head and planning everything out. But close-quarter combat couldn't be planned the way Thorne liked. Just the same, his first attack had taken Tate out the picture and it wasn't hard to believe that he could even the odds still further.

Up ahead, carcasses swung slowly back and forth as if on a breeze. Thorne had brushed past them in a hurry when he changed position. He was close. The pigs hanging to his right were moving perceptibly more than those on his left. Blake angled himself so he was facing to the right. Sara picked up on his stance and turned with him. He slowed, his body turning as he got closer. He held his hand up to Sara to stop where she was. There was something off about this, he couldn't say what. He lowered himself toward the floor, bracing himself with his left hand and looked under the dead animals. The light was gloomy and filled with a blurred icy mist, but there was no sign of Thorne as far as he could see. It was a set-up. He rolled over and fired three shots blindly in the opposite direction. One of his shell casings bounced off the floor and hit him in the face, apart from that, he hit nothing.

"Goddammit!"

He jerked his arms around trying to find his target, but Thorne was gone. After a couple of seconds, Blake heard laughter. It was deep and throaty, like a V8 revving. It sounded as though it was right on top of him.

"Cold in here, isn't it?"

"Thorne, you piece of shit. Show yourself!"

Blake waited for Thorne to speak again to reveal his position, but he fell silent. His teeth gritted, he got up off the floor. All he could hear was blood pumping in his ears. He was through playing Thorne's game, it was time to take control. He turned to Sara.

"Bring his bitch out. We'll see who's laughing then."

Sara nodded and set off back the way they'd come. He watched her walk away and was overcome with a powerful sensation he'd never see her again. She dropped her gun arm and moved casually like she was walking along a street. He sighed and went after her. His senses were dialed up to 11. Thorne's mind games were getting to him, but that didn't mean he was wrong. He was ten feet away from her when she popped out of the rows of animals and into the open floor area of the warehouse. She glanced to the side as Stockton appeared next to her, his gun raised.

"*Jay?*"

"Sorry, doll. Nothing personal."

Blake heard a gun fire, but it was Stockton who fell on the floor, half his face missing. He almost landed on Tate, they were less than a foot apart. Blake ran toward Sara, who stood unmoving, looking at the two men on the floor. He shouted at her.

"Get down!"

She aimed her gun at Stockton and fired until her Glock was empty, the slide locked back. She looked around as he grabbed her around the waist and dragged her down to the floor behind a wooden crate. He spoke through clenched teeth.

"The hell were you thinking?"

"He was going to kill me!"

"*Was!* He's dead. Half his head's gone, that usually does the trick. You just put seventeen bullets in a corpse. We're being shot at, and it's not fucking Thorne. Someone else is here."

As if to underline his point, a bullet whipped past them and ricocheted off metalwork behind them. The gunshot was loud and his eye was drawn to a burst of flame. He sunk down further behind the crate.

"I thought *you* shot Stockton."

"No."

"Why would he do that? Try to kill me."

"I guess that's why he was here. No loose ends."

She said nothing. Blake glanced around the edge of the crate, his eyes probing into the darkness where he'd seen the muzzle flash. There was a figure there. Large and shapeless. He made out a section of pale blue denim and, crossing it at an angle, a gun barrel the length of a baby's arm. The lights above bounced off it in a single long line. The thing was a goddam hand cannon. It could probably shoot both of them right through the crate.

"We need to move," he said. "Are you ready?"

Sara licked her lips. "Yes."

"You first, I'll cover you."

She ran back to the relative safety of the frozen animals, while he fired toward the shapeless shooter. When she was safely across he followed her, still firing randomly into the darkness. As he crossed the halfway mark, the figure moved forward and light fell across him. *Cabot.* He was dressed like a vagrant lumberjack, but it was definitely him. The lieutenant's arm came up, the gun like a long, silver finger pointing at him. Blake dove forward and slid across the cold, hard floor. Two shots tore into the pig above him, right where his head had been. Cabot wasn't taking any prisoners. After a moment, there was a splintering noise and he launched himself to the side. The carcass dropped onto the floor with a crunch he could feel through the concrete. He rolled onto his back and stared straight up, air rushing in and out of his mouth.

"Hey, Cabot! I think you just killed your mother."

He heard Thorne laughing again. His ears sought out the sound, but the deep bass sound made it hard to place. It still sounded like it was right on top of him. Blake blinked a couple of times and looked up, beyond the lights. There was a narrow metal walkway above the animals. That's where his old friend would be. He remembered a staircase near the office. Blake ejected the magazine of his pistol and slammed a fresh one home.

It was time to end this, once and for all.

He got to his feet and brushed down his clothes while Sara stared at him. Her face was as perfect as the first day he'd seen it in the waffle house. He held the Glock across his chest and tapped it over his heart. Her head dipped slightly in silent acknowledgement. He glanced quickly up, at the walkway, then back down to her eyes. She nodded again.

They didn't need words, not anymore.

388

SIXTY-THREE

He felt Blake coming up the stairs several seconds before he heard it. The weight of his body caused a vibration in the metal Thorne had his left knee on. He stood and crept carefully along the mezzanine toward the office wall. He'd known Blake would eventually discover his position, it wasn't like there that many places to hide. In fact, he was counting on it. Coming up here to face him down was in Aidan Blake's nature. It was also, a huge mistake. The lighting in the warehouse hung below the maintenance level, a fact that suited Thorne just fine. He'd been up here for over five minutes, long enough for his eyes to adapt to the dark.

Time, Blake wouldn't have.

Thorne reached the back corner of the rectangle and squatted back down on his left knee. He held the 1911 so that his bad arm was again resting on top of his raised right knee. He sighted down the pistol at the top of the stairs. Almost at the same instant, Blake's head appeared. Thorne adjusted his aim to line up better with the center of his body. As he predicted, Blake couldn't see him in the shadows and kept on coming until he stood at the top of the steps, a huge black void in front of the lights beyond.

Blake paused there for a second, uncertain. He had two choices; continue walking forward down the short side of the rectangle, or turn left and walk down the long side. Thorne hesitated. If he kept on coming straight the distance between them would shrink and the chances of him missing became close to zero. If he turned to the left, he became a side-on target as before, and the chances of him missing rose dramatically.

Blake turned to the left.

Thorne cursed silently, releasing the pressure on the trigger. He only had four rounds left and couldn't afford any more misses. He stood and moved forward, the Smith & Wesson out in front of him. His dress shoes had leather soles and wooden heels. They were not designed for sneaking up on someone across a metal platform, but he found he could walk almost silently on his toes, lowering the heel down carefully. He was nearly there, less than twenty feet. As was so often the case, it would come down to who fired first. Over a minute had passed. By now, Blake's eyesight would be fully dark-adapted. Ten feet. Thorne moved to the left, his gun sweeping around to cover the angle of the corner. *Five.* He heard nothing but his own heart beating. He rounded the corner, gun where he estimated Blake should've been. He wasn't there. Thorne lifted his head, looking farther and farther away, into the darkness.

The mezzanine was empty.

Thorne swung around and found Blake moving out of the space at the top of the stairs. He lifted his arm up to shoot and Blake smacked his arm away, causing the 1911 to spin uselessly out of his hand and down onto the floor below. Blake tilted his head, as if weighing something up, then put his own gun into his jacket pocket.

"You keep underestimating me, Thorne. Why is that? Should I be insulted? We had the same training you and me, the same life. Do you honestly think you're so special?"

"I guess?"

Blake punched him in the face. A light jab. He wasn't close enough to put any real power into it. Thorne nodded to himself and brought his fists up in front of him. He knew this music. He popped Blake on the cheekbone, with plenty of power. The physicality of the hit was immensely rewarding. He smiled to himself, understanding Blake a little better. This was why he'd put his gun away. It was too quick, there was no satisfaction. Blake moved forward, seeking to close the gap between them and even their power. He made an awkward swing at Thorne's gut. It was a stupid move, telegraphed in advance by his body language, and Thorne was able to avoid it with ease. The failed swing caused Blake to twist around and overbalance allowing him to hit him again in the same cheekbone. The tear from the bar fight opened up and blood ran down his cheek.

He'd hit him twice in the same spot. Time to mix things up. Using his left, he punched Blake in the kidney. It was a solid punch but it got no reaction from Blake. The man could sure take a hit. If this continued, Blake would simply out-last him. They traded blows, back and forth. The cheap suit limited his swing and bunched awkwardly around his biceps and under his arms. He noticed Blake dropped his right hand every time he moved forward. He took a step back and as Blake moved into the space, Thorne popped him again on his cheekbone. There was a crunch this time as something under the skin collapsed. Blake roared, rage overtaking him. He charged forward with no regard for self-defense, his fists swinging left and right. Thorne took a punch to his forehead, snapping his head back. He swung out his arm to open up some space in front of him, but his fist was effortlessly deflected by Blake's arm. He felt the weakness in his own

390

swing, the impact barely registering. His hands began to shake. Not just the right, his left too.

Blake smiled in the darkness, his teeth catching some light.

Thorne lashed out a simple jab and got him square in the mouth, splitting his lip. It was a cheap shot, one that would tell Blake exactly how close he was to victory. He could hear his own breathing now, it was labored, catching in his throat. He felt drunk and hungover at the same time. His limbs moved slowly, like he was swimming in honey. Blake dummied to his left, then lunged to the right as he moved to avoid it. The blow was massive and hit Thorne on the side of his face where his jawbone connected.

His ears rang and his vision swam.

He took a step to the left to steady himself and was forced to take another two desperate steps in an effort to remain upright. Blake came forward, landing a flurry of hits to his stomach. He tried to move away but his dress shoes slipped and he fell backward, the metal slats smashing into his head. For a moment he saw darkness like he'd blinked, but Blake was right on top of him, his leg drawn back. Thorne rolled to the side, but there was no time. Blake's boot crashed into his chest, forcing the air out of his lungs with an explosive pop.

His body was sluggish and unresponsive.

The platform seemed to spin around him. He was going to pass out, he could feel it. His fingers sank through the strips on the walkway and curled around underneath, holding on tight. Thorne took a deep breath, then another. The frigid warehouse air was refreshing, like it contained more oxygen than regular air. The spinning sensation eased and his focus sharpened. He forced himself to crawl forward, to maintain movement. Buy himself extra time, no matter how little. Blake had beaten him and it wouldn't be long before he decided to finish him. He remembered their last fight in the forest. *The stab wound.* He cursed himself for not remembering before. The pain Blake suffered from that leg punch had given him the upper hand. If Sara hadn't been there with that Taser, things would have turned out very differently. He saw movement out the corner of his eye and looked around.

Blake's boot coming toward his head, then nothing.

*

When he came to he was propped up against the guardrail. Blake sat opposite, smoking a cigar. There was only about half of it left, which meant he'd been unconscious for several minutes. Thorne ran his tongue around his mouth, taking stock. The all-to-familiar taste of blood gave way to the discovery of a large hole. An upper molar was missing. Noticing he was awake, Blake blew out a thick stream of smoke and flicked the cigar into the forest of pigs below. His hand came down to rest on his thigh, next to his Glock. He spoke calmly, like they were having a meal at a restaurant.

"What gives with the suit?"

Thorne said nothing.

"I guess all this *Chuck Norris* shit means you don't have the painting?"

Thorne laughed at the mention of the painting, and instantly regretted it. His ribs were cracked or broken and his abdominal muscles began to spasm. He spat blood onto the walkway next to his leg.

"Wouldn't do you any good if I did."

"How's that?"

"You never found out who the buyer was, did you? Once that first batch of money came through, you didn't care. All that mattered was that you were paid, right? *Wrong.*"

Blake stared at him with narrowed eyes.

"That's right," Thorne said. "I can see you've worked it out. Probably a part of you always knew. You shot the buyer through his windshield. He's dead. You've been chasing a dream for almost a week."

"Ashcroft."

It was a statement, not a question. Blake sighed. There'd be no million-dollar payout, no life of luxury, none of the things he'd spent weeks imagining for his future. It had appeared to slip from his grasp before, but this time was final. No new plan could resurrect his deal now. Blake would be back to sticking up convenience stores and gas stations, or whatever else had passed for work before they'd met in that bar.

Blake began to jab the side of his own head with his gun.

"That old man played us for fools since day one."

Thorne heard some mechanism inside the gun rattle every time it hit Blake's skull. It wasn't a gentle tap, like a finger on a window, it was a jarring impact like a hammer.

"At least you had a good reason, Blake. Your motives were pure. You wanted to help your sister get treatment and that's more than I can say."

The stabbing motion stopped.

"Thorne, my sister died over a year ago. She never had any disease like I said, she just walked in front of a bus. Had a note in her pocket, it was no accident."

He stared at Blake in disbelief.

"You made up a story about your dead sister to get me on board?"

"Let me tell you something, I had to identify her body after that bus was done with her. Couldn't she have taken some sleeping pills? I can still see what was left of her when I close my eyes. I used her, and it worked. I'm not sorry about it. You'd never have done any of this without that story, not even for the money."

392

Thorne shook his head.

"You are a disgusting piece of shit."

"Maybe. But I don't pretend to be something I'm not."

Silence fell between them. It was clear to Thorne that everything they needed to say had been said and only one thing was left to do. The pistol that lay on Blake's leg was no more than the icing on the cake, he was in no condition to beat him in a fight.

Blake sighed and pointed the Glock at him.

Thorne stared at the end of the barrel until everything else disappeared. It was aimed at his head, at least this would be quick. There was a fast movement in front of him and he felt his body swing around. Blake had kicked his legs. He slid over the edge of the platform, right under the wires of the guardrail. His hands grabbed desperately for something to stop his fall and found a vertical pole that connected the walkway and the rail. In a fraction of a second, he was hanging down, his hands struggling to hold on.

Blake leaned over, grinning.

"Since we've been friends so long I decided not to shoot you. On one condition."

"What's that?"

"That you let go."

Thorne glanced down at the floor. It was at least thirty feet, maybe forty.

"You've got to be kidding me."

"Do it, and I'll spare the woman. It's the best I can do."

"I'm supposed to trust you?"

"What choice you got? From where I'm standing, you're fucked either way."

Thorne looked over his shoulder at the floor area beyond the pigs. Sara Dawson stood silently watching them. She held Cabot's huge revolver in her hand and its barrel extended all the way down her leg to the top of her boot. The lieutenant lay still on the floor next to her, his arm stretched out in front of him. His fingers were spread apart in what he guessed were the same position she'd left them in when she'd taken the revolver.

He could expect no help from Cabot.

Thorne turned back to Blake and saw a hint of amusement on his face. He appeared to have recovered from the news about the painting and the end of his deal. For now, it was enough to beat him. Thorne changed his hand position, wrapping his left hand farther around, then clamping it in place with his weak right. His weight was no longer on his fingers, but the metal support was cutting into his hand. The latex gloves increased his grip level, but pretty soon it would be academic whether he let go, or if he fell.

Blake nodded.

"All right, brother. Your choice."

Blake straightened up and called across the room.

"Bring her out!"

Sara smiled and walked to the office with a spring in her step. Her body language seemed to say *finally*, as if this was what she was here for, rather than the money. He had no more plays left, he was done. Thorne looked again at the floor below. It wasn't a survivable fall, not even close. Which, of course, was the point. Blake wasn't offering him a chance to live, he was simply amusing himself. At least it would be quick. If he took a breath before he let go it would all be over before he needed to draw another.

"You know, Thorne, it's kind of funny. Your girlfriend told me only yesterday that you'd love her forever and that you'd die for her. She was quite convincing. Maybe it was all a big act, but I was interested to see if it was true." Blake shook his head. "I got to say, as a romantic, that I'm disappointed by your attitude."

"Come on, man. You don't have to hurt her. She's no threat to you."

"Time's running out, Thorne. You jumped off a building last month, this should be nothing. With your track record, you'll break a fingernail or something."

Blake smiled at his own joke, then looked up to watch Sara lead Kate out at the end of a gun. Thorne felt the air go out of him. There was no sign of the hunting knife, Kate must have decided she couldn't use it. He didn't blame her, using a knife took a certain mindset. It was more personal than a firearm. As they drew closer, Thorne noticed that Kate was considerably taller than Sara, despite her motorcycle boots. Kate was in good shape. Strong, athletic. If she could get the upper hand and disable Sara, she had a real chance to escape. She could easily make it back to Cabot's truck before Blake could catch up with her.

"Chris!"

She'd just noticed him hanging over the edge.

"Hey, sweetie."

"What's going on?"

"What's going on, Miss Bloom," Blake said, "is that I gave your man here the chance to save your life and he hasn't taken it. Isn't that right, Thorne?"

He felt his grip loosen on the guardrail.

There was no time left. In around a minute he was going to fall, he couldn't stop that from happening. Either he could fall knowing he'd done everything he could to save Kate's life, or he could fall all the way to hell knowing he hadn't. Love had to be the best reason to die, better than any other he'd avoided in the past.

"Five seconds, Thorne. Do I really need to do a countdown?"

"Wait!" he said. "I need to say something to her first, okay?"

A broad smile appeared on Blake's face.

"Of course! I'm not a monster. Go ahead."

"Kate, I was wrong before. About all this. You never needed anyone to come rescue you, do you understand? It was always within you, it's within you now."

He saw Kate give a small nod.

Above him, Blake sighed.

"That's it? I thought for sure you were going to tell her you loved her and that you're sorry for getting her into this situation in the first place. Something like that."

Thorne ignored him.

"Sooner would be better than later."

"Sooner what?" Blake said.

"I'm not talking to you, asshole."

Kate spun around and battered the end of the Colt Python with her forearm. The heavy revolver twisted sideways in Sara's hand. Instinctively, she pulled the trigger. A burst of flame shot out the end of the barrel over Kate's shoulder and the bullet screamed past Thorne and through the roof. The momentum continued to send Sara's arm wide and Kate stepped forward and punched Sara hard in the nose. The blow caused her to stagger to the side and a second later blood poured out both nostrils, and down her chin in a thick band. Sara wiped the blood away and looked at her hand, surprised. When she lifted her head again, Kate's fist missed her cheek and instead hit her windpipe.

Sara collapsed on the ground, hands wrapped around her throat. The large building filled with the desperate whistle of Sara trying to breathe.

Blake looked over the edge, wild-eyed.

"Sara?"

She looked up at Blake, her face turning blue, her eyes popping out. She jerked her hand against her throat, trying to clear the obstruction and reared back, her chest filling with air. She got another lungful of air down and managed to get to a half standing position. Kate stepped in close again and drove her knee hard into Sara's face. She tumbled backward onto the floor, her body hitting a stack of gas cylinders which crashed down on top of her.

"SARA!"

Blake's voice rang around the inside of the building. His head was twisted around trying to see where she was, but his angle was all wrong. Blake couldn't see what he could see; Sara Dawson pitched forward on the floor next to the office with a gas cylinder across her head, unmoving. Thorne turned back to Blake, he was leaning way over now.

"You gotta get down there, Aidan. She's hurt, I can see her."

"Shut up."

"I'm telling you, man. She needs you. She can't breathe."

Blake leaned over again, his eyes searching for her. The front of his jacket fell open in a large D shape and Thorne grabbed it and transferred his weight to it. Blake tipped over the guardrail, his arms flailing about. He caught one of the wires supporting a pig below and his hand slid down it before coming to a halt, leaving four or five feet of blood-red cable. Thorne heard the distant clatter of Blake's Glock hitting the concrete below.

The platform creaked and groaned around them. It was old and rusted-through and wasn't designed for any of this.

"You motherfucker!" Blake shouted.

He continued to shout obscenities, but Thorne ignored him and began to pull himself up. His arms were weak from hanging so long and his shoulder wound burned. He drew level with the walkway and he was able to reach his long arms across it and grip the thin metal slats in his hand. He rested there for several seconds, his chest gasping for air. He knew he couldn't rest long, his muscles were seizing up. He gritted his teeth for one final effort, dragging his chest, then his hips up onto the metalwork.

Below, he saw that Blake had wrapped his right leg around the cable to act as a brake and he was reaching across to a cable closer to Thorne's position. His hand reached it and he drew the two cables closer together. With his upper body strength, Blake would easily be able to climb back up and they'd be right back to fighting it out. Thorne was breathing heavily and the cold air was shutting his body down.

Another fight with Blake wouldn't go any better than the last. He needed a gun, or another weapon to bridge the gap in their fitness levels. Hell, he'd take a monkey wrench at this point. He thought wistfully about the hunting knife he'd given Kate. Most likely it was lying somewhere on that office floor, unused. It was no use thinking about it, it was gone. He looked around for anything he could use. Both the 1911 and the Glock had fallen over the edge, there were no guns. The top of the guardrail was made from a metal pipe, but each section was about ten feet long. Even if he could remove it in time, it was too long to be a practical weapon. Finally, he glanced toward the stairs. There might still be time to retreat and get Kate clear.

His attention was drawn to the warehouse floor. Sara Dawson had dug herself out from under the gas cylinders, and dragged herself across the concrete to the side wall of the office and was using it to get to her feet. She was shaky now, but that wasn't going to last. His window was closing. Thorne looked over the edge and saw Blake just below, less than six feet away. It appeared he'd stopped to catch his breath. Blake saw him and let go of one of the wires and pulled another gun out the back of his pants. He pointed it at Thorne's head.

"Easy, Thorne. You and me ain't through."

"You can't aim and climb at the same time."

"Sit your ass down. Hang your legs over the edge. I bet I can draw this and shoot you before you can stand back up."

"Why would I? You're going to shoot me anyway."

"I won't. I need you to pull me in. *Sit.*"

It was bullshit, but Thorne lowered himself back down and sat with his feet hanging over the edge. If you do what someone wants, they don't question what you're doing. *They think they're making you.* Thorne saw an opportunity, and one might not come again. Blake nodded and put the gun away. He resumed his climb. It was slow going and exhausting to watch, but it gave Thorne the chance to get his strength back. Blake had to constantly re-wrap his legs on the wires after he moved one up to take his weight off his bloodied hands.

Thorne had a theory about why Blake hadn't shot him and it had nothing to do with needing his help. It was always better to keep using the same weapon even though re-loading ate extra seconds. Each gun handled slightly differently. Once you knew your pistol, you stopped thinking about it. The weapon became an extension of your body; you aimed and fired without a second thought. You became fluid, a machine.

The gun Blake had just drawn was his backup weapon. It had been stuffed down the back of his pants all day and was for emergencies only. Blake hadn't shot him, because he couldn't. He hadn't chambered a round and he needed both hands free to draw back the slide.

"I used to think you lost a part of yourself over there," Thorne said. "That incident with the girl, I thought you changed. I thought my friend died with that girl. But you didn't, did you? You were *always* crazy. I don't know why it took me so long to see it."

Blake grinned at him. He was right in front of him now.

"You know why I call you *brother*, Thorne? It's because you and me are the same. Like peas from a pod. If I'm crazy, you're crazy. It's nothing to be ashamed of, it's who we are."

"Maybe," he said. "But I'm a lot less sentimental."

Thorne brought his foot down hard in the middle of Blake's face. He heard a crunch like he'd stepped on a cockroach, as bones folded in on themselves around the wooden heel of his shoe. When he moved his leg clear, Blake was already falling toward the floor. He was unrecognizable. A hole the size of a fist had appeared where his nose had been and a thick comet-trail of blood followed along behind. Blake's arms appeared to embrace someone all the way down. The fall lasted no more than a second but it felt longer, time stretching out. Thorne absorbed every detail: the droplets of blood that seemed to hang in the air; the swept-forward Jesus arms; and the single blink of his old friend's eyes before the back of his head flattened out on the concrete.

Sara screamed and ran toward Blake's body.

Thorne got to his feet and moved smartly along the walkway to the stairs. The fight had taken a lot out of him and he needed to use both hand rails coming down the steps. He glanced back, looking for Sara, but all he saw were the rows of frozen animals. As he reached the warehouse floor, he heard her scream again. It wasn't the kind of scream they used in horror movies, this sounded like something being ripped from inside Sara Dawson.

He'd killed Blake and hadn't left her a face to kiss goodbye.

Sirens approached. They were close, less than a block.

He ran to Cabot's side and dropped down on one knee. He removed his latex gloves and put two fingers lightly against the lieutenant's neck, right under the ear. The pulse was weak, but steady. He sighed. Cabot could still be a problem for him. All things considered, it would be a lot simpler if Cabot was dead when the police arrived. *No loose ends*, as Blake would've put it. He chewed on his lip. He could press down on the carotid artery under his fingers and hold it like that for a few minutes, starving the lieutenant's brain of oxygen. Within his dark world, Cabot would fall sleep and never wake up. It wasn't the worst way to go.

Thorne looked across to the office and saw Kate standing in the doorway watching. She flashed a smile at him as their eyes connected. Her face was pretty banged-up, but the smile was glorious and it squeezed his heart. He lifted his hand away from Cabot's neck and stood up. So much for the loose ends. Kate walked toward him then stopped, her head darting to the right, her smile vanishing.

He turned slowly, already knowing what was behind him.

Sara advanced toward him holding Ashcroft's Smith and Wesson in front of her, it's barrel pointed directly at his chest. He held his hands part way up to show her his hands were empty, and in what he hoped was a calming gesture.

"Easy, Sara, easy. The cops are about to break the door down. You shoot me and there's no way out of this for you. Lower the gun and we can talk about this."

Sara said nothing. She continued to come toward him, her gun arm straight and steady. He moved away from Cabot and began to step sideways and backward, forcing her to turn with him like two hands on a clock. The movement neutralized her forward motion, although she was too close now for that to matter.

Outside, there was a screech of tires followed by a dozen heavy doors slamming shut. She turned her head a fraction to listen to what was happening.

"There's still time to fix this, Sara. We can tell them Blake kidnapped you, same as Kate. That he forced you to do the things you did. We can do

398

this."

She jerked her head from side to side, her teeth clenched together. Sara was falling apart, but she still hadn't shot him. Tears ran down her cheeks and she wiped them away angrily using the back of her hand.

"You gotta pay for what you did to him."

"Lady, I've paid *enough*. Do you really want to spend the rest of your life in prison over that asshole? Be my guest. Just don't tell me you weren't going to kill him yourself when the money came through, because I'll never believe it."

"You got me wrong. I'd never hurt Aidan, except for pleasure."

Thorne nodded.

"I must admit, it sure was satisfying stomping on his face."

She sobbed, her gun arm dropping then coming back up.

"You're going to wish you hadn't said that."

Behind her he saw movement. He kept his eyes locked on hers.

"It's not the same, is it? Shooting an unarmed opponent, I mean. If it were, I'd already be dead. Last time around I was a threat to you. I had a gun, I forced you to defend yourself." Thorne let his hands drop to his sides. "But now...now there's nothing left to fight for. No Blake, no painting, no payout. It's over, Sara. All of it. I think we both know that he wouldn't do time for you if he was where you are now. He'd make a deal before the cops arrived. If he was consistent about anything, it was about looking out for number one."

Sara's face hardened and the pistol rose slightly.

"I guess you can ask him when you see him."

The figure behind her stepped closer, his focus sharpened. *Kate*. She grabbed Sara by the hair and yanked her head to the side before plunging the hunting knife into her neck below the ear. The gun dropped from Sara's hand, and she fell to her knees. The movement pulled the knife out and Kate stabbed it in again, this time at the front near Sara's throat. Blood pulsed out with each heartbeat, filling the air around them with the hot smell of death. The blood reached out across the floor and sprayed across his face and chest. Kate pulled the knife out again and immediately sank it straight down, into Sara's shoulder. The blade disappeared entirely, leaving only the handle sticking out behind the collarbone. Sara pitched forward onto the floor and gurgled for several long seconds, then was silent.

Make sure it counts, he'd told her. This counted.

Kate glared at him.

"Was it really necessary to bait her like that?"

Thorne had no answer for her. Instead, he went to her and held her tight in his arms. After a moment, the tension left her body and he felt her relax. He couldn't tell her the truth, he could never tell her that. Sara Dawson had to die, and Kate was the only one in a position to make it happen. He'd manipulated her to kill and he didn't feel good about it. He felt her ribs expanding and contracting in his arms and smiled.

Simple pleasures, sometimes they are all you need.

"That's the most screwed up thing I ever saw."

His eyes slid across to Cabot. The lieutenant had rolled onto his side and was watching them carefully from the floor, his head resting on his outstretched arm. His face was pale and pinched with pain, but Thorne thought he also saw a trace of humor in his eyes. He doubted Cabot felt sorry for Sara after what she'd obviously done to him; what sympathy he had was likely pooling on the floor under his jacket.

Thorne nodded at him, as if to say *are we cool?*

Cabot winked in return.

Around him, he sensed movement in all directions and close to twenty figures emerged. They carried MP5s, wore full combat gear and bulletproof vests with FBI emblazoned on the front. The machine-guns were dipped to knee level, ready to be brought up and fired in a split second. Thorne looked from one helmeted face to another, looking for Mancuso or one of the other agents he might recognize from Santa Cruz, but he saw no friendly face. This was a SWAT team, hostage rescue, not investigation.

"Hey guys," Thorne said.

SIXTY-FOUR

Thorne piled his belongings up on the bed, ready to go. There wasn't much, but it wasn't all going to fit in the backpack he'd brought with him. He'd decided to limit what he took with him to what would fit in the bag he came with, rather than what might fit in the Maserati. He knew that, logically, the simplest solution would be to load up the car and sort it out later, but that wasn't who he was. Traveling light was a way of life for him. The idea of being able to carry what he needed on his back was one of his major takeaways from serving in the military. Having arrived at this decision, he realized he could live without any of his new clothes. He moved the clothing to one side, making them into a separate pile. It was difficult for him to imagine when he might wear most of them again. Italian suits, designer clothes. The Ashcrofts had tried their best to bring him into their world, but he knew where he lived, and it wasn't here. He came across the Gap clothes Coop had bought for him after his arrest and paused. It wasn't just clothing he was going to be leaving behind.

Two days had passed since the events in the warehouse, time enough for the story to have both saturated, then disappeared from the 24 hour cycle of the national news networks. In a couple more days, he'd be able to walk down any street without fear of being recognized.

He turned his attention to his backpack.

Once he put in his laptop, charger cables, and the remaining packs of Fentanyl, there wasn't a lot of space left. He added two pairs of socks, boxer shorts, and T-shirts then fastened the compartment shut. There was a small pocket at the front with room for his battered Chandler paperback. That book went wherever he did. It had been with him to some pretty unpleasant areas of the world and, one way or another, he'd survived.

Thorne stared at the burner phone sitting next to the bag and felt his heart plunge. It tied him to Blake, to everything. He had to get rid of it. If he tossed it too near to the mansion it would be obvious who had used it. He slid it into the front pocket, next to the paperback. Best thing to do was take it with him. Find a suitable resting place for it, far from here.

He shouldered the bag and walked out the room.

Lauren's father had returned the night before, sober, clean-cut, and apologetic about his previous visit. Thorne knew a fellow actor when he saw one but said nothing. The fact was, he didn't want to leave Lauren on her own and he didn't want to stay, so Mathews' timing was perfect. Her father's absence at Ashcroft's funeral seemed to be a real sticking point with her, but to his credit the old man stuck in there and won her back. No doubt his daughter's updated financial status kept him focused on the big picture.

Thorne moved through the house to the large entrance hall. At the front door he paused to look down the passage toward the swimming pool. He expected to hear the sound of Lauren swimming laps, or the voices of her and her father talking, but there was nothing. He opened the door and crossed the driveway to where he'd parked the car. He opened the trunk and threw in his backpack. It was the first time he'd opened the trunk since Ashcroft had given him the car, and he was surprised to see that there was something in there already.

A large Nylon gym bag.

He reached his hand out to touch it.

"This isn't how I imagined this."

His hand jerked back and he closed the lid.

Lauren stood in front of him.

"I know," he said. "Me neither."

Her eyes dipped down, toward the stones that made up the driveway.

"Didn't figure you for the sneaking-away type."

He tried to put a bit of light into his eyes.

"I was just stowing my gear before I came looking for you."

"Right."

Thorne walked around the back of the car. He noticed that he'd reversed into the space, ready for a fast getaway. Shit, she had his number all right. He stood in front of her, an extra space between them now that hadn't been there for a while.

"What will you do now?" He said.

"Sell up, move back to L.A. and pick up my life where I left off," Lauren shrugged. "This was never my home, I need to be where people are. Not out here in the woods with mountain lions or coyotes or whatever. Jimmy never understood that."

"Maybe we'll bump into each other one day."

She half-smiled, the smile of sadness.

Neither of them believed it.

"What about you? Back to your TV show?"

"No, I don't care about that anymore. They're talking about shooting another season with a bigger budget, prime time slot, even bumping me to executive producer - all the things I wanted for the last five years. But I'm not doing it. Where the show ended, I realize now it was perfect. It mirrors what happened in the first episode and I like that."

"Movies then?"

"I hope so. There's been some interest. I'll just have to see where that goes. In this business, you learn not to hold your breath."

They stood for a moment in silence, looking at each other. Lauren Ashcroft was as beautiful now as she'd always been, but his feelings for her were so far gone that he couldn't find the thread to pull on to bring anything back. From her facial expression, he guessed she was on the same page he was. Despite this, there was something between them that remained, just as there had been between him and Blake after all those years apart.

Her eyes looked up, into his.

"I'd like...I'd like if this wasn't goodbye."

Thorne nodded. "I'd like that too."

They embraced, awkwardly, like two strangers.

For a moment their bodies were tense, then they both seemed to relax and let go. The hard part was almost over. Thorne saw Mathews standing in the passageway beyond, watching them through the window. His mouth was pushed up into a snarl on one side. Lauren's father hadn't changed. The old man couldn't turn off who he was for five minutes while they said goodbye. Thorne looked away and allowed himself to get lost in the moment. Their chests expanding and contracting together, the light puff of her breath into his neck. He'd miss this. He smiled and was still smiling when they broke apart.

He noticed there was color in both her cheeks.

"I forgot how good you were at that."

"In another life Lauren, you and me..."

"Just kiss me and go, don't get all mushy on me."

*

Half an hour later, Thorne parked next to the *Dream Inn* and cut the engine. He'd given Jocelyn Cooper one last exclusive at the warehouse, rewarding both her loyalty to him, and to the story. But with no new material forthcoming, he had to handle her right or risk having her expose him to the world. He had to leave her sweet and nice. Thorne reached into his jacket pocket and took out the bottle of OxyContin. Two left. He shook them out into the palm of his hand and stared at them like the result would be different. With a bit of effort, he could make two pills last for six hours a pop. He swallowed both, washing them down with half a bottle of water.

He could always go back to the Fentanyl if things got bad. He got out the car and held the edge of the door and the roof as he straightened to full height. The crunches and pops had returned. He went through the front of the hotel to the elevator.

Coop wasn't expecting him and that was probably for the best.

He'd figured he would work out what he was going to say to Coop on the drive over, but he was outside her door now and nothing had come to him. That's the way it was sometimes. He decided to take his lead from her. With the story over, she'd be moving on and her head would be in a different place. She'd used him, and now that it was over, he was fine with that. He knocked lightly on the door. After about twenty seconds the door opened. Coop stood there in a business suit with a cell phone clamped against her ear. Her face had a flash of anger frozen on it but it melted into a huge smile when she saw him.

"Listen," she said, "I got to call you back, something's come up."

She ended the call and pushed the cell into her pants pocket.

"Christopher *fucking* Thorne, as I live and breathe!"

He felt his cheeks become hot.

"You don't need to use my *full* name, we are friends after all."

"Friends, huh? We're something, all right. I'm not sure it's friends. Are you going to stand there staring at my mouth all day, or are you going to come in and kiss it?"

He laughed. He was really bad at tying things off. Maybe he should've done this by phone, but he had to see her eyes. He had to know what she was thinking, what was coming next. She reached out and took his hand and pulled him into her room. This was going wrong already. He looked down. Her hand was tiny against his, her skin hot.

Inside the room, two large suitcases sat side-by-side next to the coffee table, extendable handles pulled up. Ready to roll. He turned to her and she kissed him on the mouth.

It wasn't a goodbye kiss.

Before he knew what he was doing, his hands were around her, pulling her tight against him. He couldn't help himself. It felt good, right. His body wanted this, needed it even. It took a moment for his brain to remind him why he was really here.

Reluctantly, he pulled out of the embrace.

"Coop, stop. *Stop*. I'm not here for that."

Her face fell.

"You seem to like it."

"I *do* like it. Jesus. I really do."

"So what's the problem?"

"I just wanted to see you. Say goodbye properly."

She flinched.

"Ugh. Really?"

"I'm going to try and patch things up with Kate."

"Does she want that?"

He sighed. Coop really cut to the chase.

"Probably not, but I'm going to try just the same."

"I can't decide if that's romantic or creepy."

He shrugged, wordlessly. She made a sad face. After a beat, she walked to the desk with the yellow chair and wrote something on a pad of paper. She looked him in the eye as she passed it to him.

"In case it doesn't work out."

Thorne flipped open the paper. It was a street address in L.A. Her home. Underneath the address, she'd written the location where she kept a spare key. She trusted him completely. This was something he hadn't expected. He looked up to thank her, to say something, but saw only the bedroom door close in front of him. His cue to leave he supposed.

His heart felt heavy.

He should give her something in return, but he had nothing to give. Certainly not a home address, that was gone now. It seemed like women would always surprise him, and nearly always for the better. He took his Jake Vasco sunglasses out and balanced them on top of one of her suitcase handles. It was the most personal item he owned, and it was stolen studio property. Hopefully, they would make her smile.

He rode the elevator back down, certain he'd made a mistake. All he had to go on to make himself think any different, was a faded Top Gun T-shirt and the look of love Kate had made into Blake's camera. There was a second chance there, he was sure of it. The fact that she'd been distant and cold with him in their brief time together at the warehouse and the time since was a source of concern, but hardly surprising after everything she'd been through.

The elevator doors slid open and he got off.

He was still holding the piece of paper with Coop's address on it.

Thorne walked over to a trash can. As long as he held a parachute, he would never learn to fly. He dropped the paper into the can and walked out into the winter sunshine.

When he returned to the Maserati, he found a man in a dark suit bent over next to the car, stroking it like it was a cat. *Mancuso*. The agent had his back to him and Thorne considered turning and walking away, but he knew he'd been made by the way the old man stiffened. His reflection in the glass had given him away, just as it had for Lynch at the mall.

The agent spoke without taking his eyes off the car.

"She's a fine car, but not worth the price you paid."

Thorne said nothing. In his experience, he always put more into life than he got back out. Thinking any different was a recipe for resentment and depression.

Mancuso turned toward him.

"Leaving town, Mr Thorne?"

"Yeah."

"That's not our arrangement. You have to tell me first."

"I don't have to tell you shit, Mancuso. This isn't a western."

The old man's eyes wrinkled in amusement.

"Walk with me, we have things to discuss. I'm glad I caught you."

The way the agent presented it, he could be mistaken for assuming that their meeting here was some kind of happy accident. A more likely scenario, was that Mancuso had been hanging around his car waiting for him since he'd parked it. That he was tracking him somehow. Thorne sighed and followed the other man as he made his way around the front of the hotel. Instead of going inside as Thorne expected, he continued on, toward the waterfront.

Mancuso glanced over his shoulder as he walked.

"Is that *lipstick* on your face?"

Thorne wiped his mouth with his hand and said nothing. What he did with his face was none of the FBI's business. Above them, the sun blazed on a pale blue sky, but the air had turned cold and only a few people dotted the area. Tourist season was over. The sunlight hurt his eyes after the gloom of the hotel and his sense of humor was running out fast. His hand was going for his sunglasses before he remembered where they were. They had become so much a part of him, they were like a form of armor.

Mancuso stopped at the barrier overlooking the beach and Thorne stood next to him. To their left, the long wharf continued on out over the sand and into the sea.

Thorne allowed himself to think about Coop.

He hadn't tied that situation off at all, he realized. If anything, he'd only made things worse. She was a ticking time bomb. He was a single news report from spending the rest of his life behind bars. Was her attraction to him the only thing that held her at bay? How long could he rely on her silence if there was no movement in their relationship?

He let out a long breath. She'd said *no mikes* for their first meeting, but the more he thought about it, the more likely it seemed Jocelyn would've recorded it. She'd have him admitting he knew those involved and planned to kill them. Since they were now dead, that lined him up pretty nicely for two counts of murder in the first.

"We have a problem we were hoping you could help clear up. In your statement, you claimed to be unarmed when you entered that warehouse, yet there was an additional weapon at the scene that we can't explain."

Here it comes.

"How so?"

"We know the gang all had Glocks. They used Glock 17s at the mall, the hospital, and at the warehouse. Additionally, their leader was carrying a Glock 22 taken from a sheriff's deputy killed at the hospital. Cabot told us he was packing a Colt revolver that night, which leaves us with a Smith and Wesson 1911."

Thorne frowned. How did they know the gun wasn't also Blake's? The agent seemed to read his thoughts, his head nodding slowly.

"We ran the unidentified .45 ACP shell casings through the lab for fingerprints. Standard procedure. Got four solid hits and one partial."

"You pulled prints from spent shell casings?"

"Didn't have to, four rounds were still in the magazine."

Thorne said nothing, but instead turned away from Mancuso and looked off across the water at where the sun flickered on its surface. If they'd found anything incriminating he knew they'd be having this conversation across a desk.

"You're a cool customer, Thorne. But there's no need to be shy, we're just having a conversation. All I want to know is how you did it."

Thorne knew what Mancuso was talking about. It was clear that he'd brought the Smith & Wesson to the warehouse, hell, Cabot had probably mentioned it in his debrief. But there were no fingerprints of his on it. He'd held the pistol several times since Ashcroft had acquired it, but he'd cleaned it carefully before heading to Blake's motel. He was certain he hadn't touched it again without gloves or a cloth. The shell casings, however, were a different matter. The pistol had been empty when he'd first seen it. Later, he'd seen fresh brass in the magazine. Only one other person could have put them there.

"The truth would disappoint you."

"It usually does."

The agent's voice was casual, like he was talking to a co-worker.

Still Thorne said nothing.

"Believe it or not, you have a lot of friends at the Bureau. Partly from your TV show and the positive light it always had for us, but mostly from what we saw in that mall parking lot. You risked your life for people you'd never met before, and that carries a lot of weight. There's no appetite to pursue you for the handful of crimes we could pin on you. To do so would risk opening Pandora's Box. The world would learn of James Ashcroft's fingerprints on those shell casings and his legacy on gun control would be wiped out. Nobody has any desire for that. Equally, we see no need to release the fact that you and this Aidan Blake seemed to have known each other for a long time. I'm sure the DA might feel differently about your immunity deal if that came out."

"Thank you," he said, the words almost choking him.

"I assume Blake is our shooter from the roadhouse?"

407

Thorne nodded. "It was meant to be an exchange; a painting of Ashcroft's in return for Kate Bloom. The painting is a Picasso, it's worth over a hundred million. Exchange was going fine until Cabot showed up. Blake assumed I'd set him up and was going to shoot me until Ashcroft drove his car at him and saved my life." Thorne paused. "I guess he saved Kate's life too, his move kept everything in play."

The mention of the Picasso didn't surprise Mancuso.

"Where's the painting now?"

"In the van Cabot had towed from the crime scene. The painting was small enough to fit behind the plastic panel of the side door. Murder weapon is in there too, another Glock 17. I handled it carefully, prints will all be Blake's."

"We assumed from the beginning that there was a link between the kidnapping attempt and the gallery break-in."

"I don't know anything about that."

Mancuso looked at him side on. There was something reptilian about his eyes, like he was holding a laugh inside. He didn't believe him, but this look suggested it didn't matter.

"Who were you seeing in the *Dream Inn*?"

A subject change. The agent was giving him a pass.

"Jocelyn Cooper."

The agent nodded in acknowledgment, but again there was no surprise.

It occurred to him that every time Mancuso appeared to give him something, he answered the next question honestly. He needed to be more careful, he wasn't out of the woods yet. Thorne glanced at his watch. 11:20. It was taking the old man a long time to get to the point. He decided to ask a question of his own.

"What about Cabot?"

"He's a hero now, just like you. After what happened in the warehouse, they say he's a shoe-in to be the next sheriff. Carson is unlikely to run against him now that he's certain to lose. As far as I can tell, Cabot's interest in you appears to be over. Maybe being shot made him more sympathetic to your situation?"

Thorne grunted. That didn't sound like the Cabot he knew. More likely, he realized the danger in coming after the person who made him out as a hero in the first place. There were still too many unanswered questions about what happened and it wasn't in Cabot's interest for the truth to come out any more than it was for him. If that wasn't enough to keep him in check, there was always that felony assault frame up. Unless he played his part, jail time a real possibility for the lieutenant.

"There's something you're not telling me, Mancuso. Why come down here to tell me things I already know?"

"Isn't it obvious? We *like* you."

"And that means what?"

A thin smile cut across Mancuso's face.

"You have a lot of potential, Thorne. You are highly trained and physically capable. We figure that in return for looking the other way on a couple of things, you could help us out on a case the Bureau is working in L.A. Perhaps have some kind of ongoing relationship after that. Your conflict resolution skills need a little work, but you appear to be a natural. We're bringing you into the fold."

"I don't think so."

Mancuso's smile twisted, and his voice right along with it.

"We're not giving you a choice. Don't you see? We *own* you."

Thorne nodded.

"People have been telling me that a lot lately."

"What's that supposed to mean?"

Thorne smiled, then turned and walked away. He was through with the hero business. It didn't pay worth a damn. Behind him, Mancuso called out one last time.

"We'll be in touch, Thorne. Count on it."

He kept walking.

ABOUT THE AUTHOR

I live on the outskirts of Edinburgh with my fiancée and young son. Night Passenger is my first published novel, the previous two having been set on fire for the good of mankind.

I would like to thank my family for their support and encouragement over the years, and for saving eye rolls until I was out the room.

I would also like to thank all those who willingly gave their time to help with technical details, background, and terminology. Any factual errors are 100% my own or made with creative license to further the story or improve readability.

If you enjoyed Night Passenger, please consider writing a quick review, it would be greatly appreciated.

For more information, visit my website, Facebook or Twitter.

www.davidjstanley.com
f dstanleyauthor
t @davidjstanley

Made in the USA
Lexington, KY
23 August 2019